Letting Go

SAMSARA-THE FIRST SEASON

Volume One - Book Seven

JL Martin

Time Travellers Publishing House PTY LTD

ALSO by JL Martin

FICTION

SAMSARA- The First Season

That Fated Night- A Short Novella of Love and Loss

The Golden Glow

Unexpected Beginnings

Torn in Two

Loss of Innocence

Unconditional Love

Returning Home

Letting go

Soul Connections

Healing the Heart

Legacy and Love

Leo- Back to me!

Lilith- Utopia

SPAWNED OF SIN- Trilogy Series

Through Windows in the Sky I Fall

Tainted Blood, Poisoned Soul

The Ties That Bind Behind Me

Letting Go

J. L. MARTIN

Published by Time Travellers Publishing House Pty Ltd 2022

The series is written in British English, as the Author is Australian and the books are based in Australia. My American friends will find U's where they have no right to be, Z replaced with S, and so many double L's you may feel like throwing the book against the wall. I apologise in advance, and hope one day we can all live in harmony...

National Library of Australia

Cataloging-in-Publication data

Martin, J L, 1971-.

Letting Go

Samsara-The First Season

ISBN Print: 978-1-925852-36-3

ISBN Ebook: 978-1-925852-35-6

Cover design by Thea Atkinson

Editing and text design by Marianne Delaforce

Printed and bound in Australia by Ingram Sparks

A Note from the Author

IN READING THE SERIES 'Samsara-The First Season', I ask you to consider the era in which this work of fiction is set. In these more enlightened times, elements of this story may be considered homophobic, racist, and outright morally corrupt—along with being barbaric and downright ignorant. However; in 19th century Australia, they were not. Themes throughout the series are reflective of the times and are an accurate account of the attitude, bias and outright hate a large majority of society held towards the LGBTQI+ Community and our First Nations Peoples. In saying this, we no longer consider it appropriate for a fifteen-year-old girl to marry—forced or not—but 130 years ago, it was not uncommon.

The character of Leo is based on a real person. As outrageous, inappropriate and politically incorrect as he is—I love this soul. It is not my intention to stigmatise him or cause offence to anyone—only to remain authentic in my best effort to honour and immortalise a very dear man who left a significant imprint on my life—and who unfortunately was born without a filter and lacks all sensibilities; and can be very, very badly behaved.

Please be aware there are themes of violence, racism, and homophobia throughout this series; however, I have been mindful to write these scenes as sensitively as possible and with the utmost care.

I truly hope you enjoy 'Samsara-The First Season' just as much as I enjoyed writing it.

Dedication

To Ellie-Rose Irene.

Choose happiness in all situations
and live everyday knowing just how precious you are to so many.
You are loved, sweetheart.

Chapter One

L OUD BANGING FROM BEHIND my door pulled me from a tormented sleep, the maids employed by *The Delmont, New York* passing my suite without care or thought to the time, their trolleys rattling through the wide hallway at this God forsaken time, no different from the bushman's clock that woke me before dawn back at Willow Grove. Oh, I missed that kookaburra. Sitting majestically on Park Avenue in Manhattan with direct views over the park at its doorstep, I cast my eyes over the bustling city down below—even at this hour—thrilling and surprising me all at once. Tossing and turning all night after dining with Hamish in *The Crystal Room*, I was full of regret for agreeing to speak with him alone, my body heavy with exhaustion as I wiggled deeper into the feather mattress, my mind wishing everything and everyone away.

The Delmont in New York had been built in the way of all my hotels; however, this had a slight difference. Only finished last year, Mr Malcolm had approved the plans back in 1892 to open an exclusive, and far too expensive restaurant on the top floor of the building, their goal to attract only the wealthy and powerful of New York the sole intent. Aaron had suggested at the time they add a restaurant on the ground floor for guests who did not wish to pay the exorbitant prices charged in *The Crystal Room*, and I agreed wholeheartedly, the thriving and far too exclusive restaurant eventually placed just below the top and final floor where they built a private suite for my use alone—a waste given I was unlikely to return.

Begrudgingly, I found the building magnificent, with not a penny spared in the decoration and furnishing of the hotel—my suite even more of a surprise, possessing everything and more that most expected to find inside a grand house, including six guest bedchambers, numerous formal and informal rooms, and views over central park and the city.

Due to leave New York this morning bound for home, I glanced at the clock on the mantle, grateful our journey would soon end. Travelling for months now, the winter had well and truly set in here, the snow below covering almost everything the eye could see, leaving me pining for home and the Australian summer months. I had missed my friends and family dreadfully, and now I had attended to my business, I craved the comfort and security of Willow Grove's warm embrace.

'Bloody man,' I muttered to myself, replaying what Hamish had said to me last night. 'Damn him!' I had very little time to decide what to do after he told me in no uncertain terms he would no longer tolerate our arrangement. Threatening to court me openly on the ship, I was infuriated at the suggestion; however, he had made it clear I had no choice in the matter. I had argued with him to the point of summoning all my strength not to decapitate him with my dinner plate; however, he would not be moved.

I sighed deeply as I slipped out of bed, strolling around the room until I found my dressing gown, discovering Bessie had moved it from beside my bed for reasons only known to herself. She had been vague since we left Scotland, constantly forgetting and falling behind in her duties, and we had experienced more than one occasion where she became flustered for no reason I could see, resulting in tears and her fleeing from the room soon after. I did not mind tending to myself; however, I was highly concerned for her, and had vowed after the last incident I would find out why she was behaving in a way I had never witnessed before.

I made my way out of the exquisite bedchamber, vowing if I ever re-papered my own walls at home, I would find the same design, the embossed gold over cream and sage green with flecks of pink calmed me immensely. Wandering around the suite, stopping here and there to gaze out over the city, I found the children sleeping soundly, while Bessie and little Mary's soft snores could be heard from the sitting room. Still early, the light outside only starting to vivify, they would likely sleep for hours yet. Shuffling down the hall, I made my way to Hamish's bedchamber, crossing from one end of the suite to the other where Bessie had placed him. Knocking only once, he opened the door, his chest bare, with only the pyjama pants Collin had made him to protect his virtue, his eyelids heavy, while his long, curly hair flowed down past his shoulders, billowing out around him, and reminding me of a black lion.

'Good mornin', lass. Ye want tae come in?' He raised his eyebrows, unable to stop himself glancing behind me to ensure no one crept up on us.

'Yes. I want to talk to you.' I pushed past him, marching in to sit on the chair near the window, my shoulders tense.

'Do ye want tae come an' talk in bed?' He crossed the room in several strides, patting the bed teasingly before continuing on to sit down on the chair beside me, a smirk touching his lips.

'No, and I'll give you fair warning now, Hamish. Mock me at your own peril,' I warned, my tone sharp, while his yawn wide as he straightened up, his large hands rubbing his face several times before he glanced back at me, his eyes twinkling in amusement.

'Aye. As ye wish.' He leaned back in the chair, while I swallowed hard, the room silent for a moment before I swallowed again, forcing myself to begin, while steeling myself for his reaction.

'Is there anything I can say or do to convince you to refrain from the course of action you plan to take? I do not want Thomas and Emmy upset, or for them to think I have forgotten their father, or feel I'm betraying him. It's far too soon, and I resent being forced into a situation I do not wish to be in. If you cared about me, you would care about my feelings.'

'Och, calm yourself, lass. The twins would never think that o' ye, naw ever. If ye expect me tae continue tae put up with the likes o' Johnathon Malcolm an' Lord Harrington chasin' ye, well, yer goin' tae be disappointed.' He shook his head, reaching out for my hand before I slapped him away, much to his amusement. 'Naw, Abigail.

I'm naw changin' me mind, so we're goin' tae tell 'em this mornin' at breakfast, or let 'em find out on the ship. I warned ye from the beginnin' I was naw sure how long I could be yer dirty secret. Well, as o' last night, I cannae keep tryin' tae hide how I feel in front o' everyone, includin' Thomas an' Emmy. If I thought fer one moment it'd harm 'em in any way, I wouldnae go forward with it.' He raised his hand in an attempt to placate me, infuriating me further.

'Why are you forcing me into something you know very well I do not want?' I shook my head bitterly as I looked away and stood, moving over to the far side of the window to gaze down at the snow that had fallen heavily over the last few days.

'Because I cannae do this any longer. Do ye have any idea the torture it's been tae have tae sit back an' pretend tae everyone I dinnae love ye, an' I'm only yer friend?' He watched my reflection in the window, my fingers tracing Emmy and Thomas's name on the cold glass inside a heart I had drawn.

'But you *are* my friend, Hamish. I haven't changed my mind, and I'm not *in* love with you.' I turned back to face him, and he rose to his feet and made his way to my side, his large hands gently taking me by the arms.

'Aye, I know—but ye will be. I promise.' His eyes glistened with emotion as he guided me over to the bed, his fingers quickly untying the belt of my dressing gown, his lips on my neck as he slipped it from my shoulders, the silk gown falling at our feet, his touch sending shivers through my body.

'Please, Hamish. If you love me as much as you say, keep this between us and do not speak of it to anyone,' I pleaded, my desperation growing as he took my hands in his, and grunted to himself before placing them around his thick neck.

'Aye, an' that's why I'm naw longer hidin'. 'Cause I love ye, Abigail. This sneakin' around could go on fer ten-years if ye had yer way, so I'm puttin' a stop tae it now. I dinnae want a fleetin' romance with ye, I told ye that from the start. Ye cannae always have yer own way, Abigail. It's naw only yer heart involved in the matter. Ye knew the man Aaron was; ye also know the man I am better than most. There's naw point wastin' yer breath talkin' o' it anymore. Ye have had yer way fer over four-months now. I thought if I gave ye some time, ye would soften an' change yer mind. All that matters is I love ye. I always have. An' I always will.' He slipped his arms around my waist, lifting me from my feet, his lips on mine. Within moments, my body had betrayed me, and I kissed him back, my hands running through his hair as he carried me over to the bed and gently placed me down. He climbed in beside me and gathered me into his arms, his kiss taking my breath away. 'Dinnae think about it now. Just enjoy the few hours we have before the twins wake,' he whispered, and I nodded, his hand on my thigh as he slipped my nightgown off over my head, causing me to forget what I had been cross about to begin with.

Later, I lay next to Hamish, dreading breakfast and the twins' reaction. He remained on his side of the bed, lying flat on his back, his hands behind his head as he stared at the ceiling, smiling to himself. I wondered if all men relaxed in this way, and my limited experience gave me no answers given Aaron did the same, as did Leo when he would force his way into my bed.

'Abigail, ye are worryin' fer nought. Thomas an' Emmy will be happy their mother has someone who loves her. They do naw like the idea o' havin' strange men around ye, knowin' what ye went through with Maslow. They're very suspicious o' the men who've been tryin' tae capture yer attention on this journey, if ye haven't noticed. I cannae believe that bloody John Astor has been followin' ye around like a cattle dog. You've attracted a great deal o' attention, particularly in New York, an' I see those seekin' yer favour make ye uncomfortable. Think o' our courtin' as a way tae find some relief from yer many unwanted suitors.' He leaned across and kissed me, exploring my mouth with his tongue as he stroked my face with his fingers. I pulled away abruptly.

'I told you not to kiss me like that.' He moved over, turning onto his back, his face like thunder as he stared up at the ceiling. I felt dreadful, my stomach in knots; however, I couldn't help my reaction. Aaron still filled my heart more than ever, and I was unable to let anyone else in, not even Hamish. Silence hung heavy over us as I struggled to my feet, bending down to collect my dressing gown before slipping it on, while he lay motionless in the bed, not taking his eyes from me for a moment.

'Aye, I'll be out there soon. Ye need tae relax naw only yer body, but yer mind, Abigail. I understand ye wish tae be the one tae tell 'em, an' I respect that an' will follow yer lead durin' breakfast. Worryin' changes nothin', an' if Thomas an' Emmy are upset by the idea o' me courtin' ye, we'll forget the entire thing,' he called out, my back to him as I stepped out into the small sitting room, only turning to close the door quietly behind me.

Muttering under her breath, she abruptly rose to her feet, little Mary beside her, the dirty dishes clashing together so loudly as Bessie threw them onto the tray, I worried they would shatter. We had chosen to take breakfast in the intimate dining room, just off the small kitchen hidden behind, the square walnut table seating us comfortably, the setting far plainer than the elaborate table seating twenty in the formal dining room, while a cramped servants quarters attached to the kitchen and accessible through the staff stairwell was separated from the grandeur of the suite by only a wall. Oh, but how different these lives looked for those on each side. The guilt I carried often made me consider giving it all away, but the life I had before tormented me. My childhood had embedded a fear so deep within that disaster would befall me, poverty would call, and I would not have the means to care for those I loved—my guilt increasing a thousand fold at how selfish I had become holding on to money I would never spend, while knowing others could live well for a year on what we spent in a week at Willow Grove.

'We'll be off then, Mistress. We still have some packing to do of our own. No doubt the four of you will be needing privacy this morning to talk. If you don't mind, Mary and I have decided to make haste and use the time for ourselves?' Bessie nodded at me politely, and I nodded my consent, while little Mary picked up the enormous tray and made her way over to the door, disappearing into the kitchen. Bessie remained where she was for a moment, silent and unmoving, her eyes fixed on a black bird perching on the windowsill as if in a daze. Hamish glanced at me, then her, then back at me, his eyebrows raised, while the twins paid us no mind and continued eating, their musical voices filling my ears as they discussed the trains running through the newly built tunnels under the city—the first underground line owned by the *Interborough Rapid Transit Company* opening on the 28th of October, only last year. On the 30th of December the city celebrated the new *East Boston Tunnel*—a subject I was certain would lead to tears given they desperately wanted to go, and we were due to board the ship within hours. New York was the largest city I had ever visited, and my attempts to explain to them we would need years to see and experience everything had fallen on deaf ears, the list Emmy carried in her pocket of all the places she wanted to visit now only half complete. I glanced back at Hamish and shrugged my shoulders, reluctant to say a word given how many times she had snapped at me over the last few days, her rants and tantrums not only causing me great concern for her welfare, but I had started to fear for my own, certain she would wallop me on several occasions when I had dared disagree or speak back. I raised a glass of apple juice to my lips, while Hamish cleared his throat loudly and, leaning back in his chair, his shoulders squared, he made a guttural Scottish noise, the children pausing for a moment to stare at him.

'Och, what's wrong with ye, wee Bessie? If Leonardo were here, he would've snatched ye away from us in secret, an' we'd have tae come save ye from the asylum where they wander round much the same as yer doin' now.' Bessie jumped, startled from her thoughts. Whatever they were, I had not a clue. Confiding in her this morning when she helped me ready for the day how Hamish planned to tell the children we were courting if I did not, she had only nodded, her usual advice or straight-out orders not forthcoming. Assuming she was distracted, I repeated myself, telling her how resentful I felt towards him forcing me without care or thought for my feelings or wishes, and again she said nothing, nor did she comfort me in my distress.

'Oh, I'm sorry. I feel I'm losing me mind, and the Mistress would be justified in sacking me for it. As for that Leonardo...' Bessie's voice faltered, and she collapsed into a flood of tears, her face scarlet, her feet unsteady as she ran from the room. Silence hung over the table as I stared at Hamish sitting opposite; Emmy by his side, her mouth open, while Thomas grunted to himself as he continued to eat beside me.

'Bloody women. Always carryin' on about somethin' that usually turns out to be nothin' at all,' Thomas remarked, my hand swiftly reaching out and cuffing his left ear.

'Don't you speak in that tone to anyone, especially your elders. If someone is telling you men are calm and never have outbursts, or that women are the opposite and unable to control their emotions or behaviour due to being defective in comparison—well, they're lying to you, son. Bessie is obviously upset about something and has chosen to keep that private for now. There is no need to be snide, and I will remind you that you have not been raised to behave this way. We all have days like that, and let me give you the drum—I've seen more grown men throw down their bats and balls and refuse to play when they don't win than I've seen women prone to tantrums when things don't go in their favour.' He stared up at me, his cheeks flushing pink, while Emmy gazed after Bessie, her brow creased.

'I said nothin' wrong, Ma. An' I don't believe ya that men crack it more than the womenfolk. You're lyin' to yourself if ya truly believe ya own words, an' I doubt ya do 'cause ya the smartest woman I know. Ya only have to go an' sit in the village for half-hour an' ya'll see who has the least control over 'emselves, an' for the stupidest reasons.' He shook his head at me, raising his finger to point at my handbag. 'Take ya little notepad with ya 'cause I wanna see the results with me own eyes. The last time I was down there, I was hurryin' through the main street to say goodbye to me mates, an' I witnessed five of 'em, all women, carryin' on like pork chops.' I shifted in my chair, straightening my shoulders and steeling myself to reply; however, he raised his hand to silence me. 'An' before ya say anythin' or punish me for havin' an opinion different from ya own, the five of 'em weren't going at each other. Every one of 'em had their own crowd around 'em, includin' several furious sheilas in each. I passed 'em one after another, an' witnessed their carry on with me own eyes, so tell me I'm lyin without lyin' yerself, an' Uncle Hamish knows it well enough to back me.' Spluttering filled the room, coughing soon after, and Emmy immediately turned to pound Hamish on the back, while I narrowed my gaze at my son.

'Do not take that tone with me, young man, or speak to any woman in that manner. You are entitled to your opinion, as long as it is your own opinion, and not that of the men who surround you—who should know better, mind you—and guard their mouths when in the presence of impressionable boys. Especially when those young boys admire and rely on them to demonstrate in word and deed how to be good and decent men who treat women with the respect they deserve.' I glared at Hamish, widening my eyes to make my point as he averted his, his large hand reaching out for a glass of sparkling water, his coughs subsiding, his breathing laborious as he raised it to his lips and drank deeply. I lifted a spoon full of sweet, creamy porridge to my lips, enjoying the feel of it in my mouth. I had done everything in my power to avoid raising the subject of Hamish courting me, dawdling over the food, and once my plate was clean, I swiftly moved on to the next course, delaying a discussion I did not wish to have.

'I wanted to go to *The Olympia* near *Longacre Square*. Mr Hammerstein invited us, Mummy, and you promised him we would,' Emmy complained, rolling her eyes before raising her brows at Thomas, while he gave her a knowing look.

'It's naw called that anymore, Emmy. They renamed the section from Broadway tae Seventh Avenue *Times Square* on the 8th o' April, 1904,' Hamish interrupted, not taking his eyes from the newspaper in front of him, his free hand spooning Boston beans into his mouth at great speed.

'How do you even know that, Uncle Hamish? You never care about things like that, and you rarely remember the date me and Thomas were born.' Emmy shook her head again; however, refrained from rolling her eyes, while Hamish threw back his head and howled with laughter.

'I'm readin' it here.' He lifted *The New York Times* and shook it, while Emmy's giggles filled the room. He turned his attention back to the newspaper, appearing to settle in for a lengthy discussion. 'They've done an article about 'emselves.' He chuckled to himself again before continuing, the children interested and giving him their full attention for the first time in days. 'There seems tae be some debate whether the Mayor, George McClellan, changed the name tae favour the newspaper, 'cause they've just moved in tae *Times Tower*, their new office, an' the second tallest buildin' in the city. They've printed a quote from the owner o' the paper, Mr Adolph Ochs, so ye can make up yer own mind. Ye met him two nights past with Mr Hammerstein, remember?' The twins nodded, waiting for him to continue. I could not understand why they had renamed the square at all, given the history of the place. Dating back to the 1870s, the carriage hub known as *Longacre Square,* was called so in honour of a square in London of the same name, where carriages congregated in much the same manner. Set in the heart of a neighbourhood often referred to as *Satan's Circus* or *The Tenderloin,* by the turn of the century, from Fifth to Eighth Avenue, through to Thirty-Seventh and Forty-Seventh Street, the area was home to over a hundred and thirty brothels, alongside at least as many taverns. We had been introduced to a Mr Oscar Hammerstein in the *Crystal Room* by his daughters, Stella and Rose, who dined at *The Delmont* almost every evening, Rose confiding in me she kept a suite here at great expense to her father. A German-born composer, he had opened his fourth theatre in Longacre Square in 1895, and knew the history of the place well. Generously sharing his own experience, I found him to be a shrewd businessman, and I enjoyed his company immensely, more so than his offspring. 'I am pleased to say that *Times Square* was named without any effort or suggestion on the part of *The New York Times*,' Hamish read loudly, sniggering to himself. 'Did ye hear him say the other night how his new buildin' represents the first successful effort tae give architectural beauty tae a skyscraper in New York?' He glanced at me before returning to the paper, while I shook my head at him.

'Oh, Mr Ochs has a right to be proud of himself. He plans to hold a grand party this coming New Year's Eve to commemorate the new buildings, and I believe it will be spectacular from all reports. It may have been pure luck that he was given the opportunity to buy that old hotel and rip it down to build that tower. That was years before he could have known gentrification of the area would occur, and good for him. I would adore seeing in the start of a new year at *Times Square*, but let's hope it becomes a yearly tradition should we ever return. Mind you, he has grand plans to drop some balls out of the sky at the strike of midnight, only he is still trying to perfect his idea to make it possible, and it may not occur this year.' I rolled my eyes, the children giggling as Hamish lifted his cup and sipped his tea.

'From what I've heard on the passionfruit vine, Mr Ochs friendship with the owner o' that *Interborough Rapid Transit Company*, August Belmont, convinced him tae move there long before anyone knew they were buildin' the train lines underground. 'Twas naw pure luck at all, Abigail, 'twas a whisper in a mate's ear. Rumour has it the tunnel runs through the basement o' their fancy new buildin', *Times Tower*, an' they keep the presses under that tunnel, but it's only hearsay.' He paused, finishing his tea before pouring another. 'They're sayin' here they naw wanted any confusion with a subway stop named *Broadway*, or *Forty Second Street*, so were forced in tae it so the thousands swarming tae the place now will naw get lost. They seem tae treat their countrymen with contempt here, claimin' they cannae read a sign, an' they're naw smart enough tae get off at the right stop. Empty justifications fer not leavin' the place as *Longacre Square*, in me own opinion.' He folded the newspaper, resting it on the table before rubbing his eyes, the twins now on their second helping of beans piled on buttered toast. 'They're predictin' five million souls will pass through the terminus in *Times Square* this year alone. Mr Ochs may not have lobbied for those underground trains, but he certainly benefited from his friendship with Auld August. The thought o' that many people in one place makes me want tae run back tae the warm embrace o' Willow Grove an' never leave.' He leaned back in his chair, and smiled to himself, the snow falling heavy outside, the fire in the hearth spitting as the flame touched the sap.

'Time is getting away,' I said, glancing at the clock on the mantle. The twins continued to eat the last of their waffles, while I rose to my feet to gather the dirty dishes.

'Yer mother an' I have somethin' tae tell ye,' Hamish announced, his shoulders squared, his eyebrows raised in silent challenge. I sunk back onto my chair, my heart in my throat, while Thomas and Emmy nodded casually as they sipped their hot chocolate made especially for them by *The Delmont* chef. Hamish widened his eyes at me expectantly; however, I was unable to speak, the lump lodged in my throat refusing to budge. The room fell silent, the cutlery scraping on china grating on my nerves, the smell of maple syrup wafting up my nose surprisingly comforting.

'What is it, Uncle Hamish? Mummy looks like she just saw Daddy float down the hallway.' Emmy gazed up at him, then across at me, before staring back at him, her eyebrows raised.

'Aye, then. I've asked tae court yer mother, an' she's agreed. What that means tae ye both is I'll be around her more than usual so we can get tae know each other better an' see if we are compatible in our ways.' I grunted, my face burning, while the children widened their eyes, Emmy's brow wrinkling, confusion crossing her face.

'But you and Mummy already know each other well. Why do you have to see if you get along, when you already do? Well, most of the time.' Hamish stared back at her, his face void of emotion, his mouth silent now, yet he was unable to control himself only moments before.

'What Hamish is trying to say is he may be affectionate towards me in front of you, and we did not want you to be upset, or think I am replacing your father.' Tears stung my eyes for a moment, and I sniffed, holding them back, while Hamish relaxed comfortably in his chair, a wide grin on his lips now it was all sorted for him. I fought the urge to smack the smile from his face, forcing my hand in this way, and I summoned all my strength not to strike him where he sat.

'Are ya in love with each other?' Thomas asked, his eyes fixed on Hamish, then me, then back on Hamish, his face thoughtful.

'I love yer mother very much, with all me heart, just as I love ye an' Emmy,' Hamish answered, his voice like gravel under my feet, while Emmy's face lit up in a brilliant smile, her eyes filled with love as she gazed up at him.

'I knew you loved Mummy from when she took to her bed after Daddy died. I'm so happy you threw that Nellie over and decided not to marry her. She doesn't like me, or Thomas, and I know she's definitely not keen on Mummy. Do you love Uncle Hamish?' She gazed at me across the table, her eyes locked with mine, her smile bright.

'I need some more time. I still very much love your father,' I told them, tears now trickling down my face, while feeling the weight of Hamish's stare, the silence almost unbearable.

'Why can't you love Uncle Hamish and Daddy at the same time? I'm certain it's possible,' Emmy remarked, confusion crossing her sweet face, and my heart broke a fraction more.

'Well, only time will tell, as they say, Emmy—only time will tell.' I gazed at the three of them, from one to another then back again, their faces glowing, a sense of happiness settling over the room, while relief washed over me. Thomas and Emmy appeared pleased, and accepted the news better than I had expected, while irritation niggled at me, not ever wanting to admit Hamish may have been right.

Chapter Two

ONLY STEPPING ABOARD THE ship an hour ago, I lay on my bed while my companions settled themselves in their suites, Hamish going to his own to unpack his trunk, while Bessie and little Mary shared their own private suite. Reflecting on the last few months, I could barely believe our journey was coming to an end.

We had taken ship to France from Edinburgh, stayed in Paris for over a week, where Hamish had taken the twins to see all the sights Aaron and I had talked of. I had kept myself busy with shopping and sitting in cafes alone, sipping coffee and eating chocolate croissants, fulfilling a dream Polly and I once shared as children. I could not bring myself to go to the places Aaron and I had intended to visit together, and I had broken down a number of times when I had tried; embarrassing myself and upsetting Hamish and the children. I hoped to return one day once I had healed a little and felt stronger, and see everything we had planned to see. I would still carry Aaron with me wherever I was in the world while my backside pointed to the ground.

Sailing to New York, I was surprised by how busy it was; however, even I was forced to admit the city possessed an energy I hadn't felt anywhere else. I shopped on Fifth Avenue and walked in Central Park, only stepping out the door and across the street and I was there. I would sit for hours watching people walk by, while thinking of Aaron. Hamish would sometimes walk with me at night, describing all the wonderful places he and the children had visited, and relaying every detail of what they had seen that day.

Often, we would talk of Aaron and the memories we shared of him. It was then I was reminded how painful the hole Aaron's death had left in Hamish's life. He missed him dreadfully, too, and was doing his best to keep Aaron's dreams alive through his work on the property and by taking care of his family, just as Aaron had asked. I owed it to both of them to at least try, especially after all Hamish had done for us. The door flew open, and I jumped, startled as Bessie barrelled into the room, her cheeks flushed and clearly flustered. I wondered to myself what she had forgotten this time.

'May I speak with you, Mistress? In confidence, I mean?' She sat down on the end of the bed, her face tear-stained, her trembling hands set in her lap as I struggled to sit upright, quickly wiggling myself down to her side, panic rising in me. 'I apologise for bringing me problems to your door.' She broke down in a flood of tears, her hands covering her face. 'I'm disgusted with myself, and have ruined my own reputation,' she wailed, falling into my arms, my hand patting her back gently as I tried to console her. 'I will lose my Danny forever.' Her sobs filled the room, my alarm increasing tenfold.

'Bessie, I will always keep your confidence. Please tell me what has happened?' She pulled away for a moment, her brown eyes fixed on mine, while her tears continued to fall. Reaching into my pocket, I took a clean handkerchief and wiped them away.

'Oh, Mistress. I've made the biggest mistake of me life. On the second last night of our voyage to London, the drink got the best of me.' She blew her nose loudly before continuing. 'I can barely say the words. I... I... I woke in the morning in Jimmy's bed without a stitch on, remembering nothing. I left while he was sleeping and hurried back to our suite before dawn.' I nodded, encouraging her to go on, while biting my tongue at what a sneak she was, always warning me I would ruin my own reputation as if it were a fate worse than death. 'On the last night I went to steerage to say me goodbyes and saw Jimmy across the room, so I sought him out to ask if anything passed between us. He was rude to me, saying he got what he wanted and he never needs to see me again, just like I did to him all those years ago.' I continued patting her back soothingly, trying to calm her.

'I'm so sorry, dear Bessie. Men are such bastards. I fucking hate them sometimes, and today is one of those days where I could string them all up by the balls and twist their ears that fucking hard they would bleed. Funts,' I spat, Bessie's eyes going wide before she crossed herself, gazed up at the ceiling, and muttered a prayer for my soul. 'Put him out of your mind. I will never tell Danny, and I don't believe you should, either. It was a mistake, and it's over now. Do not allow a cunning, dunny rat such as he to make you feel less than you are. You have all of us, and we love you like kin,' I said soothingly, her sobbing now unbearably loud.

'That's not the worst of it, Mistress. I'm with child,' she howled, while I reeled back as if she had struck me, unable to stop the gasp coming from my lips. If it were true, she would be over three-months gone already, my mind racing as I calculated the dates. How she would explain her bulging stomach to Danny, I had not a clue, for she would be showing by the time we arrived home.

'Oh, my poor darling, sweet Bessie. Calm yourself, my friend. There is not one problem we encounter that does not have a solution—and we have plenty of time to think what to do on our way home,' I murmured gently, before she pulled away and straightened up, drying her tears with my now sodden handkerchief.

'Thank you, Mistress. I knew I could rely on you out of everyone in this shit filled world, 'scuse my cursing.' She looked towards the ceiling, muttering another prayer, of penance this time, as I swung my legs off the bed, placing my bare feet on the floor, our bodies touching. In a way, I was happy she would experience motherhood, as she and Danny had been trying for all these years to have a family, but nothing had eventuated, both silently disappointed month after month, year after year. I had started to question if it was too late and her time had passed, given she had just entered her fourth decade. It seemed all it had taken was one night with a different man, who unfortunately turned out to be worse than shit on her shoe; however, that was not the weans fault. Bessie would make a wonderful mother, with or without Danny.

She sighed before struggling to her feet, slowly crossing the room to where my trunks sat in the corner near the wardrobe, waiting to be unpacked. She bent down and sighed again before hanging my gowns one by one, the room silent bar the sound of the waves crashing below. Although I had spent a great deal of my time wandering through the shops of Paris and New York, I had not purchased one dress due to the many Catherine had made, and I could not possibly fit another in my trunks even if I had wanted to. I had acquired some lovely new scents in Paris, and planned to try them on the ship, given I rarely wore perfume when at home, and even then, only if it were a special occasion.

A knock shattered the silence, the door swinging open before Hamish strolled in, a wide grin on his face. Bessie barely acknowledged him, her hands moving swiftly as she sorted my daytime wardrobe from my evening wear. He pulled me up into his arms and kissed me passionately, Bessie immediately dropping the dress in her hand before turning completely to face him, her hands planted firmly on her hips, her chin pointed out, her glare murderous.

'What do you think you're doing, Hamish?' His deep laughter filled the room, his arms around me while holding me tightly to his chest.

'We're officially courtin' now, Bessie, an' we're naw bairns, ye know? We discussed it this mornin' over breakfast with wee Emmy an' Thomas, an' they seem happy enough with the arrangement—an arrangement I believe ye should be thrilled about, an' doin' a wee dance over.' She rolled her eyes at him before returning to her work, his laughter still filling the room.

'And how have you formed that opinion, you stupid boy?'

'Aye, there's naw need tae spit fire at me, as I'm doin' ye a great kindness. Ye naw longer have tae concern yerself over blokes approachin' her, or get yourself worked up like ye do, 'cause I'll keep 'em away. Ye will live far longer if ye can get hold o' that temper o' yers.'

'You rude bugger. Be gone with you,' she called out, folding a cashmere jumper before placing it in the wardrobe, and I grimaced. I detested cashmere, despite being expected to wear it due to my wealth. I was uncertain how she had slipped it into my truck without my knowledge, this being the first time I had seen it.

'This is naw a surprise tae ye, Bessie. Ye have known what's passed between us since the start.' Her face flushed deeper, his tone kind but firm.

'Well, don't you go making a spectacle out of her, do you hear me? Gossip spreads like wildfire on a ship. I don't know how you've managed to force the Mistress into this when she clearly doesn't want anyone courting her, but you got your way, boyo. You may be right about the other men, but I'm watching you. Don't you go forgetting it.' She stood to her full height, two fingers pointing at Hamish, then back to her eyes several times. 'It'll be a proper courtship, mark my words, and there will be no sleeping in her bed once we arrive home. You can bring her flowers, token gifts, and take private dinners, but that is as far as it will go until she accepts you, or kicks your backside to the driveway. I'm so wild with you, Hamish. Be aware, this doesn't give you permission to do anything other than dance and walk the decks with her while on board. You wanted a proper courtship, then you shall have it. They say be careful what you wish for. The Mistress is a respectable woman, and I will not have you ruining her reputation because you can't keep your one eyed snake in your trousers.' She turned back to my wardrobe, while he threw back his head and howled again, his deep laughter somehow comforting.

'Och, I do try with all me strength tae keep it in me pants, ye filthy mouthed fiend. I'd hate tae think I've been wanderin' around first class with it hangin' out fer all the ladies tae admire. They'd be callin' fer the smellin' salts,' he teased, still chuckling as I collapsed into a fit of giggles, while Bessie threw down my gown and marched out of the room, slamming the door behind her. 'Do ye think we're safe now, or will she return tae chastise me?' I threw myself back down on the bed, my laughter filling the otherwise silent room.

'You're safe. Once she gets upset like that and storms off, she isn't back for hours.' He lay down beside me, pushing me over to my side of the bed, and took my hand in his.

'Aye. I'll admit tae feelin' some relief that Thomas an' Emmy were so acceptin'.' He raised my hand to his lips for only a moment before placing it over his heart, his fingers entwined with mine.

'I have not been able to speak to them privately, as yet, so am uncertain of their real thoughts and feelings on the matter. I plan to spend some time with them tonight when they retire to hear whatever they wish to say.'

'Och, they have told me they're happy enough, an' they believe I'm the only man fer ye. See how bright me godchildren are? Ye need tae take more notice o' what they say tae ye.' He smirked before drawing me into a passionate embrace, my hands on his chest as I tried to push him away.

'No, not in here. The twins could walk in at any time. I will come to your suite in a few minutes,' I promised, allowing myself to melt into him as I kissed him back, but only for a moment.

I sat at my dressing table while Bessie readied me for our first dinner aboard. I watched her thoughtfully as she twisted my hair up in sections, pinning my curls up on top of my head while leaving several tendrils to fall and curl around my face.

'I was thinking about your dilemma, Bessie, and from what I can tell, you have two options. You can tell Danny the truth and pray he understands, or you and I can go away until the wean is born, and I can bring him back as mine. We could work out the details; however, you could see the child every day for as many hours as you want. I could even make you the babe's nanny, if you liked. You don't have to listen to me, it's just a thought. I'm not trying to steal your child because I cannot have any more of my own. I want you to know that. He, or she, would always be yours, and know you are his or her mother,' I said, feeling I had made no sense at all. She stopped, her eyes fixed on mine in the gilded mirror.

'You would do that for me, Mistress? Say you had a child out of wedlock and keep the baby in the main house as your own? You would be disgraced and your reputation ruined beyond repair. I cannot believe you are willing to risk all that just so I could have my wean close.' Her voice was barely audible; her eyes filled with tears as she gently placed her hand on my shoulder.

'Yes, I am willing. Without hesitation. I love you, Bessie.' She bent down and embraced me from behind for the longest time. Her attention soon returned to my hair and makeup, working her magic until I no longer recognised myself. I rose to my feet before she assisted me into a gown I had worn only once before on our voyage to France. Russet red and extremely close fitting, while low at the front with barely there sleeves, I felt it was far too loud and drew unwanted attention. I could have kicked Catherine for her wild ideas and eccentricities when it came to dressing me. Taking one last look in the Cheval mirror, I sighed deeply before thanking her once again, crossing the room and opening my bedchamber door. I stepped out into the sitting room to find Hamish and the twins waiting patiently for me on the lounge, sitting side-by-side as they chatted between themselves. Catching sight of me, Emmy's eyes went wide, their attention fixed on the revealing gown Bessie had assured me a hundred times made me look like a proper lady. A proper lady of the night trying to turn a profit, I believed.

'You look lovely, Mummy,' Emmy told me firmly, while Thomas appeared tempted to run to my wardrobe to retrieve my woollen cloak to cover me. Hamish had not taken his eyes from me since I had walked into the room, and I squirmed under his stare.

'Aren't you going to kiss her now, Uncle Hamish? Thomas and I have been waiting all day? Not on the cheek, either. A proper kiss like Daddy used to do,' Emmy demanded, while Hamish's mouth twitched.

'Aye, wee Emmy, but only 'cause it's ye that's askin', an' how can I say naw tae that?' His eyes twinkled as he rose in one graceful movement, crossing the room in two strides before taking me in his arms and dramatically tipping me backwards, his lips on mine soon after, much to the delight and laughter of the children. He stood me back up on my feet, kissing me gently on the forehead before opening the door for us to leave.

We strolled through the hallways towards the dining room; the twins running ahead, both excited and hoping to make new friends. Hamish offered me his arm, and I accepted graciously as we walked into the elaborate dining room, far bigger than the ship we had travelled over on. We were soon seated at a table with a couple and two boys a little older than Thomas and Emmy. Introducing themselves as Jasper and Lilith Arcadia, along with their sons Eros, who had just turned fifteen, and Poseidon, only a year younger, they explained they were immigrating to Australia to start a new life, and were unsure where they were going to live. They planned to start a commune for like-minded people on a large amount of land somewhere in Victoria. While living in England, Lilith would tell the fortunes of the wealthy clientele she attracted to her Chelsea terrace, while Jasper chose to care for his children at home, just as a mother would do, until they were old enough to no longer require his full attention.

I found them to be a fascinating, unconventional couple, like none I had ever met. They appeared to be honest and open, telling us how they had sold everything they owned in England, and were starting with nothing but the money they had in the bank—and from their outward appearance, they would never want for a thing. Appearing to be in their mid-thirties, they were well spoken and immaculately dressed. Feeling drawn to them immediately, they had made us feel welcome and been so very kind. I felt we were already old friends—the couple taking my breath away on sight when the golden glow surrounding Lilith caught my eye from across the room. She was a beautiful woman, extremely petite, and at least six-inches shorter than me, her golden blonde hair pinned to the nape of her neck shining in the low light, while her lilac eyes and rosebud lips were mesmerising, her skin like porcelain, her cheeks radiating a soft pink glow. I had not a clue why I felt I had known her all my life, and desperately wanted to know more. Her husband, Jasper, a handsome man, his suit flamboyant, similar to what Leo would have chosen to wear in public if his safety were not threatened for it. Friendly from the moment we sat down, they were the complete opposite of the hundreds of wealthy passengers I had met on ships before, impressing me greatly, while immediately putting me at ease in their company.

We chatted over dinner while the children became familiar. I appreciated how the ship's staff sat guests who were accompanied by their children with others in the same situation, and matched the guests who had children of similar ages, giving everyone something to talk about if they shared nothing in common, a situation that had occurred frequently in my life. Feeling Hamish slip his hand up my thigh, I gave him a dark stare; however, he only smiled and refused to move. I scraped up the last spoon of my dessert and raised it to my lips, my free hand covering his under the table before I sunk my nails into his skin. He jumped, his hand now in his own lap, a smile touching my lips.

'Aye, then, Jasper. Ye haven't settled on where ye'll live?' Hamish asked, his smile warm as he pinched the top of my leg hard, and I shrieked, causing those around us to stare. Jasper cleared his throat, his eyes sparking as he took a sip of wine until peace was restored only moments later.

'Well, from what we have just heard of Willow Grove, I think that's where we all want to live. Sounds like heaven. Your lifestyle would be a balm to our souls and provide our physical bodies with what we need without having to leave the property. Despite our wealth, we don't need much to be happy. Food in our stomachs, a warm bed, and work to do so we aren't idle. And people to love who love us back. It's quite simple, really. Lilith and I refuse to spend our lives conforming to society's expectations. They don't like that much where we come from; therefore, we have been shunned and forced to leave. We don't mind at all as we view obstacles that present themselves in life as an opportunity to start fresh and go on adventures somewhere else.' He smiled at us, while pain flickered in his eyes for only a moment, Hamish nodding thoughtfully.

'Aye, it sounds tae me ye know the path ye wish tae walk. The commune sounds interestin' enough, an' I would enjoy talkin' more o' it, an' assistin' ye tae find the type o' land yer seekin',' Hamish offered kindly, while Jasper grinned in thanks. It was clear Hamish liked them as much as I did; although, it was difficult not to, given they were so cheerful about everything, and made those around them feel better for being in their company.

The four children interacted just as easily, thrilling me no end. Seeing the surprise on Thomas and Emmy's face upon being introduced to them and hearing their mythical names had forced me to smother a smile; however, it had taken only a few moments before they were getting along like a house on fire. Eros, or Ross as his friends called him, and Poseidon, who was known as Sid, were just as easy natured and welcoming as their parents. Although they looked forward to living in the commune in the future, they were in no rush and wanted to enjoy the hustle and bustle of Melbourne until their parents purchased their land.

The music soon started, the lights even dimmer now as I watched Jasper take Lilith's hand and lead her to the dance floor. Hamish rose to his feet beside me, and I glanced up in surprise, forgetting for a moment there was no scandal in being seen together now as he gently placed his hand on my shoulder.

'Will ye dance with me, Abigail?' I nodded my consent, rising from my chair to join him alongside the other passengers, some dancing only to impress those around them. He slipped his arm around my waist, my hand firmly in his, before pulling me close. 'Are ye aware every eye is on ye? Thus, the reason it was important fer yer own peace tae let me openly court ye. I mean tae make every bloke here see from the first night that yer naw available fer dances, walks on the deck, stolen kisses, or anythin' o' that nature. Yer mine, Abigail, whether ye know it yet or naw.' His lips were on mine before I could stop him, several gasps filling my ears, and as I had broken one of the first rules of what was and was not accepted in polite society, I would again be ostracised on this voyage, thanks to Hamish, of that I was certain. Jasper and Lilith appeared amused at the reaction, kissing several times while they danced, not a sliver of light between them, causing many to point and stare.

Emmy gazed across, her eyes dreamy, her chin resting on her hand, a sweet smile on her lips as she watched us dance, while Thomas glanced over on occasion, grinning when I caught his eye. From what I could tell, they seemed happy enough for Hamish to demonstrate affection towards me, and had not once shown any signs of distress or resentment over our now public courtship. Thomas and Emmy soon joined us, and I was impressed how well they could now dance after all their lessons, not to mention how proud I was they had practised every night after dinner for months. Hamish danced us over beside them, and he took Emmy in his arms, while Thomas took me in his.

'You're getting so tall, just like your Daddy,' I murmured, glancing up to see his father's smile. 'Are you comfortable with the arrangement between Hamish and I? I mean, the fact he is courting me, and I am allowing it?' Staring up into his bright blue eyes, the colour of the ocean on a sunny day, he gazed down unblinking with deep affection.

'Yeah, Ma. I'd rather ya be with Uncle Hamish than the strangers that flock to ya. He already loves us. Most of the blokes chasin' ya are strangers to us, an' it's likely they only wanna be with ya alone, an' won't want Emmy an' me around. That's not to say I don't like Lord Harrington. I know he intends to court ya, from what Uncle Hamish told us, an' I know he isn't like the blokes I'm talkin' about.' I nodded, a lump in my throat we were even forced to have this conversation, his father taken far too soon from all of us. 'Like Neville an' Trixie, let me give ya the drum, Ma. He has Ian an' Molly with Adelaide, who died God rest her, then Trixie comes along to look after 'em, an' ends up marryin' Neville. She loved 'em like she was their own mother until she had two more of her own blood, an' now she treats Ian an' Molly like rubbish, an' expects 'em to act as her own personal servants, while her own are treated like heirs to some throne. They tell me all the time she's hard on 'em, Ma, not like ya are with us.' I cringed inside, my stomach knotting up having only heard the rumours myself a few days before we set sail; however, it was not something I had been strong enough to address at the time, nor could I brush off the guilt I felt for employing her.

'You never have to worry about that happening to you and Emmy, because I wouldn't allow it, or be with a man like that. No one will ever treat you badly while I'm around, Thomas, I promise you that. You and Emmy will always come first, and all I want is for you both to be happy in all areas of your lives, especially within our family.' I kissed his cheek, and he smiled, his eyes misty. He would be a man soon, and I hoped very much he turned out like Aaron. A strong, decent man who loved deeply and freely, and got along with most everyone he met. His son was already showing signs of this in the easy friendships he made wherever he went, his calm and laid-back manner no different. Hamish soon handed Emmy back to Thomas and took me in his arms.

'Now everyone an' his dog knows, can ye stay with me tonight an' go back in the mornin'?' he whispered in my ear, holding me at a disrespectful distance.

'No, Hamish. That part of our arrangement has not changed, and Bessie would have a conniption. I do not wish to be held by anyone. It reminds me too much of Aaron, and I'm not ready. I'm sorry if I hurt you, but I cannot help how I feel,' I said as gently as I could, while he stared down at me, his eyes so big and lovely, while dark and intense, as if he could see straight into my soul.

'Och, it's naw about hurtin' me, Abigail. Yer hurtin' yerself. Ye need tae be held desperately after all this time, an' it'd help heal ye. I willnae pressure ye, as ye will let me hold ye when yer ready.' He smiled at me, his gentle lips on mine for a moment to more gasps, dark stares, and much talk behind hands.

We returned to the table with our new friends and drank more wine, while watching Emmy and Thomas dancing, the music faster now as both tried to keep up, collapsing into laughter at times. They returned after a few more minutes, sitting back down to chat animatedly with their friends, while we spoke at length with Jasper and Lilith. Inquiring how we met, Hamish told them, causing Lilith to tear up at times while patting my hand in sympathy as she listened.

'We wish you well in your courtship, and for you, Abigail, to find some way through your grief. We read about what you experienced during your husband's trial as his case was all over the papers back home in London. I cried when Aaron was executed, and I wrote you, and you replied, thanking me,' Lilith said, and I nodded, feeling tears prick my eyes. 'We did not mean to upset you, dear Abigail. It was only I had a message for you at the time. Do you remember the letter at all?' I shook my head, my brow furrowed as I tried to think; however, I was in such pain before I left to come on this journey, my mind unable to recall any correspondence from the last two-years at that moment. More than likely, Leo had replied and signed it in my name, something he enjoyed doing quite often from what I had heard on the passionfruit vine.

'I apologise. I cannot remember a great deal from that time in my life.'

'Oh, my darling, you must know this. It was so important.' She leaned closer, her mouth near my ear, her hand covering the movement of her lips. 'Aaron came to me the day he passed. He was aware we would meet in the near future, and was told by someone on the other side he could pass a message to you, through me. I was uncertain when that would be until I saw you walk in.' She smiled, wiping away my tears discreetly with her handkerchief. 'My views on the afterlife are complicated, sweetheart, and I do not have the time to speak of it here. One day we will talk further, and I will explain more. Forget that for now,' she whispered, taking my hand in hers under the table. 'The message Aaron asked me to give you upon meeting was this, the first part word for word, 'Hiriarni is real, Abi, an' that's where I am, *mo anamchara*. Please stop breakin' ya heart over me. I'm safe, an' around ya always, an' I love ya far more than ya will ever know.' He went on to say he cannot show himself to you. He's tried many times, but you are blinded by your grief. He comes to you often, Abigail. Surely you feel him next to you? You may be unaware, but you are one of the few who has the ability to see him. Only you first have to accept he is gone and not coming back in this lifetime.' She paused, rubbing her temples for a moment before exhaling loudly. 'That was the message he gave me, my dear friend. I have only told you in the hope it eases your grief, and you find some comfort in the knowledge he is not really gone.' My eyes went wide, my heart racing, while Hamish stared at her, his mouth open, overhearing every word. Jasper leaned back comfortably in his chair and smiled, obviously used to his wife's antics.

'Thank you, Lilith. I do not know what to say.' I swallowed hard several times, lifting my glass to my lips, the sparkling water cold as I tried to gather my thoughts. 'You sounded just like him. I need time to consider all this.' My hands trembled as I wiped away my tears and sniffed, while she nodded once and sat back in her chair.

'Oh, I apologise for upsetting you. It was never my intention, and I feel nauseous over it. You are so sweet and lovely, Abigail. You deserve to find peace regarding the death of your husband. That is all I try to do for people. Bring them comfort, and give them hope they will again be reunited when their time here, too, comes to an end.' She smiled, and I nodded gratefully.

We chatted quietly for a time of other things until the music stopped and the orchestra began to pack away their instruments. I rose to my feet, thanking all at the table for their company before embracing them warmly and saying our goodnights. Following Hamish out of the dining room, the twins close behind, I felt lightheaded from the wine. It had been nice not being approached by anyone asking to dance or to become familiar with me. Maybe Hamish had been right, and our courting openly had not been such a bad decision after all.

'I want to skip, Mummy. It's been such a fabulous day,' Emmy announced, reminding me of my darling Leo, before taking my hand in hers and pulling me along to skip down the hallway alongside her, both of us collapsing into giggles, while leaving Hamish and Thomas behind shaking their heads. Catching up to us at our suite door, Thomas and Emmy hurried inside to ready themselves for bed, while Hamish and I followed, settling ourselves down companionably in the small but comfortable sitting room to share a bottle of wine. I had been forced to pay for an extra suite for Bessie and little Mary, given Thomas and Emmy had announced only last week they were far too old to share a bed anymore. Hamish had insisted on paying for his own suite down the hall, not only to ensure we did not cause a scandal, but because he hadn't allowed me to pay his passage, or any costs he incurred while accompanying us. The thought of a woman paying for anything offended him deeply. I already enjoyed the privacy of having the suite to ourselves, and planned to spend as much time as possible with Thomas and Emmy sharing special moments that would imprint on not only their minds, but their hearts. Always surrounded by others at home from dawn until well after dusk, I wanted to cherish this time without interruption, and for my children to have wonderful memories to reflect back on during their lifetime of our now smaller family long after I lay in the soil of Willow Grove with Aaron. My deepest fear after losing Aaron was they would only remember the sadness and heartache we endured once they were grown. For close to two-years I was unavailable to them—that could not be disputed, even by me—and the damage I had caused by making them feel unimportant, or unloved as a result of my despair was far too much for me to bear or think of, even now. I pushed it all to the back of my mind, my face lighting up when the children returned shortly after, both warm and snug in their dressing gowns.

They embraced us tightly, me first, then Hamish, and I silently rose to my feet while they laughed with him, patiently waiting to follow them to Emmy's bedchamber to read a chapter from *The Marvellous Land of Oz,* the sequel novel by L. Frank Baum, before settling Thomas in his own room. Only published in July of 1904, and written as an account of the further adventures of Scarecrow and the Tin Woodman, they had enjoyed the first so much—I was certain I had read it to them hundreds of times—they had told Mr Hammerstein of their love for *The Wonderful Wizard of Oz* the first night we became acquainted, and how they had insisted having their own copies. Three mornings later, two parcels were delivered to our suite by the manager of *The Delmont, New York*, one addressed to Thomas, the other Emmy, their screams of joy when they opened the packages to find the same book in each, both signed personally to them by the author's own hand. Their excitement had brought Bessie out of her room in a panic to see what the commotion was, soon calming herself enough to sit down and listen as Emmy read aloud the letter placed inside the front cover from Mr Hammerstein himself, wishing her well and thanking her for our company while in New York, a similar letter in Thomas's hand he chose to keep private. I smiled to myself, the thought of wee Isla and Ruthie warming my heart, while I waited for the twins to say their final goodnights to Hamish and followed them into the bedchamber, taking the last of the wine with me, while Hamish opened another for himself while he waited for my return.

'Aye, do I need tae remind ye it's yer birthday taemorrow? Ye said nought at dinner tonight tae our new companions. Are ye ashamed yer leavin' yer twenties behind, an' enterin' the dirty thirties, auld woman? Ye'd be called a spinster behind ye back if ye hadn't married at least once by the age o' five an' twenty. Ye have that tae be thankful fer, I suppose,' Hamish called out as I stepped back into the room, my legs heavy from the wine, my face flushed. Not too steady on my feet, I crossed the room and sat back down beside him before they went from under me.

'You hush your mouth. You left your youth behind long ago.' I smirked up at him, winking several times as he laughed aloud. Finishing the last of his bottle, another gift from Mr Hammerstein, the dense Côtes du Rhône smooth on my palette, he opened another. My eyes heavy as I yawned widely, I was tempted to sneak away to my bed and leave him here; however, could not be rude given how sweet he had been this evening. I sipped another glass while we talked of home, and how much we missed the place, along with our loved ones who we were eager to reunite with.

'Ye know I have every intention o' announcin' our courtship once we settle back at Willow Grove?' he asked quietly, slipping his arm around my waist and pulling me closer to his chest, my face only inches from his.

'Yes, I know, but you must give me time to tell the Cavanaughs', along with Dana, before you announce anything,' I reminded him, my eyebrows raised as I narrowed my gaze.

'Aye, I gave ye me word. I know I've pressured ye into this courtship, but I willnae push ye in tae tellin' yer family before yer ready. I dinnae want tae cause ye more angst than ye already suffer over the matter. I know the Cavanaughs' better than me own blood, an' I'm certain ye have nought tae fear. They love ye an' embraced ye as family from the day they met ye. They'll be expectin' ye tae love again at some time in the future. It'll naw be a surprise tae anyone when Aaron has been gone over two-years now. I've naw doubt they're expectin' it, given the blokes sniffin' around have been persistent, but they willnae be expectin' yer new beau tae be me,' he whispered before gently kissing my lips, his arms wrapped around me as I melted into him. I was confident the Cavanaughs' would indeed be happy for me, as they loved Hamish, and only wanted the best for me and the children in every circumstance.

The woman I feared most was dear Dana, and I was well aware that by choosing this path, I could damage our friendship beyond repair. Since the day Charlotte died, not once had she acknowledged Hamish, and I believed never would again in this lifetime. Allowing him to court me would enrage her, of that I was certain. It would make no difference what I said in his defence—or mine—she would make it her personal mission to remove him once and for all from my life using whatever means necessary, in her eyes for my own protection. My love for her ran deep, she was family to me, my feelings so strong I had met her in my dreams when a child still sleeping in with the weans in the nursery, only her name had been Alice. My heart pounded at the thought of meeting with her, and what would pass between us, so upsetting I felt pain pierce my heart before I pushed the thought to the back of my mind, promising myself I would only think of it when forced on my return.

We soon finished the bottle, and Hamish invited me to walk the decks, rising to his feet before offering me his hand. Walking was the last thing I felt like doing; however, he pleaded for a time, and I struggled unsteadily to my feet, believing the sooner I went, the quicker I would be in my bed. He held me firmly by the shoulder as he guided me down the hallways and up the stairs, the cold wind hitting me in the face the moment he held the door open and causing me to gasp. Stepping out onto the top deck, he gathered me in his arms, the fresh air making me giddy, the sound of the ocean filling my ears, while tasting salt on my lips as I gazed up at the full moon hanging low, the stars like diamonds on black velvet above us, the night calmer than I expected, the breeze coming off the calm water so cold it pricked my skin like needles.

'Now I can kiss ye here fer everyone tae see, just as I did when we first met.' He opened his coat, wrapping it around me as I glanced around to find not another soul present, his body warming me as he gathered me in his enormous arms, his kiss so passionate, I wished we were already in his bed. His touch set my body on fire, and I longed for him at times when I least expected to, and it still took me by surprise. 'Many happy returns o' the day, me fiery wee wench,' he whispered, his breath in my ear sending chills down my spine. I checked my watch to find it had just gone midnight, my eyes going wide.

'Oh, that was why you brought me up here. How lovely, and so very romantic. Thank you, Hamish.' I stood on my toes to kiss him, and he smiled, pulling away for a moment.

'I've somethin' fer ye, Abigail.' He rummaged around in his trouser pocket for a moment before pulling out a wrapped box, placing it gently in my hand. Opening it to find the most magnificent bracelet I had ever seen, I gasped aloud.

'Hamish, where did you get this? It's far too expensive for me. We have only been courting for a day, and not even a full one at that.' My eyes wide as I held the bracelet up to the light above us, mesmerised by the enormous stones hanging from the thick gold chain, I gasped again.

'I had it made fer ye in New York at a jeweller on Fifth Avenue. Ye seem tae ferget, I'm a wealthy man in name alone,' he teased, and I laughed aloud, 'but I still have a fair amount o' money in trust left tae me by me grandfather, God rest him. If I choose tae use it tae buy ye a bauble, then that's what I'll do. Money is useless unless ye spend it on doin' somethin' ye enjoy, or on someone ye love. I've done neither fer a long time, an' now that money's been growin' fer years with the interest paid, 'cause I dinnae have much use fer it livin' an' workin' at Willow Grove—an' dinnae let me ever hear ye say when ye receive a gift it's too expensive fer ye. This wee trinket is nought compared tae what ye mean tae me, an' I hope ye'll wear it with all me love. Happy birthday, precious Abigail.' He bent down and gently kissed my lips, his warm embrace comforting.

'Thank you, Hamish. You are so very sweet and thoughtful under those brutish looks,' I teased as he slipped it on my wrist, securing the clasp while chuckling to himself. 'Can we go to your suite now?' I asked impatiently as he nibbled my earlobe, sending shivers through me again.

'Aye, only 'cause I have another present tae give ye.' His eyes twinkled mischievously before he took me by the waist and hurried me back down the stairs and into his suite, not another soul in sight.

I woke to the twins jumping on my bed, while wishing me a happy birthday. Returning to our suite just before daybreak, I had barely slept a wink. Feeling exhausted, my head pounding from indulging in far too much wine the night before, all I wanted was to sleep. Usually one of my favourite days of the year, I felt Aaron's loss acutely from the moment I slipped back into my own bed, aware how different the day would be had Aaron been here to celebrate with us.

'Thank you, my darling babies.' I gathered them in my arms, tears pricking my eyes as I drew them to my chest in a tight embrace before they pulled me back down on the bed, their bodies close beside me.

'We bought you presents, Mummy. Uncle Hamish took us window shopping to find the loveliest things for you,' Emmy said, her eyes sparkling as she handed me three gifts, one after another from a calico bag she had placed on the bed. We lay side-by-side, propped up by half-a-dozen feather pillows as I opened the first, finding a magnificent gold tiara, set with a hundred pearls at least, and I gasped, not expecting anything so extravagant from anyone, let alone my daughter. The quality and craftsmanship was on a par with Mr Dawson, the most talented jeweller I had the good fortune to meet, not only in Australia, but everywhere I had travelled. 'It will look lovely in your hair when you wear it up to dine with Uncle Hamish,' she advised, and I smiled at her. Opening the second gift, I found a pearl necklace to match the tiara, both clearly made to complement the other.

'Thank you, Emmeline. They are exquisite, but you are far more so,' I whispered, taking her face in my hands and kissing every inch, while meaning every word. I asked her to help me open the last gift, and she giggled, ripping the paper to uncover a gilded hairbrush and ornate mirror, a pattern of tulips etched into the gold—and the closer I looked, the brush heavy in my hand, the more suspicious I became it was made of solid gold.

'The lady at the store advised us this is the finest hairbrush you can find, and it will make your hair shine with only a hundred strokes morning and night. I told her you already have pretty hair that shines, but she said it will make it shiner,' Emmy said, appearing confused as I embraced her.

'It's perfect, Emmy, and I adore everything you have given me. Thank you, my love.' Hamish's words came to mind, and I held my tongue regarding the expense she had gone to, hugging her again. Thomas passed me a small wrapped box, while Emmy took the rags from her hair and ran the brush through repetitively, while counting to herself under her breath. I opened the box to find a ring, the three dainty marquisate diamonds set in a gold band, surrounded by six smaller stones of the same quality.

'Oh, Thomas, it's beautiful,' I gasped, taking it from the box before examining it closely.

'Uncle Hamish told me if Daddy were here, he would buy white diamonds for ya thirtieth birthday. 'Cause he couldn't do it for ya, Ma, I decided to.' Tears welled in my eyes, threatening to spill over as I embraced him, determined to hold back my emotions. The last thing I wanted was to think of Aaron when our children were so very happy; fearing once I started to cry, I would never stop.

'Well, I appreciate everything you have so generously given me, including your love, time, and attention. Thank you for making me feel so special, and very, very loved. I will wear your tiara and necklace tonight, Emmy, and keep it always. Once you place this ring on my finger, I will never take it off, Thomas,' I promised them both. He grinned as he slipped the ring on my right pinkie finger, then sat back to admire his work, the ring sparkling as the light hit the flawless diamonds. Emmy and Thomas appeared satisfied and soon returned to their own beds to sleep a few more hours.

Gazing up at the ceiling, my mind went back to this day fifteen-years ago as I prepared to leave Sister and take my first train ride to a big city all by myself, not knowing a soul or what my future held. It was on this same day, Catherine entered my life, and although it felt as if we met only yesterday, it seemed I had known her a lifetime. I so very much looked forward to seeing her when we arrived home, and of course, Colin and the children, who were dear to me as my own kin. I had missed our regular chats, and pined for her company and advice a hundred times since we left. She would have known how to handle the situation with Hamish and Lord Harrington so much better than I had.

Throwing off the heavy quilt with renewed energy, I swung my legs out of bed and rose to my feet, quickly pulling on my dressing gown to go and find Hamish as it was still early, and I was confident I would not be seen. Most slept late when on the ship, particularly in first class, many often taking their breakfast in their suite just as we chose to do when aboard. As I reached up to open the door, my bracelet caught my eye, dancing and sparkling on my wrist, and I decided at that very moment pink diamonds were my new favourite thing, having never seen one before last night. Glancing up and down the passage and finding no one, I crept down to his suite, knocking only once on the door ever so quietly, and when he swung it open only moments later, still half asleep, I hurried inside, checking one last time up and down the hall no one had seen me, before swiftly shutting the door.

'I need tae get ye a key,' he remarked, yawning as I embraced him, his torso bare, his skin smooth under my hands.

'The key to the King's garden?' He threw back his head and laughed. 'Thank you for what you did, Hamish.' He yawned again before cocking an eyebrow at me. 'For buying the gifts for the children to give me.' I stood on my toes to kiss him, before he took my hand and led me to his bed, throwing himself back down while I slipped off my dressing gown and climbed in beside him, pulling the quilt over us both.

'Och, they had their own money. They come from wealth if ye dinnae know, an' are spoiled rotten by their mother.' He widened his eyes, my mouth twitching as he shook his head, yawning again. 'All I did was accompany 'em tae the store, as the Yanks like tae call 'em.

'Oh, stop making things up as you go along. Thomas does not, nor has he ever, had the money to afford a diamond ring at his age, and Emmy couldn't buy me one pearl with her own money, let alone a hundred. You seem to forget that I know exactly how much they have in their pocket at any given time. I am the only one handing it out to them once a week when they have done all that is expected of them. Unless they're asking their wealthy relatives to give it to them on the sly.' I frowned, suspicion rising in me until he threw back his head and laughed. 'I wanted to thank you, Hamish. You are a kind and generous man, and I appreciate you more than you know.' Kissing him again for the longest time, he smiled when I pulled away to catch my breath.

'Aye, ye caught me, but only 'cause I wanted it tae be a special birthday fer ye tae day, an' not sad like the two just passed. I know how much ye love receivin' yer presents on all the special days ye look forward tae every year.' He smiled as I moved closer, my hand on his chest. 'I'd never know ye turned thirty by lookin' at ye. Ye have the body o' a twenty-year-old lass still tae have bairns, an' certainly naw the mother o' a near grown son an' daughter.' He wrapped his arms around me, his eyes fixed on mine.

'I have no doubt time and food will catch up with me, and I will be fat, wrinkled, and grey before you know it.' He went to respond; however, was unable as my mouth covered his—and not for the sole purpose of shutting him up—but it was certainly part of it.

Chapter Three

I GAZED OUT OVER the ocean as I sat at the dining table on the private balcony of our suite, our breakfast laid on the table, the platters overflowing and leaving us spoilt for choice. A gentle breeze touched my face, the sound of waves crashing against the bow far louder than the engines in the ship's belly, pushing it forward at great speed.

'Many happy returns of the day, Mistress. This is from Mary and myself. We wanted to give you a gift that would mean something.' Bessie pushed a small wrapped box towards me, the ribbon tied to it bright blue, a brown paper card attached. Little Mary flushed pink as I thanked them both profusely, reading the card first before carefully taking the paper off so it could be reused, as Bessie liked to do, and opening the box.

'Oh, thank you so very much. I will wear it with pride and always think of you both when I do.' I held up the cameo brooch, taking a closer look. It appeared far older than even ancient Mr Hinkle, the gatehouse keeper back at Willow Grove. The angry old hermit refused to have anything to do with us, nor did he 'keep' the gate since we first arrived, choosing to live in a cottage that stood by itself nearby, the signs placed all around the hectare he had claimed advising anyone who trespassed would be shot on sight—it did not seem to matter the land he believed to be his was part of Willow Grove. All who worked and lived there, including myself, had assumed he was at least a hundred and ten by now, until Harry told me recently he was coming up to his eighty-eighth year terrorising those around him this coming March. My eyes widened as I turned the brooch over to look at the back. 'Where did you find this? I have never seen one even similar, and I have looked at many over the years.' Bessie shifted in her seat uncomfortably, while little Mary flushed a deeper pink, her gaze now fixed on the horizon.

'Well, Mistress. We weren't meant to say, but I can't see the harm in it given me and Mary paid for it with our own money,' Bessie said, while Mary rose to her feet and hurried inside the suite. 'It was Lord Harrington that suggested it to us. The brooch belonged to his grandmother, the late Dowager, and was left to her by your great-aunt Isabelle on her death.' She paused for a moment as little Mary stepped back onto the balcony carrying a tray, before placing a large cake down in front of me and swiftly returning to her seat beside Bessie.

'It looks even older than her,' I remarked, gazing down at the name engraved neatly on the back, 'and I know her name was not Prudence.' Bessie and little Mary nodded in unison, while the children continued to eat, both silent and appearing fascinated as they listened, as did Hamish.

'We were told it is the exact same age as your great-aunt Isabelle. The brooch was her mother's, given to her on the day of her birth as a gift from her father for finally bearing him a daughter. There were three sons much older before your great-aunt came along,' Bessie advised me knowingly, little Mary nodding her head and glancing in my direction for only a moment.

'And the likeness on the cameo is your great-grandmother herself,' little Mary added, her voice barely above a whisper.

'Lord Harrington sold this to you?' I asked incredulously, unable to imagine anything of the sort, while praying they did not steal it, the question on my lips before I bit my tongue and swallowed my words.

'Well, we didn't force him to hand it over, if that's what you're thinking going by the look on your face,' Bessie said, her eyes twinkling, 'you cheeky fiend,' she added before picking up the teapot and pouring another cup for little Mary before herself. 'Lord Harrington offered the brooch when he overheard us talking of what we would buy you for your birthday. We wanted it to be something special given it's an important milestone for you, Mistress, and one we wish you to only have fond memories of.' Bessie smiled across at me, while little Mary gave me a shy nod, the twins still silent while Hamish listened intently, his handsome brow furrowed.

'I do not wish to offend you, but I pay your wages, and I know this would cost ten-years of working from sunup to sundown without a day off, and that's if you both saved every penny. This is far too extravagant and expen...'

'Abigail,' Hamish interrupted, giving me a dark stare, his finger going to his lips to silence me.' I nodded, my cheeks becoming warm as I straightened up in my chair, smiling at them both while kicking myself for being so rude.

'It is lovely, and very thoughtful. I will keep it close always, and think of you whenever I wear it.' Bessie threw back her head and laughed, while little Mary glanced across at her as if she had gone mad.

'We're not dead yet, Mistress. When our bones lay deep in the soil of Willow Grove, you are free to do as you wish.' She giggled to herself, little Mary's shoulders relaxing, while Hamish chuckled, not taking his eyes from the ship newspaper. 'We didn't steal it either, so get that out of your mind. Lord Harrington wanted to give it to us without charge, but we refused. He settled for the money we had saved between us to purchase it, and he gave us a receipt and all.' She reached into her pocket, pulling out a neatly folded piece of paper, waving it in front of me; however, refused to open it to show me the price they had paid. I nodded, thanking them both as she slipped it into her pocket for safekeeping. 'Your aunt and the dowager were closer than sisters. It was she who found her dead in the cottage where Lady Isabelle was staying, and Lord Harrington told us she grieved her deeply. He felt the brooch should only go to you, and it was the right thing to do for his beloved granny. That's all he knows from what I can tell. You never truly know with people if they're holding something back, but the servants certainly keep nothing to themselves and know far more.' She lowered her voice, the room silent while every ear listened. 'Your mother and her sister, Anna, left

Merinda Manor the morning after you were born, but no one knew then she had even birthed you or taken you to the orphanage the night before. Your mother kept to herself, and few knew much about her, but your aunt Anna worked there, and was well liked by all. A heart was broken the day Anna left, choosing to stay by her sister's side and start a new life in York, and you know the man well. That's all I will say, or I'm as awful as that malicious gossip, Leonardo.' No matter how much I prodded, begged and threatened, she would not tell me, remaining tight-lipped, as did little Mary, rising to her feet to clear the empty platters and dirty dishes away, before hurrying to my side and lighting the candles so carefully placed on top of the cake. Surrounded by my children and my friends in the middle of the ocean on my birthday filled my heart with joy, the only thing preventing me calling today perfect was not having Aaron by my side to celebrate with us—the State of Victoria ensuring that would never happen again when they murdered him.

'Uncle Hamish had the ship's cook make this especially for you, Mummy,' Emmy sang, pride in her eyes as she glanced at Hamish, then the rich chocolate cake, covered in a thick chocolate ganache, my name written in the centre in white.

'Make a wish. After ya blow 'em out,' Thomas reminded me as I quickly brushed the tears from my eyes, threatening to spill over. I blew them all out in one breath and made a secret wish, their cheering and clapping almost deafening me. 'Make sure ya cut yerself the biggest slice, Ma.'

'Cake for breakfast? You lot always pick on me if I ever want anything sweet before the evening meal.' Hamish's handsome face split into a wide grin, the children laughing, while little Mary removed the candles, handing me a knife while placing dessert plates down in front of me.

'Aye, an' dinnae I know better than most yer weakness fer sweets? An' 'tis naw me who gets upset with ye over the matter. That's yer best friend, Leonardo, carryin' on as he likes tae do. If the wee shite knew I'd allowed it, he'd naw doubt give me one o' his famous... er, it rhymes with witch slap. Go on, ye only live once, Abigail.' He laughed aloud, glancing at Thomas and Emmy deep in a discussion of what adventures they would go on today, and I smiled to myself.

He was right after all—only now I knew life continued somewhere else—an unknown place, and far beyond comprehension. At least, for me. I cut a large slice for each of us, passing them around the table until everyone present had a plate in front of them. Tasting mine, I groaned aloud in pleasure, the heavy chocolate cake filled with caramel ganache inside, the clotted cream on top sweetened with vanilla bean. 'I'll never ferget the first night I met ye. I could naw believe a lass with yer frame could eat that much in one sittin', an' nought has changed. Ye still devour as much as a bloke o' me own size.' His mouth twitched in amusement, the children collapsing into giggles as I gave him a dark stare.

'Well, you can shift your attention away from me, thank you very much, and concentrate on your own cake. You are reminding me of Leo. Next you'll be calling me a fatty.' Lifting my fork to my lips, I took another mouthful, and he laughed. The twins finished their cake, running off shortly after to find their new friends, while Bessie and little Mary excused themselves, leaving Hamish and I alone at the table. 'I want to explain Bessie's behaviour, but you must promise to keep my confidence. I know you are worried for her.' He nodded, his brows drawn close as he sipped a cup of coffee, listening in silence as I explained her situation as best I could, and the choices she currently had available if she were indeed with child.

'Ahh, she's gotten herself in tae a bit o' a mess, the wee hypocrite.' He smiled to himself before continuing. 'Danny is a good man, an' he loves her, that I know as fact. Aye, he'll be angry an' hurt on hearin' she's stepped out on him, but I believe he'll stand by her an' the wean. It makes it far easier since the father's gone, an' hopefully will never be seen again.' He grimaced, shaking his head for a moment, a flash of anger crossing his eyes for only a moment. 'If Bessie does decide tae tell him she was actin' no different tae a tavern trollop while away from home, then I'll put me hand up tae speak with Danny about the matter, mate tae mate. I dinnae want ye going away fer months on end, or pretendin' the foundlin's yers. Remember, Abigail. What's done in the dark o' night will always be exposed in the light o' day, no matter how hard ye try tae keep yer secrets close.' I nodded in agreement, my hand in his as we gazed out over the ocean, the sun showing itself this morning for the first time in days. 'I know I'm naw who ye expected or wanted tae spend yer birthday with this year, but I hope in some way, havin' me with ye eases yer pain, if only a wee bit.' He continued to stare out over the water, a fishing boat in the distance, while my eyes again pricked with tears and I sniffed.

'More than you know, Hamish. I really do appreciate you so very much.' I squeezed his hand, and I smiled, my heart lighter simply because he was here beside me, not only as my lover, but he was, and always would be, my friend.

Bessie and I sat side-by-side on the settee, her hands in her lap fidgeting while we waited for the doctor to arrive, silence heavy over us. I had attempted to brighten her mood, speaking of everything other than the prospect she was with child. Trying to reassure her it was still possible she was going through *the change,* as some women did at her age, it was clear even that had not cheered her, while I personally looked forward to the day I no longer had to put up with my monthly visitor.

A sharp rap sounded, and Bessie and I both jumped, startled, before I rose to my feet and crossed the room. Opening the suite door to find no one there, I glanced down to find an elderly man staring up at me. Standing no more than four feet tall, he was possibly the smallest adult male I had ever seen. Pushing past my legs, he marched inside, deciding to stop in the middle of the sitting room as I closed the door behind me.

'Who am I here to examine?' he barked, glancing at me then Bessie, and back again.

'It's me, Sir.' Her voice, just above a whisper, she straightened up in her chair, squaring her shoulders as if preparing to go into battle.

'And what seems to be the problem?' he snapped again, anger starting to rise from the pit of my stomach. I had not liked the man on sight, and now he confirmed what I had suspected, finding him rude with no bedside manner, as expected of physicians these days. Bessie remained where she was, motionless and unable to speak, the way he had about him clearly intimidating my dear friend. I politely offered him a seat, which he refused, choosing to remain standing in the centre of the room, while I sat back down beside her, quickly placing my hand on her trembling leg.

'Bessie is my ladies' maid, and very dear to me. We believe she may be with child, and request you examine her to confirm or deny our suspicions. I do not want her working if this is the case.' My own voice shook in this tiny man's presence, surprising me how someone such as he commanded such power, while instilling fear by his presence alone. No bigger than a gnome, I watched him sit down on the other side of Bessie, and she recoiled slightly, discreetly moving closer to my side, the silver-haired man next to her reminding me of a ventriloquist and his puppet I had once seen at a fair. Only the puppet was on his lap, not beside him puffing out his chest, while snapping at us no different from the crocodiles that frequented the rivers and streams up the far north and across to the west of Australia—the *top end* as my adopted countrymen liked to say. Where men were men, and women were few and far between, and the ones brave enough to go, had a bravery and strength of spirit I wished I possessed. Fearsome and fearless, and I admired every one of them.

'I do *not* examine the servants. I am here for the first-class passengers alone, given the *Cunard Steamship Company* only employs the best, and I am the finest physician in their employ,' he announced haughtily, proud as the peacock Emmy had befriended at the orphanage, causing me to wonder just how incompetent the worst were.

'Well, you are here now, and I am paying you good money, so you *will* examine Mrs Bessie McCleary, and I would like you to start the examination now, please.' He stared at me for the longest time before rising from his seat, and I did the same, offering Bessie my hand, and pulling her to her feet. I nodded at her reassuringly before she reluctantly showed him to my bedchamber and opened the door, while I sat back down to wait, amused the condescending wee man was far taller when sitting than standing. Staring after them long after he closed the door, I picked up a magazine from Paris, flicking through it without seeing a picture, or reading a word, while muttering a prayer and hoping with everything in me she would walk away from that one bad decision she made unscathed.

Soon after, Bessie opened the door, a handkerchief over her face, her sobs filling my ears as she hurried to my side and collapsed next to me on the settee. Slipping my arm around her shoulder, the doctor followed her out, picked up his leather bag, and left without as much as a see you next Tuesday.

'Did he harm or hurt you, sweetheart? Tell me, and I will chase the little bugger now and sit on him. Wouldn't take much to smother the bastard with the backside I have on me,' I called out loudly as the door slammed behind the irritable prick. She calmed a little and smiled weakly through her tears that continued to fall.

'Oh, Mistress. He says I'm over three-months gone, closer to four. That's how long it's been since we first arrived in London, and this trollop hasn't opened her legs since.' She screwed up her face in disgust, pointing at her chest with both hands, her fingers jabbing violently into her own flesh. I grabbed them and held her trembling hands in mine, trying to calm her as she wailed like I had never heard before. 'I will be known as a moll and a mad rooter from Melbourne to Geelong if that Leonardo finds out and has his way.' Collapsing onto me, I encircled my arms around her, her body quivering as she sobbed. I waited in silence until she calmed enough to sit and wipe her face with my handkerchief.

'He will not do such a thing, or he will be forced to deal with me. Even one word and I will show him just how violent I can be. He accuses me now of abusing him, spouting off to anyone who will listen that I'm a danger to everyone around me. Well, I've only tickled him compared to what I will do with his ears and balls should he make mischief for you.' A smile touched her lips, brighter this time, the tears continuing to slide down her face.

'I'd been praying every minute of the day, and into the night, that it was the change of life, stupidly believing it couldn't possibly happen now after trying for so long—and at my age! Can you imagine it, Mistress? I'll be an old woman, and close to meeting me maker before the bairn is grown.' She lowered her head, placing her hands on her face, while I stroked her back, trying so very hard to console the inconsolable.

'All will be well, darling Bessie. The bad passes just as quickly as the good in this bloody life, and I give you my solemn promise. I will always stand beside you when you experience one or the other, and everything in between. You can ask me for anything, and I will always give you that and more. Come to me whenever you need to talk, or just a shoulder to cry on, and I will be there. Always.' I clasped her hand in mine tighter, and she nodded, so obviously miserable. I felt a sharp pain in my heart for only a moment, but long enough to take my breath away, knowing deep in my soul, there would be thousands more tears shed—and they would not only be hers—before anyone knew the path Bessie would be forced to walk now her entire world, and life as she knew it, had changed forevermore.

Standing in front of Bessie, she put the final touches to my gown, the heavy cream satin trimmed in gold, while pinning the brooch just below my breasts, complimenting the handsewn gold beads covering the bodice, sparkling in the electrical light above—a luxury—but one I wouldn't miss, preferring the lamps and candles we used at home. I exhaled loudly, unable to stop fidgeting or adjusting the full skirt, until she slapped my hands away. Only our second night aboard, dressing for dinner had already become a chore. I had sat for an hour while she styled my hair, taking care as she applied my cosmetics far heavier than I liked, soon finishing after pinning the pearl tiara to the crown of my head, before gently slipping the strand of pearls around my neck and securing the clasp. I had not wanted her to remove my gold locket Aaron had given me when we first married, and had not taken it off since the day he gave it back to me at the gaol; however, reluctantly agreed it did not compliment the gown and, given her current situation, knew my refusal would only lead to another argument between us, and consented for her to put it away for safekeeping until I returned to ready for bed.

'Thank you, Bessie. As always, you have transformed me from a caterpillar into a butterfly. Stay off your feet and go to bed after you have eaten, please. Hamish will help me undress.' I embraced her warmly for only a moment before she pushed me away, holding me at arm's length.

'Not bloody likely. Now, get away with you. Have no fear, Mistress. I'll be here on your return, and for his own sake, tell Hamish the same.' I smothered a smile as I made my way out into the sitting room.

Emmy beamed up at me when she caught sight of the tiara and necklace, jumping to her feet to embrace me, while Hamish and Thomas rose, both slipping on their waistcoat and tails, Thomas adjusting his several times and grimacing.

'Are we off?' Hamish asked, politely holding the door to our suite open for us to go ahead of him.

'Like a bucket of prawns left out in the sun,' Thomas called back over his shoulder as I followed them, Hamish closing the door behind us, his loud laughter echoing through the hallway and beyond.

Strolling into the dining room, the twins ran ahead to our table to greet our friends, while the maître d' tapped Hamish on the shoulder as we passed the front desk, asking him to step away to speak in private. I followed them off to the side, concerned how nervous the young man appeared as he stared up at Hamish, his left eye twitching more than once.

'I do apologise, Sir. We have received some information regarding an incident that occurred last night here in the dining room. There have been a significant number of complaints made by the first-class passengers you were, er... oh... ah... I'm unsure how to say this politely.' He paused, glancing at me for a moment before turning back to Hamish, his eye twitching again. 'There were concerns expressed that you and Mrs Cavanaugh acted, well, er, lewdly while dancing, and offended many that were present. We ask if there is any truth to the matter, you would be, er, kind enough to refrain from repeating this behaviour tonight and in the future. It would be greatly appreciated. Thank you kindly, Sir.' The poor man appeared terrified under Hamish's stare, relaxing only when one side of Hamish's mouth turned up, his brown eyes twinkling and he nodded. The poor man turned to me and nodded politely, his cheeks flushed, far less noticeably than my own. 'Madam.' I nodded back, fighting the urge to strike Hamish dead where he stood, while hoping the ship would split in half and swallow me; however, he appeared unfazed by it all, politely thanking the nervous young man before offering me his arm and escorting me to the table.

Feeling the weight of the passengers' stares, my gaze fixed on our table across the room hidden away in the far corner, sat the only friendly faces on the ship, their smiles wide, their manner so very welcoming. No matter how hard I tried, I was unable to ignore the whispers, or several women we passed gossipping loudly, most in the room far more polite, ensuring they spoke of us in hushed tones, glancing at us at times, their eyes full of judgement. Walking quickly, although most would consider my pace a slow run at the very least, I sat down heavily next to my new friend, my face now on fire. Jasper and Lilith greeted us warmly, ignoring the stares as Hamish and the children made themselves comfortable, while I shifted in my chair, slumping down as far as possible in the hope no one could see me.

'Och, I feel as though I'm a twelve-year-old lad again, an' have just been reprimanded by me auld headmaster. Kept me hands in me pockets the whole time on the off chance I'd be given the cuts without warnin',' Hamish complained, a smirk on his lips as Jasper threw back his head and howled with laughter. Lilith, only slightly more restrained, collapsed into a fit of giggles, while the children laughed and teased each other over whose parents would be escorted from the room before dinner even started—only causing more of our dining companions to stare in our direction, some wrinkling their noses in disdain, while others openly mocked us. Overhearing a conversation while walking the decks this afternoon, two ladies had been discussing a table in the dining room filled with strange children, and even stranger adults they assumed to be the parents. I stopped to listen, ensuring I was discreet, while thinking the family they spoke of may be like-minded, and considered inviting them to our table given it could seat at least four more. It was only when they described Emmy's glorious red hair did I realise the vile things they were saying were about us, causing me to cringe and swiftly return to my suite, where I had remained in hiding.

'How wonderful to be back in your company,' Jasper exclaimed, his eyes glinting in the candlelight. 'You two certainly don't go unnoticed in a room, no matter how big the crowd surrounding you.'

Chatting over dinner, while enjoying course after course, my wine glass always full no matter how quickly I drank, thanks to the efficient footmen hovering around every table. Out of the corner of my eye, I noticed the maître d' reluctantly making his way towards our table, a large tray in his hands. I panicked, quickly scanning the room to find a way of escape, but there was none, other than jumping to my feet to flee through the main entrance, and I would cause yet another scene and disgrace myself, of that, I was certain.

'Many happy returns of the day, dear Abigail. We wanted to make this one memorable for you in a new way, compared to the past,' Lilith said just as the maître d' arrived, a tendril of dark hair having escaped its binding at some point between the kitchen and our table flopping over his twitching eye. The footman cleared a space near the end of the table, allowing him to place the heavy tray down, his hand immediately going to his forehead to brush back his hair and tuck the rogue strand back in under his cap. My eyes went wide as I gazed across at the tiered cake, the largest on the bottom made of chocolate, the slightly smaller in the middle, vanilla, while the top tier was raspberry, all beautifully decorated into an elegant masterpiece that would feed at least fifty people. Lilith waited for the staff to excuse themselves before continuing. 'I have a small gift here for you, Abigail.' She rummaged around in a burlap sack hidden at her feet, an enormous contradiction to the sparkling handbag she carried, now resting discreetly on her lap, the diamonds covering it handsewn with fine silver wire to ensure they stayed where they were meant to.

'You are far too generous, and you did not have to go to all this trouble. Your company alone makes the day special.' Jasper grinned at me, the children in deep discussion about the trout in the rivers that ran through Willow Grove, soon organising a fishing trip together on the property. Finally, finding what she was looking for, Lilith straightened up, heaving an ivory silk bag onto the table with some effort, the contents thudding heavily on the linen tablecloth. I embraced her, and thanked Jasper profusely before she lifted it gently with both hands, placing the heavy gift into mine. I undid the ribbon binding the top of the silk bag, slipping it off with a flourish before placing what looked like an emu egg down in front of me, the exterior like jagged stone. Although I was uncertain what it was, or what I would do with it, I smiled brightly before continuing. 'Thank you, Arcadia family, for your thoughtfulness. It is so very lovely.' Lilith collapsed in a fit of giggles, while Jasper chuckled to himself. Hamish appeared confused as he reached out and took it from me, studying it closely, while Lilith took my hand in hers under the table, her body trembling, her laughter louder now.

'Looks like a rock tae me, except fer the wee touch of purple at the bottom where 'tis chipped away, by accident it seems if ye take a closer look,' Hamish remarked, Thomas and Emmy glancing up at him in amusement before returning their attention to the object he was able to cradle in one hand, while a regular sized person required two at the very least.

'Oh, Abigail. You are just the sweetest, sitting here trying not to offend anyone,' Lilith gasped, attempting to catch her breath and calm herself, her lilac eyes full of affection as she gazed into mine, my cheeks starting to flush. She leaned back comfortably in her chair, her hand smoothing her hair before she adjusted her bodice. 'Please do not be embarrassed. You are among friends, and most in the world would not have a clue what it is, or its purpose.' I swallowed hard, my shoulders relaxing as a peace settled on me, confident now they would not mock our ignorance—and I loved them just a little more for it. Lilith kissed my cheek before leaning forward in her chair. 'It's a raw Amethyst. This,' she said, reaching out to Hamish, who obediently placed the heavy stone in her cupped hands, 'is a powerful grounding gemstone that radiates positive energy. If you split it in half, you will find the purple crystals said to ward off evil, and they enable healing from past wounds, along with protection from sickness.' I nodded, fascinated by an object so ugly on the outside, yet held such treasure hidden inside. Considering myself a woman of the world these days, I had admired Amethyst stones before, but only ever polished and worn as jewellery. Lilith gently placed the stone back on the table in front of me, my hand unconsciously reaching out to run my fingers over the uneven surface. If I had stumbled across this in the bush back home, I would have continued walking, thinking I had stepped too close to an emu nest, the shape and look of it so similar.

'What am I meant to do with it? Use it as a doorstop for my bedchamber, or as a weapon to strike an intruder down? It's certainly heavy enough, and would likely keep Leo from bothering me when I sleep. Looks to me it would be effective whichever way I choose to use it,' I said in jest, the children's musical laughter filling the room. Lilith leaned in to me, shifting her chair closer, her mouth near my ear.

'This crystal will protect you from spiritual attacks, and believe me when I say there has been a war raging against you that you've no knowledge of. You are gifted, Abigail, far more than anyone I have met in this lifetime, only somewhere along the way, these gifts have been dismissed, and now lay dormant within. By you, whether you are consciously aware or not. At some point before you were even born, you made the decision to reject the supernatural, within yourself and in everything and everyone around you. You now must reconnect with and develop the powerful metaphysical abilities you still hold deep inside waiting to be woken. I am confident keeping the stone close will help ease the grief, fear and nervousness of the body and mind currently tormenting you.' I nodded, ignoring the fear sitting heavier than this stone in the pit of my stomach.

'Does it do anything else, Lilith?' The children accepted another slice each when offered, barely making a dent in the enormous cake, while I nodded my consent when the footman offered me another slice, choosing raspberry this time.

'Oh, yes. If kept in your home, it provides you great security, and due to its vibrational frequency, Amethyst will bring peace and stability of mind.' She paused, lifting a crystal glass to her mouth, and drinking deeply, her rosebud lips stained deep red when she placed the glass back on the table. 'You need to find someone to at least cut it in half. Leave one piece on display in your bedchamber, and break the other into smaller pieces to have jewellery made. When feeling melancholy, wearing it close helps the body and mind recover, and it will ward off evil around you if secured to your person.' I swallowed hard, finding it difficult to believe a rock dug out of the ground was able to do so many wonderful things, but forced a smile, not wanting to be rude given how thoughtful they had been. 'Place a piece under your pillow, and the children's. They won't notice it's there, and it fights off sleeplessness and bad dreams. The added benefit is you'll remember dreams vividly and understand what they mean. Only put a small piece though, or you may bruise that lovely face of yours.' I embraced her again, grateful we had met, and for Aaron sending her to me.

'Thank you. For everything,' I whispered, many around us finishing the last of their drinks, some already leaving to find their beds before the night was over. The musicians had taken a well earned break, and many took that to mean they, too, were retiring.

'You are welcome, my dear Abigail. I would also like to give you a reading as part of your birthday gift. Not now, but when the time is right, I will sit down with you in private.' Unsure what this entailed, I thanked her profusely, anyway. Attending a 'psychic' at Dana's insistence not long after we arrived in Australia, I had been left far from impressed by the woman's predictions, and found the entire experience odd; however, I trusted Lilith and was drawn to her uniqueness, feeling safe in her company to speak freely, while confident she was not a gossip.

'Mummy. I have made a new friend. She is from Melbourne, and invited me to sleep in their suite. May I please?' Emmy pleaded, my eyes widening as I stared back at my daughter.

'You've got Buckley's chance, my girl. I do not know her family, nor even the young girl's name, and I suspect you don't either.' She collapsed into a fit of giggles, while several at the table looked at her with affection.

'Oh, of course I know her name. It's Madeline. Now you know, please may I sleep there, even for one night? Her parents said it was fine as long as I have permission from you. I don't know how they thought I would sleep there without it. I am only thirteen.' She shook her head in disbelief, wrinkling her nose indignantly, while I smothered a smile. 'And, Mummy. That saying about William Buckley does not make sense to me. We learnt all about him and his adventures with the Wathaurong people, mostly from you and Daddy when we were small, but if the truth be told, we hear more at school about Captain Cook and how wonderful he and all the explorers were who civilised this country. I never realised how famous Mr Buckley is around Geelong, well, not until I heard Alinta Bradley talk about him from stories passed down by her elders. Although Mrs McGinty still bunches all the tribes into one and calls them blacks or natives, sometimes much worse. You need to go talk to her again, Mummy. She doesn't treat the Bradley children well at all, and is doing everything she can to make their lives so miserable at school they will choose to leave.' I nodded, uncertain where this was leading, dread sitting heavy in my stomach at the thought of our friends being treated poorly by anyone.

George and Regina, along with their twin girls, Killara and Alinta—born the same year as my own—and their two boys, Jarrah, a year younger than his sisters, while Jiemba, or Jimmy as everyone knew him, completed their family only a year after his brother, had become firm friends to us all over the years. Regina's parents' property sat only two miles from our own, where they were forced to live under the protection of the name her parents carried, given marriage between a white man or woman and a 'native' was illegal, unless permission was granted through the Aboriginal Protection Board, and consent was rarely given. What was worse, the Bradley's were shunned by most in the district, although Regina's parents were tolerated only because of their wealth, a situation that broke my heart, yet one I could never truly understand or relate just how soul destroying, humiliating and painful it would be to be judged by the colour of your skin. Given I was rarely treated with suspicion, or outright rudeness when away from Willow Grove doing what I pleased without restrictions, I was well aware my freedom was only because of the colour of my skin, along with my wealth. If I were female and poor, I would still be treated with more respect than anyone with a drop of Aboriginal blood in their veins, and the darker their skin, the worse the treatment they received.

Originally from New York, Mr Henry Morgan and his wife Alice, along with their only daughter, had settled in Geelong five-years before us, and Regina had fallen immediately in love with George, a Gunditjmara man employed by her father as a farmhand, while forced to take an English name given to him by the family where he had been taken by force as a boy of ten to work the land under their supervision, earning three meals a day and a bed at night in the shearers quarters—four to a room during shearing season—and not much else until he ran away at fifteen, taking labouring work where he could find it until employed by Mr Morgan, a fair man who paid equal wages no matter what the colour of your skin.

'Mrs McGinty calls 'em half-caste to their face, an' says she would kick 'em off the property if it weren't for the Mistress runnin' the place,' Thomas interjected, arching his eyebrows at me, his tone sarcastic, 'an' she says education is wasted on 'em 'cause they don't have the same brain we have, an' are only good for domestic service an' labourin'—an' even then they need a firm hand standin' over 'em to make sure they work at all. I'm sure in her own mind, she's imaginin' a stockwhip in that firm hand she believes they need due to their laziness an' poor character, an' takin' great pleasure from it.' I grimaced, pushing down the rage ready to explode from every part of me, while adding this to the long list of things to be addressed by this *Mistress* on my return.

'I will speak to Mrs McGinty in private when I have had time to calm myself. What's most important is you both know it is now called racism to judge a person by the colour of their skin, or where they were born. I want you to promise to tell everyone who will listen until I can put a stop to it one way or another, at least within the boundaries of our own property, which is the extent of any power I hold. I can do nothing outside of Willow Grove, other than speak my mind if I'm witness to the mistreatment of anyone, no matter where they come from or what they look like.' They both nodded, Emmy squirming in her seat. A word only new to me, and uttered for the first time in print in 1902 by an American man by the name of Richard Pratt—a good man in my opinion fighting the evils of racial segregation—there was finally one word to describe the unfairness and cruelty I witnessed daily if away from the protection of Willow Grove. I was not alone in my disgust of how colonisation had impacted on those to whom the land had belonged for thousands of years, while acutely aware the treatment they received would continue while it suited so many to use and abuse those left who had not been slaughtered en masse over the last one-hundred and seventeen-years of English occupation.

'Of course we know Mrs McGinty is a racist, but so are most of your fancy friends, Mummy, and they're not bad people, only daft and following along like the sheep in the paddocks,' Emmy remarked, fixing her gaze on me.

'I disagree with you, Emmy. Anyone who believes someone else is inferior because of their race, well, they may not be bad in the true sense of the word, but they are ignorant, mean-spirited, and a hundred other things that come to mind, and I include several of my friends. I will always find it unacceptable, and I tell them so.' I crossed my arms, feeling slightly defensive regarding the company I kept.

'Getting back to what I was saying, if you don't mind?' She jutted out her chin, determination in her brilliant green eyes. 'Mr Buckley obviously had a far better chance than most expected when he escaped, along with enormous luck emerging from the bush like that in 1835 after thirty-two-years missing. So, in fact, I have a better chance than most to gain your permission to stay with Madeline. That is what you are really saying, Mummy, and we all know it well.' Hamish choked on his wine, Thomas pounding him hard on the back while I stroked my temples, feeling a headache coming on.

'I must meet Madeleine's parents first, Emmy. I would prefer you invite her to sleep in our suite first, before I will allow you to stay in theirs. Once that is done, I will give you my consent.' She nodded, her smile brilliant, her face shining as the music started for what would be the final time before we retired to our suite for the night.

'Do we dare?' Hamish asked, offering me his hand. I smiled and took it, not caring anymore what these strangers thought. They had already formed their opinions of us, and I had not the strength or inclination to change their minds. He led me to the dance floor and held me at an appropriate distance, his manner proper and that of a gentleman as he swept me around the floor, while I fought the urge to laugh aloud. He had never behaved so politely in public since the first night we boarded the ship in Melbourne, leaving me wondering just what point he was attempting to make. He kept this up for three more dances, while every eye was on us, glistening in anticipation of what scandalous things we would do. The music ended, and he elegantly led me from the dancefloor back towards our table, halting abruptly in the middle of the room to turn and kiss me passionately, loud gasps and frenetic whispering filling my ears before he released me and moved forward, my hand firmly in his, while the strangers surrounding me watched *us* return to the *strange* table. 'Och, dinnae fash, Abigail. We naw did anythin' lewd *on* the dance floor.' He kissed my forehead, pulling out my chair before I reached up and touched his handsome face, smiling to myself as I lowered myself down next to the people I loved.

Back in my suite, Thomas and Emmy were already sound asleep, unable to stay awake long enough for me to read one page, let alone a chapter, from *The Marvellous Land of Oz,* before tucking them in, leaving Hamish and I with nothing to do but drink wine in the sitting room.

'How about I take ye tae a proper party?' He rose in one elegant movement, pulling me up with him. 'Go an' change yer dress. They'll laugh at ye, an' think the King's consort jumped aboard tae visit with 'em especially.' He held me by the shoulders, chuckling to himself. 'Can ye wear the one that sits just off yer shoulders with the long wispy lookin' sleeves?' He released me, and lowered himself back down on the lounge, making himself comfortable for what appeared to be a long wait, while I stood in front of him, gazing down, my eyebrows arched.

'Well, I'm going to need help, unless you want me to disturb Bessie?' His face broke into a grin as I shook my head and turned to walk away. He followed me into my bedchamber, clumsily helping me strip off my gown, before I hurried to the wardrobe to look for the dress he was talking about, finally finding it hanging in the back. His gaze had not left my near naked body, my shift flimsy and transparent, and I swiftly slipped on the simple dress before he could drag me into bed, lust in his eyes. I returned to his side, his thick fingers securing the buttons down the back easily, his hand slipping down to my waist as I adjusted the skirt, his lips on the back of my neck sending tingles through me. Catherine had continued to make the buttons on my dresses larger out of habit, and I had not requested any change. When Aaron was alive, he struggled with his fat fingers to undo some of the more delicate buttons, and Hamish's hands were just as big and clumsy; however, he had been able to secure these without difficulty, thanks to my dear friend. I made my way over to my dressing table and sat down, waiting patiently.

'What are ye doin'? Ye have enough o' that face paint on, an' look far more beautiful without it,' he called out, before throwing himself down heavily on my bed, a faint crack sounding somewhere in the room.

'God help you if you broke my bed, Hamish.' I turned around in my seat to glare at him, now laying back on my pillows, his legs crossed at the ankles, his shoes on the floor. 'I refuse to go to steerage in a tiara and a pearl necklace worth more than most poor souls earn in a lifetime. Unless you are secretly taking me to a ball, I will need your help to take my hair down and the jewellery off, if you would be so kind?' Turning back to stare in the mirror, I considered washing my face, then glanced at the clock above the fireplace and thought better of it. 'Surely you undressed and redressed some of those ladies you courted over the years?' He came up behind me without warning and kissed my neck, removing the necklace before taking the pins one by one from my hair, allowing it to fall down my back in loose curls.

'Och, naw. They had their servants tae do the undressin'. I was only welcome once all that was done an' they were in their bed fer the night. Even the lassies without maids tae serve 'em did the same. Naw one o' 'em would ever think tae let me see 'em stripped naked in the light o' day. They were quick tae open their legs, but only in the dark. Well, the women I've known in the biblical sense o' the word.' He shook his head for a moment, his eyes fixed on mine in the gilded mirror. 'This dress would have tae be me favourite on ye, Abigail. Ye remind me o' a gypsy princess.' Taking the last of the pins from my hair, he placed the tiara down on the dressing table alongside the necklace and helped me to my feet, leading me from my room and through the empty suite out into the wide hallway.

Holding his hand, we descended flight after flight of what seemed to be never ending stairs, soon arriving in steerage where I stopped at the door to catch my breath, the Irish music drifting down the hallway from within. Stepping into a large room filled with tables and chairs, almost identical to the ship that first carried us to Australia, Hamish left me sitting at a table, approaching the busy barkeep to order refreshments, while I listened to the music, my mind filled with memories of happier times—and of home, where those I loved waited for our return. To watch those around me dancing and singing songs from their homeland brought me nothing but happiness, seeing them all so relaxed and joyful in comparison to our companions in first class, most who wouldn't have known what a good time was even if smacked in the face with it. Hamish returned, a bottle of whisky and a jug of beer on a tray with three steel mugs, and bent forward to place them on the table in front of me, before sitting down opposite.

'We're goin' tae celebrate what's left o' yer birthday with Aaron, now the day is almost done.' A lump lodged in my throat, his kind gesture bringing tears to my eyes for the thousandth time today. He poured three whiskies, placing one in front of me, one in front of himself, and the third in the middle of the table in remembrance of Aaron. We held them up, steel clashing against steel, before drinking it all in one swallow. Burning its way down my throat into the pit of my stomach, the rough spirit soon created a warm fire, radiating through my body, my legs already heavy from the wine. 'Aye, I'll go first, an' tell ye a story ye possibly dinnae know,' Hamish offered, his brown eyes full of emotion, a wry smile on his lips, and I nodded, unable to speak for fear I would break down and humiliate myself. My fears were unfounded, and as Hamish recounted a number of memories he held close, I laughed until I cried tears of joy that my Aaron experienced such a wonderful time when he was here, surrounded by genuine mates, and all who knew and loved him well. My turn soon came, and I quietly spoke of a night long ago when he became so drunk at the pub, he was carried home by four strong men, two of them Hamish and Angus, while I followed along behind believing we had a lifetime ahead of us, amused and quietly confident it would not be the last time he would be carried home like a pig trussed to a branch ready for the fire. We spoke back and forth for the longest time of all the wonderful memories we had of him over the years, and there were many, while we drank one whisky after another, the room lit by lanterns and candles, casting a romantic glow over all present.

Surprising even myself, I did not feel as melancholy as I expected speaking of him in such depth and at great length, although I missed him as much as the day he left, and still cried myself to sleep every night—but tonight was a celebration, and I was enjoying talking of him with someone who knew him nearly as well. I appreciated having Hamish with me. He had really made my birthday special, and I treasured what he had done in thought and deed to make it so.

Finishing the last of the whisky, he stood and took my hand, leading me towards the front of the room where a group danced and laughed while holding hands, forming a line as they followed the person in front of them. We joined them at the end of the line, Hamish taking a dark haired woman's hand in his, mine in the other as we followed their steps, soon dancing the jig with the best of them. A tall man came up beside me without warning and took my hand; however, he did not bring along a partner. His grip tightened, his finger stroking my palm, and fear overwhelmed me as I looked up at him to see George Maslow's eyes staring down at me.

Pulling away, my heart racing, he would not release his grip no matter how hard I tried, my other hand now clawing at his frantically. Grabbing my other arm with his free hand, he pulled me to his chest, a silent scream coming from my lips, my body shaking, while I could not run even if he did loosen his grip, my legs buckling underneath me. His face only inches from mine, he bent forward to kiss me, while I remained his hostage, my body limp in his arms, terror consuming every part of me. Hamish came from behind me without warning, his fist connecting with the man's nose, the crunching of bones and blood splatter causing my stomach to lurch as the man released me, his body crashing to the ground before me, the back of his head hitting the floor with a thud. The room was silent, the musicians on their feet appearing confused as a small crowd formed around us.

'Stand up!' Hamish roared; however, the man refused to move, remaining motionless on his side at my feet, his knees pulled up to his chest, his arms covering his bloodied face and head. 'I told ye tae get on yer feet! How dare ye touch her,' he roared again.

'Hamish, he's had enough, and is bleeding badly. Let's go back to the table. Please?' I reached out and took him by the arm, and he relented, stepping away before escorting me back to the table. Several of the man's friends helped him to his feet before hurrying him out of the room. I could not bear violence of any kind, and fighting was only one vice Hamish was known for when drunk, and when sober if he felt justified. Sliding back into my seat, I waited for him to calm, my body still trembling; however, my heart had started to slow and my fear dissipated knowing I was safe and the man was a stranger to me. I raised my mug of beer, as did Hamish, his full lips turning up slightly at the corners as I took a deep breath. 'Wherever you are, my beautiful man, may you be as happy as you were here, and feel the love I send from my soul to yours every single day. I miss you, and I adore you. Always will.' We drank to Aaron, my lost love and his best mate before Hamish left me to order another bottle, while I gazed down at Aaron's glass of whisky in the middle of the table, so many memories running through my mind, some making me smile, while others hurt my heart.

Hamish soon came back empty handed, and I smiled at him, pleased to see the anger had passed and he had returned to his usual self, other than the knuckles on his right hand, damaged and bruised. I watched him drink the last of the beer, drawn in by his beautiful dark brown eyes staring straight into my soul, truly making me believe he saw what lay deep within and hidden; his long black hair loose, his curls billowing down like silk, his full lips I could kiss forever.

'Aye, it's time we went tae bed an' finish celebratin'.' He handed me Aaron's whisky, and I nodded before drinking it in one swallow, my face twisting in disdain as he reached across, grasping my hand as I looked up at him and smiled, grateful to whomever had sent him my way so very long ago.

The last night of our journey had arrived far quicker than any of us expected, and we were now steaming towards Melbourne down the east coast of Australia. We had experienced an enjoyable voyage, and become even closer to Jasper and Lilith, while Thomas had become great mates with their two sons. Emmy had been inseparable from her friend, Madeline, spending their days together, and taking it in turns to stay the night in the others' suite.

Bessie had made her decision regarding her unborn wean, and had already prepared herself to suffer the consequences, whatever they may be. Over five-months gone now, closer to six, she knew she had my support come what may, while secretly, I was overjoyed she would soon become a mother, despite the circumstances. I would do anything for her and her bairn, even if that meant losing her as my maid, and I had decided I would pay her wages even if no longer in my employ until the day she took her last breath. After all she had done for me in the last fifteen-years, I owed her that at the very least. I knew having your own child changed everything the moment you held them in your arms for the very first time, and despite Bessie vowing she would continue in service as my ladies maid, I had decided to prepare myself if, in fact, she ultimately chose to stay home to raise her babe.

Begrudgingly, I was forced to admit Hamish had been right, and by allowing him to court me we had become closer, along with the fact I was not forced to endure unwanted attention from even one gentleman on board. I was not in love with him in the way he wanted or deserved; however, I had formed a stronger romantic attachment to him, enjoying the time we spent together inside and outside of his suite. I allowed him to hold my hand, or stroke my face for only a moment when in public since embarking on the ship; however, there were times I would pull away when he tried to kiss or hold me a certain way, yet he had been patient and loving towards me, despite my rejection of him on occasion.

Although I felt sick to my stomach about Hamish openly courting me once home, my nervousness mingled with excitement at the thought of returning to the safety and loving embrace of Willow Grove, and all who lived there. Being able to wear the clothes in which I was comfortable, to ride Delly bareback with nothing on my feet, to embrace everyone I loved, and a hundred more things I had missed filled me with joy—and I could barely stand the wait until the morning. To be able to take flowers to my boys' grave and tell the three of them about the voyage, and the exciting adventures we had been on only made me miss and think of them more the nearer we drew to home. I wanted to tell Aaron how I made it through the journey, only just, as he wanted me to, asking me to make him proud—and I felt I had—along with an all consuming gnawing inside my heart to tell him how I had missed him so very dreadfully, unable to feel his presence at all the entire time we had been gone.

Hamish and I had kept to ourselves during the voyage home, socialising only with Jasper and Lilith, while making friends with several passengers we had met in steerage. Due to our *lewd* behaviour the first night in the dining room and the constant scrutiny from the other passengers, we had chosen to spend most nights in steerage if we felt like dancing, leaving first-class as soon as the last course was finished, often accompanied by Lilith and Jasper.

Never seeing Hamish so relaxed, his softer, sweeter side on display more often than not, I had struggled to not be drawn in too deeply. I cherished our friendship, and how he trusted and confided in me in ways he had not before, and I felt the same towards him. It was an easy and comfortable arrangement between us—for me, at least—as I was not forced to explain a thing about myself as I would if I were to allow a stranger to court me. Hamish knew me far better than most, and he still cared for me despite my faults.

We had only returned to our suite after sharing our last dinner onboard with Lilith, Jasper, and their boys, agreeing it was far more sensible to say our farewells tonight, rather than attempt to find each other when disembarking at Port Melbourne in the early hours of the morning. Not only would there be hundreds of passengers eager to step foot on Australian soil, some for the first time, there would be the same, if not more, waiting on the pier for their loved ones' long awaited return, along with those onboard immigrating to reunite after years of separation from friends and family who settled here before them. It was the ones who came alone I felt sorry for the most, but I was quietly confident they would find their feet fairly quickly, and meet others in similar situations. One thing I knew for certain was that the majority of Australian people were a friendly and welcoming bunch, and they would reach out to give someone a hand up more often than not. We were fortunate to have a wide circle of friends and family who looked out for us, and made life easier, Richard only one of them, thoughtfully arranging for *The Delmont* carriages to collect us from Station Pier and transport us to Flinders Street Station, where we would take the train home. I had not wanted anyone to travel such a distance when they could welcome us once we arrived back in Geelong a few hours later, and had sent word while in Scotland. Richard had sent me a telegram only days before we left New York, advising me he had it all in hand and our transport had been confirmed.

I relaxed back on the settee, nowhere near as luxurious or comfortable as what we were used to at home, Thomas laying next to me silently staring at the ceiling, while Emmy sat close to Hamish opposite us, her delicate body pressed into his enormous side as they flicked through a magazine he had picked up in Paris.

'Are ya goin' dancin' down steerage tonight?' Thomas asked, while I shook my head, the light above flickering, the ship shuddering violently for a moment, while Hamish glanced across at the large porthole to check the horizon, certain we were headed into a storm.

'No. We said goodbye to new friends and acquaintances there last night. We wanted to spend our final evening with you.' He grinned up at me, my finger gently stroking his cheek, his jaw becoming more chiselled with each passing day, his features so very much the image of Aaron at the same age.

'Aye, then. Tell me what ye enjoyed the most durin' yer adventures away. Only the best parts.' Hamish asked, his voice low, our suite pleasantly quiet other than the sound of the ocean below, the room swaying ever so gently I was at risk of falling asleep, an imperceptible hum from the engines deep within the belly of the ship so soft I no longer noticed.

'I adored the orphanage where Mummy grew up. Sister is my very dearest and closest confidante now, and we have decided to exchange letters until she has permission to visit with us. Of course, meeting my very best friend, Madeline, was only one of the best parts as I have far too many to list,' Emmy replied, and Hamish nodded in agreement. Thomas appeared thoughtful as he lifted his head from my lap.

'The best part for me was the voyage over to England. We made good friends, an' had a beaut' time,' he murmured wistfully before laying his head down again, Hamish and I exchanging a knowing smile.

'Aye, well, the best part fer me was spendin' all me time with the three o' ye. I could naw have hoped fer better company.' Hamish glanced across at me and winked, Emmy now turning the pages of the magazine on his lap while pointing out the new Rolls Royce advertisement taking up an entire page.

'I enjoyed every part, because you were all by my side; however, I particularly enjoyed the journey home from New York.' I stared back at Hamish, holding my gaze for the longest time, his handsome face creased in a gentle smile as he stroked Emmy's back while she read aloud to him in French, her accent the worst I had ever heard.

A loud bang startled me, and I jumped in fright, the door flying open before Bessie hurried into the room, little Mary close behind her, her face pained. Thomas and I made room for them, and they soon settled down next to us, making themselves as comfortable as possible on the hard settee.

'Everything is packed, Mistress. I've left out your clothing for the morn', and Mary has done the same for the bairns. We dock before sunrise, I've been told by a kindly steward. I asked a favour of him, being such a sweet lad and all, and he agreed to make our trunks a priority, and gave me his solemn oath that our belongings will be taken tonight and unloaded first thing, to ensure we are on time to meet the early train.' Her cheeks flushed, my dear Bessie stopped to take a breath, while I leaned over and took her hand in mine.

'How are you feeling?' She stared back into my eyes, quickly brushing away a tear before anyone noticed.

'I am looking forward to planting my feet back on the solid soil of Willow Grove, the place I will always call home, but my nerves are shot and I feel sick to my stomach, Mistress.' Unable to contain her emotions any longer, she broke down, little Mary quickly slipping her tiny arm around her friend in an attempt to console the inconsolable, while Thomas and Emmy ignored us and Bessie's tears, having become used to the outbursts that came without warning, both speaking of the Bradley family, and their plan to visit them first upon arriving home.

'Oh, Bessie, my dear friend. All will be well in the end. Whatever happens, you will soon hold a beautiful babe in your arms who will belong to you forevermore. It makes no difference who planted the seed because you will be the most wonderful mother any bairn could be blessed with. One, I have no doubt, will protect and adore her child fiercely and without measure from now,' I said, pointing at her bulging stomach, well hidden under her uniform, 'through to eternity—and you will do a fine job of it all.' I smiled reassuringly, patting her leg before she rose to her feet, little Mary beside her. She bent down to embrace me, before sniffing loudly and straightening up.

'Oh, I'm just wrung out, and my mind will not stop racing even when I sleep. I will retire now, though, Mistress, if you don't mind? Only so I can be fresh for tomorrow and what is to come.' I nodded, kissing her hand before she made her way to the door. 'May you all rest well, and I love you, my darling Thomas, and Emmy,' she called out as we bid her goodnight before stepping out into the hallway, quickly making her way to their suite next door, little Mary following behind.

I stroked Thomas' sandy blonde hair, like silk running through my fingers as it fell down past his collar, the sides and front only slightly shorter, no different than the way his father wore his the entire time I had known him. Emmy snuggled into Hamish's side as we all chatted animatedly about the near seven-months we had been away from Willow Grove. I often wondered what had gone on during the time we had been absent, and dreaded to think what havoc Leo had left in his wake. Shaking my head, I pushed the thought to the back of my mind, wanting to enjoy the last night where I was not responsible for anyone other than my children. I would deal with it all when it found me, no doubt within minutes of our arrival home.

'Ma, I'm goin' to bed. I know it's an early day tomorrow, an' I'll be flat out like a lizard drinkin' once we get back 'cause I wanna catch up with me mates first thing.' Thomas struggled to sit up, kissing my cheek before rising to his feet and making his way over to Hamish, thumping him on the back, while Emmy came to me, lowering herself down onto my lap, her arms wrapped around me.

'I'm off to bed, too, Mummy. It's fabulous to be returning to our beloved Willow Grove, and I cannot wait to see my darling Uncle Leo. He will have made so many sweets for us, and it will be such a fantastical celebration, although I do dread what he's been up to without us there to keep him in line.' I smothered a smile as she rolled her eyes. 'Not to worry, the sooner I sleep, the sooner morning will arrive.' My mouth twitched, amusement in my eyes, my hand squeezing her waist one last time before she went to hug Hamish goodnight.

'No truer word has been spoken, my wee Emmeline. I will come and settle you in for the night.' I was pulled to my feet with ease by Thomas, and followed them into Emmy's bedchamber, where I lay down between them to read the last chapter of *The Marvellous Land of Oz*. Emmy was soon asleep; however, I continued on to the end, Thomas listening intently. Once tucked up in their own beds half-an-hour later, I returned to Hamish and sat down beside him. He slipped his arm around my shoulders, pulling me close to his broad chest, his eyes fixed on mine as he lowered his head and kissed my lips so very gently, my hand on his cheek, my fingers caressing the stubble along his chiselled jaw.

'Will ye come tae me suite an' spend the night? I dinnae know when the next time'll be when we'll have the chance tae be alone once we settle back home. Since ye dinnae want anyone tae know what lies between us fer a time, I feel 'tis only right I sleep at the cottage with Angus an' Polly fer the sake o' yer own reputation. I dinnae wanna be seen sneakin' up tae the house, causin' a scandal an' bein' tae blame fer the workers losin' all respect fer yer. Ye haven't told me how long ye'll need, an' I dinnae knew how much time ye plan tae take tae announce our courtship.' I stared up into his eyes, a flash of uncertainty unsettling me, although passed in a moment before his eyes sparkled again, his mouth turning up into a slow smile.

'You will not wait for long, of that, I give you my word. I only require a few days to tell the people who are important to me in person, and I will not make you suffer as I did during our time abroad.' He lowered his head, kissing my brow, his arms tightening around me.

'Aye, ye better naw, or I'll give Leonardo permission tae take out a full page in *The Geelong Advertiser,* announcin' our betrothal before we're officially courtin'.' He threw back his head and laughed while rising to his feet, lifting me up in one graceful movement before crossing the room in three strides, cradling me in his arms. Opening the door slightly, he used his boot to push it wide, stepping out into the hall, my arms wrapped tightly around his muscular neck as it clicked shut behind us. Walking with purpose towards his suite, we passed several passengers, one turning up her nose in disdain, her friends widening their eyes as they watched Hamish turn the key in the lock before carrying me inside, the door slamming in their faces louder than usual thanks to a little help from Hamish's foot. Carrying me through the sitting room, he said not a word until he gently placed me down on the bed.

Much later, as I lay naked beside him, my hand wrapped tightly in his, I drifted off into a comforting slumber, my dreams filled with kangaroos and their joeys, a charming cottage by a river, and Aaron. Always Aaron.

Chapter Four

THE CARRIAGE SLOWED, THE four Martarinos panting loudly, their ebony coats lathered in sweat as they drew the carriage through the elaborate arched gates at a walk, the gates always left open given we had never appointed another gatekeeper, the blue-stone lodge standing proudly to the side, empty as the day we arrived. The large plaque with *Willow Grove* and underneath, *Est 1838* engraved deep into the solid silver shimmered in the sunlight as we passed, appearing to have recently been polished. Set into the bluestone pillar to my right, the sign had been there long before we arrived, the intricate iron gates held strong by the twelve-foot high columns, measuring five-foot square at the base, the left pillar holding a newer, matching plaque with *Cavanaugh* inscribed, along with the year *1890*. Underneath sat a similar plaque, this one far older, the inscription *Residence of Lady Isabelle Delmont* alongside *1840-1875* chiselled into the polished, weathered silver. A sense of peace settled over me, my gaze fixed on the bluestone cottage in the distance behind the gatekeepers lodge inhabited by Mr Hinkle, the carriage gently rocking from side to side. Hamish sat beside me holding my trembling hand, while the children pressed their faces against the window, their smiles wide, before Emmy opened the latch and leaned out, her plaits swaying gently in the breeze.

Movement caught my eye, and Mr Hinkle himself emerged from the thick scrub behind the cottage he claimed as his own. Reminding me of an older, thinner version of Mad Dan Morgan—a notorious bushranger shot and killed in April of 1865 after he terrorised and robbed Peechelba Station near Wangaratta—this man squatting on our land as light as Morgan was dark, his thick hair and bushy beard white as snow, his tall, lean frame looming large in the distance, a spade in one hand, while his other stretched out in front of his tattered overalls giving us the one-fingered salute, his deeply lined face distorted in rage as he loudly sucked the phlegm from his nose into his throat, a guttural sound causing me to jump in my seat before he violently spat in our direction.

'Oh, hello, dear Mr Hinkle. It's so lovely to see your backside still pointing to the ground, and you look well enough from where I'm sitting. Must be the bush tucker you grow, and the 'roo meat you cook ever so nicely.' He lowered his hand, his face like thunder, relaxing only slightly when he nodded once at my daughter, my eyes widening, while I shook my head in disbelief. Harry slowed the horses to almost a stop, his eyes twinkling in amusement as he glanced across at the old hermit whom he knew well, while Bessie gasped from her seat beside him, her hand darting up to cover her mouth, the thought of her sweet Emmy left alone in the company of the ex-gatekeeper far too much to bear. 'I worried for you while away, and I dreamt of you often. I wanted to be the first to tell you of our return, and just how thrilled we all are to be home. I hope you enjoy working in your garden today. I'll pop over for a visit as soon as I have settled myself back in,' Emmy sang out to him, and I grimaced, mortified and unaware until this very moment my Emmeline had been within cooee of the place, or they were even familiar, let alone on friendly terms. Every single soul who lived and worked at Willow Grove knew to give the gatekeeper's lodge and the cottage a wide berth, particularly the children, and to make haste when passing down the driveway, this entire situation taking me by surprise, the thought of my own child's betrayal almost amusing. Hamish chuckled quietly to himself as the old hermit straightened up, still holding the shovel, his gaze fixed on Harry before he glared at me, his old boot kicking the ground several times, creating a small mound of red soil visible fifty-yards away, the carriage painstakingly creeping past *his* property.

'Yeah, then brin' me another tin o' that *Billy Tea*, an' I'll give ya some o' 'em Muntries ya so fond of,' his deep voice boomed across the distance, frightening me a little, although this was not the first time I had been at the end of his sharp tongue. I had attempted to approach him a number of times over the years, intrigued by the golden glow surrounding him, while confident we would become fast friends once we had the opportunity to speak. How wrong I had been, and he had chased me from the acre he claimed as his own every single time, shotgun in hand. The last time when he had shot the ground only inches from my boot, I had made a firm decision to wait him out and not return, believing he would go to God at any time given the age of him. That was twelve-years ago, and his arse was still pointing to the ground, as my daughter has so eloquently observed. The fact we knew barely anything about him had caused me years of frustration, and those who did would speak very little regarding the subject no matter how much I prodded and probed. Mr Hinkle raised his hand again to wipe the snot from his nose onto his worn shirt sleeve, his eyes meeting Emmy's as he nodded at her once more, and she nodded back just as solemnly, confusion overwhelming me, my mind racing as to how I had not known my own daughter had befriended this odd man. 'Welcome home, nipper, an' I'm only sayin' it ta ya, an' not them livin' where they shouldn't. Now, get yerself gone from 'ere before I get me gun an' shoot those ya got beside ya in *Lady Isabelle's* carriage, an' the ones on top laughin' an' thinkin' they're all Lords an' Ladies o' the manor. Disrespectful fiends, the lot o' ya.' He turned away, disappearing back into the native scrub as quickly as he had appeared.

'Thank you for the warm welcome home, Mr Hinkle. Have a fabulous day,' she called out, a loud growl drifting back from the bush through the window only a moment later, causing me to jump again.

'An' stop talkin' like that irritatin' cook ya dafty Ma keeps 'ere, or I'll be forced ta shoot ya in the foot next time I see ya, Mistress Emmeline.'

Laughter filled the carriage, my face blank as I stared at my daughter, holding her stomach as she collapsed into giggles, while Thomas and Hamish howled no different than the dingoes occasionally roaming the property in the night. Harry chuckled to himself before moving the horses forward, their pace only quickening slightly as they ambled down the mile-long driveway, the paddocks on both sides vivid green, one filled with merino sheep supplying us with wool and meat throughout the year, the other holding highland cattle I was certain were not here when we left—the dozen or so heifers, all with a calf or two at foot, ignoring us as they grazed on the lush grass, their long black coats shimmering while vacillating in the gentle breeze. The bull, almost double in size to his female companions, had been secured in a far paddock, the fences reinforced with steel rails and posts since we had last been here. I had often considered importing a small herd of *Bò Ghàidhealach* from my homeland, and had even discussed doing so on several occasions over the years with my beloved Aaron, and despite his enthusiasm and support on the matter, I had felt it unfair due to the climate. A hearty breed known for its long horns and shaggy woolly coat, they were able to withstand the coldest of winters, and I was uncertain if they would acclimatise to the harsh summers we endured in Australia. Why they were here, I had not a clue, and I knew for certain I had left no instruction or given my consent for anything of this magnitude to be purchased in my absence.

Once our trunks had been loaded onto a second carriage at the Geelong Terminus, Bessie and little Mary had chosen to sit up front with Harry, both wanting to enjoy the sweeping views and beauty of our adopted homeland, while catching up on all the gossip they had missed.

Our ship had docked even earlier than expected, the dawn yet to break, allowing us more time than required to catch the first train to Geelong from Flinders Street Station. Collected by a *Delmont* carriage, we were taken to one of the few places open at that hour, *The Victoria Coffee Palace* in Collins Street, adjacent to the Melbourne Town Hall. The bleary-eyed server, Ronny, appeared happy to see us, warmly welcoming us in, and once settling us down at a long table by the fireplace, he returned soon after with four mugs of steaming coffee, two glasses of sweetened warm milk with cinnamon for the children, along with two loaves of bread, still warm from the oven, and a porcelain butter dish, the slab inside freshly churned this morning, a knife beside it, before placing a small plate down in front of each of us . Given there was not another soul in sight, he lowered himself down on a seat in between Bessie and little Mary after we invited him to join us.

Speaking with affection of his parents, Ronald and Peggy Bramhall, now well into their sixth decade and still living above the shop, they had immigrated from Liverpool in England, arriving in Melbourne in 1879 before purchasing the solid, elegant building in 1880 from the owner of the *Victoria Club*—first opened in 1877, while forced to close and move from the premises only three-years later. Starting their coffee palace when the population of Melbourne was far smaller, and the Temperance movement far stronger, the Bramhall family now held fears they would be forced out of a building and the business they so loved, and were proud of, after twenty-five-years of blood, sweat, and many, many tears to earn enough to live comfortably—all as a result of whispers the town hall would soon be expanded.

Hamish had left a substantial tip, something we had recently learned was not only common in America, but expected, along with our details, should they ever need financial assistance or advice. The dark-haired, handsome young man, no more than thirty, immediately became suspicious of us, and we were asked to leave shortly after. Wandering down Swanston Street, past *The Delmont*, we were soon climbing the sweeping stairs under the clocks, the mood jovial as we strolled around the grand terminus to pass the time, before hearing the call for the Geelong train. Hurrying to the platform to find our seats in the first-class carriage only moments before departure, it had taken a good twenty-minutes for my heart to slow. The journey passed quickly, our compartment filled with cheerful banter from the time we pulled away from Melbourne, right up until the moment we arrived at the station in Geelong, all present filled with varying degrees of excitement at the prospect of reuniting with our family and friends after more than seven-months apart.

Although Thomas and Emmy had enjoyed the journey immensely, they had desperately missed their family at times, particularly their grandparents, and were clearly overjoyed to be home, both bent at the waist, their upper bodies hanging out of the carriage windows, a squeal filling my ears as Emmy caught sight of the main house in the distance, the clip-clop of the hooves crunching on the gravel as we continued on down the long oak lined road I had always wanted paved with stone, but felt the time, money and labour involved not worth such effort.

Harry slowed the horses as we came into the circular paved driveway, pulling them up directly out front of the main entrance, Thomas and Emmy already out, their feet on the ground before we had come to a complete stop. Relief swept over me as I gazed up at the basalt mansion, the deep blue of the stones bringing me such comfort to be finally back where I belonged, a sigh escaping my lips, my shoulders relaxing for the first time in days. My face lit up at the sight of Mr and Mrs Cavanaugh, along with my brother and sisters-in-law pouring out of the front door to greet us, my nieces and nephews, our dear friends, and many of the staff following behind, the cheering and loud shouts welcoming us home filling the carriage, the twins already wrapped in their grandparent's arms, held tight in a warm embrace, soon after disappearing from my sight as their loved ones surrounded them.

'Aye, then. Are ye ready, lass?' Hamish asked, his voice low, my hand tightly in his, the noise outside deafening me once Bessie and little Mary joined their friends, not even Harry paying attention to us as he watched them greet each other with great excitement while lighting his pipe, his backside leaning against the front of the carriage.

'As ready as I will ever be, I suppose,' I murmured, my legs trembling slightly. 'Please don't forget you gave me your word that you will keep control of yourself in thought, word and deed, and allow me the time to tell those I must before what lies between us becomes common knowledge.'

'Aye.' He nodded, chuckling to himself as he jumped down from the carriage, his boots landing heavily before he turned to help me, politely offering his hand. I accepted with grace, carefully climbing down and thanking him before he stepped away, placing a respectable distance between us. I turned in his direction and smiled, unable to keep my eyes from his backside, the style of his moleskins relaxed, an easy fit he was most comfortable in; however, there was nothing relaxed about the way in which he wore them, the cut only emphasising his hips, the serviceable thick cloth clinging to his strong, solid thighs. The taupe, neutral colour of the fabric was not neutral at all on him, the hue strangely provocative in the way it highlighted his well toned form, almost making it appear as if he wore no trousers at all, and I felt myself blush, quickly averting my gaze.

'Oh, Abigail, we have missed you all so desperately,' Mrs Cavanaugh called out as she rushed towards me, her arms spread wide. Embracing me tightly, tears streamed down her lovely face, Emmy and Thomas at her side, their arms wrapped around her. I heard someone jumping up and down nearby, frantic clapping, and soon after, loud screeching pierced my ears. Opening my eyes, and quickly pulling away from my mother-in-law, I stepped off to the side for her own safety, opening my arms as Leo ran towards me and into my embrace, nearly knocking me off my feet.

'Oh, my sweet Abigail. If you knew the torture I've endured during your absence, you would break down right this very moment and sob.' He pulled away, his hands on my shoulders before he gently pushed me back a step, his eyes studying me from head to toe. 'It appears you have been in the good paddock, but your maid over there looks like she's had the chaff bag strapped to her head permanently since you've been away.' He glanced across at Bessie suspiciously as I violently shook him off, slapping his hands away. 'Welcome home, Abigail. You are still my best friend in the entire world, even if you have turned into a fatty.' My hand flew up to his ear, and I twisted hard, pulling his face close to mine, his shrieks for help going unheard due to the chaos and noise around us, the joyful laughter and loud greetings drowning out any hope he had of rescue.

'If you've been tortured in my absence, I have no doubt you deserved every moment of it. Say another word about the size or shape of any woman, and I will poke out your eyes with the stoker, and you will never have the privilege to see anything or anyone again in this lifetime,' I snarled, shaking his head one last time for good measure while twisting his ear with all my strength, his screams deafening me.

'You violent slag. Let me go,' he screamed, those around paying us no mind. I released him, roughly pushing him away, and he stumbled for a moment before finding his feet and fleeing at great speed through the crowd, his voice rising above the noise, although I could no longer see him. 'Abigail is an evil, unfortunate looking fatty!' He soon emerged on the other side, climbing the stairs and barrelling back into the house, only pausing once inside to gather his strength before slamming the heavy door with both hands behind him. Twice, but only to ensure I heard it above the ruckus of the crowd—still hugging, still laughing, still loving each other without limits—all connected by an invisible thread winding its way through their hearts, while binding their souls together without their consent or knowledge.

I exhaled deeply, Mr and Mrs Cavanaugh coming to my side to take my hands and lead me through the grand entrance, our family and friends soon following us into the sitting room, the one room where we all felt most at home and could truly relax without interruption, or the need to comply with the social niceties expected from those of our station when outside the boundaries of Willow Grove—while Mr Masters ran a tight ship, and did not tolerate inappropriate behaviour from anyone at any time. Leo and I topped his list of lawbreakers, Leo having far more infractions recorded in the small notebook he kept in his breast pocket. Yet I was still in second place, I had shockingly realised when going through it once when he had carelessly left it on his desk when called from the room by Maisie, during one of our meetings.

I made myself comfortable between Polly and Catherine, both embracing me for the longest time. Those who could not find a seat took the large cushions scattered around the room on every chair, making themselves as comfortable as possible on the floor, while most squashed together on the deep, wide, velvet lounges, some sitting on their husband's laps. Emmy and Thomas strolled in with Hamish behind them carrying several large bags filled with gifts they had chosen, separate to the presents we had brought home for each of our loved ones, child and adult alike. After leaving the bags next to the fireplace, Hamish made his way back across the room, sitting down heavily next to Angus opposite me, his brother ferociously guarding the seat he had saved for him, my children now on the far side of the room handing out every wrapped gift to their cousins and our friends' children, all sitting together on cushions near the hearth, while squeals of excitement filled the room as they unwrapped their presents, soon playing together with their new toys on the carpeted floor, while listening in silence to Thomas and Emmy talk of their adventures, their eyes wide as they spoke about far off places they had never seen or heard of, along with great ships no different than floating palaces.

Turning my attention back to those around me now the children were settled, I picked up the mug filled with coffee Sally had kindly poured me, Leo nowhere to be seen, before raising it to my lips to take several long sips.

'Oh, dear Abigail, you look so very different. Far happier than when I last saw you,' Adele said from her chair near the door, her smile bright as I beamed back at her. She jumped to her feet and ran to me, her arms around my back in a tight embrace. She straightened up and returned to her chair before someone took it from her. 'We are all beyond thrilled our sister has finally been restored to us.' The cheers filling the room from the Cavanaugh clan alone deafened me, restraining myself from placing my hands over my ears to not offend.

I noticed Bessie standing in the doorway, her face flushed, her hands bright red from wringing them together almost constantly since leaving the ship. I nodded to her, and she quietly came to my side, unnoticed by most, still laughing and teasing each other, all so obviously delighted to be back in each other's presence. Bessie stood behind me, her hands on my shoulders as she leaned down to whisper in my ear.

'I apologise for the interruption at such a happy time, Mistress, but may I please speak with you for a moment in private?' I nodded as she straightened up, quickly rising to my feet and politely excusing myself before leading her out into the wide hallway. 'I am more than sorry for interrupting your homecoming, but I don't know what to do. Should I go and see Danny now, or do I wait until you have time to sit with us?' Her hands trembled as I clasped them in my own, her lovely eyes looking up into mine with complete trust.

'I will do and say whatever you ask of me if it would make this situation easier for you, dear friend. Tell me what you need?' I glanced up and down the hallway several times, the hall-boy gasping when he saw me as he came around the corner in the distance, before disappearing back from where he came almost instantly, the young waif obviously taken into our employ while I was away. We had taken in several young orphaned boys over the years to fill the role of hall-boy who had grown into men before my eyes, all but one going on to become farm or stablehands here at the property—and every single one of them had been terrified of me from the day they arrived up to this—my belief as to the reasons behind this pointing to Leonardo every time; however, I was unable to prove my suspicions.

'Oh, Mistress. It would bring me great comfort to have you by my side should he become angry and unreasonable, which of course he will, being a bloody man, as you say.' Tears filled her eyes as she collapsed into my arms, sobbing silently, her body heaving, my hand patting her gently on the back as I whispered soothingly to her until she had no tears left to shed.

'Would you like me to keep you busy here until later this afternoon when we can speak in private once everyone has gone?' She nodded, wiping her tear-stained face with her crisp linen handkerchief, a weak smile touching her lips.

'Thank you, Mistress. I have more than enough to do. First, I must unpack your trunks, then there is your bedchamber to clean and organise.' She paused, her finger going to her temple, tapping it several times while deep in thought. 'What would you like done with your old wardrobe? Many of the gowns and dresses are outdated, and then there are the mourning clothes?' It was my turn for tears to prick my eyes, and I sniffed loudly, willing them away.

'I have decided to have my entire wardrobe packed up and placed in storage under the house with the rest, before the trunks are un-packed, but you will not be the one to do it. I have already arranged it with Mary, so there is nothing more to be said about it. I want you off your feet until we meet with Danny, and I am ordering you to rest on my bed while Mary organises everything. You can still bark orders from there, I promise.' Her eyes went wide, alarm crossing her pretty features, while I smothered a smile.

'All your wardrobe from seasons past? I did not mean they are *all* out of fashion, maybe a quarter, if that. Most have years of wear left, and look fine on you, Mistress.'

'All of it, right down to my shifts and undergarments.' Her eyes widened further, my hands in hers as movement caught my eyes, a looking glass inching its way around the corner in the distance, the hall-boy's eyes locking with mine for only a moment before the hand holding the mirror disappeared. 'I came to realise while away that everything I have, I wore throughout the time Aaron was in hiding, or at his trial, and of course, what came after.' My voice faltered for a moment, willing myself to continue without breaking down, I swallowed several times, running my tongue along my dry lips. 'I do not wish to be reminded daily of the loss we have suffered, or the memories attached to every garment.' She nodded, her face softening, an understanding in her eyes. 'I have so many beautiful gowns thanks to Catherine, and I only have to ask and she will make a few more plain dresses for home.' She embraced me tightly before turning to go. 'I meant what I said about resting today. Mary has already made it known to anyone who will listen that you are organising my wardrobe and are unavailable for the rest of the day. Now, get up there before you make a liar out of me.'

I could still hear her laughing to herself as I stepped back into the sitting room to find Hamish the centre of attention, his deep voice filling the otherwise silent room as he told his captivated audience of our journey, every ear listening intently as I settled myself back down between Polly and Catherine.

'I cannae explain it tae ye in words, only 'tis beyond what ye can imagine when lookin' at the picture books, or the photographs they print in the papers with their articles about the place.' He continued on, telling them of the sights of London, Paris, and New York, while only briefly mentioning Scotland given we had spent the majority of our time there either at Emiliani House or Merinda Manor. 'The most enjoyable was the return journey from New York tae Melbourne.' He glanced across at me, his eyes twinkling, while I grimaced, hoping he would not give us away, especially in front of Dana and the Cavanaughs' before I had time to speak with them, knowing it would not be today, or even tomorrow, as I was far from ready, Yet here he was, not half-an-hour home, dropping hints to anyone paying attention.

'Abi, I have missed you so much more than you could possibly imagine. Never in my wildest of dreams did I realise the work involved to keep the place running. I've had to put up with Mrs McGinty and Amelia arguing daily over her Mathew's behaviour at school, taking me close to a fortnight to sort, and if that wasn't enough to make me want to hide in the cellar with a bottle of brandy, I've had Trixie and Patty at each other's throats over the treatment of Neville's two eldest—at the hands of Trixie herself. It has been on for young and old, and almost drove me to the point of madness.' Polly shook her head, taking my hand in hers. 'I don't know how you do it, my dear sister, but somehow you do, and you make it look far easier than it truly is. I'm utterly and completely exhausted, and I'm beyond relieved you have returned to us safe and in good spirits. I need to sleep for a week now I'm free of them all, thank the Lord above. I truly missed every part of you.' She leaned in and kissed my cheek, before lowering her voice to a whisper. 'I promised myself I would not speak to you of Leonardo on your first day home. The things I must tell you would take days, and we don't have the time for that while everyone is here to welcome you home where you belong.' She smiled weakly, the loud banter in the room drowning out our private discussion. 'It is such a relief, Abi. I've hardly seen Angus. He leaves before the bushman's clock calls and does not return until well after dark. I know he's relieved to see Hamish.' She leaned back, her eyes heavy, resting her head on the cushion behind her.

'Thank you so very much for everything you have done, and what I can only imagine you have been forced to deal with, dear Polly.' She nodded, closing her eyes for a moment, before looking up into mine. 'I have so much to tell you about the orphanage and all the Sisters, but now is not the time.' She yawned, nodding before closing her eyes again, and within a moment, she was snoring softly beside me.

Closing my eyes for a moment, too, I inhaled deeply, the smell of the beeswax candles taken from our own hives burning sweet in the air, while every part of me felt so very deeply loved by every soul present in the room. I appreciated them coming today to visit with us, and relaxed back sipping my coffee as I listened to Hamish continue to speak of our time away quite competently, while relishing the fact we were now home and surrounded by the people we loved, and who loved us back just as ferociously.

Dana and Martin had ignored Hamish since he stepped down from the carriage, and continued to do so, choosing to talk between themselves while Hamish had the full attention of all present, including the children, silent now as they played together on the floor listening intently. I understood why Dana couldn't bring herself to look at him, let alone hear what a wonderful time was had, and I decided in that moment, I would make time to visit with her later in the week to explain what lay between me and the man she despised most of all. Aware this could fracture our friendship forever, if not destroy it entirely, I felt she deserved to hear the news from my own lips, rather than discover by accident, or through gossip, Hamish and I were courting. Hoping she would understand I had no plans to marry, nor was I in love with him, the last thing I wanted was to lose her friendship. She was more than a close confidante and friend. I had always looked up to her as the mother I never had, always seeking her approval, while hating even the thought of ever disappointing her.

Mr Masters came into view, pausing at the door before bowing politely in my direction, a hint of a smile on his lips when he silently greeted me before formally announcing that luncheon was served. I remained where I was, allowing those present to stand and make their way to the dining room before I rose to my feet and followed at my own pace, their cheerful voices floating through the halls. Passing the open drawing-room door, an arm reached out, quick as a flash, the large hand grasping my waist and pulling me off my feet and sideways into the room, my strangled scream stuck on my throat, the wind knocked out of me.

'What... the... bloody... hell... do... you... think... you're... doing?' I tried to catch my breath, bent at the waist, panting, my hands on my knees, while Leo's laughter filled the room.

'I'm no longer cross with you, and have decided we love each other again.' He patted my back until I was breathing fairly normally once again, before straightening up to my full height and glaring at him.

'Oh, have you?' I eyed him suspiciously, his face lighting up, his eyes full of affection as he kissed my cheek, and I softened a little towards him, hating myself for it.

'Of course, Abigail. I adore you nearly as much as I adore myself.' He shook his head, pulling a face as if I was the simplest person he had come across this week.

'Only until I upset you, almost always for no reason at all.'

'We only have a few minutes, and I must talk to you about the women who live here at Willow Grove, particularly many whom you naively call friends.' He slipped his arm around my waist and guided me from the room into the hallway, strolling side-by-side towards the dining room, passing portraits of people from long ago who were strangers to us; however, someone must have loved them enough to display their likeness within these walls.

There were hundreds upon hundreds lining every hallway, the grandest of them hanging in many of the formal rooms. Some I recognised as great-aunt Isabelle herself, alone in formal and informal portraits, alongside many with friends or family beside her, while others were certainly her kin, their features similar to her own. Representing people from every class, it had surprised me when we first arrived to find less than half were white skinned, the rest made up of men, women and children from places such as Great Qing and the East Indies, a number who hailed from what could have been any one of the hundreds of islands in the Oceania, along with countless Aboriginal and Torres Strait Islander people, some in their native dress, while others wearing clothing not so very different to my own.

I assumed most had been part of the mysterious community rumoured to have lived here decades before I was born, while some portraits were clearly shipped over from great-aunt Isabelle's family home in York, and many I believed were friends and lovers she had met throughout her long life, one in particular a handsome captain of a ship, his blonde hair pulled back neatly into a plait, the artist capturing the twinkle in his eyes as he stood at the bow of a ship named *Freedom,* and underneath in the same script, only smaller, *Come Hell and High Water*. I had come across some so old they had faded in their frames, while others were hand sketched in charcoal and preserved perfectly under the glass, many appearing to be kind souls as they stared back at me, immortalised forever.

'They are horrid, and it makes no difference what you say in their defence.' He stopped abruptly, jolting me back, his palm up only inches from my face.

'Stop doing that, you rude prick.' I slapped his hand away, and he slipped it back around my waist, moving us forward again, slower now.

'I have no doubt they have formed a coven in your absence, and I'm certain there is an enormous cauldron out there somewhere simmering on a fire where they gather in secret to cast their evil spells.' He waved his hand in the direction of Polly's cottage, widening his eyes further while forming a cross with his thumb and index finger, placing it on his forehead, then mine, to bless and protect us both from evil. 'I'm buying them broomsticks the next time I'm in Geelong. They can then fly their fat backsides around the property without bothering me, removing the risk I may have to gaze upon the ghastly creatures should they be allowed to walk. They have done nothing but torment and tease me, especially that Pollyanna, the queen of the coven, and the essence of my favourite word that rhymes with witch.'

We turned into yet another hallway, this one leading directly to the dining room, a portrait catching my eye of a young boy of no more than four, possessing the same eyes as Mr Hinkle, only this child was smiling, his tiny frame painted standing in front of a shop, his boots, overalls and thick coat immaculate. I stepped closer to inspect the painting I had never once taken notice of before today, the initials *B H* signed on the bottom right corner, the large sign above the shop in the background written in black, naming the business inside as *K & B Hinkle Fashion House*, and in gold lettering underneath *Milliner, Tailoress, Dressmaker*, below that in black cursive, the final line, *Finest Seamstresses in Hobart Town*. I lifted the frame from the wall, hung far above my eye level, and turned it over, the inscription so faded it was barely legible, *Henry's 3rd Birthday*, and underneath, *17th day of March, 1820*.

'You're not listening to a word I'm saying, and you look simple minded since I last saw you. What are you doing?' He shook his head, startling me from my thoughts.

'Nothing.' I stood on the tips of my toes, reaching up to place the painting back on its hook next to a portrait of a pretty young girl, dark-skinned and dark-haired, standing in front of what appeared to be Polly's cottage. Dressed in a plain skirt and white shirt with a shawl over her shoulders, she was flanked by an older aboriginal woman in native dress, their arms around each other, a strong resemblance between them. They appeared familiar, but from where, I had not a clue. Ensuring the frame hung straight before turning back to him, I rolled my eyes.

'Bloody hell, Abigail. You must get rid of her, or I will. She did terrible things to me while you were away, and no one would play with me like you do. They're as boring as dry toast. Nothing special about any one of them, and I have no clue what you see in the sloths compared to the friendship you share with me. I have cursed them all after what they did to me last week.' He remained silent as we continued on, strolling arm-in-arm towards the grand arch, the double doors to the dining room below opened wide, voices filtering down the hallway, quieter now, the conversations lighthearted.

'All right, Leo. I'll take the bait, and suffer the consequences. What did they do to you last week?' He stopped again, turning to me, his arms flapping frantically in the air while attempting to emphasise his point.

'Polly set that feral pig, Hades, onto me when I was walking past the pigsty, minding my own business. Remember that, no matter what lies she tells you. I really am innocent this time.' I raised my eyebrows at him, remaining silent. 'Anyway, back to me. *Your* friends were standing around the pen looking at the sow and the new piglets, fourteen in all if no one's told you, and all they did was laugh when that boar chased me down, knocking me straight into the mud. Well, it was more like quicksand if I were to be honest. I came close to drowning in the puddle where I landed face first, unable to get myself up. Not one of them came to help me, and by the time I saved myself from certain death, I was covered in slime and pig shit. Not one even offered me a handkerchief to wipe my eyes so I could see where I was walking. They humiliated me, Abigail, and pointed while laughing and mocking me as I continued to slip and fall, trying to escape before Hades massacred me. I hate them all,' he spat as I narrowed my gaze suspiciously.

'What did you say as you innocently walked past my pagan friends?' The draft in the hallway caused me to shiver for a moment as I tried to hurry him along, his face thoughtful, his finger resting on his chin.

'The only thing I said was the weather was fine, and I had not seen such a beautiful day in weeks. They agreed, and I remarked how appropriate it was to find them sunning themselves beside their cousins, and how difficult it was to tell them apart due to their similar skin tones, unfortunate looking snouts, and fat rumps. I was happy for them that they had found their tribe, yet in the next moment they cast their spell on Hades, and I'm attacked and nearly killed.' I shook my head in disbelief before continuing on into the dining room, Leo scurrying behind me to ensure my friends were punished severely.

Crossing the room, we were greeted loudly by those at the table, a feast laid out in front of them from end to end, the footmen already appearing worn out before lunch had even begun. I was aware the kitchen staff had been preparing since the early hours, my stomach knotting up knowing I must go in there to thank them afterwards, or it would be considered the height of rudeness.

Making myself comfortable across from Angus and Polly, they told me they had continued the Sunday lunches without us, our family and friends attending religiously, while Tamara and Brian, along with Victoria and Eric, travelled down regularly from Melbourne while we were away. I was thrilled to hear they had all stayed in touch, many forming friendships with each other separate to my own years ago.

'What's with the cattle, Angus?' I inquired, lifting a spoonful of vegetable broth to my lips.

'Aye. I had planned to speak with you of it later after lunch.' His eyes twinkled as he leaned forward in his seat, lowering his voice. 'Do you remember Samuel Amess?' I nodded, my mouth full of bread, while lifting the spoon again to my lips. Mr Amess had made a fortune in the goldfields soon after his arrival from Scotland in 1852 with his wife, and by late 1853, he had started his own business as a building contractor in Melbourne, going on to build *Customs House*, the *Kew Lunatic Asylum*, the *Government Printing Office*, and many of the railways stations across the state of Victoria. I remembered reading somewhere he had been contracted in 1883 to build the west facade of *Parliament House*, but lost the job due to a dispute over the facing stone. Eric had told me Mr Amess, a personal friend and mentor to him, was elected as the first president of the Builders and Contractors Association in 1873, and had once been the Mayor of Melbourne long before we arrived.

'I know who he is, but I've never met the man. I thought he passed away decades ago,' I replied, taking a large serving of roasted lamb from the platter that lay between us.

'Aye, he did, but only seven-or-so-years-ago. Caught a chill an' up an' died at the ripe old age of two an' seventy. I've been mates with his son, Sammy, fer years now, an' he came to visit while you were away. I dinnae know fer certain if he's runnin' from the law, but he's as game as a pissant, that one.' I nodded again, uncertain how this was connected to the cattle out in the paddock, widening my eyes at him. 'Ye impatient wee troll,' he teased, before settling back in his chair. 'He offered us a small fold from the herd his Da kept at Churchill Island, down Westernport bay. They've owned that island fer decades, an' kept it well stocked with pheasants, rabbits, an' quail for shootin', an' horses, of course, along with the highland beasties, far more in number than when his old man started breedin' them. I'm hopin' the money we paid goes where it's supposed to, an' the rest of the Amess family know of the sale. The price he asked was far too reasonable to knock back.' He threw back his head and laughed loudly, as did Hamish.

I rolled my eyes, their humour lost on me given I had no idea of whom they were referring, and turned to listen to Amelia as she talked of Mrs McGinty, the words *old* and *moll* scattered through the conversation, and I smothered a smile. They had never gotten along, and I believed they never would. Amelia, strong minded and well used to people doing as she wanted them to do given her aristocratic upbringing, while Mrs McGinty was just as stubborn, despite being raised in poverty, rarely bowing down or yielding to Amelia in particular—all the while refusing to allow anyone, including me, to dictate how or what she taught the children. From what I could ascertain, they were currently at a stalemate, and I would need some time to consider how to manage what had now become a war, along with a number of issues only coming to my attention in recent times, before I said or did anything that could make this battle far worse.

Catherine sat to the left of me, the corners of her mouth turning up into a smile as she served herself a roasted quail from the tray Colin held out to her, while Dana sat further down with Martin by her side, her face lighting up when she caught my eye, her plate holding a quarter of the food piled on my own.

'Thank you for the beautiful gowns, Catherine. Everyone commented on them, and many asked the name of my seamstress. I hope you do not mind that I passed your details on to all that inquired.' She elegantly placed her cutlery down before embracing me tightly.

'I'm thrilled you were satisfied with them, my dear friend. I am well aware already, as I have taken a substantial number of orders from women who were on the voyage over to England with you.' She lowered her voice, taking my hand in hers under the table. 'I heard a great deal of gossip, Abigail. Now I'm waiting with bated breath to hear if any of it was true.' I felt my face flush as she turned back to her meal, sipping a glass of wine before picking up her cutlery once more.

'Aye, ye did bonny, Catherine. 'Twas naw only the blokes unable tae take their eyes from her, but the women were far worse. I heard that many compliments an' opinions about these gowns, I feel like a wee bit o' a fashion expert meself these days. The amount o' eligible gentlemen, among the naw so eligible wearin' a ring, that were tryin' tae gain Abigail's attention was overwhelmin', even fer me,' Hamish remarked, his eyes on mine for only a moment before I averted my gaze. If he gave even a hint of what lay between us, I would smack him square in the face, of that I was certain. I glared across at him, and he immediately lowered his head and resumed eating, taking up his conversation with Patrick where they left off only minutes before.

'I hate asking, but I need more house dresses as my old ones are being packed up as we speak. Only to wear around the property. If you would kindly agree, I will come to you so we can catch ourselves up on what we've missed without interruption. Unlike here, where I often cannot get five-minutes to myself.'

'Oh, Abigail. So much has happened since I last saw you, and I cannot wait to meet with you in private to talk. Of course I will make some simple dresses for you, a hundred of them if it means we can spend more time together.' She leaned over and kissed me on the cheek, her brow furrowed slightly, concern in her eyes.

'Is there something you need to speak about now? We can go to my bedchamber once lunch is finished, if you wish?' She hadn't been herself since I had arrived, and her attempts to smile through whatever was bothering her hadn't fooled me for a moment.

'No, it can wait until you call on us. It is of no significance, for today we celebrate you all being returned home safe to us. That is far more important.' She again turned back to the table and resumed luncheon, while I nodded to myself.

I gazed around the long table, the children sitting down one end together where extra chairs had been placed so as to fit our growing brood. Patrick and Scarlett were the worn-out parents of four now, as were Victoria and Aiden, while Luke and Adele were blessed with two who rarely gave them trouble, all not much younger than Thomas and Emmy. The close-knit cousins sat alongside Catherine and Colin's two beautiful young ones, who smiled at me when they noticed my stare, before I glanced at Willy and Bella, both like my own children living so close, Amelia and Tommy's two joining in the cheerful banter. Tamara and Elizabeth had not been able to attend today, but had sent their apologies, along with advising of their intent to visit in the next fortnight. Had Tamara's four and Elizabeth's two children been here today, there would have been twenty-four of them, and so much louder than they were now, their voices rising well above the adults. It was so lovely to see them all together again, talking, laughing and eating as a family once more. Thomas and Emmy would soon turn fourteen, a fact I found hard to believe, and refused to accept they were not far off adulthood, my gaze fixed on them, my heart about to burst with pride as they continued to ignore me.

'We must know immediately, dear Abigail. Did anyone catch your eye? Was the smell of romance in that sea air?' Victoria asked, a wicked glint in her eyes, while my face became warm, wishing she had seated herself closer so I could have twisted her ear.

'We met many lovely people on the voyage, there and back, but as for romance, I am sorry to disappoint you,' I murmured, averting my eyes and concentrating on the dessert in front of me.

'That's naw true,' Hamish called out, my stomach knotting up before hitting the floor. I had no hesitation in taking the carving knife to him below his belt if he said one more word, while I willed my face to remain void of any emotion. 'Aye, there was one particular Duke who made it well known he wanted tae marry our Abigail, even before we stepped foot on British soil. An' he had every intention o' whiskin' her an' our Thomas an' Emmy away tae England tae live in his castles an' preside over his grand estates. An' I mustn't ferget his mansion, but he calls it a terrace, built smack bang in the middle o' the swankiest part of London.' He leaned back in his chair, his large frame relaxed, no different than his brother beside him, his brown eyes sparkling. 'He's naw a bad bloke. We were guests o' the man at his castle in Scotland fer a time, a grand place called *Merinda Manor*, an' he treated us well, much tae his credit.' A hint of teasing in his tone, gasps filled my ears, the room now silent, some shaking their heads in disbelief, while others were unable to hide their admiration. Out of the corner of my eye, I noticed Mr Masters as his head snapped around towards us, his eyes widening for only a moment before he regained his composure, his face the colour of whipped egg whites and sugar, yet everything else about him was the same as it was before his lapse, whatever the reason for it.

'I refused him, of course,' I quickly interjected before continuing to eat my dessert, the weight of their stares almost unbearable, while the urge for a slice of pavlova rather than the warm spotted dick filling my bowl consumed me, the steaming pudding covered in thick clotted cream from the milk of our own Jersey cows. Our herd had grown significantly since Aaron first purchased several for milking fifteen-years ago when the number of mouths to feed on the property had increased dramatically, and without warning, resulting in a shortage of milk for several months, along with the cream, buttermilk, cheeses, and butter the kitchen staff made from it, while leaving us at the mercy of our neighbours for a time, most happy to sell their excess on to us.

'My darling daughter, Abigail.' Mrs Cavanaugh smiled affectionately, pausing for a moment to gather her thoughts, Mr Cavanaugh nodding his consent to her before she continued. 'The last thing any of us want is for you to move away, but we do want you to find happiness again. If that means living as a Duchess back in England, then so be it. We have enough boats of our own to come visit, and you have enough money to buy your own shipping company. If you love him, then that is what you must do.' Hamish raised his eyebrows knowingly, then nodded to himself as if in confirmation the Cavanaugh family would not object to him courting me should it mean we would stay, while I shook my head at how simple-minded men were.

'You will find him just as delightful as I do, of that I am certain. You will meet him in the coming months as he plans to visit with us here at Willow Grove when in Melbourne to attend his business. I want to be clear, there is nothing more between us. He understands I am still grieving Aaron, and he graciously agreed to remain friends, and no more, for the moment.' Hamish narrowed his gaze at me, his brow furrowed, while I glanced across at Mr Masters standing by the sideboard, his tall frame rigid, his attention on the conversation at the table rather than the footmen clearing away the dirty dishes, while several maids carried the platters of leftover food back to the kitchen.

'Are ya yankin' our chain, Abigail? Are ya sure this is a *real* Duke wantin' ta marry ya? Why?' Aiden asked, his eyebrows raised suspiciously before his expression changed to one of surprise, a bread roll hitting him hard on the forehead, thrown by Patrick, before Luke launched another in his direction, Aiden appearing confused, this time catching the roll expertly after it rebounded off his chest.

'Apparently so, and I have no idea. I doubt the poor man knew what he would be taking on if I ever said yes,' I teased, while Luke and Angus chuckled, many losing interest and turning back to resume their conversations.

'Abigail, don't go puttin' yerself down like that. This bloke saw the beautiful soul ya have inside ya that Aaron saw in ya too, an' loved ya so dearly for. Ya can't stay by yerself forever. Aaron never wanted that for ya, or the nippers,' Patrick said, his voice low and gentle as I sighed deeply, fed up to the back teeth of hearing the same thing over and over from different people, while being forced to repeat the same answer—over, and over, and over again.

'I'm not ready, Patrick. I cannot give my heart to anyone, now or in the future. I love your brother just as deeply now as when he was here beside me.' He nodded, changing the subject, much to my relief, while I wiped my mouth with a napkin, the urge to escape out into the fresh air so overwhelming, I rose to my feet and politely excused myself.

I relaxed back in the sun lounge, the sound of children playing near-by, while a dozen conversations swirled around me, my forearm resting across my eyes. I heard heavy footsteps running in my direction, and opened my eyes to find Emmy and Thomas standing at the foot of my lounge, both attempting to catch their breath.

'Mummy, may we go down to the village to visit with our friends, and take the presents we have for them? We have missed them all so very much,' Emmy asked, her emerald eyes pleading with me, a loving smile touching my lips as I struggled to sit up.

'Are you all going?' My gaze flitted between them, Emmy nodding, while Thomas appeared uncertain.

'Oh, yes, and then we are going to sit by the river together to talk.'

'You have my consent, Emmy, but only if the others have permission from their parents. It would be rude to leave your cousins and friends here.'

When Emmy and Thomas told their cousins, children went running from everywhere to their parents to beg for permission, and it was granted, before they bolted towards the stables and over the hill, disappearing from my sight, their laughter floating back in the breeze. Hamish sat several chairs away, deep in discussion with Angus and Luke, a relaxed smile on his lips, a calmness about him now he was back among friends.

It had come time for me to thank the kitchen staff for their hard work an hour ago, my stomach becoming increasingly nauseous the longer I delayed, while my mind made every excuse to stay where I was; however, my failure to attend the kitchen in person to express our gratitude would certainly have been noticed by now. I reluctantly struggled to my feet, excused myself and walked towards the house. My hand trembled as I stepped through the open back door, tears stinging my eyes as I stared down at Dingo's empty bed, still where it always was despite him dying in his sleep a month ago, the gut-wrenching pain I felt over losing another part of Aaron he had left me almost unbearable. They had buried him at the foot of his grave, and I knew Aaron would be pleased knowing his loyal old mate now slept at his feet. I stopped beside the basket, reaching down for a moment to touch the soft blanket covered in golden hair, a prayer on my lips before I straightened up and continued on towards the busy kitchen, the cheerful banter continuing until Leo noticed me standing in the doorway, several gasps coming from the maids before silence descended on the room, Leo's hand flying up to his mouth, his eyes wide.

'Oh, Abigail, you're white as a sheet. You look even more unfortunate than usual. You need to sit, because if you dare faint, I'm quite aware I do not have the strength to hold you up with the size of that backside on you.' He gently took me by the arm and guided me over to the table, my legs trembling as he lowered me down onto the chair, then slid onto the one beside me. 'You're shaking. Would you prefer if I take you to the sitting room to talk?' He rose to his feet, offering me his hand; however, I shook my head, my heart slowing only slightly as I tried to gather my thoughts and compose myself.

'Not just yet. Just give me a moment.' Although my mind was filled with so many memories and times we had shared in this room with my beloved, being back in the kitchen was no longer unbearable as it had once been, and I no longer saw him sitting at the table as I did the first time I returned after his death. Not stepping foot in here for nearly two-and-a-half-years, so many emotions I could not explain to Leo, or myself, filled me and overflowed for all present to witness. Sally placed a bottle of wine down on the table, winking at me before pouring me a glass, a sympathetic smile on her lips as she returned to her duties, while Leo took my hand in his large one.

'Abigail, we all know returning here is hard for you. I miss the man constantly; far more than you, now I think about it. Anyway, back to me. We are now at the part where I am being helpful and very kind, so you do need to listen—and stop guzzling that wine like you're sitting in a gin house spending the quid you just earned hedge creeping.' I drained the last of it before placing the glass back on the table,

Leo sighing deeply as I picked up the bottle and poured another. 'I'm grateful for the time Aaron spent here with us, far more time than you ever have in any kitchen, and he has left many wonderful memories behind for us all to treasure. Instead of feeling sad and full of regret, absorb the love and fun times we all shared with Aaron within these walls, and create more fabulous memories as you and my babies move forward with your lives. I know how much you still love him, Abigail, not more than me, but it's a lot. You're a good wife, Abigail.' His voice low and full of affection, he squeezed my hand, while I lifted the glass to my lips, drinking deeply.

Feeling far more in control of myself than when I had first entered the room, I glanced around at the staff as they continued with their work, most avoiding my gaze, while not wanting to upset me further. No longer used to my presence in the kitchen, it was clear I now made them uncomfortable, and I hated myself for it. I quickly stood, making my way over to the workbench in the centre of the bustling room, while raising my hand to get their attention. Within moments, the room was silent, the staff standing motionless as they stared back at me while waiting for me to speak. I swallowed hard several times, the wine slowing my mind, although, relaxing every part of me.

'Thank you all so very much for your hard work and dedication while I was away. We are grateful, and appreciate the luncheon you prepared for our homecoming. Every dish was beautifully presented and enjoyed by all. Again, thank you for...' My voice faltered, Sally slipping her hand over mine as I composed myself once again.

'You are very welcome, Mistress. I can't imagine working anywhere else and being so content. It's such a relief to have you back.' I heard several claps, her eyebrows arched while narrowing her gaze in Leo's direction. '*Someone* thought himself the boss cockie of everyone and everything in your absence. I can't speak for others, or tell you all were happy during your absence, but I'm certainly beyond excited to welcome you home,' Sally said, her mouth twitching, the staff surrounding us, most nodding in agreement. I returned to the table set off to the side of the kitchen, the room warm, while Leo rolled his eyes at the staff as I sat back down beside him. He poured me another glass of wine, a mischievous smirk on his lips as he passed it to me.

'Tell me what you really got up to on that journey? You appear to have been well-bedded since I last laid eyes on you.'

'Leo!' I spat my wine, my eyes wide, my cheeks starting to burn. 'We are surrounded by people listening to every word. How can you say that to me?' I wiped my mouth before running the napkin over the splatter of red liquid on the table.

'Because you do. Please tell me every detail. I miss our filthy talks so desperately since you and Goliath haven't been here swinging your dicks around,' he pleaded, his voice barely audible, and I forced a smile.

'What makes you think I have done anything of the sort?' I whispered teasingly, the staff paying us no mind as they finished the last of their tasks, before bidding us farewell one-by-ones to sit down to a late lunch in the large dining room in their quarters, a place for them alone where they could relax without feeling anyone was looking over their shoulder.

'I know you far better than most, Abigail, and I remember how you looked after being with Aaron. I could always tell when you were fornicating.' His mouth twitched again, his hand over mine, his eyes twinkling wickedly. 'Tell me what wonderful, disgusting adventures you got up to while away?' I leaned over and murmured in his ear, his giggles soon turning into loud laughter, my hand reaching out instinctively before I pinched him on his nipple, twisting it for only a moment to quieten him. 'Ow! You old tavern trollop. When I suggested you take a lover, I meant to entice a man you have no feelings for into your bed. What a simple minded idiot you are.' Snorting no different from the pigs he hated, he choked on his wine, some spurting out of his nose. I laughed aloud, my mood so much lighter than when I first entered the kitchen, while he continued to cough, wiping his face soon after and taking a long drink, draining every drop of wine from his crystal glass. 'Should we be reckless and have another?' The room now empty, a peace settled over me, the birds outside singing their native songs, a sound I hadn't realised I missed until this very moment. The sound of home.

'Why not? What could it hurt?' I held up my glass, affection in his eyes, his face lighting up in a brilliant smile as he poured the last of the bottle between us, before raising his own glass.

'Welcome home, dear friend, but more importantly, welcome back to the kitchen. You've been missed.'

I returned to the garden feeling warm all over, my body relaxed from the wine, along with Leo's company. It seemed a decision in my absence had been made, and we were all attending the village pub this evening to celebrate our homecoming. Facing one of my greatest fears, I had successfully returned to the kitchen; however, I did not feel strong enough to do much more today, and stepping back into the pub where Aaron and I shared countless moments and had made thousands of memories I would keep forever without him was far too much for my damaged heart to bear. I strolled back towards my friends, many dotted around in groups chatting while enjoying the unusually warm autumn weather, the gum tree above the largest standing in the eclectic garden, a mix of English and native plants and trees, their branches swaying gently in the soft breeze. Lowering myself back down onto a lounge next to Dana, I smiled across at her, while her face lit up at the sight of me.

'Oh, my dearest Abigail. I worried for you the entire time you were away.' She reached across and took my hand in her, sympathy in her eyes. 'I know better than most just how much you were dreading this journey without Aaron, and I am so very sorry you were forced to put up with a low-life lout to support you through such a terribly difficult period of your life. I should have made the time myself to accompany you.' She shook her head bitterly, her eyes fixed on the yellow crested cockatoos in the distance pecking at some leftovers put out by the kitchen staff.

'Hamish did support me well, as did Bessie and Mary.' I leaned across and kissed her gently on the cheek, her face softening. 'I know your feelings on the matter when it comes to Hamish, and it is not my place to convince you differently. I do ask you to understand he has been a good mate to Aaron and a friend to me, and is the godfather of my children. I will never take sides between you under any circumstance. You are both important to me, and I value both friendships equally and would be devastated if I were to lose one or the other.' I leaned back on my lounge, my hand still clasped firmly in hers, while she gazed up at the sky and exhaled loudly, pausing for the longest time before closing her eyes.

'I know, and I would never make you choose. Nor would I selfishly place you in that position, only because your friendship is so very important to me, and the last thing I would ever want is to hurt you, dear friend.' She brushed away a tear with the back of her hand before anyone noticed, the laughter around us loud at times, while most talked animatedly, all far too busy to notice us. 'I *hate* him with every part of my being.' She glared across at him next to Angus and Tommy, too far away for us to hear the lightheartedness behind their chuckling, before closing her eyes again, a hateful scowl on her pretty face. 'The prayer on my lips every single morning is the same I mutter at night when on my knees next to my bed—he will suffer far worse than my Charlotte, his mind tormented with thoughts of her he cannot escape from in the dark of night, and he will never find peace. If there is another life after this, I hope she finds him and seeks her vengeance.'

I nodded silently, aware no words would ease her, and closed my eyes for only a moment before heavy footsteps filled my ears, what sounded like hundreds of them running towards me, no different than a herd of cattle. Struggling to sit up, I saw Mr Masters out of the corner of my eye making his way towards me, albeit at a far slower pace than the children now standing around my lounge, some panting as they tried to catch their breath.

'You're all filthy. Go inside to Mary and wash up for dinner. I have no doubt that is why Mr Masters is on his way.' Most scattered towards the house, while Thomas stayed a moment, bending down to hug me.

'I'm happiest here at home, Ma. There's no better place in the world.' I hugged him back tightly before he straightened up, ready to go and catch up with his friends.

'So am I, Thomas—and you're not bloody wrong, son.'

After dinner, we retired to the sitting room with the children, waiting for their bedtime to arrive. Leaning back on the lounge, far more comfortable than anything I sat on while away, I watched the children play on the floor near the hearth, a near empty glass of wine in my hand.

'Tell us, Hamish. How did you and Abigail get along while away? I'm only one witness to how much you both argue, or should I say, how much Abigail argues with you? Was she difficult to manage, or was she easy?' Leo's eyes glinted mischievously, while several in the room stopped to listen. 'To get along with, I mean.' Hamish gazed across at him thoughtfully, lifting the dram of whisky to his lips and taking only a sip.

'I was wonderin' much the same about ye. How did *ye* get along here while we were gone, as we all know how much *ye* like tae argue? I've already started tae hear about some o' yer antics, an' I have naw doubt there's more tae come. Ye should hang yer head in shame, ye daft-heided idjit. I already know what ye did in the village with the slingshot.' Leo gasped, his hand flying to his mouth, while the room quietened further. 'How can ye lay in wait tae hurl rocks at 'em passin' by? Ye hit old Murray on the head, an' he needed Dr Richards tae come out an' stitch him up. Ye can pay the bill, as I dinnae see why Abigail has tae keep dishin' out money hand over fist tae save yer sorry arse. She gave Ronny five-pound the last time he came cryin' tae the house, sayin' ye had tripped him over an' called him illegitimate. How can ye say that tae a bairn whose parents were married fer ten-years before they birthed him? Now he's questionin' everyone who'll listen about the matter. Yer lucky 'twas Angus who was left here tae deal with ye.' Leo glared back at him, before rolling his eyes indifferently, dismissing everything Hamish had said with a flick of his wrist. I closed my eyes and let out a deep sigh. I had avoided listening to any tales of what Leo had got up to while I was away, choosing to pretend he had behaved himself just as he promised me he would.

'Excuse me, Hamish, but I have an excuse about the slingshot. I was helping this time. You always assume the worst of me,' Leo complained, while Hamish arched his eyebrows suspiciously. 'I was innocently walking through the village,' he said, raising his hand to his mouth before lowering his voice, 'after looking at the most recent unfortunate looking wean born last week.' He lowered his hand, his voice now louder. 'Little Johnny stopped me in the street and asked me to show him how to use his new toy. He wanted to shoot balls into the air. Boring. I explained that slingshots are not effective unless you hide, then lay in wait to shoot rocks at people, understanding only then if they see you, they can move out of the way, causing you to miss your target. It was only under my guidance that he was able to find us a good hiding spot.' I shook my head in disbelief, the urge to place my fingers over my ears overwhelming. 'Anyway, back to me. I went and hid, lying in wait until we were soon flinging fabulous rocks around the village. The slingshot was the best I have ever used, so it is perfectly understandable that once I started, I couldn't stop. At least Johnny knows how to use it now.' He puffed out his chest, proud as a peacock, while I cringed. No doubt tomorrow I would be dealing with Johnny Black's parents, who fortunately for me were sensible people and understood the burden I carried regarding Leo.

'Weel, then, it's bonny ye enjoyed yerself, an' that ye have fond memories tae keep fer always, 'cause ye'll be payin' fer the seven broken windows on the terraces, an' the three in the dinin' hall, naw tae mention two o' the pub windows. Dinnae look at Abigail like that. She's naw goin' tae save ye. I manage this property when it comes tae situations like this, Leonardo, an' I'll make sure ye dinnae see a penny o' yer wages 'till all the damage is paid fer an' ye compensate auld Murray fer his pain an' sufferin'. I think five-pound should do it, given ye did it deliberately, ye wee pain in me arse.' Leo smugly slipped his arm around my shoulder, and ignored him, those around us continuing to chat, most on their second whisky, while I sipped another glass of wine, listening to the many and varied conversations in the room.

Little Mary came down an hour later, hurrying the children all upstairs to ready for bed, the extra mattresses already down on the floor in both Emmy and Thomas's room to accommodate them all.

Well aware she was a braver woman than me, and none of them would settle to sleep for hours being so very excited to be back together, I wished her well, and meant every word. I had wanted twelve of my own from as far back as I could remember; however, twelve Cavanaugh children together were far more than even I could cope with.

'Well, I suppose we should all go and get ready,' Scarlett suggested, her face lighting up in a brilliant smile as Mr and Mrs Cavanaugh rose to their feet at once, hurrying to my side

'We've come to say our goodnights as we need to get on home before the dark sets in. I feel my long lost daughter has returned, and my heart is set to burst,' Mrs Cavanaugh said, tears in her eyes as I embraced her affectionately. 'I want you to be happy, my dear, but I would have hated it if you had married that Duke and been taken from us, despite what my husband forced me to say. I don't want you and the children to ever leave us, as we love you all so very much. I couldn't bear it.' I hugged her tighter, promising her fears were unfounded as we loved them just as dearly and couldn't bear to live so far apart. Mr Cavanaugh took his wife by the shoulders and guided her to the side before bending down and embracing me warmly, kissing my forehead.

'Don't listen to her. She's a darlin' woman who has become far too sentimental in her old age.' He grinned down at me as she slapped his arm playfully. 'You only need to concentrate on what makes you an' the twins happy, an' we'll accept your decision, even if that means marryin' your new Duke.'

I walked them out to the driveway, kissing them again, while promising I would visit in the next few days, leaving them thrilled. Staring after them long after their carriage had disappeared, I turned on my heel and hurried to the sitting room to find most had returned to the guestrooms to ready themselves for the evening. I crossed the room, deciding not to sit as I picked up my glass of wine in one hand, and the near full bottle of wine with the other.

'I'm staying in tonight. I will excuse myself, as I am retiring to my room and intend on having an early night.' I quickly bid those present goodnight, and scurried from the room, pausing in the doorway, their disappointment clear as they begged me to stay, none more so than Hamish. 'I'm sorry. I'm just not feeling up to it.' I turned and hurried down the hallway, climbing the stairs two at a time, now running through the hallways towards my bedchamber. Bursting through the door, I kicked it closed behind me, my hands on the sideboard as I gasped for breath, tears trickling down my cheeks. Taking a moment to compose myself, I kicked off my shoes, placed the wine on my side table, and threw myself down heavily on Aaron's side of the bed. Relief to be back in my bedchamber alone for what felt like the first time in years gently slid over me, yet I could not feel Aaron's presence when I had most expected to. Closing my eyes, a loud knock on the door sounded, and I grunted to myself, calling out to enter, thinking the intruder Bessie, only to find Hamish looming over my bed when I opened my eyes.

'I'd like ye tae come tonight, Abigail, if naw fer yerself, fer yer workers. It's been a long time since ye've been there, an' everyone is lookin' forward tae seein' ye again. Yer their Mistress an' Boss Cocky now, an' they need tae know yer here an' functionin' fer their own peace o' mind. I'll be beside ye, as will all those who love ye. The firsts o' everythin' are always difficult, but we'll support ye. I give ye me word.' He nodded his head encouragingly, a sympathetic smile on his lips. Silence hung over the room for the longest time, while he remained as he was, waiting patiently.

'Oh, I know I must go back sooner or later, and you're right. I'm best to do it when those I love are there rather than popping by one day on my own and falling apart.' I sighed deeply, struggling to sit up. 'All right. I will try, but if I'm unable to cope, I'm leaving.' He sat down on the bed beside me, slipping his arms around me before kissing my forehead for the longest time.

'Yer brave, me wee wench, an' that's only one o' the tiny pieces o' thousands I love about ye.' He leaned down and placed his lips on mine, kissing me deeply, my body melting into his. 'I've wanted tae do that ever since we returned, but dinnae have even a moment tae get ye alone.' A knock on the door startled me, before Bessie stepped inside. She had decided earlier to wait and speak to Danny tomorrow given she was sleeping here tonight, helping little Mary with all the children. Danny had been there to welcome her home, and although she was now showing, her dress and cloak hid her secret well. Crossing the room, she stood over us gazing down for a moment, her hands on her hips, a sheepish smirk on her face as she greeted Hamish sitting beside me before turning her attention to me spread out on the bed.

'Those little fiends. There are feathers all over the bedchambers, which will take forever for the maids to clean. I could belt them all on the backside tonight.' She shook her head in exasperation, while Hamish snorted with laughter.

'I've naw doubt wee Emmy an' Thomas would get the shock o' their lives if ye did such a thing.' I laughed out loud, as they had never once been smacked, while Hamish continued to chuckle at the thought.

'Oh, they would. Thomas and Emmy are perfect children in thought, word and deed, except when all the cousins get together. Then it's a disaster. None of them listen to us at all.' Poor Bessie screwed up her face in frustration, while I tried to smother a smile, and failed miserably.

'Would you like me to come in and speak with them?' I threw my legs over the side of the bed, rising to my feet to go and have a stern talking to with all of the Cavanaugh children, including my own.

'It would be pointless, Mistress. They're far too excited at seeing each other again, and I doubt they will settle to sleep for hours yet. Mary and I will manage. You go with your friends and enjoy your night.' She paused, turning to Hamish, who now stood near the window gazing down over the garden. 'I hope you'll take care of her, Hamish, without being overly caring in the presence of witnesses.'

He nodded solemnly, picking up his hat. 'Aye. I give ye me word.' Bessie nodded back, shooing him out of the room to ready me for the evening. I made my way to the ornate dressing table, once my great-aunt's, leaving me often wondering what it could tell me should it have the power of speech. Bessie emerged from my wardrobe with a gown the colour of toffee, my old clothes now gone, the new ones hanging in their place. Placing it on a hook, she came up behind me, her hands on my shoulders as she prepared to style my hair and paint my face.

'Mistress, may I ask you something?'

'You can ask me anything, dear friend.' Her eyes stared into mine for only a moment before she averted her gaze and stepped forward to organise the products on the table.

'If you were to find out something you believed would help another find peace, would you tell them? Even if it was none of your business to stick your fat beak in and start squawking?'

'Hmmm... I'm not sure. It would depend if it would hurt more than help, I suppose.'

'It may be better to let sleeping dogs lie. I mean, you and Pollyanna have created a beautiful life here, and the secrets of the past of those that came before you shouldn't be allowed to sully that. They can stay where they are as far as I'm concerned.' She nodded her head determinedly, as if only making up her mind at that very moment, my eyes widening for a moment, her gentle fingers covering my face with liquid powder.

'If it is about me and Polly, you must tell.' I straightened up in my chair as she applied a touch of rouge before darkening my eyebrows, then my lashes, finishing with a light coat of lip paint.

'Oh, don't listen to me. I don't know where me head is of late.' She picked up the brush, now silent and refusing to talk as she styled my hair. Her moods had been all over the place for months, and I believed nothing could be done about it, nor would she change, until she held her child in her arms. Soon after, she had me dressed and presentable, not overdone, but how she felt the owner of such a property as Willow Grove should present in public, although I fidgeted in front of the cheval mirror, wondering if I really should go, when Catherine strolled into my bedchamber, a smile lighting her pretty face.

'I hear you weren't keen on coming tonight?' She crossed the room, taking my hands in hers, a sympathetic glint in her eye as I nodded, sadness overwhelming me. 'I will be there to hold your hand, and if it's all too much, I will walk home with you. We can raid the kitchen and eat it all in your bed.' She embraced me tightly, and I nodded before she took my hand and led me from the room, calling out our farewells to Bessie and wishing her luck. Strolling hand in hand through the wide hallways, we spoke not a word, a comfortable silence between us. Taking a deep breath, I hugged her again, before taking her hand and marching into the sitting room to try—and that was all I, or anyone, could do—never stop trying.

Chapter Five

WE MADE OUR WAY past the stables and over the hill, pausing at the top to see the cosy village lit up and bustling down in the valley. Several groups walked on ahead, while others remained for a time to take in the magnificent view, the light fading as the sun dipped below the horizon. How many times I had taken this walk with Aaron over the years I couldn't count, most of the time too drunk to walk, but always making an enjoyable night of it. Here I was surrounded by people who loved me, and whom I adored, yet I felt so very alone without him. I had returned to the village a handful of times before we departed for London; however, the pub was beyond what I could endure, holding far too many memories I was certain would slice through my still unhealed heart. I had promised I would try, and try I would, my hands lifting my skirt slightly at the front before I hurried after my friends, the half-moon lighting the way

Arriving in the town square within minutes, still quite busy with a steady stream of workers making their way from the dining hall towards their homes, several of the younger ones catching my eye as they sat around on the verandah of the pub gossiping while listening to the music drifting out of the open windows, their parents inside. I gazed up at the building, one Aaron had spent so much time working on, and I felt the urge to run, unable to summon the courage to step inside. Catherine and Polly stood to each side of me, my hands in theirs, both silently waiting until I was ready to go in and join the others.

'Take a deep breath, and just remember you are here in 1905 with us. The past is gone, Abi, and we can never get it back,' Polly reminded me, my nose wrinkling in annoyance, despite the polite nod of my head.

'I'm not an imbecile, Pollyanna. I know where I am and what bloody year it is, and I'm sensible enough to know there is no such thing as time travel. Let's just get this over with.' I straightened my shoulders, lifted my chin, gathered my skirts, and marched towards the pub, climbing the stairs, Polly and Catherine hurrying behind me. Stepping onto the wide verandah, I reached for the oversized door handle, turned it hard, and pushed it open, stepping into the crowded room feeling far more determined than I had for the longest time, just as my boot caught on the corner of a carpet, my body stumbling as one foot tripped over the other, gasps filling my ears as I lost my balance and crashed forward into a small group of people, none of whom put their hands out to steady me as I spun through the air, landing hard on the floor at their feet. The music continued, while those around greeted me where I was on my back from their standing positions, beer in hand, all appearing pleased to see me as Polly and Catherine pulled me to my feet.

'How embarrassing for you,' Polly murmured as they guided me through the crowd and towards the table where our friends and family waited.

'Oh, bang it up your backside, Pollyanna. You had every opportunity to grab me, but you were far too busy fixing your hair while flirting with your husband across the room,' I snapped, sliding my sore bottom onto a chair, Catherine lowering herself down on the one next to me, while Polly wisely chose to sit on the opposite side of the table as far away from me as possible. Adelaide approached, a tray in her hand.

'This here is from Peter. He wanted to be one of the first to welcome you back, especially after witnessing such a grand and fitting entrance by the Mistress herself,' she whispered, her mouth twitching as she placed a glass of beer down in front of me, while I grimaced, glaring at Polly for a moment before thanking Adelaide for her kindness, along with Peter for his generosity. Soon the table in front of me overflowed with pots of beer, along with a bottle of whisky sent over from the staff and workers. All around me were merrily imbibing, so I poured myself a whisky, and drank it down in one swallow, followed by a beer, warming the pit of my stomach.

Everywhere I looked I saw Aaron in this very room by my side throughout the years, dancing and drinking, while always enjoying every moment spent here, from the early days of our marriage through to the very week he went into hiding over that sorry business. As the memories flooded my mind, bringing tears to my eyes, I poured another whisky in an attempt to numb not only my heart, but my aching body thanks to Polly, and Catherine's lack of attention hadn't gone unnoticed. Hamish watched helplessly from afar, unable to come to me despite my miserable countenance, or his concerns over the whisky I continued to slam down my throat, warning him earlier that should he dare expose me in front of everyone, I would throw him over before we even began.

I leaned back in my chair, my eyes following Patrick and Scarlett as they walked hand in hand to the dancefloor, as had many from our group. Catherine stayed beside me, always steadfast and true, and watched me pour another drink, her eyes widening as I drank it again in one swallow, followed by another glass of beer.

'Maybe drinking is not what's best for you at this time, Abigail. We all worry for you, and I know throwing yourself into an ocean of whisky and beer may ease you for now, but it will not ever fix a broken heart.' She embraced me, tears pricking my eyes.

'Can you not see I hate the fact I'm falling apart the moment I stepped back in here? It feels like no time has passed at all, and I cannot stop glancing at the door expecting Aaron to stride in like nothing ever happened and it was all a bad dream.' She held my hand tight in hers, remaining silent as we watched Nellie approach the other end of the table where Hamish sat with Angus and Leo, her face lighting up at the sight of him. Maybe there was still a chance for them, and for him to have the family he always wanted, as I knew I would never be in the position to love him the way she did, or give him what she could. I continued to drink, one after another, as she attempted to sit down on his knee. He pushed her back onto a chair next to him, fury crossing her face for only a moment, before Hamish turned to her, speaking in hushed tones. It was clear to every man and his dog they were arguing, although I couldn't hear a word and was clueless what passed between them.

Catherine and I spoke of William, movement catching my eye, both of us turning to see Nellie raise her hand before bringing it down hard across his face, seeming to take offence to what he had said. Grabbing her arm, he pulled her to her feet as she screamed filthy words at him, attempting to hit him several times while he marched her out of the pub, her shrieks still floating back through the windows long after they were out of sight. Catherine raised her eyebrows at me, and I shook my head, confident he would never harm or hit her, while acutely aware he would not tolerate being shamed in front of anyone, either. Dana sat across from me, smiling to herself as she stared after them.

'I see he is reaping what he has sown. He will never stop messing about with any woman who will have him. Nothing will ever change.' I remained silent, drinking the last of the bottle I had refused to share, before rising unsteadily to my feet to go and get another one. The dance floor was full, and all appeared to be enjoying themselves very much. Well, all except for me, and possibly Hamish, still stuck outside with Nellie. Catherine hurried to my side and dragged me back to the table empty handed, refusing to listen to my pleas for more whisky and beer, gently pushing me back down onto my chair, while Polly stood up, appearing concerned before hurrying down to the end of the table where the men sat. Bending down, she whispered in Angus's ear, his eyes fixed on me as he nodded before she returned to her seat. I could no longer stand under my own strength, my body heavy, my legs like stone, my mind so very far away.

'It's time we go home, dear Abigail. It's been a long night, and I think you need to rest now,' Scarlett murmured in my ear before sitting back down at the table, her and Patrick both out of breath after finishing the last dance, the music now slower, the light appearing dimmer.

Angus rose to his feet, as did those around him, draining their glasses before striding over to us. He slipped his arm around my waist, standing me up as best he could before guiding me towards the door, my body stumbling out onto the verandah supported by his strong arm, while tears streamed down my face as I called out to the sky filled with stars reminding me of diamonds on black velvet, demanding my husband be returned. Angus carried me down the stairs, my hoarse voice screaming his name, needing desperately for Aaron to come. Leo hurried to my side, pushing my friends out of the way.

'Excuse me, hot stuff coming through,' he shouted as they rolled their eyes, several hands attempting to shove him away. He pushed back harder, knocking Polly off her feet and onto her backside in the dirt.

'Stuff and nonsense more like it, you pig of a man. How dare you push me.' Polly's face twisted in rage as he stared down at her, appearing unconcerned as he dismissed her with a wave of his hand.

'You forget the most important thing, Pollyanna. I'm not like the other men in your life. I will shove you back, and if you force me to, I will show you my famous slap.' He slipped his arm around my waist, his nose pointed in the air, while Dana helped a furious Polly to her feet.

'You're beyond lucky Abi is as pissed as a mute and I don't have time for your shite now. I will get you back when you least expect it,' she snapped, rubbing her backside. Angus continued to hold me upright, while Leo tried to push him away from me.

'Leonardo. The only reason I dinnae smack ya for layin' yer hands on me wife is I'm far too busy, an' then there's the fact ye'd only cry an' whine about it tomorrow. Move away now before I show ye me naw so famous punch,' Angus growled, Leo immediately releasing his grip on me before walking back to Aiden and Luke without a word of reply. My friends and family surrounded me, some sobbing, but none louder than my own, my body wracked with grief. Heavy footsteps came running towards us from the side of the building, Hamish appearing from around the corner, Nellie close behind, her eyes swollen and red. Within moments, he was by my side, Angus on the other. 'We need to get her home. We cannae calm her,' Angus said, Hamish leaning down to take a closer look at me.

'I'll carry her on me back. She cannae even stand, let alone calm herself.' Hamish bent down, while Angus lifted me up, his large hands tucked up under my knees to prevent me falling until Hamish gently grasped my legs, now wrapped around him.

'I knew you were in love with that bitch. You are, aren't you?' Nellie screamed as she ran towards us. I rested my head on his back, closing my eyes as I continued to sob, only quieter now, my only wish to have my husband back here with me.

'Och, fer cryin' out loud! Bugger off, ye irritatin' wee woman,' Hamish called out, stepping away towards the terraces.

'Get away from us. We don't like you. Not because you are unfortunate looking, but because you have a hideous core to you, and are the biggest whiner I know. Just stop it, Nellie, and go home. You have given me a headache, forcing me to set eyes on you without warning,' Leo called out over his shoulder, but she paid him no mind, her attention on only Hamish.

'You're throwing me over 'cause you're in love with some other woman, and it's her, isn't it?' She continued to scream, while my friends and family ignored her, most making their way down the cobblestone street away from the pub. Hamish remained silent, following the others while Angus and Polly walked beside him, his hands holding me in place firmly, my sobs filling the silent night.

'I can't do this without him. It hurts to breathe in and out,' I cried as he continued to stride up the hill, showing no signs of strain carrying me, while those around us breathed heavily as they tried to keep up.

'All will be well, lass. I'll have ye home an' in yer bed in naw time. Lay yer head, an' try an' breathe. Aaron is here beside ye, Abigail. He loves ye still, an' will always be around ye. Just calm yerself an' try tae rest yer mind. Naw long now 'till yer safe inside yer home.' No one paid any attention to the fact he had run to me earlier, and now carried me, knowing we were close friends, and had been for the longest time. They would be shocked if they knew he now shared my bed; however, they would be even more surprised when I eventually told them I was allowing Hamish to court me.

Hamish carried me up the stairs while everyone else made their way to the kitchen to eat whatever they could find. Carrying me against his chest through the wide hallways, my arms around his neck, my head on his shoulder, my sobs for my dead husband startling the hall-boy as he came around the corner, his eyes wide at the sight of me, before running past us and down the hall at great speed without a word. Hamish stared down at me as he stepped into my bedchamber, his eyes full of concern. Polly and Catherine followed him in as he gently lay me on top of the heavy quilt before straightening up, his large-frame looming over me, his brow furrowed, my friends now at his side. Several lamps burned brightly, so bright I kept my eyes closed, my body heavy despite feeling I could drift away into nothingness.

'Thank you, Hamish. How was she when you were away? Did she break down like this when drinking?' Catherine asked, her voice trembling slightly as I turned and sobbed into Aaron's pillow.

'Aye, the poor lass suffered through some difficult times, but naw, naw like this. Do ye have anythin' ye can give tae ease her? I know when she lost the weans, Dr Richards left some calmin' pills here.' He stared down at Catherine, her blonde hair still neat as a pin as she shook her head ruefully.

'That is true, but she cannot have them with a skin full of alcohol. We will kill her by the morning.' Polly sat down next to me, reaching out to stroke my forehead, my rambling cries making no sense, even to my own ears. 'Thank you for getting her home safe, especially in the state she's in.' Catherine placed her hand on his forearm and patted him several times, while Polly glared up at him.

'I thought Nelly was going to attack Abi; she was that wild at you. You really need to straighten up, Hamish. Commit to the poor lass. I know she loves you. She visited with me often while you were away and told me so more times than I can count. Stop playing with her heart and grow up. Get gone with you and make sure you talk to Nellie tomorrow. I don't see why we should all have to put up with that scaffy just because you are playing your games,' Polly snapped, before turning her attention back to me. He said nothing, his face starting to flush as he slowly turned and strode over to the door, unable to even kiss me goodnight in front of them.

He closed the door behind him as Polly and Catherine pulled me to my feet, stripping me within minutes and slipping a nightgown over my head before placing me under the covers, tucking me in tightly. Polly stayed next to me, her hand on mine, while Catherine went to change into her nightclothes, soon returning and slipping into bed beside me. Polly kissed me goodnight before walking around the room and extinguishing the lamps, picking up the last one to guide her back downstairs, calling out goodnight over her shoulder.

'I'm not leaving you alone tonight, Abigail. You are stuck with me, and always will be,' Catherine murmured, her fingers gently stroking my hair as I continued to cry for the longest time, my heart breaking, until I had no more tears left to shed. Eventually drifting off into a tormented sleep, dreams of Aaron holding me in his arms and dancing with me at the pub filled my head, soon turning to a field in which I danced alone, lost in a place unfamiliar to me.

My head throbbed as I gingerly opened one eye, the dim light starting to brighten, my memory of the night before blank. Finding Catherine had slept next to me left me slightly unsettled as I turned to see her still snoring softly. Groaning to myself as I rolled out of bed, I struggled to my feet, unsteady as I made my way across the room to my dressing room. Slipping on a skirt and shirt that required no assistance, I laced up my red ankle boots and threw my woollen cloak over my shoulders before quietly leaving the bedchamber, creeping down the hallway and stairs towards the kitchen.

Stepping out the back door without drawing any attention, to my great relief, I picked up my basket and made my way down to my rose garden, albeit slowly, my stomach churning and a pang of regret I hadn't taken a cup of coffee with me, Wombles following along behind. Cutting only the best stems, I reached down and scratched her on the head before placing the flowers carefully inside my basket, made in Geelong by a master basket weaver. Her joey was seven-months old, and barely fitted in her pouch; however, when he did squeeze inside, her pouch extended so far, Wombles was forced to stay where she was, or drag the now heavy burden along, near touching the ground. The joey was nameless for now, the staff waiting for our return to do the honours, but I was still in two minds and was considering Willow, or Wonky, the wombat. The way I felt this morning, the second choice seemed far more fitting.

I made my way down to the island, rowing myself across feeling every part of me ache, while missing Dingo's company dreadfully. Tying the boat to the pier, I struggled up onto the bank, my basket over my arm, before stopping to bend down and vomit, my stomach heaving. After some time, I straightened up, wiping my mouth with my handkerchief before leaning against a tree until the lightheadedness passed. It had been so long since I had been here, and I took my time as I wandered over to Adelaide's grave, leaving two roses, one each for her children, before making my way towards the enormous marble headstones where my family lay. Sitting down on Aaron's grave, I placed my basket down next to me, observing what a wonderful job Margaret and Jenny had done keeping the graves tidy, fresh flowers in the vases, the marble cleaned and polished to perfection.

I placed my hand on the headstone, telling him of our journey, and how very deeply he was missed, my heart breaking again as I burst into tears, while allowing every thought, feeling and regret to tumble out of my mouth. After the longest time, I composed myself as best I could and rose to my feet, kissing his name on the elaborate headstone, before moving over to the small slab of marble beside Aaron's that held my boys underneath. I sat with them for a time, sobbing until I had no more tears left to shed. They would have turned five only months ago, the thought setting off such a deep yearning within me to hold my children who had never taken a breath.

I gathered my things and stood, sighing deeply, before wandering over to the base of our tree next to the water to calm myself. I was to meet with Bessie and Danny later in the morning, and it was not something I looked forward to, dreading it even more so due to the state of me. I held only vague memories of last night, disjointed and fragmented; however, without doubt whatever had occurred would haunt me, and to find Catherine sound asleep and holding my hand this morning only confirmed what I had already come to believe.

I rowed myself back over the water, slowly making my way towards the house, while enjoying the fresh morning air, helping to clear my cluttered head. Making my way across the manicured gardens, a renewed energy in my step, I placed my basket back on the table under the verandah and entered through the back door, walking through to the large kitchen. Leo turned and smiled brightly at me, the kitchen warm and bustling, before bringing me a coffee, following me over to the wooden table where I sat down to wait for my children to arrive for breakfast.

'You need this.' His voice low, he smiled sympathetically as I nodded, accepting the mug gratefully.

'I do not want to know the details, Leo, but on a scale of one to ten, how bad was it?' I closed my eyes for a moment, cringing inside, wanting to know, but not wanting to know.

'It was a sixty-nine, Abigail, and that's about all you need to know.' He stood behind me, patting my back, while I lowered my head into my hands and shuddered, my face on fire, my only wish for the ground to open up and swallow me whole, while vowing I would never drink again.

Bessie's hands trembled, her work-worn hands red from wringing them over the last weeks, Danny beside her on the comfortable lounge opposite where Hamish and I sat, the low table between us. Danny appeared unsettled, suspicious of why he had been called to speak with us, his shoulders tense as he sat back in silence waiting to hear why he was here instead of out working and the reason his wife did not return home last night. Comfortable with us, Hamish was great mates with him, as Aaron had been, he and Bessie spending enormous amounts of time with us at the main house for celebrations, and gatherings for no reason at all.

Bessie had requested Hamish be present, concerned Danny would lose his temper, as she knew full well Hamish would calm him given their friendship. Waiting for Bessie to begin, silence hung heavy over the sitting room, her mouth opening and closing several times, although she did not utter a sound.

'Bessie has something she needs to tell you, Danny. Please stay calm, at least until she finishes.' His eyebrows shot up as he stared back at me, his face visibly paler than it had been only moments before, while Bessie took a deep breath, her body tense.

'Danny, darlin'. You know I love you more than anything or anyone on this earth. I want you to know that before I tell you.' He nodded, taking her hand in his, his eyes fixed on hers. 'There's no point me delaying any longer. I've decided what will be will be.' He nodded again, while she swallowed hard several times. 'I made a mistake, love. One I will regret forever. I was unfaithful to you once while we were away.' I could have heard a pin drop, Danny's face blank, his complexion grey. 'I'll never see him again, and it wasn't something I did on purpose, or that I even remember.' Her usually cheerful, confident tone had been reduced to barely a whisper, while he stared back at her, his eyes wide, the shock on his face no different than if she had told him the Pope had converted to Buddhism.

'No, Bessie, love. I can't believe it. You'd never do that ta me, me darlin' girl. I trust ya with every part o' me.' He leaned back for a moment, exhaling deeply before turning back to her. 'What the bloody hell has gotten into ya? Ta go an' let another man touch ya?' His voice broke, tears in his eyes as he lowered his head into his hands. Resisting the urge to go and embrace him, I cleared my throat, swallowing hard, the urge to break the silence almost unbearable.

'I'm sorry, my darlin'. You're my heart, and my only love. I will understand if you hate me from this day forward, but there's more. I'm with child, over five-months gone, six in a fortnight, and I plan to keep the bairn; whether you stand beside me or not. I love you Danny, love, but I already love this child growing inside me. I hate the man who planted the seed, but I'll never think of him again. The wean is my priority now, but I am so very sorry I've hurt such a good, decent man, whom I love deeply.' He rose to his feet, silent, his face like stone, turned on his heel, and left without a word. Hamish jumped to his feet, bending down to kiss Bessie on the cheek before crossing the room in several strides.

'I'll go after him. He only needs some time tae digest what ye just threw at him. I dinnae know if I can help ye, lass, but I can tell him o' me own mistakes, an' the pain they caused me, an' those around me. There's nought tae be done other than listen tae him, Bessie. I cannae promise I'll be o' any benefit, but I'll go after him now, an' take him fer a beer.' He quietly stepped out into the hall, while Bessie silently sobbed, gasping aloud at times as I moved to her side, lowering myself down and encircling her in a warm embrace.

'He will calm, and Hamish will talk to him just as he promised. It may take some time, but until then, you are always welcome to move back into the main house 'till it is sorted one way or another,' I suggested gently, holding her until her tears stopped.

'I've lost him, Mistress. All over one stupid mistake. Now I know how Hamish felt when you caught him with Charlotte, and he lost you as a result of it. I feel ashamed of meself how hard I was on him back then.' She sniffed before continuing. 'Now I understand how easy it is for these things to happen with too much grog in you.' I nodded, sympathising far deeper than I usually would, my hand on hers as we sat side-by-side in silence, the minutes passing quickly. She soon stood to return to her work.

'Bessie, you no longer need to work now you are this far along. You need to rest through the day so you're not exhausted when the bairn does arrive,' I remarked as she wiped her face, nodding before smiling down weakly at me.

'I know, but I would much rather keep myself busy. I'll rest when I need to. You're not the most demanding employer when it comes to my workload. I get plenty of time off, so don't fret. I have a lot to do under the house with your clothing that needs storing, so I'll go about my day, if you don't mind? The solitude down there is just what I'm craving.' She bid me farewell, and I stood to embrace her, while wondering what would happen between her and Danny. I knew how much they loved each other, and I hoped that would be enough to get them through.

I released her, and she bid me farewell again, hurrying out of the room as I settled myself back down on the lounge, pulling a thick woollen blanket over me, and let sleep take me.

Hamish returned to the sitting room an hour later, waking me from my nap. Closing the door behind him, he came straight to my side, bending down to kiss me awake. I placed my arms around his neck, pulling him closer, his eyes level with mine.

'Hello, lass. It's nice tae see ye with a bit o' a spark back in yer eyes.' He smiled to himself, kissing my lips again, his tongue running along my top lip before he slowly explored my mouth.

'Whatever happened last night, I do not wish to know. I am confident you out of everyone would have helped me in some way, so thank you for that.' Kissing him passionately, I ran my fingers through his silky hair, letting it loose from its leather bind. A sharp cough startled me, and I pushed him away with both hands. He slowly sat up beside me, appearing amused as he assisted me up into a sitting position beside him. I straightened my clothes, running my hand over my hair to smooth it before glancing across at the door to find Mr Masters, my face flushed as he bowed formally before stepping inside, an envelope in his hand.

'I apologise for the disruption, Mistress.' He turned, nodding at Hamish politely. 'And to you, Mr Makenzie. Detective O'Neill called, and he left a letter for you. I explained that you were unavailable, as per your instructions, and he departed not ten-minutes ago. Would you like morning tea brought in here?' He avoided my gaze, his own cheeks flushed, while Hamish appeared pleased with himself.

'Morning tea would be lovely; however, I wish to take it in my bedchamber with Bessie, if you do not mind?' He nodded, his shoulders relaxing. 'Please ask Leo to include several desserts for us to choose from.' He nodded again, preparing to leave. 'How is Maisie? I haven't seen her since we arrived home.' He paused, turning back, a smile touching his lips.

'You saw her last night, Mistress, but it matters not, given the state of your distress. She was overjoyed to see you returned safe to us, and cried tears of joy to hear of her kin, Alasdair and Archie.' My eyes widened for a moment, Hamish shifting uncomfortably in his seat beside me.

'Oh. Was it Bessie who spoke of them with her?' Mr Masters stared down at me, silent for a moment, his eyes full of sympathy.

'No, Mistress. It was you.' I closed my eyes, cringing inside, my mind racing as I tried to remember.

'I hope I said nothing to offend or upset her.' I swallowed hard, glancing across the room and out the pane glass window looking out over the garden, before returning his stare.

'Of course not, Mistress. Maisie gets the odd letter from them from time to time, and she writes them often. She believes it was serendipity itself that you made the acquaintance of Lord Harrington, and secretly hopes you marry the man.' He chuckled to himself, while I pressed the palms of my hands to my cheeks, Hamish's grunt not going unnoticed. 'I served for a time myself under Lord Reginald Harrington the third. Not for long, but long enough to know he is a kind and decent man, very much like his grandmother, Lady Charlotte.' I nodded, far too embarrassed to say another word, while he nodded again before striding out of the room, discreetly closing the door behind him. I often wondered if he suspected Maisie was my aunt, or that Anna, a woman he was rumoured to be familiar with fifteen-years before he met Maisie, was in fact her eldest sister, suspecting he knew far more than he would ever let on. Hamish threw back his head and howled with laughter, while I turned, narrowing my gaze at him.

'Oh, stop it, you fat headed moron. I'm never drinking again.' I threw myself back on the lounge, closing my eyes. 'Do not assume I am so blind I cannot see how thrilled you are every time someone else becomes aware of what lies between us. I am not.' His eyes twinkled as he took my hand in his.

'I cannae help it. Ye know I want everyone tae know about us. I've never hidden the fact.' He smirked, touching my nose with his finger, and I couldn't help but smile back at him.

'I offered for Bessie to move back to the main house until things are sorted one way or the other with Danny.'

'Aye, seems she may need tae take ye up on that. He's gone home tae pack her things fer her. I'll spend some time with him over the next few days, an' try an' help the poor bloke come tae terms with such a betrayal. I'm hopin' they sort it out. They've always made a good team, them two.'

'Oh, so do I. They have always been a wonderful couple. So dedicated to each other for so long now.' He nodded, slipping his arm around my shoulders, the room silent bar the birds scavenging the kitchen scraps left out on the lawn.

'I've somethin' tae ask o' ye, an' dinnae say naw straight away as ye usually do tae me.' I stared back at him, narrowing my gaze suspiciously, my hand on his knee.

'What do you want this time? Leo does this to me. Tries to get me to commit to something before I even know what it is. Believe me, the amount of regrets I have over agreeing to things I have no knowledge of I cannot even count.' He threw back his head again and laughed loudly, a smile touching my lips.

'I need tae take ye somewhere after lunch. Dinnae ask any questions, just agree tae come with me.' I relented after only a moment before he rose to his feet in one elegant movement, turning to blow me a kiss from the door. He disappeared into the hallway, his footsteps fading as he made his way back to the stables, my mind clearer now as I struggled to my feet, feeling far more prepared to face the rest of the day.

Stepping into my bedchamber, I found Bessie already waiting. Crossing the room to where our morning tea had already been laid out, I slid onto the ornate chair beside her, the walnut table seating four.

'I hate to be the bearer of bad news, but it's best to get it over with so we can enjoy what's in front of us.' She nodded, helping herself to a roasted beef sandwich smothered in Leo's special mustard pickles. 'I spoke with Hamish, and it seems Danny would like you to move out of the terrace for a time. You can either take a guest room in the house, or return to your old room in the staff quarters. It's only become available again as unbeknownst to me, Mabel left us a month ago, and I was sad to hear it, but it was not unexpected. She secured the head maid position with the Mulhulland family in Geelong, and I completely understand why she accepted with Maisie here. She would never have risen up the ladder of the household hierarchy, but I do wish her all the luck in the world.' Surprised Bessie did not break down, she poured our coffees, fixing her attention on organising the plates of cakes and juices still on the trolley.

'I'll be far more comfortable back in my old room in the staff quarters. I don't want any of them thinking I see myself as their better.' I nodded, accepting her decision without question. We took our time, talking of other things far more cheerful, while enjoying every morsel the kitchen staff had provided with such care. Stacking the dirty dishes back onto the trolley, we walked side-by-side down to the kitchen, leaving the silver cart at the top of the stairs near a dumb waiter used only for this purpose, a feature of the home I at first believed would never be used, but oh, how wrong I had been.

Embracing in the hallway, Bessie left me to collect her belongings from the sitting room sent back with Hamish. He had left them on the table, not wanting to give them to her himself should he upset her further. Stepping into the bustling kitchen, I paused in the doorway for a time, watching as they cheerfully went about their tasks, their banter loud, far more rambunctious than if they noticed my presence in their kitchen. Most had been here from the start, although over time we had employed younger staff to fill the positions as the more experienced staff were promoted. Bessie brushed past me, smiling weakly as she made her way towards the staff quarters, two heavy canvas bags in her hands, a small box under her arm. Erin hurried along in front of her, opening the door before reaching out to take one of the bags from her, following her in, the door closing firmly behind them. I made my way across the now far quieter room, sitting myself down at the well used wooden table, the grain more beautiful as time passed, the carved legs and engravings so very intricate. Heady spices filled every inch of the kitchen, the dish familiar and one Leo had learned at the knee of a chef from the East Indies who stopped for a time in his village, staying six-months with his family. Leo strode towards me in his pristine uniform, only the right sleeve appeared to have been torn from the shoulder, sympathy in his eyes.

'How are you feeling, you tavern trollop? You do not look as unwell as I was expecting.' He appeared eager to speak with me, lowering himself down onto the chair opposite, while Sally brought several bowls of curried meats and vegetables to the table, soon placing down warm flatbread, along with mango chutney, and a small pot of yoghurt, a half-cucumber chopped finely mixed in. Returning a final time with a large platter of steaming yellow rice, she nodded at me before returning to her duties.

'What the hell have you done to your uniform? They are all practically new, and cost me a small fortune. You better not be trying to start a new fashion in the hope of becoming famous like you tried to do last year. I told you then that pink, purple and lemon coloured suits for men would never catch on, but would you listen?' Crossing his legs before folding his arms across his chest, he rolled his eyes, his face like thunder.

'It's that hateful Pollyanna you choose to continue to call friend, despite me telling you for years you must get rid of her. Do you listen?' He shook his head, while I gathered all the strength in me to not smile. 'No, of course you don't. I blame you for what's happened, Abigail. I'm certain you keep her on here because you know she is the only person at Willow Grove, other than Mr Masters, who torments me on purpose. They even look alike.' The room now silent, I sighed deeply, not wanting to ask but knowing I must.

'What happened, Leo?' He shifted in his seat, settling himself in before pouring me a glass of apple juice.

'Well, I rose this morning and went about my usual routine while tending to my personal hygiene. I'm surprised you did not hear my screams when I opened my wardrobe to find every shirt, coat, jacket and jumper had the right sleeve cut off.' I collapsed into a fit of giggles, laughter in the adjourning room from the kitchen staff filling my ears, while Leo sat forward, shrieking at me, his arms waving frantically in the air. 'I will seek my revenge, Abigail. Laugh. Keep laughing. Pollyanna is an awful person, and I have no doubt she is spawned from evil. Jack the Ripper could have fathered her for all we know, and if not him, someone just as maleficent. The worst part is she took the sleeves with her, and I am unable to ask a favour of Bessie to sew them back on.' I sighed deeply, the room silent once more bar his moaning, and leaned forward to serve myself lunch, while narrowing my gaze at him.

'What did you do to her?'

'This time, I swear, absolutely nothing, Abigail. She fell down drunk on her backside last night like the drunkard she is, then blamed me; however, I had nothing to do with it. Angus didn't even go and help her because he was shamed publicly by his slovenly wife. I still believe living with the Makenzie's would do her good. We don't need her here. She doesn't do anything productive or have any purpose around the place, so I believe you need to lighten the load. Unless she starts working as a farmhand, she must move on.' I smothered a smile at the thought of Polly ploughing the paddocks, his arms folded across his chest as he continued to glare at me, going on to list a hundred other qualities he detested in Polly.

'I'm sure you will sort it between you, as you usually do,' I replied, my mouth full, while his face twisted as if he were in physical pain.

'Abigail, how many times must I tell you? Do you have any idea what rice and yoghurt look like chewed up in your mouth? No. Well, it's better I don't say it in front of ladies.' He cocked his head to the side, nodding towards the staff, his eyebrows raised as Hamish entered the kitchen, striding across the room to join us at the table. I watched as he piled his plate with rice, adding ladles of goat curry, along with a lamb and pineapple stew. 'Tell me, Hamish. Did you enjoy your time away?' Leo inquired, a smirk on his face, while Hamish returned his stare.

'Aye, I did. I'm glad tae be home, though. We all missed the place.' Leo raised his eyebrows wickedly, while Hamish remained blank of any emotion, a sparkle in his eye I did not recognise.

'You look to me like you have been bedded well while away, Hamish. You have a certain spring back in your step.' Hamish narrowed his gaze, straightening his shoulders while continuing to eat. 'All your stories are filled with the children and Abigail, and I wonder where you got the time to romance the ladies while away.' Leo leaned forward, raising his fingers to his temples and rubbed them for a moment. 'I once knew a soothsayer, and she often remarked I was far more gifted than she.' He looked up, widening his eyes at Hamish, a smile on his lips. 'I know without doubt you are sharing Abigail's bed in secret, you mad rooters.' He collapsed in a fit of giggles before I leaned over and smacked his bare arm for betraying my confidence.

'Did ye tell him?' Hamish asked, his eyes twinkling in amusement.

'Oh, dear. Hamish, never fall for that again. Whenever Leo says anything, it makes no difference what it is, never confirm or deny. Most of the time he has not a clue and is just fishing for information.' I shook my head while Hamish grinned, placing his hand on mine for only a moment.

'At no time did you ask me to keep your rooting a secret from Hamish. I'm sure he knows even more than I do about it, Abigail.' I rolled my eyes, ignoring him while he fixed his attention on Hamish. 'How about you, Adonis? Abigail already told me all the dirty details, but you need to understand I must hear it from your lips to know for certain. She is prone to exaggeration, you know?' Hamish threw back his head and laughed, several giggles erupting from the direction of the kitchen. 'As her one and only best friend, you must go through me for everything Abigail related. When you wish to spend time in her company, this must be arranged and approved by me. If there are certain preferences you have in the bedchamber, tell me and I will ensure she complies. Treat me well, I will force Abigail to treat you better. If you irritate me, then I will throw you over on her behalf. It's all really quite simple once you understand how our friendship works,' Leo advised him, his brow furrowed, his legs crossed, while Hamish laughed again, my face burning.

'Leo, I dinnae believe any sensible person on this earth understands the relationship between ye an' Abigail. I dinnae even try anymore tae work it out. Hurts me brain the more I think about it. As for...' I raised my hand, shaking my head.

'Stop. Don't say another word, Hamish. I told him nothing. Not one detail. Do not get caught up in the tangled web he weaves,' I warned, smiling weakly as he laughed louder. We continued eating companionably, Hamish and I behaving no different than we always had, our friendship the same as it had always been.

'Thomas and Emmy are feeling left out at the moment,' Leo remarked, and I flinched.

'Why?'

'Well, they told me they are the only ones who no longer have a father. It's made them feel different.' Leo sighed, while tears pricked my eyes. 'For the first time in my life, I didn't know what to say to them.' He sniffed, while I brushed away a stray tear. Changing the subject, Leo spoke of what he had recently heard on the passionfruit vine, entertaining us for an entire hour. Finishing his coffee, Hamish turned to me and smiled, his brown eyes staring into mine, his hand slipping down onto my thigh.

'Are ye ready tae get goin', lass?'

'Yes, I will just finish my drink.' Draining my glass, we stood to leave, Leo glancing at us knowingly before returning to his work, while I followed Hamish across the room, ignoring them all while fully aware they knew far more of my private business than I wanted.

Hamish glanced around the back room, or mudroom, as we called it, where boots and coats were stripped off and hands were washed in the corner trough kept full of warm water from the kitchen next door. He opened the backdoor wide, brushing his lips against mine as I stepped outside into the afternoon sunshine. Taking my hand in his, he led me towards Delly, saddled and standing tied to a bench seat in the garden, a magnificent stallion, Simi, sired by Goliath standing next to her.

I approached her, my hand out as she turned towards me, an excited whinny echoing around us. Giving her a rub, my head against her neck, I reluctantly pulled away to mount her with some difficulty. I hadn't known he intended to take me riding, or I would have worn my riding clothes, for now I was stuck in a cumbersome skirt that would no doubt ride up my bare legs, exposing the flesh of my lower thigh, scandalous should I be seen. Hamish swung up on his horse, moving him forward past Angus and Polly's cottage, while I followed, walking the magnificent beasts through the woodlands on the far side of the property.

A quarter of an hour later, we came into a cleared area by the wide river, a charming cottage I never knew existed settled comfortably on the riverbank, the tall native trees and shrubs surrounding it protectively, hiding it from view until you came upon it. We rarely frequented this side of the property, preferring to use the river near the village to fish and swim.

'When did you find this, Hamish?' I dismounted, leaving Delly grazing on the grass, while Hamish hobbled them both near the water, removing their bridles. I wandered over to the quaint building, reminding me of one from a storybook I had read to Thomas and Emmy when they were small. I had seen this cottage before, a number of times in my dreams, yet hadn't a clue where it was, the building exactly as I had seen it right down to the colour of the stones used, and the pane glass windows. 'It's truly beautiful, and it looks new, not like it has stood here since my aunt bought the place. How did I not know this was here?'

'Weel, that's 'cause it was naw here 'till recently. Let me show ye the inside.' He came up alongside me and took my hand, leading me to the front door. I followed him in to find a comfortable sitting room, the floor to ceiling windows looking out over the fast flowing river. Showing me through to the small kitchen, a warm fire burned in the hearth, a small bathroom built off to the side with running water and a flushable commode. Stepping into the bedchamber, the room decorated in purple, lilac and cream, an enormous four-posted heavy wooden bed pushed back against the far wall, a different but no less beautiful view of the river just outside the window, the trees swaying gently outside, the birds singing their chorus from their strong branches.

I assumed Hamish had tired of living with Polly, Angus, and the children, and was now seeking a place for himself, something more private given he almost ran the property single-handedly, and I felt he deserved at least that after how he had cared for us and Willow Grove. He led me by the hand out onto the wide verandah surrounding the entire cottage, several cane chairs placed outside to take in the fresh air, the cushions thick and luxurious. Gazing down at me, the muscle along his strong jaw twitched several times, he shifted from foot to foot, clearing his throat several times.

'Abigail, ye know I love ye. Always have. I've come tae suspect over the years there's naw other woman on this earth fer me, an' as every man an' his dog knows, I've looked.'

'What's wrong with you, Hamish? You have gone all soft and giddy headed.' He loomed over me, his hands gently holding my shoulders.

'Aye, maybe I have. I know yer naw *in* love with me, Abigail, but I do know fer certain ye love an' respect me as yer friend. There are partnerships that have started with far less, an' they've gone on tae be happier than they thought they could ever have been. I've loved Thomas an' Emmy since I first held 'em in me arms 'cause they were part o' ye, but as time went on, I fell in love with 'em in their own right. I want tae be with ye fer the rest o' me life, an' be there fer Thomas an' Emmy, naw tae replace their father, but tae love 'em an' guide 'em just as Aaron would have done had he been here tae do it. I want all o' ye, Abigail, an' if I dinnae have ye honestly, an' in the open, I cannae stay at Willow Grove any longer. It's tearing me apart, lass.' I swallowed hard, tears pricking my eyes as he dropped to one knee, both my hands clasped in his as he stared up into my eyes. 'I love ye a million times more than me words can express, an' I promise tae make yer life easier than it would have been every day we're together, an' I will always make ye feel loved, an' be ye best friend, an' I'll protect ye with me body, an' love ye with all o' me.' Pulling a small box from his pocket, he held it up toward me before flicking it open. Rising to his feet, his eyes fixed on mine, he ran his tongue along his dry lips. 'I know I dinnae deserve ye, an' there are far better men out there than me, but that only makes me try harder every single day tae be the best I can. Fer ye an' the twins. Ye make me want tae be a better man, Abigail. Naw one walkin' this earth will love ye more than I, an' I want tae ask ye tae be me wife?' Tears filled his eyes as I reeled back, taking several steps away from him, my hands raised, my palms facing him as I shook my head.

'Oh, Hamish. I cannot give you any children,' was all I could mumble, my mind racing with a thousand thoughts, none of them making any sense.

'Ye've already given me two bairns, an' I'll always consider 'em mine tae love an' guide, an' that's all I'll ever need.' He waited patiently, a small distance separating us, the rush of the water flowing over the river rocks filling my ears.

'I do not know what to say.'

'Take yer time, lass. We've nowhere tae be.'

I would never find another who loved me and my children the way he did, that I knew for certain, and I did love him dearly, not how he needed or deserved, but my attachment to him was strong. My heart sank at the thought he could leave forever and never see us again, and I slowly wandered over to the river, stopping at the bank, while he remained where he was, gazing across at me from the verandah, the silence broken by the native birds, the sound of the water calming as it slowed at the elbow into a swimming hole before continuing on downstream and out towards the ocean.

If I agreed, Thomas and Emmy would have a father again, a strong and loving man who would take his responsibilities to them seriously, an empty void they so desperately needed filled after the loss of Aaron, and after the brief discussion with Leo earlier, I had only come to realise just how desperately they craved for life to return to what it had once been. Aware I too needed to feel close to another, and craved intimacy and love no different from the next, I trusted Hamish with my life, and my children's, despite what a lot of people thought of him. What I couldn't get away from was Aaron had wanted me to marry Hamish after he was gone, and had not only given his blessing, he had almost blackmailed me into agreeing. He knew without doubt he would take care of us, and I trusted my husband to this day. I marched back towards him, a determination in my step that hadn't been there before. Standing in front of him, I stared up into his eyes, my thoughts racing, although soon after stopping at one.

'I will marry you, Hamish, and I will do right by you and make you a good wife, but I hope with everything in me I make you as content as you seem to believe I will.' He threw back his head and roared, lifting me up off the ground and into his arms, swinging me around the veranda and out onto the grass, his lips on mine.

'Abigail, ye've made me the happiest man alive.' He continued to spin me around, kissing me again, before slowing to a stop in the middle of the small garden, still holding me off the ground. I gazed down at the large diamond ring fitted snugly alongside the wedding band on my finger. I had never taken them off since the day we married. Hamish placed me back down on my feet, and I gently removed them, placing them on the fourth finger of my right hand, while Hamish slipped his arm around my shoulder, holding out the box before I took it, my hands trembling. Inside sat the biggest pink diamond ring I had ever seen. Truly beautiful, he slipped it on my finger, a satisfied smile on his lips. 'I had it made fer ye in New York with the bracelet fer yer birthday, but wanted tae propose tae ye here at Willow Grove. Here is where I want tae make memories with ye, Abigail, an' took the chance tae ask ye, naw really expectin' ye tae accept the first time.' He chuckled to himself, his arm around my waist as we looked out over the river. 'I was certain I'd be forced tae ask at least another fifty-times before ye got sick o' me an' agreed under sufferance.'

'I must talk to Thomas and Emmy before anything is official. I want to make sure they agree to me marrying again so soon after losing their father,' I warned, however, he shook his head, his eyes twinkling in amusement.

'They already know. I asked fer their permission days ago.' I turned and looked up at him, widening my eyes while he laughed aloud. 'Abigail, many widows marry again within the first year o' their husband's death, an' ye have nothin' tae feel guilty about. I would naw have asked ye tae marry me without talkin' tae Thomas an' Emmy first.' He leaned down, kissing my neck, the sun warm on my skin as I turned my face to the sky and closed my eyes.

'What did they say?' He slipped his arms around my waist, my back on his chest, my arms raised back up around his neck.

'Aye, they were beyond acceptin', an' loud an' cheerful about it, an' they made it clear if ye refused me, they'd talk tae ye themselves an' convince ye, come hell or high water, ta be me wife.' He laughed loudly, and I smiled to myself, my eyes still closed as I let myself melt into him, my body lighter somehow now I had someone beside me to share the load.

Later that night as I lay in his arms in our new cottage, the sound of the river gently flowing past outside the window, I drifted off into a deep slumber, my dreams filled with a pink diamond, a white diamond, and Aaron. Always Aaron.

Chapter Six

T HE SOUND OF RUNNING water drew me from sleep, the sky only starting to brighten, our Kookaburra just starting his morning laugh in the distance, echoing across the property as the land started to wake. Still wrapped in Hamish's strong arms, it felt nice to be held again by someone who loved me. I snuggled my head deeper into his shoulder, not wanting to wake him.

After I had agreed to marry him yesterday, he had promptly gone to the kitchen to retrieve a bottle of champagne, along with two crystal flutes. I had teased him on his return regarding his cockiness, confident I would say yes, while he preferred to call it hopeful at best. He had not told a soul of his intention, other than Thomas and Emmy, even keeping it from Angus, believing I would reject him.

Hamish had been so very thoughtful, ensuring there were several large, comfortable lounges furnishing the place, all big enough for two or three people to stretch out on. Placing a lovely purple lounge out under the verandah, we had spent the afternoon reclining on it while gazing out over the water, the conversation comfortable and animated. He had told me he had written to Angus when we first arrived in London to request he have the cottage built, and specified where, including an intricate plan of what he wanted, asking Polly to furnish the place, the only instructions he had given. Angus and Polly had done the rest without question, thinking the cottage for him alone.

We had drunk three bottles of Bollinger Champagne by the time Leo arrived, arranged earlier by Hamish if we had not returned within two-hours, bringing with him our dinner packed in a basket, still warm from the oven, along with a box packed with breakfast food for the morning. After unpacking it all in the kitchen, he had returned to speak with us for a time, noticing the pink diamond on my finger almost immediately. Truly happy, he had hugged us both, promising to keep our secret until we formally announced our betrothal, before skipping back to his horse, singing at the top of his lungs as he kicked her forward, trotting back towards the house, his voice floating over his shoulder long after he was out of sight, still causing me to cringe and cover my ears no matter how soft.

We had taken our time over dinner, drinking far more champagne than I intended, before he took me to bed. I had allowed him to make love to me for the first time slowly, and with emotion, and let him hold me after. I felt safe, comfortable and loved again for the first time in years. It seemed Aaron had made room in my heart to open just a little for Hamish. It was only a small piece, but it was a start.

I felt him stir beside me, his lips on my neck before I lifted my head to stare at him. 'Good morning.'

'Och, yer awake? I thought ye were still sleepin' soundly.' He kissed my shoulder, his fingers running gently up and down my arm. Turning to kiss him, I ran my tongue along the inside of his lip, passion overwhelming me. Pushing me away after a time, breathless, he held me at a distance, amusement in his eyes. 'Ye've never kissed me like that before.' He leaned closer, kissing me again for the longest time.

'Well, you weren't going to be my husband before.'

Delly wound her way through the native trees, soon trotting out into the paddock leading down to the sea, and the homes of Aaron's family. I had left my pink diamond at the cottage in Hamish's safekeeping, slipping Aaron's rings back onto my left hand before departing soon after breakfast, my nerves already frayed. I not only wanted their blessing, their consent was something I needed given I loved and respected them as my own kin. Trotting through an open gate leading into Scarlett and Patrick's yard, Delly slowed to a walk as we came up the side of their substantial home, before turning the corner and making our way to their grand entrance.

'Scarlett,' I called out at the top of my lungs from where I sat in the saddle, calling out again just as the front door opened, a dishevelled Scarlett hurrying out onto the verandah, her eyes wide.

'What's wrong with ya, yelling out like a fisher wife?' She threw back her head and laughed while slipping on her coat before pulling the door closed behind her.

'Good morning. I have a favour to ask of you.' She nodded, silent now, the sounds of the bush and all it held awakening around us, the waves in the distance crashing against the shore. 'I have some important news, and I need to discuss it with the family. Do you mind gathering the tribe at our parents' home?' Agreeing immediately, she waved me off as I rode on to Mr and Mrs Cavanaugh's larger plot set near the ocean, looking out over Bass Strait.

Dismounting in their driveway, I hobbled Delly near the water trough before making my way to the front door and knocking twice, my hand trembling. Their housekeeper, along with their new maid, Rose, greeted me cheerfully, taking my cloak before welcoming me in. Aaron's parents hadn't changed their way of living much since coming into more money than they would ever spend when they expanded the business over a decade ago, the only notable difference being the amount of staff they now employed at home, their house busier than mine.

'Your mother is in the sitting room, Mrs Cavanaugh. I will take you to her, if you would like to come?' I nodded politely at Rose, thanking her, before following her in to meet with Aaron's mother, her face lighting up at the sight of me as I went to her side.

'Oh, my darling girl. You're visiting with us far earlier than expected. I thought you would come in a day or two after you settled yourselves back in.' She motioned for me to sit beside her near the hearth, the love seat she sat on built for two, while embracing me before I made myself comfortable.

'I have come as I need to speak with you all.' I raised my hand to my chest, my heart pounding hard as Rose poured us both a cup of tea.

'Are you well, Abigail? Has something happened to the children?' The blood drained from her face, her hand grasping mine, and I turned to her, shaking my head.

'The children are fine, and all is well. I just need to talk.' She visibly relaxed, squeezing my hand before preparing to stand.

'Oh, blessed be. I will just go and get your father, and he can send for the others.'

'There is no need. Scarlett is already gathering them up. You only need to get Da.' They were in their late fifties now, and I worried for them, even more so today and how they would feel about my news. Afraid they would believe I was replacing Aaron, and would forget him, I not only wanted to reassure them that would never occur, I wanted their honest opinion if I was making the right decision, not only for me, but for Thomas and Emmy. Aiden and Victoria soon barrelled into the room, both breathless as they sat down heavily on the lounge, while Patrick and Scarlett arrived within moments, followed by Luke and Adele.

'What's happened? Are you an' the nipper's okay? Aiden asked, the rest of my family gathered around the comfortable room in silence just as Mrs Cavanaugh returned with her husband, still wiping the sleep from his eyes, an overcoat thrown over his flannel pyjamas.

'Yes, we are all well.' I cleared my throat, my hands fidgeting in my lap. 'I do not know how to start...' My voice faltered for a moment, Adele reaching out from where she sat on a large cushion on the floor in front of me to place her hand on mine as I inhaled deeply, willing my heart to slow.

'Oh, my dear Abigail. Whatever it is will never change our love for you. You became our child the day Aaron brought you here to meet us. Remember?' Mrs Cavanaugh's eyes glistened, a mixture of joy, longing and grief clear for all to see. I nodded, my hand in hers as she stared into the fire, the logs burning ferociously, while Mr Cavanaugh perched on the arm of the love seat, his hand on her back. 'What larrikins they were, teasing you like that.' She shook her head, a smile touching her lips. 'But I knew then Aaron loved you, and a knowing settled on me that day you were given to us as a gift, and a precious one you have shown yourself to be. You are our daughter, their sister.' She pointed to her sons' and rolled her eyes as their wives giggled. 'And you are the mother of our grandchildren. Nothing, not even when parted by death, will ever change the fact we *are* family.' I swallowed hard, closing my eyes for a moment.

'Hamish has asked me to marry him, and I have accepted. I want to know if it is too soon. I don't ever want any of you to think I love Aaron any less than the day I married him.' I promptly lowered my head and burst into tears, Mr Cavanaugh swiftly moving across to sit on the arm of the seat next to me, his large hand gently patting my back. 'I will reject him if any of you are against the match.'

'Abigail, me sweet girl. I think I can speak for everyone here, an' say no, it's not too soon. Aaron loved an' respected Hamish, as we all do, an' it was his wish for you ta marry him when he was no longer here with us. He told me himself the last time I saw him. Ya do have our blessin', an' we'll always regard ya as our eldest daughter. Ya belong ta our family forever. I hope ya can find happiness again, darlin'. It's been unbearable ta watch ya suffer like ya have for so long.' Mr Cavanaugh leaned down and kissed my cheek, and I smiled up at him through my tears.

'I was told by a stable boy what happened at the pub, and if my heart wasn't broken enough for you before, it completely shattered when I heard of you screaming and sobbing for Aaron like that. He cannot ever come back to you, or us, Abigail, no matter how hard you pray for it to be. I will admit, I sobbed in my drawing room for hours. It brings me great comfort to know you will no longer be alone, and now have someone beside you who loves our grandchildren. He loves you deeply, and I'm confident will care for you well, just as my Aaron wanted. You have nothing to feel guilty or ashamed of, my dear. You have grieved my son so very deeply, for so very long now. You loved our boy well, and he loved you, a stronger love I have rarely witnessed. Now it's time to find the same with Hamish.' Mrs Cavanaugh kissed my forehead, while my sisters-in-law embraced me all at once before Patrick picked me up and gathered me into a warm embrace, my feet dangling inches above the carpet, passing me from brother to brother. Sitting me back down in between their parents, I wiped my face with a clean handkerchief, relief washing over me.

'Abigail, this is such wonderful news. I cried all the night, and well into the next day for you after witnessing you so very distraught. Now I think about it, Hamish *was* very caring towards you, despite that woman screaming abuse at him,' Adele remarked thoughtfully, and I heard Patrick snort, setting Aiden and Luke off until they were all laughing uproariously.

'Hamish has made a lot of mistakes with a lot of women, but I doubt very much he'll make one with Abigail. She has that ear an' ballsack twistin' down ta a fine art,' Patrick teased, the room loud with laughter and cheerful banter.

'Aaron was the one who told us Hamish was in love with ya, an' he was the only man he wanted ya ta be with after his death,' Aiden remarked, while his brothers nodded thoughtfully. I stayed to take an early morning tea, enjoying their company so much I forgot the time. Standing to leave, they walked me out, the long hugs and goodbyes taking longer than expected.

Standing together on the verandah, they waved as I rode out the driveway and back towards the cottage, a peace settling on me. I may have been marked an orphan at birth, but I never truly had been without family, nor would I ever be while the Cavanaughs' backsides pointed to the ground. I was grateful.

I unsaddled Delly, throwing her saddle up over the post and rail fence sectioning off the small plot around the cottage before letting her loose. Wandering up towards the house, I noticed Leo's favourite horse grazing on the native grass. Opening the front door, I called out, making my way through to the kitchen where I found Leo sitting at the table with Hamish, both sipping a mug of freshly brewed coffee. A box filled with what I assumed to be our lunch sat on the bench, while Leo appeared to have made himself at home already.

'Can I talk to you in private, Abigail?'

'Why?' I narrowed my gaze suspiciously, pouring myself a cup of coffee before leaning against the meat safe.

'It may embarrass Hamish if I should say it here.' Hamish grimaced, raising his hand and pointing towards the door.

'Go. I have naw desire tae hear anythin' ye have tae say between ye.' I lowered myself down onto Hamish's lap, slipping my arm around his neck before brushing his lips with mine.

'Oh, my. I feel you are running around on Goliath with Adonis, and it's giving me a strange feeling in my tummy. Stop kissing him. I feel the urge to run and tell Aaron on you, Hamish. He would belt you for touching his wife, far worse than that time he beat your backside years ago when you touched her dangerous parts.' He paused for a moment, widening his eyes at me before turning his gaze back to Hamish. 'Abigail promised me she would never marry again, and I now find she's deceived me. Do you believe you can trust her after that, Adonis? I wouldn't be hitching my wagon to the tired old troll when you could have had me. I was next in line for you, and Abigail pushed in yet again, shoving everyone out of the way so she could get her hands on the most eligible bachelor in the district,' Leo complained, leaning back in his chair as I settled myself deeper on Hamish's lap, his arms around my waist.

'Aye, I heard about someone shovin' someone else, an' it was naw Abigail. Ye pushed me sister, Pollyanna, on her arse at the pub. She told me herself 'cause Angus willnae touch a hair on yer head, an' she asked him tae do far more than that, but when he refused, she came tae me beggin' fer help.' Leo's eyes went wide, his mouth opening and closing several times before he composed himself.

'What did she want you to do? She already paid me back by cutting off all my sleeves. What does she want? My blood? My firstborn?' He wrinkled his nose indignantly as I smothered a smile.

'Ye should have left it at that, but ye had tae retaliate after she took yer sleeves, did ye naw?' Hamish held his gaze, Leo's eyes widening further, his voice going up several octaves.

'Oh, I did one small thing.'

'Aye, ye did, but I'm sure Abigail would like tae hear it.'

'All I did was sneak into her cottage when Angus left for work. There was no harm in it. She was sleeping late, as expected of the slovenly trollop, and I was far from surprised she did not wake despite my presence.' He stopped, turning to me. 'You must do something about her, Abigail. She lays around here like the Queen of the castle, and everyone here knows that's me. Anyway, back to me. I have far more important things to discuss than that wretched Pollyanna.' I put my hand up to stop him, while Hamish shook his head.

'What did you do to her?' I glared at him, while he dismissed me with a wave of his hand.

'Not enough, in my opinion. I took every dress she owns, and cut the backside out of them. How was I to know she wouldn't notice before leaving the house and walking down to the village to work in the general store? Anyone else would feel the cold breeze around their buttocks, but not Pollyanna. She's solid ice inside, therefore, the weather has no effect on her. She walked around for half the day with her bum hanging out before anyone summoned the courage to tell her. Even the villagers are frightened of her, Abigail. I cannot see how any of that was my fault at all, and you would be best to take her to the asylum in Ararat. I wrote to them while you were away, several times in fact, to advise of her impending arrival.' I hadn't seen Polly since all this was supposed to have occurred, laughter bubbling up inside me.

'She wants more than just yer blood, Leo. She's out fer yer sausage an' eggs served on a silver platter tae shove down yer throat. I'd stay out o' her way. She'll hurt ye, an' I willnae protect ye from her,' Hamish warned, taking my mug from me before drinking deeply and handing it back empty.

'I do not believe you understand just what your new position is here, and that is only *if* I allow you to marry my Abigail. You are now obligated to protect me from everyone and everything, especially your mad sister, Pollyanna, and we will throw Jemima in there for good measure, as she is not only mad, she's bad. As for your future wife, well, I do not think you realise just what you are signing up for. Poor Aaron was forced to spend half his workday following her around to ensure she stayed out of mischief,' Leo warned him, while Hamish snorted loudly, his brown eyes twinkling.

'Aaron spent most o' his time chasin' after ye fer leadin' his wife astray, so dinnae give me that scaffy. I know very well what I'm in fer, an' am adequately prepared fer it.' I smiled at Leo before brushing my lips against Hamish's once more, Leo's groans filling the kitchen before he rose to his feet, stomping off into the bedchamber, while I remained where I was, an almost unrecognisable feeling of happiness settling on me, and in that very moment, I knew I had chosen well.

I lay on the thick, feathered mattress, the heavy quilt underneath me, silent as I waited for Leonardo to entertain me with yet another story, the last one regarding a man of royal blood caught in a Molly house, the other of a famous writer he had once known who had been born as a woman, but lived as a man, taking his secret to the grave, it seemed, as I had read every book he had ever written, and I had never heard even a whisper. He stood near the window, a canvas bag in his hand he had brought with him from the main house.

'I was going through your things to find your nightclothes to ensure you are comfortable, but I found this instead,' he teased, tipping the bag upside down and spilling its contents on the bed next to me, while I rolled my eyes.

'Catherine refers to these as *negligees*, or *linge*, but has always used a made up word she learned when very young through a friend of her father when referencing erotic wear. *Lingerie*. Have you heard of Lady Duff-Gordon?' He raised his eyebrows suspiciously, shaking his head before sitting down on the end of the bed to listen. It wasn't often I knew of people he hadn't met or known at some time in his life—true or false, I was never certain. I struggled to sit up, leaning back against the pillows as I settled in to gossip. 'Well, she was Lucy Sutherland when Mr Montague took her under his wing in 1880 when only seventeen, but she married James Wallace in 1884, and birthed a daughter, Esme, the year after. She left her position as seamstress with Mr Montague, but was fond of him, and his family, and kept in touch over the years. Her husband was a drunkard, and they separated in 1890, just after the Montagues immigrated here. He was notoriously unfaithful.' He widened his eyes at me, grunting to himself.

'Why do you think I would care about anyone but me? Have we even met?' I giggled to myself, dismissing him with my hand.

'Oh, you will care. Bear with me.' I laughed again, watching as he dramatically threw himself down on the bed beside me, groaning loudly. 'From what Catherine told me, Lucy had her own liaisons, including a love affair with the renowned surgeon, Sir Morell Mackenzie, just before his death. Can you believe she started divorce proceedings in 1893, and they granted it two-years later? I'm telling you, Leo, unless you are a wealthy woman, or have a wealthy benefactor supporting you in secret, it's impossible to get rid of a shit husband legally.'

'Are you suggesting they do it illegally?' We both collapsed into loud laughter, the bed shaking.

'Of course not. But the divorced daughter of a civil engineer would not be married to Sir Cosmo Duff-Gordon had she come from poverty, and not established herself as a leader in women's fashion in the years before she met him. We were introduced to her in New York where she was visiting with friends, and I found her fascinating. She endured some hard times to get where she is, and I admire that in a person. Catherine had already told me so many lovely things about her, and spoke of her so often I felt I knew her when introduced at *The Delmont* the day before we departed for home. I came within a bee's dick of humiliating myself, but she was so overjoyed to hear the Montagues were well, and are close friends of mine, she took no notice of my faux pas.' He nodded, staring blankly at the ceiling.

'Boring! Back to me!'

'Oh, stop and let me finish. She spent seven-years before marrying well working her fingers to the bone to support her daughter, opening *Maison Lucile* in the West End in 1893, and it took her another four-years to open a larger shop in Westminster. Only last year she incorporated the business and moved to Hanover Square, and is now in a building ten times bigger than where she started. My point is, despite her success in fashion, no one uses her word *lingerie,* except Lady Duff-Gordon herself, and of course, Catherine. These here were gifted to me by her before we parted, and I must say, they are the rudest negligees I have ever laid eyes on. I had no idea there were other deviants out there creating very similar items to what Catherine has made in secret for her friends for so many years now. Well, not as many as I've become aware of in recent times. I can barely look at them without blushing, let alone put one on.' He giggled, rolling off the bed and onto his feet before picking up several items, holding them up against his body one after the other while staring into the cheval mirror next to the dressing table, throwing what he liked into a pile on the bed, and what he did not onto the floor.

'Do you mean to tell me Hamish has never seen you wear one of these? Why did you even accept them?' He lifted what Lucy called a brassiere to his chest, the matching black bloomers so small they barely covered his groin as he held them against his trousers, admiring what he saw.

'She is a dear friend to the Montagues' and a woman I would be reluctant to say no to. Catherine would never have forgiven me, and I could never be so rude.'

'Why? She is the rudest person I have never met, going by these.' He held up an emerald green negligee, the lace beautiful but completely transparent, alongside a white slip with barely there straps, again, hiding nothing. 'Which one?' He twisted and posed in front of the mirror, before turning to me, holding them out to me, one in each hand.

'For what?' I shook my head, confused for a moment.

'For me to parade around this cottage in front of Hamish.' He rolled his eyes, shaking his head at me. 'For crying out loud, you can be scatty in the head, Abigail. For tonight? Which one do you want to wear? I think the green if you are going to be really trollopy, and the white if you want to look virginal—pure trickery, mind you, and it may be difficult to pull that one off,' he teased, jumping on the bed and landing on top of me, his arms around me so tight I found it hard to breathe. 'Why did you really accept them if not for Hamish?' We lay together, our legs entwined, while he stroked my face, the only sound filling the room from outside the cottage—the river, the bush, the native animals—all vying to be heard.

'Well, they *are* comfortable. It's not like a corset when you have two separate pieces. It's far less restrictive compared to what everyone is wearing under their gowns here in Australia. I'm uncertain if Hamish would admire them, or think me a filthy whore. Aaron was never too bothered by the risque nightwear Catherine made, and preferred them off rather than on me.'

'Hamish adores everything about you, Abigail. These will be no different, but I must say, while I have you here alone, I cannot believe you agreed to marry him when you were so strongly opposed to telling a soul you were even stepping out with him. That's a fabulous leap from one side of a cliff in Melbourne to another in Adelaide, and only ever undertaken by a lunatic. What's got into you, dear girl?' His face only inches from mine, I stared back at him thoughtfully.

'I'm still uncertain. I've been against the idea from the start, yet my mouth said yes, then my heart agreed. Once I heard it from my own lips, it sounded right, and I firmly believe it's the best thing I could do for Thomas and Emmy at this stage of their lives.' He gazed into my eyes for the longest time, the corner of his mouth turning down, sadness settling on him.

'And what about you, Mistress Abigail? Will he make *you* happier than this Lord Harrington would? I only want to ensure you are doing this for the right reasons, otherwise you could both end up miserable, and then I would be miserable. You told me yourself you would not be forced into anything. Nor make decisions due to pressure or obligation, but I feel you are. For Thomas and Emmy. The last thing I wish to do is rain on your parade, but keep it in mind. We'll talk more when you return.' He kissed my lips gently before rolling off the bed once more, landing on his feet before straightening up. 'You can never hide a thing from me, you old sea hag.' He pulled me to my feet, embracing me tightly, before lifting me off the ground and carrying me to the kitchen, my screams filling the cosy cottage. Placing me down on Hamish's lap, much to his amusement, Leo gathered his belongings, while Hamish rose to his feet, letting me slip back down on the floor before taking my hand in his and following Leo out onto the verandah.

'Aye, so ye'll be off, then?'

'Yes, I must tear myself away and return to my kitchen. We were not all born under a lucky star like Abigail here, but I will return with your dinner to get me out of work for at least an hour this evening, so do not fret.' Leo turned, kissing me on the cheek before turning back, quick as a flash planting his lips on Hamish's mouth. Pulling away, he ran to his horse faster than I had ever seen him run before. 'Farewell, my Adonis. I just took your lip-er-ginity. You now belong to me more than you ever will to Abigail. So many women came before her.' He swung up on his horse, tipping his hat. 'And if you want to live to see old bones, eat nothing your future wife cooks. Not even the once, or it could be the end of you.' Confident atop his horse, a safe distance between them, he waved his hat in the air before turning the mare's head for home, kicking her into a canter and disappearing into the scrub within moments.

'The cheeky wee bastard. If Polly naw manages tae kill him, I'll accept the burden from her.' He wiped his mouth on his sleeve one last time, while I slipped my arms around him. 'Yer cook seems tae be comin' up with more filthy names fer us, each day worse than the next. He called me a fabulous fornicator. Do ye think he'll stop once we're married?' The poor man appeared so innocent, and lost when it came to dealing with Leonardo, and I couldn't help but reach up and place my hands on his cheeks with some sympathy.

'You've Buckley's chance.'

Sitting at the elegant dressing table, I stared out over where the river slowed into a round pool, the pristine water continuing on far less ferociously once flowing into the river bend, several trout swimming just below the surface, the gentle hum of the bush calming me. Slipping the pink diamond back on my left hand, Aaron's rings on my right, Hamish strolled into the bedchamber, turning to close the door firmly behind him.

'Yer naw leavin' this room again 'till taemorrow. I warned Leo naw tae disturb us taenight when he brings the food, or I'll strangle the wee bastard with me bare hands.' He crossed the room in two strides, his hands reaching up to unbutton the back of my dress, sending shivers through every part of me at his touch. 'But prevention is far better than lookin' fer a cure, so ye'll notice a lock on the door.' He grinned at me, my dress falling to the floor. Left standing in my flimsy shift, my arms around him, I fumbled, trying to pull his shirt off over his head. Unable to reach up far enough, unless he bent forward for me as Aaron used to do, I tried again with his assistance. After several attempts, I threw it down on top of my dress, kicked into the corner earlier, my fingers nimbly unbuttoning the front of his trousers. 'Ye haven't changed yer mind after visitin' with yer family, have ye, Abigail?' Shaking my head, I let his pants drop to the floor, and he shook them off, my hands firm on his muscular body, my fingers caressing his firm thighs, my kiss deep.

'No, I haven't. Stop talking.' Pulling him down onto the bed, I let myself melt into him, sinking deep, and he was all I could see.

Much later, as I lay in his arms, he spoke of our time away, the afternoon sun still high in the sky.

'You have nothing to worry about. Aaron's family not only gave their blessing, they were beyond thrilled.' Relief washed over his face, his arms holding me tighter for a moment.

'Do we have tae get married in the kirk? The priest at Saint Mary's likes ye well enough tae come out an' marry us here in the garden.' I struggled to sit up, propping up the pillows behind me before leaning back against them, while he remained where he was, staring up at me, a smirk on his lips.

'Father Donnelly much prefers to work from home. He only made an exception when it came to burying our sons. It still hurts me he wasn't allowed to conduct the service in the house of God because they were unbaptised. I know of other parishes where this has been allowed, so it never made sense to me. Although I am beyond grateful to him for everything he did, especially blessing the island so all who rest there are in consecrated ground, I'm angry at those above him, and have no wish to marry there for a second time. I only agreed to Aaron's funeral being held at St Mary's due to the public interest, along with the fact my journalist friend, Cain Stephenson, warned me Willow Grove would be overrun by thousands of strangers if insisted on a private funeral.' He nodded, a sadness settling on him, and I realised I was ruining what should have been a very special moment. 'I always wanted to marry here in the garden, Hamish. Aaron and I did what everyone around us expected, and we enjoyed every moment, but you and I have the privilege of choice, and can have it our way alone. There have been a number of ministers from a range of faiths who have performed marriage ceremonies here over the years. We are spoiled for choice.' His face lit up in a smile, and he pulled himself up next to me, settling back against his pillows, his arm around my shoulders.

'I know yer naw one fer fancy parties, but I'm keen tae celebrate every part. I'd like tae throw a betrothal party; a proper *rèiteach* with close friends an' family here tae bless our union.' I nodded, agreeing immediately only because he had never married before, although the thought of an additional party tired me already. Leo had always referred to the period between a betrothal and marriage as an engagement, just as the Romans did, and soon after, he had us all calling it the same before we had even stepped off the ship the first time all those years ago.

'It will be lovely to have something joyful to celebrate.' He leaned over, kissing my forehead before gently stroking my cheek with his finger.

'Aye, it will. There's somethin' I've been meanin' tae say tae ye, lass.' I turned to him, placing my head on his shoulder, my hand covered by his, our fingers intertwined while resting on his stomach. 'I dinnae want ye thinkin' I naw have an original thought in me head, or made this cottage tae replicate what Aaron built fer ye when ye first married.' I felt tears prick my eyes, my cheek pressed against his chest, his strong heartbeat thumping in my ear. 'I wanted tae have me own place, just fer us tae come an' take a rest from the world, an' make our own memories in a place so very special tae the both o' us. I wanted tae make it different tae yer honeymoon cottage, an' asked Polly tae ensure the furnishin's dinnae resemble what ye have there. An' Eric had it clear in his mind tae build this opposite in every way, selectin' the best spot beside the river, rather than the ocean.'

'Does it bother you? The honeymoon cottage, I mean.'

'Och, naw. I respect what ye had between ye, an' that'll never change. Aaron was by yer side fer over a decade, an' he loved ye well. He's the father o' yer children, an' he belongs in yer memories an' yer heart. Tae speak o' someone after they're gone with affection honours them, an' keeps 'em alive in a part o' ye deep down ye keep just fer yourself.' My heart opened a fraction more to him in that moment as he continued to speak of the difference between the two cottages, this one built from basalt, the bricks far smaller than the main house, the cosy building reminding me of a fairytale, *Little*

Golden-Hair, published in 1889. I had read it to my children many times when they were small, the picture book filled with images of a near identical cottage. It was only last year I had come across the same story, renamed *Goldilocks* in a children's book I purchased in London *Old Nursery Stories and Rhymes,* leaving it at the orphanage with the boxes upon boxes of books I had sent before we arrived. I had never realised just how many versions existed of the tale since first published anonymously as *The Story of the Three Bears* in 1837, discovering at least five in recent years, although I suspected there were far more that could be considered interpretations of the original story, decades later revealed to be written by poet Robert Southey.

'You are far sweeter in private than in public,' I teased, his face breaking into a wide grin.

'Aye. I cannae have anyone thinkin' I'm a soft touch 'round here.' He tightened his arm around me while I nuzzled my face deeper into his chest. 'The day we marry will be the happiest o' me life. I never thought fer a moment ye'd accept me, an' now ye have, I worry I'll wake an' find it's all been a dream.' He kissed the top of my head several times, his fingers stroking my hair.

'I feel calmer, and at peace for the first time in so very long. I think I may have fallen just a little in love with you, Hamish.' Turning my face up towards him, I covered his mouth with mine, my fingers caressing his chiselled jaw. Pulling away after the longest time, he stared down into my eyes, his own glistening.

'Aye, a little is far more than I was hopin' fer, an' beyond anythin' I was expectin' o' ye, Abigail. Ye make the world a far better place fer bein' in it, an' I now naw only understand the true meanin' o' home goes far beyond a buildin' tae hang yer hat an' rest yer weary body, along with yer mind. I never knew 'till now that home was a feelin', warmin' every part o' ye an' bringin' an indescribable joy—naw a place—it's ne'er been a place.'

We relaxed around the large wooden table, only arriving back from the cottage a half-hour ago, the kitchen hot and bustling, the staff

preparing afternoon tea, every window open in an attempt to catch even a whisper of a breeze. Leo sat at the end of the table, several trays of sandwiches, cakes and fruit laid out in front of him, a pot of tea left to steep in the middle of the table, while he poured himself a cup of coffee. Heavy footsteps came through the door, Thomas and Emmy rushing through the kitchen and straight to my side, both gasping for air, their cheeks flushed from running the entire way home from school the moment the bell rang, the summer sun scorching anything and anyone stepping outside of the shade.

'How... was... ya time... away... Ma?' Thomas inquired, breathing hard as he slid into the seat next to Hamish. 'Ya were gone a lot longer than we expected.' He grinned at Hamish, then across at me, his breathing slowing significantly as he reached for a large slice of cheesecake, the mixed berries on top in a sweet syrup picked only hours ago.

'Did you miss me then, Thomas? It's only you wouldn't normally notice my absence, with you and Emmy being so busy these days with your friends,' I teased, his laugh loud as Emmy sat down beside me, a drink in her hand and far more composed than her brother.

'Yeah, of course we missed ya, Ma, but we knew you'd be back eventually, an' are always safe when ya with uncle Hamish.' He glanced at Emmy knowingly, then back at me, widening his eyes only slightly.

'Was your time away exciting, Mummy? Is there anything Thomas and I should know about?' Emmy probed, her green eyes sparkling, while Hamish chuckled, reaching across to touch her cheek for only a moment. My mouth twitched as I lifted my hand up from under the table, showing them the pink diamond. Jumping to their feet in unison, they screamed, first hugging Hamish before pulling me to my feet and into a joyful embrace. 'Oh, Mummy. I have never seen anything more beautiful than this.' She ran the tip of her finger over the diamond while Thomas returned to his seat, thumping Hamish on the back. 'I now need one the exact same or I will *die*!' Emmy collapsed into giggles, as did I, while Leo gazed at the four of us, tears in his eyes before returning to his work, giving us our privacy. Returning to my seat, I leaned forward, cutting myself and Emmy a slice of cheesecake, along with a second for Hamish and my son, a hearty appetite on him like all the Cavanaughs'. 'Thomas and I have been talking, and we are only forced to tell you because you have agreed to marry.' I nodded, waiting for her to go on, her long auburn hair unusually dishevelled today. 'We believe people will think us strange if we continue to call Uncle Hamish...' Her voice, barely above a whisper, she paused for a moment, her rosebud lips redder than usual. 'Well, Uncle Hamish. Once you're officially married, we mean. We love him so very much, and have decided, if it's acceptable by you, to call him Da instead?' Emmy placed her little hand in his while tears welled in his eyes, his gaze moving back and forth between them. 'Do we have your consent, Uncle Hamish?'

'Aye, ye do, wee Emmeline, an' 'tis me privilege, an' an honour I'll always treasure, if ye were tae call me yer Da.' Leo stood by the sink, tears streaming down his face as he whisked the cake batter, unable to hide his feelings at all today. I rose to my feet and quickly made my way to his side, slipping my arms around his waist as he lay his head on my shoulder and sobbed. Wiping away my own tears while stroking his back, I murmured reassuringly in his ear, my gaze fixed on Hamish across the room, Thomas on one side, Emmy on the other, their heads close together, their conversation low, although animated. A contentedness descended on me, and those around me appeared to relax, feeling it just as strongly as I, a sense of peace and a joy I hadn't felt in so long settling on me. Although Aaron was always on my mind, and filled my soul no different from when here beside me, I had started to stumble upon times like this where my heart made room for happiness to enter, if only for a short time. When in the company of Hamish, my thoughts were with only him, but when alone, my mind overflowed with memories of my Aaron. I felt I was somehow splitting into two distinct parts, half of me belonging to one here on earth, the other half remaining with the other somewhere in the great beyond. Returning to the table, I gazed down at them, a smile touching my lips.

'How about we take a ride down to the sea?' All three cheered, drawing the immediate attention of the staff. 'It's the hottest part of the day, and the closer to the ocean we go, the cooler it will be. I know how much I would enjoy our first outing as a family to be swimming the horses down on the shore.' They were both on their feet before I had finished, and I glanced at them lovingly as I collected their empty plates from the table, gathering them all together in front of me. 'Go and get your bathers, and we will meet you in the stables in half-hour, and don't forget your towels.' They had run from the room before I had even finished, while I smiled after them, then at Hamish. 'I must find Bessie. I hate to disturb her, but it is impossible to get into my own swimming costume and then put my dress back on over it. Everything takes so much time when you're a woman, and is far more complicated than it needs to be,' I complained to no one in particular, although several of the maids nodded to themselves as they cleaned the worktable in the centre of the kitchen. 'I need to ask Catherine to make me a wardrobe like she would for the average bloke. It looks far more practical. I'm sure she could tizzy it up.' I rose to my feet, picking up the tray now filled with dirty dishes.

'Naw, ye dinnae need Bessie. I'll help ye so ye dinnae have tae disturb the poor lass. If this new wardrobe ye plan tae request is anythin' like them ridin' trousers ye insist on wearin', I'll be forced tae follow ye around tae make sure none o' the workers see ye in 'em.' Hamish rose to his feet, taking my hand in his and pulling me to mine, before leading me across the kitchen, past Leo and towards the door.

'Pure trickery, but my admiration overflows, Adonis. Respect,' Leo murmured, and Hamish threw back his head and laughed aloud, our footsteps fading down the hallway as those in the kitchen returned to their work, all smiling, most uncertain why the room felt lighter, happier, and somehow filled with a feeling of family. An invisible silver thread connecting us all, some stretching back generations to a time and place full of people those here now had no knowledge of. Yet the choices made by the men and women who came before us affected every single soul who had ever lived and worked at Willow Grove—without their knowledge or consent.

I sat on the edge of my bed, gazing out the window at the stars twinkling like diamonds on black velvet above, my foot twitching as

I waited for Bessie to help me ready for bed. Hamish and I had settled Thomas and Emmy in their bedchambers for the night together for the first time, and it had been sweet. Although he had disappeared soon after, I was aware he was hiding somewhere close by, no doubt waiting impatiently for Bessie to retire for the night. Despite the fact we were betrothed, we had not announced the marriage banns in the local newspaper declaring our intent, nor made anything official. There would be a scandal if anyone knew I had taken him to my bed before the wedding, and it was not something I wanted the world to know, keeping it between only a handful of trusted friends—Bessie, little Mary and Leo the only ones who truly knew the truth of the matter. I had endured enough, my private life strewn all over the papers for years for the world to read and judge. Now all I wanted was some privacy, and as much peace as I was blessed to find.

Bessie kicked open the door, startling me before hurrying into the room; several freshly laundered dresses hanging over her arm. I stood, moving over to the dressing room, my hand brushing her shoulder before I sat down in front of the mirror.

'Apologies for me tardiness, Mistress. I've been running behind from the moment I put me feet on the floor this morning. I don't know what's wrong with me.' She picked up the silver hairbrush, smiling weakly at my reflection before setting to her work.

'You're creating a wee person is what's wrong with you. A miracle so grand always requires some sacrifice.' I laughed aloud, and she smiled, running the brush through my hair before plaiting it down my back, winding it up, then finishing off by pinning it securely to the top of my head. 'Oh, dear Bessie. You must slow down and rest. Not everything needs to be done each day, and nothing is a priority over your good health, and that of the wean.'

'You have nothing to concern yourself with, Mistress. Everyone has been taking very good care of me downstairs. In all honesty, you are far from demanding of my time or attention. It makes no difference how big I get; I plan to continue right through until the babe arrives. I don't want anyone else looking after you.' She pulled me into a tight embrace, only releasing me to strip my clothes before leading me into the washroom, the bath filled with warm water, vanilla and cinnamon punching me in the nose, my head giddy for a moment.

'We can worry about it when the time comes.' I dismissed the topic with my hand, closing my eyes in bliss as I slid into the water. Despite my persistent offer of a guest room close to mine, thinking she would be far more comfortable, she had refused me each time, preferring to return to her old room in the staff quarters where many of her friends lived. She still kept in touch with the wives in the village, many of them her neighbours for near on a decade-and-a-half. Some were reporting Danny's comings and goings to her several times a day, Bessie's fear she would lose him to another not unfounded. We often had single, attractive women attend Willow Grove for the sole purpose of finding a husband among our workers, and many had over the years. Employees were known to earn good wages, and live in conditions well above the standards of most, and well able to support a family. There were women amongst them whose sole intent was to catch themselves a wealthy *married* man, one prepared to keep them as his mistress in the lap of luxury, a number of them looking among my male friends and acquaintances, much to my chagrin.

Surprised she hadn't noticed, I raised my left hand from the water, waving the pink diamond around under her nose. Her eyes flew open, and her backside dropped onto the side of the bath, her hand clutching mine, bringing it up to the light to examine it closer.

'Jesus, Mary, and Joseph, bless 'em one and all.' She stared down at me, her face flushed, her eyes sparkling. 'It's Lord Harrington, isn't it? Oh, of course it is. Who else do we know could afford a diamond the size of this? If it is a diamond?' She narrowed her gaze, her brow drawn in concentration. 'It's pink? Oh, just like your bracelet. How sweet of him, but I do wonder how Lord Harrington knew the children gave that to you.' She continued to chat incessantly, while I scrubbed myself with the washcloth, the soap, made from goat's milk far gentler on my skin than anything the laundry maids brewed in their cauldron and expected everyone to use for every single cleaning task on the property, including their personal hygiene. 'Well, he couldn't possibly have known, could he? We had left him by that time.' I released the plug, the water starting to drain as I rose to my feet with Bessie's assistance; a thick towel quickly wrapped around me. 'Oh, congratulations, Mistress. I knew he was the right man for you from that first night aboard. I'm thrilled the children will go to only the best of schools, and rub shoulders with the aristocrats they, too, will soon be.' She helped me dry off, slipping a robe over my shoulders before leading me back into the bedchamber. 'And such a kind man at that. I don't know how he convinced you, but I am overjoyed that he did. The life we will lead, and it will be a fresh start for me and the bairn.' I gently raised my hand to calm her, swallowing hard several times.

'It's Hamish I've agreed to marry.' Her eyes widened, and she sat down heavily at my dressing table, my nightgown in her hand, her mouth open, silence hanging heavy over the room as she tried to compose herself.

'Oh, Mistress. After all these years of him loving you so very deeply, you've softened towards him. He will make you a fine husband, and a good and steadfast father to Thomas and Emmy.' She paused for a moment, rising to her feet, swiftly helping me finish readying for bed. 'I'm sorry for what I said about Lord Harrington. It was only I pictured you as a Duchess in my mind, and my imagination ran wild for a moment. Seeing myself as the ladies' maid to the most famous woman in the world was too much to bear.' Smiling shyly at me, I giggled as she gathered me into a warm embrace. 'I really am so very happy for you, Mistress.'

'Thank you, dear Bessie. I always knew you would be. It will be a relief once word gets out, eligible men will stop calling on me to seek my affection.' I sighed deeply, smiling across at her as I made myself comfortable at the table, inviting her to join me and share my supper, sent up on a tray every night before bed by my darling Leo. Her eyebrows drew together as she lowered herself down on the chair opposite me, pouring us both a cup of warm chocolate from a silver pot.

'I'm sorry to say it, but I don't think even a wedding will keep Detective O'Neil away from you. I'm told he called in nearly every day to check if you were here when we first left, and didn't believe for a minute you were away. Took close to three-months for him to believe it, and stop bothering Mr Masters. There must be at least thirty letters he left here for you, though. Did you get them?' She had always detested the detective, concerned to this day he would abuse his power; his manner clear he thought himself above the law. I had given my word I would never allow myself to be alone with him for that very reason, aware of what had now become an obsession.

'Yes, I have the letters. He left another one yesterday; however, he is still unaware I am home, to my knowledge. You do not need to concern yourself, dear Bessie. I have no doubt once he knows I am marrying Hamish, he will turn his attention to the next poor woman who crosses his path. The fact he is still intent on convincing me he is a good and decent man who only did the job he was paid to do sickens me. And he has the nerve to think I would accept his visits.' She shook her head in disbelief while I rolled my eyes, sipping the sweet cup of chocolate before picking up a crumpet drizzled with honey; a pat of butter melted on top and puddling underneath on the plate.

'You've given him no reason to believe you even like him, and have treated him with nothing but contempt, yet he is starry-eyed and clearly in love with you no matter how many curse words you spit at him. I will never understand bloody men.' I took her hand in mine, holding it for a moment before passing her a warm biscuit dotted with chocolate, the crumb soft and chewy.

'You know, everything will turn out as it should. Danny is a good man, and he loves you deeply. Give him some time to recover from the shock of it all.' She wiped away a tear that slowly slipped down her cheek, before taking a large bite out of the biscuit, rolling her eyes in bliss.

'Thank you, Mistress. I only hope I haven't lost him forever, but there is nought to be done about it, and worrying isn't good for the wean, like you say.'

She lifted the heavy quilt as I slipped underneath, tucking me in before wishing me a peaceful sleep, extinguishing all but one light, and closing the door behind her, her footsteps lightening as she went to find her own bed. Within moments, the door opened and Hamish stepped inside, quietly pushing it closed before crossing the room.

'Take that nightgown off. I get all tangled up in 'em, an' I cannae see the parts o' ye I've become fond o'.' Throwing himself down on the bed beside me, he tried to pull it off over my head, failing miserably as I pushed him away, rising to my feet to remove it myself, placing it carefully over the chair before returning to my bed. Gazing at me as I slipped back under the covers, he gathered me into his broad arms.

'I dinnae think I'd ever get used tae seein' ye in the nuddy. Seems I notice somethin' new about ye each time.' His breath heavy in my ear, he gently sucked my lobe, sending shivers through me, rolling onto his back and taking me with him. Gazing down, I smiled, his hands gently tracing the outline of my body, as if trying to memorise every part of me. Leaning down. I placed my lips on his, while he pulled me closer, our bodies melting into one.

As I lay in his arms much later, I wondered what tomorrow would bring, my impending visit to Dana causing my stomach to drop to the floor. Eventually drifting off into a restless sleep, sugarplums danced through my dreams, alongside a blue-tongue lizard, and Aaron, there was always Aaron.

Chapter Seven

I WOKE TO FIND Hamish still in my bed, panic rising in me immediately. The sun, already brighter than I would have liked, glowed
orange as it broke through the dark sky, turning night to day, the
gentle breeze caressing the lace curtains already warm. March, one of
the hottest months of the year in Victoria, was always unbearable for
me, and no doubt would be until I took my last breath. We had come
from the freezing cold winters of Scotland and America to what felt
like the pits of Hell itself.

'Hamish, what are you still doing here?' I shook him by his enormous shoulder, one of his eyes opening for only a moment before
slamming shut.

'It's naw even daylight. Stop yer fashin'.' He wrapped his arms
around me, pulling me close to his chest, my face pressed up against
his neck.

'Are you blind? The sun is well up, Hamish. What if you get caught
in here? Thomas and Emmy could walk in at any time.' I shook him
again, his arms wrapped around me so tightly I was finding it hard to
move at all.

'They're old enough tae know, an' are naw weans anymore, Abigail.
More importantly, we're tae be married soon enough.' He placed
small kisses all over my face, then brushed his lips across mine, turning his face to the window for a moment, a gentle glow casting gold-
en shadows across the bedchamber, the morning light brightening,

while the native birds started to wake. 'Dinnae worry yerself. I'll go down tae the kitchen long before the twins open their eyes.' I sighed, hoping today was not the morning they chose to crawl into bed with me earlier than usual. 'The nerve o' ye kickin' me out o' yer bed. Ye dinnae seem tae appreciate how fortunate ye are tae spend yer nights with me, an' use an' abuse me body fer yer own pleasure, ye lucky wee wench.' He held me close, his head resting on his pillow, his eyes closed as if he were still sound asleep.

'Oh, is that what they call it?' I teased, kissing his lips, my hand pressed against his cheek.

'Aye. I've kept meself tae meself in the last few years, an' I was ready tae give up on ever havin' me own family. Even when I was steppin' out with Nellie, I knew the end would come before any serious promises were made, an' I was prepared tae remain alone after that. I'm givin' all that up fer ye,' he teased back, and I smiled.

'Are you going to tell Nellie yourself?' I pushed myself deeper into the mattress, the resident kookaburra starting his morning laugh, his song filtering out over the property.

'Naw, she can find out with everyone else after the way she behaved. Ye need tae consider sackin' her. She has naw respect fer ye.' He stroked my face with his thumb, the room silent other than the land waking outside the windows.

'No. I cannot sack her over a situation you created. She lives and works in the village, and it's not as though she is forced to have much to do with any of us at the main house. I'm sure in time things will settle. She is hurt now, and rightly so. You never have understood women, Hamish. You may not have cared as deeply for them as they did for you, and although you had no intent to cause harm, many of your past sweethearts are not so easily able to forgive or forget you as you are them. You promised them everything, then walked away without a second thought, and are now surprised by the way they behave? Some held strong feelings for you, no different from you hold for me. As for Nellie's opinion of me, I'm not concerned. No one will pay her any mind knowing she is a woman scorned, but she is certainly entitled to her pain.' He rolled his eyes at me, while I nudged him towards the edge of the bed.

'Yer too kind fer yer own good at times, Abigail. Anyone else would have sacked her then an' there at the pub. I suppose ye were too drunk tae remember.' He stroked my hair, sadness in his eyes. 'I wanted tae come tae ye a thousand times that night, but had given ye me word, an' I could naw go back on it. Yer mine, me love, me heart, an' soon, me wife.'

'All right. Thank you for all that. Can you go now before we get caught?' He threw back his head, laughing so loud I placed a pillow over his face, his muffled howls still filling the room, a smile touching my lips in spite of myself.

Nearing Dana's mansion, my hands trembled, a million thoughts running through my mind, my breathing shallow. Filled with worry I would lose her friendship the moment I opened my mouth, the urge to cry overwhelmed me before I even arrived. The horses slowed, turning into her driveway, the mid-morning air warm on my skin as the carriage came to a stop in front of the grand entrance. Harry's boots crunched on the gravel, a smile on his face as he opened the door. I hesitated, my legs like the jelly coloured with saffron, and flavoured with sugar and lemon juice, Leo still insisted on preparing the same way they did a century ago, forcing it on us far more often than anyone truly enjoyed.

'There you are, Mistress. Just take me hand.' His eyes full of sympathy, he assisted me down, still holding me by the arm as I leaned back against the carriage, unsteady on my feet. 'You've gone as white as a sheet. Here, sit yerself down, an' put ya head between ya knees. Breathe in an' out real slow, an' all will be well in no time.' He took a small stool from the back of the carriage and lowered me onto it, waiting patiently as I did what he ordered. My heart indeed started to slow, my breathing coming easier now as I straightened up.

'How kind of you to notice my distress, Harry?' He had always had a way about him that calmed the worst storms brewing within me. 'I already feel better. Thank you.'

'Oh, say no more about it. Your great-aunt suffered with nerves much the same as you, Mistress. It may be a family trait ya inherited. Not everything our kin leave behind for us is of benefit.' He grinned, his eyes twinkling teasingly as he helped me to my feet. 'Isabelle was unable to hide a thought or feelin', an' everythin' showed on her face, as it does you.' He placed the stool away before escorting me up the stairs to the front door, the house silent, appearing empty from the street. 'I hope whatever is worrying ya eases, an' ya burden is lifted.' He tipped his hat before returning to the carriage to wait for me, while I called out my thanks before knocking hard on the door. Within moments, the new under-butler, Mr Swizzle, opened the door, welcoming me far more warmly than his superior; guiding me through to the drawing room. Dana rose to her feet, her face lighting up at the sight of me as I crossed the room, embracing her warmly before she sat back down in her armchair, offering me the one beside her.

'Oh, Abigail. My dear, dear friend. It is so lovely to see you. I have missed your company and conversation so very much. It feels as if you have been gone for a year.' Well into her sixth-decade now, age had started to slow her, as had the many years of grief she had endured, her once unlined face now creased, her bright orange hair streaked with silver in places. While she outwardly showed signs of her suffering, she was still robust and strong, her voluptuous frame standing straight and tall, the core of her tough as old boot leather, her sense of humour sharp and bawdy. A true and loyal friend to me for what felt like a lifetime, I hoped for many more years of friendship. I spoke for a time of my travels, along with Lord Harrington, leaving out all references of Hamish when relaying several incidents she found amusing, Dana's laughter filling the room as two maids hurried in, both carrying trays. Watching them set out the morning tea on the table in between us, I closed my eyes for only a moment as vanilla and coffee wafted up my nose. 'You are such a unique soul. To go to steerage every night to dance instead of staying in first class, well, it is exactly what I would expect, you delightful creature. I cannot wait to meet these new bohemian friends of yours. They sound terribly interesting. I know you mentioned they like to be at one with nature, but do they really go about without a stitch on? Quite brave of them if they are out visiting with family and friends and there are children present.' Her mouth twitched as I collapsed into a fit of giggles, feeling like a child again at my mother's knee.

'That is why they plan to purchase a substantial plot of land out bush. They intend to create a safe place for themselves and like-minded people.' She nodded, sipping her tea while urging me to continue. 'They do not believe in the sanctity of marriage, despite being married in the eyes of the church and the law, and have given each other permission to have relations with others. Only on the condition they do not allow themselves to love or prioritise another.' She nodded again, her eyes twinkling in amusement. 'I must say, they are the most fascinating couple I have ever met. Although I could never behave so freely, I find their courage to live as they choose without guilt or fear quite admirable.' Mr Swizzle quietly entered the room, closing the windows then drawing the drapes to keep the heat of the day out before going to Dana's side, pouring us both a glass of iced lemonade before excusing himself, his eyes kind as he carried a tray of dirty dishes from the room, the plates in front of us replenished with cucumber sandwiches and scones still warm from the over, the cream whipped with sugar and vanilla, the strawberry jam made only yesterday. 'I have invited them to stay at Willow Grove while they search for their new home, or commune I suppose I should say.' Dana threw back her head and laughed, a memory flashing through her mind before she composed herself, taking a deep drink.

'You do know your great-aunt established a commune herself?' I nodded, the room quiet now, her tone becoming serious.

'But was it, though? It is often mentioned, but very little is known if I were to believe those around me purported to have been there.' I raised my glass to my lips, draining it before pouring another.

'I visit old Mary Chirnside from time to time down in Werribee. She is still of sound mind, despite being only three-years off her eighth-decade, and she has confirmed Willow Grove was once a commune and considered so by all who knew of it. It saddens me that her hatred for your aunt far exceeds all sensibilities that you are not responsible for the sins the woman supposedly committed.' She grunted to herself, and I sighed, aware Dana had been trying for fifteen-years to get the truth of the matter on the bad blood between the Chirnside family and Lady Isabelle Delmont, and had little success to date.

'Do you think my aunt had an affair with her husband, Andrew? It is the only thing that has ever made sense to me,' I remarked, while she shook her head, appearing thoughtful as she leaned forward and offered me another sandwich. Long and thin, the hard crusts removed, the bread soft and white, the cucumber crisp; if I were to eat my fill, the plate would be empty, and another already ordered.

'More likely with his brother, Thomas. Well, that's what I have come to believe. Mary loved him, and still does. She has always regretted not marrying him when she had the chance. The man was obviously tormented, being forced to live alongside the woman his brother stole out from under his nose—for decades. Can you imagine?' She shook her head in disbelief while I took another sandwich. 'You would have to be slightly sad, or mad, to blow your brains all over the ceiling of the laundry house after Sunday luncheon with the family, now wouldn't you?' She wrinkled her nose as I shuddered, a chill running down my spine. 'She's been alone now since 1890 when Andrew died, and Thomas three-years before that, yet she still hasn't softened towards you. I have tried to convince her to visit with you; however, she refuses to step foot on the soil of Willow Grove to this day. Mind you.' She leaned forward, lowering her voice to a whisper despite not another soul being present. 'Mary admitted to me it was Thomas who stole the design for their Werribee mansion from your aunt. Although she did not say it with her own lips, she alluded to an affair between them that lasted years, and suggested he built the house based on Lady Delmont's design purely out of spite to enrage her. And from the whispers I've heard from others, he was successful. Without much effort on his part, at all. It seems they shared an intense bond, but it was complicated and fraught with difficulties. The servants at Werribee Park are far friendlier than the family, and willing to discuss events of the past, although it has been thirty-years since your aunt was here amongst it all.'

'Are there many staff still in their employ from back then?' She nodded, her eyes lighting up.

'Oh, yes. I have managed to speak with several of their servants in the past few years. It's such a shame the world is changing so fast.

Those willing to go into service are dying out, and I fear there will be no such thing in the coming decades. How will any of us survive if they all choose to work in factories and live in their own homes?' Her tone teasing, a smirk touched her lips, and I smiled, taking another sandwich. 'Their cook started as a scullery maid when the house was completed in the 1870s, and she likes to talk.'

'I doubt she could tell me one way or the other if there was a commune on the property. Many believe there was, including a hierarchy of residents and a leader running the place. Others refute this, saying Willow Grove was a private home my aunt shared with only her family and friends, and not one living there was a stranger to her.' She nodded, shrugging her shoulders.

'It matters not what you call it. Several have confirmed in your presence that Willow Grove was home to a thriving community long before you arrived. I do not understand why you will not take me at my word, Abigail.' She raised her hand, dismissing me with a wave. 'The Chirnsides connection to your family is far more interesting and goes back decades.' I relaxed back in my chair, curiosity rising in me, although I often found some of the retellings and stories of my aunt difficult to believe. 'Apparently, Thomas met your aunt on the ship when he immigrated to Australia in 1839, but she didn't officially settle at Willow Grove until 1840. Went on to Tasmania for a time while that lovely cottage Polly and Angus live in was being built. I heard she was a frequent visitor to a number of properties he and Andrew owned together, and their alleged romance spanned right up until she left Australia for the final time in 1873. It is difficult to know for certain what stems from a seed of truth and what is gossip for gossip's own sake.' She lowered her voice again, glancing around before raising her eyebrows mischievously. 'I do know as fact Thomas was a man of twenty-four when he arrived in Victoria, and the notorious *Lady* Isabelle Delmont just shy of fifty that same year.' Her laughter filled the room while I swallowed hard, trying to dislodge the lump in my throat.

'Dana, there is something I must tell you.' I promptly burst into tears, while she appeared alarmed, sitting forward in her chair while clasping my hands in her own.

'Abigail, calm yourself. I am always here to listen, and help you in any way I am able.' I nodded, swallowing again as I tried to compose myself, quickly brushing away my tears.

'Hamish has asked me to marry him and I have accepted. I have wanted to...' My voice broke, while she sat back in her seat as if I had punched her in the stomach, the colour gone from her face, her eyes filled with tears. Silence hung heavy over the room as I reached into my pocket and pulled out a fresh handkerchief, my gaze fixed on a vase in the corner of the room, my hands shaking.

'Why him, Abigail?' Her voice barely above a whisper, I cringed, closing my eyes for a moment, my cheeks warm. 'Why him?' She paused for a moment, attempting to compose herself. 'Why him, when you could have your choice of far better men than he?' Her voice louder now, I held back the tears that threatened to flow once again. 'He is a lying, cheating, piece of shit who doesn't deserve you. He will discard you without guilt or thought when he meets the next floozy who takes his attention. Please, I beg you, Abigail. Do not choose this path. He will ruin you with his poison. Just as he does everything he touches.' I remained where I was, silent and unmoving, unable to utter a word even if I had wanted to. 'Do you love him, Abigail? I mean, really love him? Two nights ago you were screaming for your husband, and were in such a state, I was unable to stop my own tears.' She paused again, wiping her tear-stained face with a handkerchief, honey bees embroidered on the fine linen cloth. 'Aaron was a good man, and he adored you. He always placed you first above everything, even the children. Hamish isn't a fraction of the man Aaron was. He does *not* deserve a woman like you to love him, nor does he deserve the lifestyle your wealth would provide him.' She shook her head bitterly, pain clear in her eyes, while I wondered why she could not see she was behaving no different to her hateful friend, Mary Chirnside. I cleared my throat, my gaze meeting hers.

'You are right. I am not *in* love with Hamish, but I trust him with my life. He is one of my closest friends, and he loves Thomas and Emmy, and they love him. They miss Aaron dearly, and Hamish will make a kind and loving father to them. They need that, Dana, especially Thomas. He has cared for us since Aaron was taken, asking nothing in return, and I feel I may find happiness again in the future with him beside me.' She nodded, remaining silent, her eyes fixed on mine. 'It has been you I've been most worried about. Telling you, I mean. The last thing I want is to cause you pain, knowing how much you despise him. He makes me feel safe, and very loved. I know that doesn't sound like much, but he makes a difference to me.' She sniffed, straightening her shoulders before pouring another lemonade, one for me first, then herself.

'If you wish to marry for companionship, why did you not consider Lord Harrington? Although I have never met him, he sounds like a good and decent man who would have loved you and the children well. If you are only marrying for Thomas and Emmy's sake, he would certainly make a better father, and has the means to provide them with opportunities so few ever have. Hamish has nothing to offer you, or them. He has no family, nor is he of good name or reputation, and has very little to give you in the way of financial support, other than a small inheritance left to him by his grandfather, a pittance compared to your wealth, Abigail. You are not in love with Lord Harrington either, but he would make you a far better match. Anyone would make a better match.' She shook her head, screwing up her nose in frustration.

'Oh, so you would rather see me and the children living on the other side of the world, separated by an ocean from our family and friends?' I jutted out my chin, while she shook her head, sighing deeply as her shoulder slumped.

'Of course not, sweetheart. I'm only pointing out that you have your choice of so many suitable men. I'm simply stating a fact. You can do far better for yourself and the children than settling for Hamish.'

'I have made up my mind, Dana. I cannot explain myself, other than it feels like the right path for not only myself, but for Thomas and Emmy. Hamish has restored some hope within me that I will once again find some happiness, no matter how small.' Tears trickled down my face, while she stared back at me in silence, not without sympathy.

'I have always said I would never make you choose between our friendship and Hamish, and it still holds true.' She leaned back in her chair, her shoulders straight, her face softening. 'There are certain things you must know if you do marry him, Abigail.' I nodded, grateful she had not asked me to leave the moment I mentioned Hamish's name. 'I will always consider you my friend, no matter what is going on around us. Martin and I will continue to visit with you, and spend Sunday lunch in your company, but please do not ever ask, or expect, me to acknowledge Hamish. I will never say another word against him in your presence, and will keep my opinions to myself, but do not expect me to attend or celebrate your union, or acknowledge you are married to him.' I nodded slowly, and rose to embrace her, relief washing over me we would remain friends. 'All I wish for you is happiness, and some relief from the grief you carry. If that man can heal even a small part of you, then I am satisfied, my darling girl. Do not fret over our friendship, or my love for you, as that will never change. Things will remain as they are between us.' She kissed my forehead, releasing me to return to my seat, as did she. Another hour passed before I rose to my feet, gathering my things before she walked me out to the carriage. Embracing her one last time before climbing into the carriage, I clasped her hand through the window for a moment.

'Thank you, my dear friend.'

'Be happy, sweetheart. I will always be here for you when you need me, and you will need me, of that I am certain.'

I strolled into the kitchen, finding Leo and Hamish at the table, a pot of fresh coffee sitting between them. Passing Hamish to find a seat, he reached out and grabbed me by the waist, pulling me onto his lap, his lips on mine.

'Oh, stop.' Leo put his hand up, the other covering his forehead. 'I feel I must wash my eyes out with tallow soap after being forced to witness such offensive behaviour.' He shook his head while Hamish chuckled to himself, pouring me a cup of coffee before placing the mug in my hand, kissing my cheek. 'Anyway, back to me. Well, you really, Abigail. How your visit with Dana went is far more interesting to us all. Have you come to call off the wedding because she does not approve, or is she on her way over here to commit murder, and return to the home she once loved?' Leo collapsed into a fit of giggles, while I rolled my eyes.

'Our visit went far better than I expected.' I slipped off Hamish's lap into the chair next to him, raising my cup to my lips before drinking deeply, while he arched one eyebrow.

'Aye, she took it well, then?' He raised his hand, tucking a stray strand of hair behind my ear, while Leo continued to laugh to himself.

'Well, no, but our friendship remains as it always has, and for that I am grateful.' I leaned in closer, lowering my voice; the kitchen busy as the staff prepared luncheon. 'Dana still holds a deep grudge against you, which is her right, and has decided to continue to ignore your existence. I do not believe she will ever soften towards you, and I'm sorry for it. I have made no attempt to change her opinion, and I would be wasting my breath if I tried. Once she makes up her mind on the matter, there is no changing it.' He nodded, his face thoughtful as I picked up a piece of gingerbread, nibbling the corner before dipping it in the coffee.

'Aye, like someone else I know.'

'Well, never a truer word spoken,' Leo teased, flicking through the *Geelong Advertiser*, while Hamish laughed, pouring himself another cup of coffee.

'I've sent word fer every employee on the property tae gather near the stables after lunch. Better they hear from us directly we are tae be married, rather than on that passionfruit vine Leonardo is so fond of.' I supposed they had to know, and nodded; however, I did not understand why Hamish felt the need to ensure every man and his dog, near and far, knew of it before the sun went down this evening. 'Would ye come with me tae tell Angus an' Polly? I dinnae want me own brother findin' out with everyone else, an' I'm sure ye feel naw different towards Pollyanna.' He grinned, while Leo rolled his eyes in my direction, cursing Polly under his breath.

'Of course. I have no doubt they will be thrilled.'

I had already written to Tamara and Elizabeth, telling them of our betrothal, along with Mr and Mrs Malcolm, and had sent a lengthy explanation, and apology, to Lord Harrington, while sending Sister

Josephine a thick envelope filled with every thought I'd had over the last few days. Catherine was expecting me in the morning for tea, and I would see Richard and Jas later in the week to tell them of my news in person. Feeling far more relaxed than I had since our return, I was confident I had made the right decision, despite the doubts rising up in me on occasion that I quickly pushed to the back of my mind.

Hamish rose to his feet, turning to take my hand in his before pulling me to mine. 'No fornicating on the lawn, and tell Pollyanna I will be calling on her when she least expects it,' Leo called after us as we made our way out of the kitchen and towards the back door; Hamish chuckling to himself.

'I hope I can make ye as happy as ye make me.' Stepping outside, he slipped his arm around my shoulders, holding me close as we strolled down the path leading to the cottage, Wombles following along behind, her joey running alongside to keep up.

'Hamish, you have already made me far happier than I have been since I lost Aaron. I never thought I would ever feel anything other than grief.' He halted abruptly, pulling me into his arms, his lips on mine.

'Yer me whole world, Abigail. Everythin' I do, an' the choices I make from here on in, will always be with yer best interest at the forefront o' me mind. I'm naw the man Aaron was, an' naw bigger bastard than me has walked the earth, an' I dinnae deserve ye. I never once felt the same way about marryin' Angelique or Nellie as I do ye. With them, dread sat in the pit o' me stomach at the thought o' it, but with ye, I feel nothin' but excitement, knowin' I'll soon be wed tae the woman I'll love fer the rest o' me days.' He kissed me again, the gardeners tending to the lawn glancing over several times before continuing with their work, pretending they hadn't seen us at all.

'We better move on before Angus and Polly hear the news from a worker here, and we are at risk of Leo throwing a bucket of water over us like he does to the dogs.' I stood on the tips of my toes and kissed his cheek, taking his large hand in mine before continuing on down the meandering path, winding its way through the garden and towards the two-story bluestone cottage in the distance, a third level containing only small, triangular windows of the cluttered attic barely noticed from the ground. Always reminding me of something from a fairytale, its lead light windows intricate, the cobblestone walkways winding around an acre of private gardens, my biggest regret was not taking it for myself and raising my own family there from the beginning. Although not stately or opulent in comparison to the main house, it was far larger than most grand homes in Geelong owned by the wealthy, holding four bedchambers for the family, along with a staff quarters large enough to house five tucked away behind the spacious kitchen. The sitting room, parlour and library were far smaller than ours, although, just as elaborately decorated and furnished, and a small office sat next to the comfortable dining room, a large table seating twelve already there when we first arrived, covered in sheets and dust.

Polly and I would often spend hours going through the attic, the room spanning the entire floor and holding hundreds of treasures we believed had been left by my aunt. Polly had used only pieces she selected from the attic when asked to furnish the cottage, built under Angus's supervision and her sharp eye, and had done a fine job of it, proving herself to be talented in the way of decorating. I had asked her if she would come and freshen up several rooms at the main house, and she had agreed, but when was an entirely different matter.

Following Hamish up the path to the front door, he walked in without knocking, strolling through the house until he found Angus seated outside on the verandah enjoying lunch with Polly. Surprised to see us, Angus smacked the tabletop with his hand cheerfully, his voice loud in greeting, while inviting us to join them.

'What brings us the pleasure of your company? We've barely seen either of you since you've been back. I suppose there have been a lot of people to catch up with since you returned.' Polly stood to hug me, pulling me down on the seat beside her, while Hamish lowered himself down on the chair Angus pushed out opposite with his foot, a grin on his face as we made ourselves comfortable.

'It's lovely to be back with everyone. Travelling has shown me just how much home really means.' Polly nodded, patting my hand before turning her attention to Hamish, narrowing her gaze as she selected several sandwiches and placed them on a plate, handing it to him before doing the same for me.

'Hamish, you must go and talk to Nellie. She cornered me yesterday in the village, and begged me to speak on her behalf and tell you she's sorry. She loves you more than life itself, and will agree to anything if you will have her back, and will await your response. She's a sweet lass, Hamish, and I am of the firm opinion you need to grow up and stop putting her off. You're five-and-thirty now, and the right age to have your own family, but you'll need to hurry it up as poor Nellie isn't getting any younger,' Polly lectured, while Angus rolled his eyes discreetly at his brother, Hamish chuckling to himself, his eyes twinkling in amusement.

'Aye, Pollyanna. I dinnae disagree with ye. Yer right, 'tis time fer me tae settle down, an' tae take meself a wife.' She stared back at him, her nose wrinkled in suspicion before glancing at Angus, returning her attention to Hamish within moments.

'You'll go sort it with her, then?' She appeared relieved until he shook his head, his mouth full as he chewed the roast beef sandwich, the yellow pickles dripping onto the plate.

'Naw, I willnae. We've somethin' tae tell ye, an' wanted ye tae be among the first tae know. I've asked Abigail fer her hand, an' she's agreed tae give it tae me.' He straightened in his chair, Polly's eyes wide as she jumped to her feet, her screams piercing the silence, several yellow-crested cockatoos screeching before frantically flying from the oak tree sheltering the oasis of flora and fauna in their backyard.

'Oh, my. I cannot believe you are telling me true. Here I was ordering you to go find and marry that dreadful Nellie, when you've gone and caught our sweet Abigail, just as you always wanted. I'm beyond happy for you.' Polly embraced me for the longest time, then went to his side to do the same, Angus on his feet and enthusiastically thumping him on the back before picking me up in a tight hug, my feet dangling inches from the floor. 'Finally, after all these years, you'll be together. How bloody romantic.' Angus released me to return to my seat next to Polly, my hand in hers, her smile lighting her face.

'Well, brother. I'm happy fer ye, an' I hope this settles ye down after all these years of tormentin' yourself over a woman ye could naw have.' He paused, turning to me, a gentle smile touching his lips. 'Abigail, ye'll naw find anyone on this earth that loves ye more than Hamish. I know fer certain that Aaron, God rest him, would be happier than a pig in shite knowin' yer loved an' have someone beside ye takin' good care of ye, an' the bairns. Me fat headed brother adores Thomas an' Emmy naw different than if he planted the seed himself, an' yer his whole world, an' always have been. Naw matter how he's behaved in the past towards others, he'd never dare do any of that tae ye, Abigail—an' if stupid enough tae do so, he'd be forced tae face me.' Angus smiled again, his eyes shining, his hand on his brother's shoulder.

'Tell us when you will marry? Will it be soon?' Polly spoke quickly, unable to hide the excitement in her voice. I spoke of our plans for a small party to celebrate our betrothal, and how we would marry in the garden a few weeks later in the presence of family and friends. Lifting my left hand from under the table, she gasped, her eyes widening, her hand clasping at mine before pulling my finger up to her face to examine the ring. 'Oh, Abi. It's truly beautiful. I've never seen a pink diamond before, and this one is far larger than any precious stone I've looked at. The way it's been set so elegantly into the gold band with the small pink diamonds surrounding it is magnificent.' She glanced down at my right hand, confusion crossing her face. 'I notice you still wear the bands from Aaron.' She appeared uncomfortable for a moment, glancing across at Hamish, who stared back, clearly unperturbed, his large frame relaxed, his smile easy.

'I'll always wear Aaron's rings. He is part of me, and will be until the day I take my final breath and join him. I am wearing all the jewellery Aaron gave me on the right side of my body, and what Hamish has given me stays on the left.' I showed her the watch, along with the diamond bracelet now on my right wrist, the ankle chain filled with diamonds Aaron gave me dangling down onto my right foot, the pink diamond bracelet and engagement ring on the left.

'Oh, Abi. What a lovely idea. That way, you have them both with you for always,' Polly murmured, overcome with emotion, tears in her eyes she quickly brushed away.

'I will never remove my locket.' I caressed the solid gold heart with my fingers, the gold chain it hung from thick and strong, while reflecting on my wedding day so long ago now when Aaron presented it to me. Running my fingers over the six tiny diamonds embedded in the smooth gold he added just before he passed, the bauble always hidden where it nestled between my décollage, tears pricking my own eyes as I tucked it back safely under my dress.

'And nor should you have to. Hamish would not expect or demand it of you.' She smiled at me before rising to her feet and hurrying off to the kitchen to retrieve the trifle she had made with her own hands, while I leaned back in my chair, feeling all was well in the world.

Hamish stood on top of a cart used to transport our groceries home from Geelong, left just outside the stables looking back up onto the garden, the house staff and farm workers gathered around, a perfect platform to be seen above the crowd, numbering well over a hundred souls. Gazing up at Hamish from where I stood on the ground alongside him, I admired how striking and confident he appeared, his ruggedly handsome face and strong, muscular frame not going unnoticed by the women who lived and worked here.

'Thank ye all fer takin' the time tae meet here tae day.' A hush fell over them before he continued. 'I've an announcement tae make, an' wanted ye tae hear it directly. I've asked yer Mistress, Mrs Abigail Cavanaugh, tae marry me. An' she's accepted.' Cheers rose up, and many clapped loudly, several whistling, while others whispered between themselves, clearly surprised. Once they had quietened, he continued. 'Aaron was me best mate, an' I'll do me utmost tae continue his vision fer Willow Grove, just as he wanted. I've come tae know ye all well while in me position here as manager over the last few years, an' I want tae thank ye fer the hard work ye do while I'm up here.' Several clapped again, while he nodded at me. 'I know I've big boots tae fill comin' along after Aaron, but I hope ye feel just as comfortable comin' tae me over any problems that crop up, just as ye did with him.' I heard someone laugh, many turning to see who would dare.

'Ya seem to 'ave been tryin' ta fill his shoes for a while, mate, lurin' his widow in ta ya bed. How long ya been workin' on that, ya bludger?' Hamish remained silent, his face like thunder as he gazed out over the crowd, while many gasped, some appearing amused, others as if they would have a conniption.

'Who said that? Show yourself now.' Straightening up to his full height, his broad shoulders rigid, his hands curled into fists, he demanded an answer, not backing down for a moment, while my stomach knotted up, worried he would lose his temper after being so publicly shamed. The crowd, so quiet I could hear the birds singing in the trees, my gaze on Hamish as he jumped off the cart, landing elegantly on his feet before wandering through the crowd towards a group standing at the back. 'If yer not brave enough tae stand by yer own words, ye have naw right tae express yer opinions.' His voice boomed at them, echoing out over the paddocks, while I jumped, startled by his fury, the workers now silent, not one daring to move, let alone speak.

'I'll stand by me words 'cause it's the truth of it. What kind of mate were ya ta the great Aaron Cavanaugh? Not a bloody loyal one, trickin' his grief-stricken wife in ta marrin' ya.' Hamish turned, his glare finding the man in moments. 'There isn't a person at Willow Grove who can't see the sufferin' the Mistress is goin' through, an' we all feel sorry for her an' the little ones. Seems ya took yer chance while travellin' as the family's chaperone ta take advantage of a wealthy, greivin' widow. An opportunist I'd call ya, at best,' the man called out defiantly, and I felt my stomach tighten further, my heart starting to race away from me. The man, tall and solid, his dark hair long and loose, was a stranger to me, and I wondered if he were in our employ, or a friend of someone who was.

'How long have ye worked here?' Hamish snapped, striding up to him, his face now only inches from the man, who did not appear to back down for a minute despite Hamish' fury.

'Four-months.' His voice calm and strong, this man had balls of steel. He showed no fear of Hamish, despite his size or the expression on his face, frightening me a little.

'Ye've slandered yer Mistress's good reputation in front o' witnesses, an' I demand ye apologise tae her now,' Hamish roared, his face so close their noses almost touched.

'Oh, tell the truth, ya lyin' swine. It's not the Mistress I've offended, an' we all know it well enough. Yer as cunnin' as a dunny rat, an' not a soul in the district is ignorant of yer reputation with women, so I'll be makin' no apologies ta anyone. Ya likely to use the poor woman, an' take what you can before discardin' her like the rest ya've ruined, includin' me sister, but ya wouldn't remember her. She was just a tavern trollop ta ya, like most. Now ya think ya the Laird of Willow Grove 'cause yer swivin' the dead boss's wife?' Hamish pulled back his arm before striking him with his fist, the man doubling over, gasping before he fell to the ground, his body crumpled in on itself, his arms clutching his stomach.

'Shut yer mouth an' be gone from Willow Grove within the hour, or I'll come lookin' fer ye. I'll warn ye now, the next time we come face tae face, I'll damage ye badly,' Hamish spat down at him, the man's friends lifting him up and hurrying him away. Hamish returned to the cart, apologising to all present before thanking them. Soon after, he was by my side guiding me towards the house, his body tense, his pace quickening. Stopping at the back door, I placed my hand on his cheeks, forcing him to meet my gaze.

'Thank you for defending my honour. It was kind of you, but pay him no mind, whoever he was. I've had far worse said about me in the papers, and it's best to ignore it.' Following him into the kitchen. He paused in the doorway to kiss me, Leo coming upon us while carrying a sack of flour to the pantry.

'Oh, must you? I've already heard everyone in the district thinks you're a golddigger.' He stopped, throwing the sack on the bench to leave for someone else to put away, his finger pointing at Hamish. 'And as for you, Abigail.' He ordered Erin to clean the bench and put everything away, before pointing the same finger in my direction. 'Well, it seems everyone believes you just lay about day and night with your legs open.' I stepped towards him, but he was too quick, ducking away. Unable to pursue him due to Hamish's grip on my upper arm, I allowed him to lead me over to the table, settling myself down on a chair.

'You mustn't allow people like that to get under your skin, Hamish.' I smiled up at Sally as she placed a pot of coffee down in between us, pouring us both a mug, while Sarah brought a plate of scones to the table, Leo still nowhere to be seen.

'Aye. He stepped on me last nerve taeday. I'll be glad when it's done.' He kissed me gently on the forehead, pulling me close, his arms wrapped protectively around me. The time passed quickly, and by the time he rose to his feet, he had calmed significantly. 'I have tae go back tae work, but meet me when I knock off?'

'Of course. As soon as I have finished my errands in the village, I will come find you,' I promised, kissing him farewell before skipping down to the stables to spend the afternoon with Delly.

Chapter Eight

I STEPPED INTO THE shop, the bell tinkling overhead announcing my arrival, the streets outside busy, the air already stifling for this time of the morning. Catherine stood behind the counter with a young seamstress unpacking a recent delivery from London when she noticed me, her face lighting up as she ran to embrace me.

'I have so much to tell you, dear friend. Come with me so we can speak in private.' She hurried me upstairs and into the sitting room, closing the door behind us before inviting me to sit. 'Nanny died while you were away.' I gasped, my heart skipping a beat as tears filled my eyes. Opening my mouth to speak, she shook her head, putting her hand up for a moment. 'I didn't want to ruin your homecoming, and kept silent on the matter when I visited with you on your return.' Sadness filled me for the beautiful soul that was their Nanny, more of a mother to them than their own. Unable to imagine how Catherine, William and Beatrice would cope losing the only person who had consistently been there to care for and comfort them, while loving them without measure, I sniffed, composing myself before blowing my nose.

'Oh, Catherine. You all have my deepest condolences. I cannot imagine how terrible this must be for you and William, but poor, poor Beatrice.' She nodded, blowing her nose daintily before dabbing at her eyes with her handkerchief. Beatrice had not spoken a word to this day since the attack she endured in London all those years ago, and men continued to terrify her. She had grown into a lovely woman, polite, sweet and kind, and visited Catherine often to help with the children, and around the shop when needed.

'Beatrice wrote me a letter the day after Nanny passed asking to live here with us, unhappy our parents are never home. She felt so very alone, the poor darling. Of course we agreed immediately, and we all adore her living here.' There was a soft knock at the door, and Catherine called out her consent before a maid stepped inside carrying a tray. Greeting us politely, she laid out our morning tea before quietly excusing herself, leaving us to our privacy without further interruption, just as Catherine liked, and expected, of her servants.

'I'm pleased Beatrice is here. My Emmy just adores her.' I accepted the cup of tea she poured for me, her musical laughter filling the room.

'Oh, sweet Emmeline has been telling anyone who would listen since she could first talk that Beatrice is her bestest friend in the entire world. What a lovely friendship they have. Reminds me of us in so many ways.' I nodded, lifting my left hand up from under the table, her eyes going wide. 'Oh, Abigail. You have accepted your Lord Harrington.' Her face lit up in a brilliant smile before gently lifting my hand to inspect the ring. 'How very exquisite. I have never seen anything like it, to be honest, and I've seen some trinkets in my time. It's perfectly matched with your bracelet.' She let go of my hand and leaned back in her chair, her face falling. 'Does this mean you will leave us to live as a Duchess in England?' Her eyes shone with tears as I shook my head, smiling reassuringly before taking her hand in mine.

'Of course not. The ring isn't from Lord Harrington. It's from Hamish.' I waited for her to scream with joy, or congratulate me; however, she remained silent for the longest time, her cup to her lips as she sipped her tea, her eyes fixed on mine.

'Are you in love with him, or have you accepted his proposal only for the sake of the children? I know what you are like when it comes to Thomas and Emmy. You must be honest with me, Abigail. Does your heart desire this, or have you made your choice because you believe they need a father? Or is it the fact Aaron asked you to? I respected and liked Aaron very much, but it has always upset me that he burdened you with such an emotive request only hours before he...' I exhaled slowly, hiding my impatience at being forced to repeat myself a hundred times to what felt like a hundred people since agreeing to marry Hamish, feeling it would have been far easier to announce to everyone at once and bugger the consequences. Explaining everything as best I could, from taking him as a lover the first night onboard right up until this morning, she relaxed back in her chair and listened without interruption, tears in her eyes at times. Opening my heart to her, I confided my innermost feelings, my fears, and the sense of peace and contentment that had found me again over the last few days.

'I may not be *in* love with him, whatever *love* means, but I care so very deeply for him. It's comforting that we have such a solid foundation of friendship before we even embark on marriage, and I appreciate knowing he is there to share the difficult times and bear some of what burdens me, along with celebrating the triumphs I am confident are ahead for all of us.' She smiled, sadness in her eyes, before leaning forward and taking my hand in hers.

'You deserve that at the very least. All I have ever wished for you is happiness, and if you can find that again with Hamish, you have my blessing and full support.' The young maid knocked before silently entering the room, quickly collecting the dirty dishes on a tray, another soon following her carrying a pot of coffee, two clean teacups, a small jug of milk and a pot of sugar, alongside an unopened tin of *Arnott's Famous Biscuits,* Catherine's favourite. Although displaying what many assumed was a parrot, native to Australia, I had been told by Sister Josephine—her mother a distant cousin of the founder of the *Arnott's Biscuit Company,* William Arnott—the inspiration was in fact a brightly coloured Macaw, gifted to him by a captain of a ship returning him to Australia after a visit to his homeland. Said to be drawn by his daughter-in-law, Leslie Arnott, the parrot was first registered as a logo in 1888, and had adorned their packaging ever since.

Born on the 6th of December, 1827, in Fifeshire, Scotland, the first of eight children, William Arnott, arrived in Sydney with his younger brother, David, on the 17th of February 1848. Their parents, and four of their siblings, had left Scotland before them, settling at Peels River near Tamworth in New South Wales. The brothers travelled there post haste to reunite with them after being forced to remain at home to complete their baker and confectioner apprenticeships, soon following their family to explore the many and varied opportunities their new homeland held. Working as a baker for a time, along with spending a short period trying his luck on the goldfields, William opened his first bakery in High Street, Maitland, five-years later, and was successful enough; however, after a number of floods, the last the most devastating of all in 1861, he and his wife, Monica, decided to sell the property and establish their business elsewhere.

His brother, David, opened his own bakery in Swan Street, Morpeth, in 1862, and William and his family joined him a year later, but his bad luck had only begun. Another flood came through in 1864, and Monica passed away suddenly and without warning in April of 1865, leaving him two young sons and three daughters to care for. At the point of bankruptcy, he recognised Newcastle held opportunities far greater than where he's been so far, while aware the town was expanding rapidly, he took an enormous risk and loaned money from friends and family and relocated again, opening up a small bakery on Hunter Street where he thrived, supplying pies, bread and biscuits, not only to the locals, but to the ships docked in the port of Newcastle to replenish their supplies.

Word spread, and he had repaid the debt he owed to his loved ones within the first year, and from all reports, his business thrived. A religious man, and a philanthropist, William did not remain alone for long after Monica died, marrying Margaret Maclean, and in the following years fathered two more daughters with Margaret, while running the business alongside his sons, continuing right up until 1899 when he retired.

After successfully establishing *The Arnott's Steam Biscuit Factory* in Newcastle in 1875 to produce a range of plain and sweet biscuits and cakes, by 1882, the man no longer needed to work, sending his products to Sydney by ship. Only recently, they had begun to retire their distinctive horse drawn carriages that once delivered biscuits to the traders to sell in their shops by the pound, along with 'broken biscuits' at a far cheaper cost to the customer, all to be replaced by motorised vehicles painted in red and black with their instantly recognisable biscuit eating parrot on the side. I had heard they were in all the large cities and towns throughout Australia, and I had seen two of them in Melbourne with my own eyes before travelling to England. Since our return, the Arnott's cart, its driver Bert, and its single horse, Matey, were nowhere to be found around Geelong, replaced by a smaller motorised carriage and a new driver I was yet to meet. Sister had been beyond excited when in 1894, the first *Arnott's Biscuit Company* factory opened in Forest Lodge, Sydney, to meet demand not only from Australia, but across the water. It was only five-years ago I started to send her a package every month filled with tins of biscuits, not only because she was fond of them, but I knew she was proud of her family's connection, and liked to share them around with the Sisters and bairns—well, she shared them with everyone, other than Sister Mary Monica if she could help it.

Arnott's, as the company was referred to by almost everyone, had only begun to package the biscuits in tins in 1900, not only to keep them fresher for longer, but to prevent breakage while providing an interesting and ever changing patterned container to store them. Leo kept them all for himself, storing everything from marbles and buttons to lollies or coins inside them, although I had managed to sneak several up to my bedchamber while still full of biscuits, and refused to return them to the kitchen when empty. Sister had mentioned in a letter when William died in the July of 1901, leaving the business in the hands of his two sons, James and Samual, who were reported to be doing a splendid job and looking to expand yet again, their five sisters watching on without any influence, although their father had been generous to all his children.

'I doubt very much Hamish will behave towards you in the same manner in which he has to every available woman in Geelong. There wouldn't be many he hasn't been with,' she said, jolting me from my thoughts of Sister, while her face flushed, appearing upset. 'Oh, I'm sorry, Abigail. That was mean spirited of me. I know Hamish loves you, and I'm confident he would never treat you in the same way.' I nodded, taking a malt o' milk biscuit from the tin before dipping it into my coffee. 'I mentioned before you left that I believed Hamish was not for you, and I based my opinion purely on his past behaviour.

I'm sorry for it now, as it seems I was wrong.' She stood, coming to my side and embracing me. 'I am truly happy for you, my dear friend, and for Thomas and Emmy. He will make them a wonderful father, of that I am certain. He truly adores them as if they were his own blood.' She linked her arm through mine, leading me downstairs to show me several dresses she had nearly finished for me. I ran my hand over the fabric, the cut of it comfortable and feminine, and more importantly, plain just as I had asked. My cheek became warm as I turned to her, glancing around several times to ensure her staff could not overhear.

'Would you consider making a few negligees for my wedding trousseau? To take away on our honeymoon? Not that I'm even sure we will leave the property.' She clasped my hands in hers, her face lighting up, while a wicked smile touched her lips.

'Oh, I would adore it, Abigail. I have just the cloth for them.' Leading me over to a table by the window, she showed me bolts of the finest silk, the colours resembling gemstones, allowing me to choose my favourites. Walking me out to the carriage, she embraced me on the street, while Harry jumped down to open the door. 'I truly am thrilled for you, dear Abigail, and I wish you only happiness in your union with Hamish for the rest of your days.' Embracing her once more, we said our farewells, and I stepped up into the carriage with Harry's assistance, settling myself on the seat before opening the window to wave to her as the horses moved forward, pulling out onto the busy road, Catherine standing alone and staring after us long after we turned into the next street to head home to Willow Grove.

I tied Delly up near the school gate, tethering her to a post next to the concrete water trough. A wide-brimmed hat shielded my face from the sun, my boots crunching on the gravelled path as I reluctantly walked towards the charming white schoolhouse, several younger children lagging behind on their way home for the day waving, while greeting me cheerfully as they passed by. Glancing over at Mrs

McGinty's well kept cottage in the distance, I reached up and pulled the cumbersome hat from my head as I stepped into the shade of the verandah. Throwing it down on a chair, I wiped the sweat from my brow, grunting as I waved at the blowflies swarming around the entrance. Several March flies were among them, one taking a bite from my hand as I reached out to open the door, always kept tightly shut in the warmer months when at their worst, not only to keep the filthy creatures out, but the heat of the mid-afternoon sun.

'Hello there,' I called out, the heavy door clicking shut behind me, the small entrance room where the children kept their bags on the wooden pegs on the wall almost empty, the place oddly quiet. The fireplace was spotless, cleaned of its ash months ago, the wood left neatly stacked outside to prepare for the coming winter, while someone had already come through and swept the floor clean of the dirt traipsed in on tiny shoes and boots since this morning. Above the mantle hung ten large photographs, all pressed behind glass in identical native cypress pine picture frames, fashioned by Harry in his own time. Leo would trudge down to the village once a year with the heavy, and extremely expensive, photography equipment on his back, complaining the entire time of his tormented life here at Willow Grove, while wishing Aaron back from the dead to anyone who would listen, if only so my husband would continue to take the annual portrait of the most unfortunate looking children Leo ever had the misfortune to lay eyes on. Taken every February of the students and Mrs. McGinty gathered out in the schoolyard, all dressed in their Sunday best without a hair out of place, Thomas and Emmy's faces beamed back at me from every single photograph, although this year, they were not present. My heels clicked on the floorboards as I hurried across the room, soon pushing open the door to the much larger hall where the children took their lessons. Finding Mrs McGinty at her desk, her head lowered, her pencil moving quickly as she recorded something in the thick book laid out before her, I exhaled slowly. The door slammed shut behind me, and her head snapped up, her spectacles askew on her nose, her greying hair pulled back severely into a bun as was her usual habit, while I gasped, startled, the bang still echoing through the room.

'Good afternoon, Mrs Cavanaugh. Thomas and Emmy were amongst the first to leave.' She stood, inviting me to sit on the chair opposite her, while I nodded, crossing the room to her desk before lowering myself down onto the hard wooden chair. 'If you are looking for them, there was some talk of swimming in the river just out of the village before going home to do chores.' She smiled affectionately to herself as she closed the leather-bound book in front of her and placed her pencil down on the desk, before resting back in her far more comfortable chair, her hazel eyes gazing into mine, a slight smile touching her lips. I had always respected Mrs McGinty, and I liked her very much, feeling we shared a friendship of sorts. Not close, but there was an ease when in each other's presence, while many uncomfortable discussions had passed between us with no ill feelings lingering afterwards. There were times over the years I felt she enjoyed my company, although I would never know of it given she kept everything between us so very formal, treating our interactions no different to a business meeting—cordial, always friendly enough, but never overfamiliar.

'Good afternoon, Mrs McGinty. Are you well?' She smiled, pouring us both a glass of water from the metal jug on her desk, the pane glass windows high above open to allow the hot air to escape.

'I am well, thank you.' She straightened her spectacles, her gaze going from my face down to my hands resting in my lap and back up again. 'I must say, you look the best I have seen you in years, my dear. I am thrilled you will marry again, at least for your own sake, and you have my very good wishes. I am more aware than most just how difficult it is without a man to speak on your behalf. You have my congratulations that will no longer be the case. Now, tell me what brings you to my door?' I raised the glass to my lips, taking a deep drink of the tepid water before meeting her gaze.

'I'm here to have an honest discussion with you.' She nodded, silence hanging heavily over the room, while I took another drink, my throat tight. 'It's about the Bradley children.' She wrinkled her nose in disdain before gently pushing herself back from the desk. Rising to her feet in silence, she straightened her plain brown skirt, her white shirt showing patches of sweat down her back and under her arms, before strolling over to the window, her gaze fixed on the birds in the distance shitting on the swings and seesaw in the playground, a deep sigh escaping her pursed lips.

'What about them?'

'Oh, come on, Albertina. You know very well. Stop treating me like you treat the Bradley family.' She turned back to me, shaking her head before moving around the room, drawing the drapes on every window except for one. Returning to her seat, she placed her elbows on the desk, her hands cupping her chin, her brow wrinkled as she raised her eyebrows.

'Are we to speak bluntly?' Her manner calm, her tone polite, I nodded, aware if anyone could be blunter than she, I had not met them in this lifetime.

'If you mean without consequence, that I cannot promise.' She arched her eyebrows further, nodding once more before relaxing back in her seat.

'May I ask you a question first, Mrs Cavanaugh?

'Of course.'

'What do you care? Do you really think they need, or even want, a white woman like you swooping in to save them, all to ease the guilt you carry living on the land they call theirs? Are their complaints about *your* countrymen slaughtering them one after another and raping their women, while trying to breed them out, upsetting to you, Mrs Cavanaugh?' She only paused long enough to take a breath, my eyes widening slightly, her cheeks a soft pink. I raised my hand while straightening up in my seat.

'They are not *my* countrymen, thank you very much. I was born in Scotland, and you know it well, Albertina.' I narrowed my gaze, my eyes glinting dangerously, while she scoffed, rolling her eyes sarcastically, her laugh mocking.

'Oh, you speak like an English woman, and you are a direct descendant of Charles Howard, the first Earl of Carlisle in the Howard lineage. They may have abandoned you in Scotland, Mrs Cavanaugh, but you're as English as your great-aunt, Lady Delmont, who I understand felt a similar sympathy and affinity towards the blacks. Going against the morals and values accepted by most will only harm you, as it did her, if you were to go by the rumours that swirl about the place.' I forced a smile, not wanting to argue over less important matters when I had come to address a far bigger problem. Pushing down the anger bubbling up inside me, I crossed and uncrossed my legs, feeling restless, while considering if I should leave and return when I felt calmer. 'Heed me when I say you should tread lightly. If you must help these unfortunates and believe it's your Christian duty, do it in silence, or you *will* suffer for it in the long run. You do know that Lady Delmont was forced to flee for her life from Willow Grove in 1866, abandoning all who lived here? Mrs McPhee rarely speaks of Willow Grove when we visit, but when she does, I believe every word spoken. There is not a malicious bone in that woman's body, and she has nothing to gain by lying. Her husband, on the other hand...' She paused, aware she had said too much; however, I was well aware of her friendship with the McPhee's, and had remained silent on the matter. She leaned forward, lowering her voice, although not another soul was present. 'Lady Delmont was driven out of Australia with threats of death as a direct result of mixing with the natives as if they were her equals. You should avoid following in her footsteps, Mrs Cavanaugh.' I placed my palms on my cheeks to cool them, before picking up a small book left on the edge of her desk and fanning myself with it.

'My opinions, values, and morals are my own. I never met the woman, but I have no doubt we would have been friends.' I continued to wave the book, the warm air hitting my sweaty skin providing some relief from the stifling heat.

'If not for Christian women like you and I, these lamingtons would be walking around naked with spears, killing us and each other for no reason other than they are wilder, and far more dangerous, than the native animals surrounding them. They would be living in humpies and eating nothing but wombats, kangaroos and emus, not to mention the weeds they forage from the bush and call food.' She screwed up her face as if tasting something bitter, while I forced myself to remain in my seat and not punch her in the throat. This was the newest of the derogatory terms Mrs McGinty used when referring to the Aboriginal people, and I cringed every time I heard it. The vanilla sponge-cake, cut up into squares and covered in chocolate, referred to their dark skin, while the coconut it was rolled in represented dandruff as a result of poor hygiene, the first published recipe appearing in *Country Life* newspaper in 1900, and the term picked up and used as an insult soon after. 'Yet all they do is whine about the past, present and future, while doing nothing to help themselves. If it were up to me, the English would have herded them all up a hundred-years ago and sent them south west to Kangaroo Island. Would have saved both sides a great deal of trouble.' I reeled back in my chair as if she had slapped my face, then spat in my eye.

'How can you be so cruel to wish such things upon anyone?'

'My opinion comes from experience, Mrs Cavanaugh. The natives would have been far better off without colonisation, I agree, and given they were not strong enough to fight in any actual way that made a difference, they should have considered gathering together in one place away from civilisation. Only then would they have been stronger, and far safer, and could have lived however they so chose without interference. Their ways are complex, and rarely understood by the civilised.'

'It seems you do not understand them any better than the next, but if I'm not confused, you appear to believe this would have protected them, and would have been in their own best interest? Do I detect some sympathy underneath such harshness?'

'Oh, I could not care any less than I already do about any of that lot, but in saying that, there are many I dislike in this world, no matter what their colour. Nor do I have any ill feelings towards the Bradley children directly. I wish to make that clear. It's not their fault their father saw an opportunity and took it. The same thing happened to my own Papa.' Tears filled her eyes, the only thing preventing me from sacking her where she sat.

'Your father was an Aboriginal man?' She shook her head at my confusion, a wry smile on her lips while she dabbed at her eyes with a white linen handkerchief before blowing her nose.

'Oh, no, of course not.' She composed herself, placing the sodden cloth in a basket at her feet, while I drained the last of the water in my glass, accepting another, no matter how awful. 'I agreed to speak plainly, so I will.' I nodded, expecting nothing less of the woman I had grown fond of over the years. 'You are unaware, but I am not from these parts. I was born in 1840 in Adelaide, the only child to Albert and Victoria McGinty, but my parents arrived in South

Australia a decade before from Ireland. I was my mother's only child, but not my father's.' I swallowed hard; her stare fixed on the only window not covered by the cheerful blue drapes, allowing a beam of bright light into the darkened hall.

'I'm sorry. You are not obligated to tell me your private business, Mrs McGinty, but we *do* need to discuss your treatment of the Bradley children. You are right in saying I should not have to stand up for anyone around me, no matter what the colour of their skin, but it's the way of the world, and will continue to be if those witnessing injustice remain silent, or worse, become apathetic and follow along.'

'I must defend myself regarding the matter, Mrs Cavanaugh, given you have raised the subject, and I feel attacked by your manner. I have always been a fair woman in every area of my life; however, I am acutely aware my views on certain subjects may be considered harsh by a minority, particularly when it comes to the natives. I'm certain you will not disagree that we are all somewhat influenced by our personal experiences.' I nodded, encouraging her to continue while she nestled herself in her chair. 'My parents were not wealthy, but my father earned a decent enough living as a blacksmith, and my mother, a seamstress with her own shop, worked long hours—long enough to justify employing a housekeeper and a scullery maid five-years before I arrived. The maid, Ruby, was thirteen when she started with us, and barely eighteen when she delivered a daughter, sired by my father, the month after I was born. I never understood why my mother was such an angry woman. Well, not until Ruby ran away in the night when I was ten, taking her three daughters with her.' Tears pricked my eyes, not only for Ruby, but watching a usually sensible woman like Mrs McGinty torn apart by hate from the sins of those who came before her. Tears trickled down her face as I stood, swiftly moving around behind the desk before passing her a clean handkerchief, my hands grasping her shoulders for a moment in comfort.

'I did not know, and I'm more than sorry for it.' I poured her another glass of water, waiting until she composed herself before I sat back down opposite her. 'I understand now why you feel the way you do; however, I have a responsibility to the children first and foremost.' She nodded, remaining silent. 'All who attend this school must be treated equally, no matter what the colour of their skin or where they hail from, Mrs McGinty. Black, white, yellow or rainbow, I will not stand for anything less.' She jutted out her chin defiantly, meeting my gaze with a glare.

'This is the only school I know of that allows the blacks to attend as students, and I will say it now as no one else seems to have the backbone to tell you to your face, Mrs Cavanaugh.' She leaned forward, sneering as I narrowed my gaze, fury rising in me. 'You are a laughing-stock, not only in the district, but all over the country. There are laws against it, and for good reason, and you break every one. I've done nothing wrong, and if you are thinking of sacking me, you've got another think coming. I will go screaming to every politician I know, along with every reporter from every newspaper in the country, and I will visit with Janet and her husband myself to ensure he no longer allows her to consider you a friend or receive your visits. You will not be supported in the matter like you were when your husband went to trial.' I raised my eyebrows, widening my eyes sarcastically as I crossed my arms against my chest, while she returned my stare, not backing down for a moment.

'I have no intention of sacking you, Albertina. That would be far too easy for you, and you will not have learned the lesson you were so clearly sent here to learn. Not to mention, I could not send you back out into the world with a clear conscience to treat other children in this manner, no matter what your excuse. I came here to tell you I have employed another teacher to assist you.' She sat back in her chair as if *I* had slapped *her*, while I straightened my shoulders further, holding her glare.

'I won't have it.'

'You have no say in the matter and are no longer entitled to an opinion. You are free to leave if you so wish.' Shaking her head in disbelief, the headmistress abruptly rose to her feet and returned to the window. She knew that I knew that she knew she would be mad to walk away from a position such as this, and given her age, it would be difficult, if not impossible, for her to gain employment in a school under the same conditions with the benefits she received here. She paid for nothing, and collected wages well above what any of her peers teaching at schools or working as governesses in private homes earned, and if she chose to leave, she would not sleep on the streets.

I was confident she had enough savings to buy a cottage of her own somewhere and retire comfortably, given I had rarely seen her spend a penny whilst in my employ.

'Who have you hired?'

'Mr David Unaipon. You may know of him and his wife, Katherine? They've only been married three-years, and moved here twelve-months ago from Adelaide.' She nodded, rolling her eyes before marching back to her desk and lowering herself heavily down onto her chair.

'He's a labourer, not a teacher,' she snapped, her eyes glinting dangerously, while I remained silent. Little did she know, David Unaipon was far more than she would ever give him credit for, and in my mind, his intelligence bypassed her own, as did his kindness and manner. Born at the Point McLeay Mission in South Australia on the 28th of September 1872, he was the fourth of nine children. His father, James, and his mother, Nymbulda, hailed from the Ngarrindjeri tribe and were both native Yaraldi Yaraldi speakers, their children fluent in the dialect by the time they could walk. I had gone to visit with David and Kate at their terrace soon after arriving home, seeking his counsel regarding Mrs McGinty, and he had been more than generous with his time and advice. Presenting as an educated man, I had been unaware he attended a mission school up until the age of thirteen when he left to go into service for a Mr Young, a kind employer who encouraged his interest in music, literature, science, philosophy and art. Leaving his employment to return to the mission in 1890, he learned boot-making, played the piano and read widely. A conservative man in his habits, David expressed his frustration at the lack of work available for Aboriginals, particularly when he was often far more educated and qualified than many applying alongside him. Dissatisfied with what the mission could offer, he returned to Adelaide in the late 1890s, successfully gaining employment as a storeman, then a bootmaker for a time, before taking up a book-keeping job back at Point McLeay where he met the love of his life, Katherine, a Tangani woman, whom he married on the 4th of January 1902. I hadn't hired David the day he and Kate arrived at Willow Grove seeking work, Hamish had, but I was glad of it, finding the man not only clever, but sensible, with a curious mind. I had offered him the teaching position, and he had accepted; however, had been clear he was unsure how long they would stay, the pull of family in South Australia strong.

'He's a preacher, actually. As was his father. His grasp of the written word is better than mine, and his intellect far superior, of that I am certain.' She rolled her eyes again, her usually pale cheeks flushed.

'You cannot have a darkie teaching white children for the benefit of a few half-castes who shouldn't be here in the first place. No matter how rich or powerful you believe yourself to be, there are people far more so who take a dim view of what you allow on this property,' she spat, leaning back in her chair, 'and I certainly will not be supervised by a man with no formal education, let alone a savage. That's what you're doing, isn't it, Mrs Cavanaugh? He is not there to assist me. You're putting a boong in my classroom to undermine my position, and report all my perceived sins back to you.' She shook her head bitterly while I remained silent, my face void of emotion. Rising to my feet, I picked up my small bag, slipping the strap over my shoulder before stepping away. Pushing the chair back under the desk, she glared up at me, her hands shaking, her face a deep magenta.

'I will deal with the matter however I see fit while I'm the Mistress here and my backside still points to the ground. You do not need to decide today if you will leave Willow Grove, Mrs McGinty. Personally, I hope it is the latter and you can soften regarding the matter, and change your views and treatment of those you view as less than you. We have always valued and appreciated you, and what you do for the bairns. I would find it extremely sad if your time here was to end in this way purely as a result of an unhealed wound you carry. A wound that appears to have festered with hate over time, growing so large and heavy, you'd be best to lay it down for your own sake.' She exhaled sharply. Avoiding my gaze, she nodded; her trembling hand reaching out for the pencil while opening her thick book before lowering her head to write. Feeling there was nothing left to be said, I turned on my heel and made my way across the expansive hall to the heavy doors.

'When does Mr Unaipon begin his position?' I paused, my hand on the door, the room silent, bar the sound of the blowflies buzzing around the ceiling.

'You can expect him tomorrow morning at eight o'clock.' Without turning back, I stepped through the door and hurried out onto the verandah to find my hat, relief washing over me. Swinging myself up onto Delly, I headed for the main house, grateful for the distance that lay between the village and the sanctuary of home.

The room dark, only a dim glow from the half-moon lighting the bedchamber; I lay naked in Hamish's arms. Doubting myself and my ability to care for and protect the souls living on the property, I stared up at his chiselled features, his eyes closed, his breathing slow, his snores soft. Laying flat on his back, his long black hair falling down around him like silk on the white pillow, I admired how handsome he was even in the dark, unable to stop myself from kissing his cheek. His eyelashes fluttered, and he turned his face towards me, his lips on mine, before opening his eyes.

'I love ye, me precious girl.' Melting into his arms, several hours passed before I drifted off to sleep, my dreams filled with visions of a bottle of arsenic, a girl named Ruby, and Aaron. Always Aaron.

Chapter Nine

I STRETCHED OUT ACROSS the bed, the daylight starting to filter in through the open windows, the gentle breeze touching my face as I rose from sleep, yawning loudly before opening my eyes. Today I would marry Hamish. Leaving me yesterday with a long passionate kiss, he had dragged his feet back to the cottage to stay one last night with Angus and Polly.

We had decided to hold our wedding breakfast in the dining hall, and the reception party at the pub. Inviting every soul who lived and worked at Willow Grove, past and present, along with Aaron's family and all our friends, I wanted my wedding to Hamish to be different to my first. Concerned I would not cope being in the pub—clearly proven the one and only time I had been there since Aaron died—Hamish had accompanied me several times a week leading up to today to prepare and ease my nerves.

Mr and Mrs Makenzie had heard on Leo's passionfruit vine that I had accepted Hamish's proposal of marriage, and had called on us unexpectedly soon after. Gritting my teeth while forced to visit with them in the sitting room, it was no surprise it was Mr Makenzie who did most of the talking. Now they thought him respectable once again, they wanted to welcome him back into the Makenzie clan and reinstate him as their son and heir, and it enraged me. My poor friend, Harriet, had sat through the entire visit, unmoving and silent, while gazing at Hamish with tears in her eyes, the joy at seeing her son after so many years reflected in her weary smile. Feeling nothing but resentment towards his father, the cruel and callous man who had pressured his son into a marriage he hadn't wanted, then disowned him when he was true to himself and walked away, left me sick to my stomach. I was disgusted how easily he had discarded his son, behaving as if Hamish had never existed. Wanting to throw the man out of my house before I let him through the door, I restrained myself, biting my tongue so hard it bled, not only for Hamish's sake, but for Harriet, along with the fact I had not seen Hamish as thrilled as he was in that moment when they first embraced after so many years apart.

Mr Makenzie may have thought me a daft orphan with the intellect of a mosquito; however, I was well aware he had only come to gather Hamish back into the fold to feather his own nest, aware I had been generous with the Cavanaughs'. They had attended our engagement dinner three-weeks ago at their son's invitation, and although I felt a bond of friendship with his mother, I detested his father in every way. Doubting I would look on Mrs Makenzie as a mother in the future—as I did Mrs Cavanaugh from the day we first met, and would continue to do until I took my last breath—I was hopeful our friendship would be rekindled and strengthened without interruption or interference from Mr Makenzie, whom I had no doubt would cause Hamish heartbreak in the impending years.

Jemima was the spit of her father, and the thought of seeing her today caused my stomach to drop to the floor. Widowed twice, and now a year into her third marriage to a man ten-years older than her own father, she was the mother of two small children, although I was unsure who sired them. Now wealthy in her own right as a direct result of inheriting everything her dead husbands' owned, she no longer needed the financial security of marriage, surprising me she had chosen to wed another so soon after losing the last. Only weeks ago, I was outside in the kitchen garden collecting herbs at Leo's request, the staff unaware I could hear the gossip they cheerfully shared while preparing our Sunday luncheon, animatedly discussing how Jemima was seeking to outdo me—for what reason, no one was certain. Not only at Willow Grove, but throughout the district, most were aware of Jemima's grudge against me. She had been determined to blacken my name over the last fifteen-years, and deliberately spoke badly of me at every opportunity, whether to her servants and labourers, or the grocer in Geelong. Recently heard stating when at a baptism in Melbourne she had set her mind to become wealthier than me, while telling anyone who would listen how an orphan did not deserve the life so generously placed in my hands on a gilded platter, I could only hope her forked tongue exposed to all around her how petty and vindictive I believed her to be.

Considering my age, and I was a widow with two children, I had not wanted to dress as a bride as I had with Aaron; however, Catherine had insisted, arguing with me for days over the matter. Wearing me down while making me feel terribly guilty, I relented when she pointed out Hamish had never married before, and how pleased he would be to see me in a wedding dress. If it had not been for Queen Victoria wearing a gown as white as snow when she married Albert in 1840, I could have married in any colour I wished; however, everything she did was copied by her subjects soon after, cursing the rest of us to keep up with the fashions she set over the last six-decades. The perambulator Aaron had bought before Thomas and Emmy were born was a replica of the one the monarch had used for her own children and grandchildren, mine now gathering dust under the house, alongside the clothes I was unlikely to wear again.

Emmy had been thrilled when I asked her to be my maid a week after accepting Hamish's proposal and had not stopped talking of it from that day to this. She had stayed in touch with Madeline since we returned home, and although she lived in the city, Madeline would cheerfully travel down by train to Willow Grove most Friday afternoons to visit, returning to Melbourne on Sunday evening. They had great fun together riding around the property, often swimming in the creeks and the sea when the weather was warm, while passing the time doing what young girls enjoyed—sharing secrets. At least half the time they were together was spent gossiping in Emmy's bedchamber, sometimes for hours, while reminding me of my bond with Polly. Madeline, although offered a guest room, always chose to stay with Emmy, often whispering into the wee hours of the morning before sleep found them. Thrilled to see my daughter develop such a close friendship with a girl her own age, I also felt a certain sense of relief. I had always felt guilty she was surrounded by so many boys at Willow Grove, along with her younger cousins, and had worried for her over the years she would never form any close friendships outside of our family, or the boundaries of our property.

Maggie and Irene had visited with us several times to stay, along with their children, and we had all enjoyed being together again, but not more than our offspring, the six of them delighted to be reunited. Ron and Irene had fallen in love with Willow Grove and the district far more than they expected, soon deciding to buy ten-thousand hectares just out of Ceres to start their sheep property. Wealthier than most, they planned to build a grand house, the construction soon to commence; however, they were frustratingly stuck in the planning stage, the architect only recently finalising the drawings. Inviting them to stay with us until their home was complete, they accepted graciously, agreeing it would be wonderful for the children to spend an extended period of time together. All three Delaforce children were now attending the village school, and it seemed Thomas and Hannah had become even closer, choosing to spend the majority of their free time in each other's company. Feeling I needed to speak with my son in private, I had waited for the right moment before leading him to my bedchamber, soon slipping under the quilt with him beside me. Laying his head on my chest, I stroked his hair as I talked of the sweet things his father would say, and the little things he would do that meant so very much, while explaining how much respect his father held for women, never raising his hand once to the fairer sex, while believing they deserved to be protected and cherished, and hoping our son would be no different.

Although excited for our wedding night to arrive, I was beyond nervous. I had decided not to wear any of the lingerie gifted to me from Lady Duff-Gordon in front of Hamish before today, choosing to save them for after we married when it mattered not if he thought me a tavern trollop. Catherine had been a woman of her word, and delivered six dresses and two evening gowns, along with a box filled with negligees, including several of the most risqué she had ever made. After studying her friend's lingerie I had shown her, Catherine immediately wrote to Lady Duff-Gordon asking her permission to design items in a similar fashion—and that consent was given in an affectionate letter arriving from London, alongside bolts of material and paper patterns. Catherine had never once fooled me with her quiet manner and the conservative way about her, recognising a rebellious spirit and a lusty wickedness she managed to disguise in front of most; however, this hidden side she could not help but express through her designs. Orders for her lingerie and negligees had always been by special request, and only available to her friends, along with several customers whom she now considered friends, while most women were unaware items like these existed.

Hamish had decided to take me away on a proper honeymoon, but wouldn't tell me where, only that I wouldn't need evening gowns, and to bring warm clothes I was comfortable in. I was relieved we weren't spending it here as Aaron and I had, despite how much we loved Willow Grove. Hamish had taken into consideration how it may make me feel and done everything in his power to ensure the entire experience was different from what I had shared with Aaron.

He had wanted desperately to take Thomas and Emmy with us; however, I had immediately refused him, first, because they had missed far too much school, and second, we were meant to be going on a romantic honeymoon, and I had collapsed in a fit of giggles when he had raised the subject. Excited to be a family, he believed we should include them in everything, but I stood my ground over the matter, much to his disappointment. Thomas and Emmy hadn't seemed to care at all, both more than content to stay at home, as they had missed it so very much while away. They were more mature than Hamish, deciding they were not comfortable intruding on what they considered private time, and I thought it lovely of them. We had only been home from our voyage for just over three-months, and they refused to leave their friends again so soon, especially now the Delaforce children were living under our roof.

Although Hamish was aware of the space under the house, he did not know about the money stored down there. When I had led him downstairs and unlocked the door to what Aaron and I referred to as *the vault*, he had been rendered speechless for several minutes, silently wandering around while running his fingers over the wads of notes, all neatly bundled up side-by-side and stacked on top of each other. I had sat down on a wooden chair and explained how I had come across the room and its contents so many years ago now, believing it was left by my great-aunt Isabelle, along with confiding we paid the staff their monthly bonus from it, along with purchasing any luxuries needed. Explaining how Aaron managed the farm account, I officially handed it over to him to do with as he saw fit, bringing tears to his eyes as he had embraced me, while confirming my trust in him.

Although the new terraces had been completed and we had moved the married workers in, there were still a number of them vacant. I had furnished them all carefully with only the best beds and finely crafted pieces throughout, and was pleased with the result. Cheerful new drapes hung in all the terraces, old and new, while Hamish had ordered that the older residences were freshened up when Eric's company were building the new street of terraces, ensuring any maintenance issues were addressed, the shingles on the rooves replaced, along with new paint and wallpapers inside, the exteriors all freshly painted. They had replaced all the fencing at the back of the terraces, creating a separate and private backyard for each.

I had started to get to know some of the new families while reacquainting myself with those I hadn't spoken to for years. I no longer saw Aaron when I stepped into the pub—in fact, I no longer saw him anywhere, upsetting me greatly. I missed him dreadfully, and would have given anything to see him again in my mind's eye. I was terrified he was fading from my memory, despite doing everything in my power to hold on to him.

I heard the door quietly open, and turned to watch Emmy creep across the room, sliding into bed beside me; her arms soon wrapped around me as she gently kissed my cheek.

'I wanted to spend some time in here with you, Mama. This is the last chance I have before Da moves in with you.' Her voice far too cheerful for this hour, I squeezed her tighter, enjoying the warmth of her in my arms. Stroking her back, I gazed down at her beautiful face, her hair piled on top of her head tied up in rags just like my own.

'I love you, my Emmy. You make me so proud, sweetheart. You may look like me, but you have your father's thoughtful, loving nature.' I kissed her forehead, and she smiled.

'I get that from you, too, Mummy. You don't realise how lovely you are on the inside.' She affectionately ran her finger down my face. 'I don't think I will ever marry when I'm older. Would you be terribly disappointed in me if I chose not to?' Staring into my eyes, I gently touched the tip of her nose, and she giggled.

'Of course not, but may I ask why you feel this way, sweetheart? You have only ever been around happy marriages, with the exception of only a few.'

'Mummy, I don't want to ruin your wedding day.' She turned away, and I reached out and took her chin in my hand, directing her gaze back to mine.

'Oh, Emmy. There is nothing you could say that could ruin any day I spend here on earth in your company, nor could anything change my love for you. You could tell me you committed cold-blooded murder, and I would help you hide the body *and* provide you with an alibi,' I teased, trying to get her to smile as I held her close, her large green eyes welling with tears.

'I don't like boys the way other girls do. I view the sensible ones here at Willow Grove as friends, but nothing more. I have known most of them my whole life, and I mostly enjoy being around them, but I do not want one as a husband.' She started to cry and I held her close, knowing in my heart what was coming. 'I like girls the same way you like men, Mummy. I've tried to change how I feel but I cannot, no matter how hard I try. I want to be held and kissed by a girl the way Daddy used to hold you, and to have her look at me the way Da now looks at you.' She paused, her voice breaking, while my heart felt as if it were being squeezed, my chest so tight I could barely breathe. 'I will understand if you and Da hate me and never want to see me again. You must feel completely disgusted in me as I am nothing but a filthy pervert, a deviant, just like what those about the district call Uncle Leo.' She pressed her head against my chest and sobbed, my fingers gently stroking her cheek, my arms wrapped tight around her.

'Do not ever let me hear you say that again, Emmeline. You are none of those things, nor is Uncle Leo. We could never hate you, or feel anything but love for you, my darling wee girl. We love you more than anything in this world, and if loving another girl is what makes you happy, then your Da and I will help and support you in every way we can. You are only young, and many say feelings change as you mature, but that is not something I agree with. I was curious about boys at your age, and when I thought of romance, it was boys who featured in my daydreams. I didn't grow out of it. I still like boys,' I teased, and she hiccupped, her sobs now silent tears she was unable to stop. 'Your Da and I will always be here to help as you find your place in the world, and you will. You have nothing to feel bad or horrible about, or even guilty. I believe everyone is born a certain way, and there is nothing to be done about it. You cannot choose who you love, sweetheart. Look at Uncle Leo. We love him for who he is, and those who truly call him friend do not care who he shares his bed with. The others, well, they can suck my...' I stopped, not wanting to ruin the day with my foul mouth, while she nodded, sniffing as I wiped her face with the hem of my nightgown. 'We love you exactly how you are, Emmy. For the generous heart you have, the special soul that is the essence of you that no one else in the world has. No matter what you choose to do as you grow, or who you choose to spend your life with, we will always be here for you.' My tears mingled with hers as she sniffed again, her hand on my cheek as her tears started to slow.

The last thing I ever wanted was for my children to carry shame or guilt that wasn't theirs to bear. We did not live in a world that was kind to anyone who differed from societal norms, or refused to behave as expected, but I would give my life to protect her, and do all I could to minimise her suffering at the hands of another. As would Hamish, a ferocious man when it came to his Emmy. I had not suspected for a moment Emmy had been struggling with this, as we were close and confided in each other often. She lay in my arms, her breathing slower now, her body relaxing ever so slightly. Within minutes, she was sound asleep. As I held her close, I wondered if Hamish would keep his word and stay away from the house until we met in the garden after lunch for the service, and smiled to myself, aware it would drive him mad before breakfast. He made me feel as if I were the only other person in the world, and I was all he could see. Whenever I was with him, my grief lessened for a time, and I felt content and at peace. Pondering what today held for all of us, I drifted back to sleep, my dreams filled with magpies, a large island covered in blood, and a man called Rupert.

Bessie came waddling into the room, kicking closed the door behind her before slowly moving around the bedchamber pulling open the heavy drapes, the room suddenly filled with the early morning light.

'Today is the day, my little sweethearts. You will be a family again, with a husband for you, Mistress, and a father for little Miss Emmy. Oh, it lightens me heart to know that such a good man will be looking after you from today onwards, because I must tell you, I'm exhausted.' She paused near the small table and chairs, her hands on her hips, her breathing slightly laboured. 'Dr Richards said yesterday that despite being a week over me time, this little one shows no sign of wanting to join us. Not that I blame the wee thing, given the way of the world at the moment. And as for trying to reprimand me for not staying at home and resting, he said walking here and back each morning could help bring the child on.' She straightened up, composed now, her hand on her enormous stomach, well hidden by her apron. 'You've no idea how hard it was to keep all those men away who wanted to court you. Far more than the crowds those Geelong football matches draw.' She laughed to herself before making her way over to Aaron's side of the bed to check on Emmy, still sleeping soundly. 'Now I have nothing to fret over, as it would be a courageous man who would even try to get within cooee of you with a husband like Hamish. He isn't like Aaron, who was slow to anger.' She paused, cringing for a moment as a smile touched my lips. 'Well, that boy hid his temper far better than Hamish, now I think about it.' She shook her head, sadness in her eyes before she forced a smile. 'Hamish has that Scottish fire in his belly when it comes to the people he loves. I can't imagine him to be any less than a protective and jealous husband.' She crossed to my side of the bed before bending down to kiss me good morning.

'Hmmm, a little less of the jealousy would be nice though. He punched a man from another property last week for putting his hand on my backside. If he's not careful, he is going to get himself a reputation,' I complained as she narrowed her gaze, a deep crease in her brow, her finger wagging in my direction.

'I say good for him. How dare anyone lay their hands on you in the pub in front of witnesses? As the Mistress of this property, they should have more respect. I heard about it in the village, and I must say I congratulated him the next time I saw him. That Robert O'Brian is nothing but trouble, and he's had his eye on you since Aaron went into hiding. You must understand, despite you being such a progressive woman, we live in times where you need a man to protect you and speak on your behalf. Women are treated and taken notice of as much as the chickens we keep out in the coop. All the money in the world will never change that. Even the customers who purchase your horses will only deal with a man, and Harry has been generous speaking on your behalf on the matter, but Hamish will now take that in hand and complete your life in more ways than you even understand.' I smiled at the thought of him, while she wandered around the room tidying as she went.

'Progress is being made, no matter how slow here in Victoria. It has me stuffed how every other woman in every other state has the right to vote, and in South Australia women have been able to run for parliament since 1895, yet here, we have no voice or influence at all. They have always been ahead of their time, though. Did you know, it's the only state in the country where women who own property in their own name have been given the right to vote in local elections since 1861, and Aboriginal men were enfranchised when all men gained the right to vote in the colony in 1856? David Unaipon told me. He is like a walking encyclopaedia when it comes to all things interesting. He has the brain of a scientist, yet a heart for service to all around him, no matter what you look like or what class you sit in. We had quite a long conversation about the draconian political leaders of this country, and how they still refuse to include the true owners of this land as residents on the census. Shameful. I will miss him dreadfully when he and Kate leave, but I applaud South Australia and may consider packing us all up and moving there with them,' I teased as she shook her head, a smirk touching her lips while refreshing the water in a crystal vase filled with white roses picked from my own garden.

I had avoided surrendering my property to Hamish, along with all money and future wages earned, only because I had a lawyer insisting on a legal contract between us in my own best interest before I entered into marriage. Before the 1870s, women had no access to divorce no matter what the grounds, and despite legislative changes in the 1880s, it was still a difficult path to walk given men were the legal guardians to any children from that marriage, and could remove them from their mother at any time without reason or explanation, and had the right to bequeath them to whomever they saw fit if they should unexpectedly pass away. Abandonment was common, and there was nothing in place financially to support any of them, forcing women into paid employment, while earning two-thirds less than a man doing the same job.

'My point is, Mistress, you have nothing to fear. Now you will have a husband to stand up for you in every situation, whether you can vote or not. Hamish is not the type to take advantage, and I believe he will always represent you well, not only in business, but personally as the head of your family, here at Willow Grove and in the district. He is well liked and ferociously loyal to you.'

'Yes, but most women are not as fortunate as me. It is like betting on the Melbourne cup. They all look magnificent as they parade around before the race, but how they perform on the track is an entirely different matter. Anything could happen, and you could end up with a donkey and losing all you had, no matter how little, or gaining more than you ever dreamed.'

'Oh, you've backed a winner, of that I am certain,' she called out, ambling over to my dressing table to tidy the cosmetics and jewellery left out yesterday, while putting aside what she intended to use today. He certainly protected me in thought, word and deed, and he made me feel safe. When I was with him, I held no fear of any man, and was confident I would never be in the position to be attacked again by anyone, including Maslow, the thought of him causing me to shudder. Hamish's love for my children had always been strong; however, he had drawn closer to both of them now he was about to become their step-father. He had taken on the role with great enthusiasm, thought and care, ensuring Thomas and Emmy felt part of everything, not wishing them to feel excluded, or form the opinion he was only interested in me. He spent an enormous amount of time with them—when they would fit him into their busy social calendar.

'Leo is preparing a special breakfast for you that should arrive shortly. Don't get up yet. You have hours before you must get ready.' She yawned, appearing tired as I motioned for her to sit beside me while I fluffed my pillows, relaxing back on them to take our morning gossip.

Hamish had spent months supporting Danny, spending time with him at night at the pub, or visiting with him at his terrace. Poor, lovely, kind Danny had started to see that even though the child was not of his blood, this could be his only opportunity to have the family with Bessie he had always longed for. It eased him knowing Jimmy would never have contact with the bairn, allowing him to raise the child from the beginning as his own. He still loved Bessie deeply, and was trying his utmost to forgive her for straying, and although he was softening day by day, he still found the situation too much to bear at times. He had asked her to return to him only last week to see if they could be a family, and she had delightedly agreed, moving back into the terrace that very same day.

Carrying a child this late in life had taken its toll the closer she came to her time, although she refused to admit it to anyone, least of all herself. She refused to stop working despite being overdue, frustrating me no end. Insisting she only come in the mornings for an hour or two to complete the tasks she felt could not wait—or be conducted by another—there was not a day I was not forced to order her home to her terrace to rest and put her feet up. Our doctor had told her walking could help bring the child on, and she had used this against me every day since in an attempt to justify her presence. Most days, I could call on Hamish to help me dress and undress given the clothes I wore at home were plain; however, Bessie was far more efficient and helpful when it came to my wardrobe. Emmy struggled to sit up beside me, her eyes heavy as she blinked several times before staring up at me, yawning wide without even attempting to cover her mouth.

'Do you really still love me, Mama?' she murmured, while Bessie went to the door to collect a small tray from Erin holding a pot of coffee for me, and a pot of tea for Bessie.

'Of course I do. More than anything. I meant everything I said this morning.' I leaned down and kissed her nose, and a slight smile touched her lips.

'Do you promise to not tell? Not even your best friends. I don't mind if you tell Da while you are away, only so he has time to adjust. Would you do that for me, Mummy?' She snuggled into my side, while I held back tears threatening to spill down my face.

'Yes, Emmy, I will.' Swallowing hard several times, my arms tightened around her slender body. 'I know for certain it will change nothing between you. I give my solemn oath to keep your confidence. It is your own private business, and it's up to you who you want to share that with. I would never betray you, baby.' I swallowed hard again, my throat tight, and she smiled, brighter this time.

'It's comforting to know I can trust you, no matter what the subject, Mama. The other girls I know keep so many secrets from their mothers, and never talk to them about anything worthwhile. You will always be my best friend.'

'And you will always be mine.' Pride welled in me as I gazed down at her, so very brave to tell me her darkest secret, risking rejection as so many like our dear Leo had suffered, disowned by those they loved and forced to leave and create a new life as far away from the old as possible.

A knock sounded at the door before several young maids from neighbouring properties here to help for the day came scurrying in, all carrying trays while greeting me cheerfully. Bessie met them in the centre of the room, quickly ordering them to place the trays on our laps, first mine, then Emmy's, while a tray holding a pot of coffee and two carafes of juice was placed on the sideboard. Seeing them out, Bessie waddled into my dressing room to organise my clothes for the honeymoon, singing an Irish love song to herself. I had heard on the passionfruit vine Hamish had given her strict instructions on what he wanted packed, and she was determined to please him, no doubt to my own detriment.

'Thomas and I are going to walk you up the aisle and hand you to Da, then we will stand beside you both,' Emmy remarked for the hundredth time in the past week, her sweet face beaming up at me as we sat side-by-side eating our breakfast companionably. Relieved how happy the twins appeared to be since the announcement of our betrothal, I could not have gone through with the marriage if they were unhappy in any way. I had been worried they would forget their father, but my concerns soon evaporated when they continued to visit Aaron's grave to talk and sit by him, along with their brothers they never had the opportunity to meet or grow alongside. Often they would go without me, although, sometimes I would find one of them walking alongside me in the garden wanting to tag along. Hamish would often visit Aaron alone, and on the very rare occasion with me; however, preferred to allow me the privacy to grieve alone with my memories, and it seemed he wanted to do the same.

Emmy kissed me before swinging her legs out of the bed and rising to her feet to dress and visit with friends in the village before she had to return and ready for the wedding. I lay back on my pillows, listening as her footsteps faded down the hall, thinking a thousand thoughts. I could always spend some time with Maggie, who had arrived yesterday to stay for the wedding, along with Lilith, She and Jasper, along with their two boys, had come to stay at Willow Grove as our guests shortly after we returned from New York in March, and would remain with us until they found the property they were seeking. I glanced at the clock on the mantle, aware they would have already taken their breakfast in the dining room with our friends and family members as a direct result of Leo's strict timekeeping, all staying here as guests over the weekend. Bessie strolled out of my dressing room, her face shining and unable to hide the happiness she felt, whether over her reconciliation with Danny, or the upcoming wedding, I was uncertain.

'I know you aren't *in* love with Hamish, but I truly believe that will follow in time. How could it not when he treats you the way he does? Without him, the children would have been without a father, but he has tried his best to be that and more, and well before you let him into your bed. Now is the time to let him into your heart. It doesn't mean you must stop loving Aaron, as in my mind, that will never change, but your heart is bigger than you realise. There is just as much room in there for Hamish as there is for Aaron.' She pointed to my chest before offering me her hand, helping me out of bed and onto my feet. I knew she was right; however, I couldn't change how I felt. I was unable to force myself to fall in love with Hamish as I was when I married the first time, but I truly believed I would love him in my own way and be just as good a wife as I had been to Aaron.

Helping me into a simple house dress before shuffling back into my dressing room, she bid me farewell before resuming her song. I worried everyday she would give birth while going about her duties, but she was a stubborn woman and refused to listen to anything I had to say.

My hair tied up in rags, I had been threatened with death if I touched them before I was ready to put on my gown this afternoon, and Bessie frightened me more than usual at the moment. I made my way downstairs barefoot, as was my regular habit when inside the house, and often around the property when I could get away with it. I could not see the need for shoes when not out and about in public, only ever wearing them these days when I was forced to travel into town for business or pleasure, or to visit with a friend outside of the boundaries of Willow Grove. Strolling through the wide hallways, down the elaborate staircase and towards the sitting room, I found Irene and Maggie relaxing comfortably side-by-side on the lounge closest to the fireplace, chatting animatedly until they noticed me standing in the doorway.

'Good morning, bride to be,' Irene called out as I smiled, crossing the room to embrace them.

'Are you nervous, dear friend?' Maggie asked, her eyes twinkling, her smile infectious.

'A little, only because I feel so very self-conscious when people stare at me, but as for marrying Hamish, I have no doubt this is the right thing to do for everyone's sake.' I made myself comfortable opposite them, soon leaning forward to pick up the silver pot of freshly brewed coffee placed on the low table between us by Mr Masters, before taking a clean cup for myself, topping up theirs, then filling my own.

'Lord have mercy on us all, Abigail. Could you be any more romantic?' Irene remarked, rolling her eyes sarcastically, while Maggie giggled to herself.

'You could at least say you're marrying him because you like the poor man. And from what you have told us, he is quite competent in the bedchamber.' Maggie arched her eyebrows wickedly, a smirk on her lips. 'Who wouldn't be thrilled to honour and obey that man? The body of a highland warrior, and blessed with the face of an angel, any woman would think themselves the luckiest on this earth taking him to their bed? Oh, the things I would do to him. Well, if I told you, it would burn your ears right off, and you would never receive my visits again. You are such a fortunate woman.' Maggie threw back her head and laughed aloud, while Irene giggled, her eyes fixed on mine.

'To think of the night we met and our voyage to London, we all believed him to be your brother-in-law. I must say here and now, even back then I was suspicious there was something more between you. The way he would look at you at times when he thought no one was paying attention, and how obviously he despised Lord Harrington caused me to wonder. Now it all makes sense,' Irene remarked thoughtfully, moving a cushion from behind her back so she could lay down.

'I am nervous about tonight. I am trying to select what I will wear to bed, and I am uncertain if he will think me a whore. Aaron couldn't have cared less what I slept in.' My cheeks started warm, and I shook my head, dismissing the conversation while wishing I said nought about it.

'What is it?' Irene asked, while Maggie nodded eagerly, leaning forward in her seat, while I sighed deeply, unable to find the words.

'It's probably best I show you, rather than try to explain.' I drained my cup before rising to my feet, while they did the same, accompanying me up to my bedchamber. Locking the door after they followed me inside, they ran to my bed, throwing themselves down heavily to wait while I crossed the room to my wardrobe. Picking up a silk bag filled to the very top with lingerie and negligees made by Lady Duff-Gordon and dear Catherine, I returned to my friends. Upending the bag onto the bed, their eyes went wide.

'I wanted to wear one of these for him tonight, but I am in two minds about it.' I held up a short chemise and the matching frilly bloomers reminiscent of what the Parisienne Can-Can dancers had been wearing for decades. Their eyes widened as they touched the soft lace trimming the silk, Maggie picking up each item individually and examining them closely, while Irene held a black negligee up against her petite frame, admiring it from where she sat in the cheval mirror in the corner of the room.

'I've never seen anything like them. This thing here I imagine is meant to hold your breasts up somehow with the small straps that go around you. It's so small compared to a corset, and I cannot imagine this provides the same support.' Maggie picked up the matching bloomers, shaking them in the air. 'You may as well be naked. They leave nothing to the imagination, and that can only be good on your wedding night. Where did you get these, Abigail?'

'From Lady Duff-Gordon. They are her own creation, and she warned me I would find them nowhere else, which I have discovered to be true. Not like what she creates, anyway. Catherine's been making similar items for years in secret.' They nodded, appearing impressed as they continued to study each item. 'I've been worrying myself sick Hamish will think me a nymphomaniac if I were to wear any of these. He has only seen me in simple nightgowns that cover me well.'

'Any man who is lucky enough to see you in any of these will lose his head, and all control, and will be unable to stop himself ravishing you,' Irene reassured me, while folding each one carefully and laying them on the bed.

'Choose one you like and go put it on so we can see it and give you our honest opinion,' Maggie suggested, a sapphire blue brassiere and bloomers catching her eye. I picked up a white silk negligee that Catherine had made, the thin lace straps delicate, the fabric soft. Returning to my dressing room, I slipped out of my dress, pulling the negligee over my head before reluctantly making my way back to stand at the end of the bed, feeling embarrassed exposing myself, even to my friends, let alone Hamish. 'Oh, it's lovely, and very sweet, but also seductive and slightly wicked. Now, tell us immediately how to contact Lady Duff-Gordon to order these for ourselves. They are truly beautiful.'

'Catherine made this one, and several others here.' I ran my hand over them, all laid out on the heavy quilt, while pointing out which was which.

'Does she sell them, or make them only for you?' Irene asked, her eyes lighting up.

'She does take special orders from time to time if asked. They are not cheap, but are of the highest quality and so very comfortable to sleep in. You don't wake up tangled in yards of fabric like the old nightgowns.' Aware cost was the last thing either would consider, I returned to my dressing room to change back into my house dress, Maggie following me in to assist.

'You have nothing to be nervous about, Abigail. I would even try to lure you into my bed dressed like that.' Her musical laughter filled the room, her teasing lighthearted as we returned to Irene.

'I'm thinking of ordering a few to put the lead back into Ron's pencil. Not that it's gone blunt, but it does need a little sharpening,' Irene called out, making me smile. Since she had been spending more time with me since moving in with her family, along with many of my friends, she had started to open up more, appearing far more interested in joining our bawdy conversations than when we first met, and I wondered to myself if her lovely husband Ron was benefiting from any of it, my smile widening. I threw myself down on the bed in between them, both moving quickly to each side to prevent me landing on them.

'Do you know yet where he is taking you on your honeymoon?' Maggie inquired, her eyes sparkling as she gazed up at the ceiling, slipping her hand into mine.

'I have not a clue, other than I do not need to take an extensive wardrobe. I like that he likes to surprise me.' We spoke of the wedding, and gossiped for a time before I struggled to my feet, packing up the garments from the bed to put them away. As I crossed the room, there was a knock on the door, and I jumped, startled before hurrying to answer given I had locked the door.

'Ahh, just the person I was about to go looking for,' I exclaimed, opening the door wide before Lilith pranced into the room, throwing herself down on the bed where I had just been. Placing the bag on my dressing table, I returned to my friends, lowering myself down onto the side of the bed.

'How are you this fine morning, Goddesses?' They smiled at her, both quickly becoming accustomed to Lilith's eccentricities and her views on the world, despite having met no other like her. I adored having her stay, and would miss her very much once they left, aware how selfish I was for wanting to keep them all here instead of feeling the excitement I should at seeing them so very happy once they found their new home.

'I am more than looking forward to the ceremony, although I did want to bed the man myself the moment I first laid eyes on him.' She paused, her face thoughtful. 'As did every woman onboard, single, married, and undecided, I will remind you all before you think *me* the trollop.' Maggie sighed, while we all collapsed into loud laughter. She openly admitted to still having a small crush on Hamish for the simple reason she thought him the most handsome man she had ever seen, and I didn't mind, teasing him often, much to his chagrin. Lilith sat up, reaching across for my hand.

'I came to find you as I need to speak with you in private, and it is fairly important, dear Abigail.' Irene and Maggie rose to their feet before politely excusing themselves, leaving Lilith and I to our privacy, the door clicking shut behind them. She pulled out a small bottle of polish from her pocket and set about painting my toenails while we talked. 'Aaron came to visit with me this morning just as I was waking. I cannot *see* those who have passed; however, I can hear them as clearly as I do you when they decide to come to me. He must have been on my mind to draw him to me in this way because of the wedding today. Often I've sensed him around you, but he has never spoken to me since that one time shortly after he died, and long before we ever met.' My eyes widened, my heart pounding, while uncertainty overwhelmed me.

'You can have a proper conversation between you? How do you know for certain it is him and not in your mind when you cannot even see him?' I shook my head in disbelief, my gaze fixed on the magnificent golden glow surrounding her petite frame, her exquisite lilac eyes sparkling, a rare beauty not often found in many women.

'Oh, Abigail. Ye of little faith.' She laughed to herself, pulling my other foot down onto her lap to paint my nails to match the other, the soft lilac polish now drying as I hung my leg over the side of the bed. 'I know it's Aaron because he introduced himself, and a lovely and polite man he is, I must say. Only you will know whether to believe it is him or not by what I tell you.' My throat tightened, and I swallowed several times before reaching for a glass of water on my side table and taking a deep drink.

'Stop dragging this out and keeping me in suspense, Lilith. What kind of friend are you?' She giggled to herself while dipping the tiny brush in and out of the paint before expertly placing it on my big toe, her strokes quick and clean.

'One of your best friends, Mistress Abigail, and a good one to have on your side. Far more than you realise.' She paused, and I groaned, urging her to hurry herself along. 'Aaron told me to tell you that everything makes sense to him now. The auras you see, all that you have been told about past lives and how souls are connected, and a place called Hiriarni, which I have never heard of. He says it is all true, and you would know what that means. You are apparently what's called an evolved soul who is able to keep your memory from lifetime to lifetime, of which you have had many. He tells me you haven't spent a great deal of time in between your lives at Hiriarni, a planet he assures me is not unlike this, but without all the problems that go with life here on earth. It sounds absolutely fascinating, Abigail; however, when I went to question him more, he changed the subject.' She pouted at me, and I smothered a smile. 'From what he told me; you chose to wipe your memory of every lifetime prior to this at the very beginning of this life cycle for reasons he was not allowed to reveal. You are one of the few souls able to recognise those you have shared a previous life with by the auras that surround their body, only you are unable to remember who they were to you. Those you see with a grey aura are not evil; however, they were known to you in a past life and have come back to cause mischief in this one, while those with a black aura have also been a part of a previous life, though, they are dangerous and have come back to do you harm for whatever reason. For some of them, it is because they felt wronged by you and have developed an obsession to seek their own vengeance. Aaron refused to reveal where evil souls go when they pass over, only saying that is *not* where he is.' She shrugged her shoulders, clearly uncertain what he meant. 'Those with the golden glow are very much loved and dear to you, as you are to them. Their soul is connected to your own by an unbreakable thread pulling many of you back together, while most reincarnate back into another life cycle for the sole purpose of being alongside those in their soul group.' She exhaled loudly before tightening the lid of the polish and slipping it back into her pocket, my feet now placed carefully at the end of the bed on a pillow to dry as she lay down beside me. 'The connection to each other we have in life does not disappear in death. Love is what draws them all back together in the next life cycle, if they choose to return to complete another. Those that you love without any visible aura are new souls to you, who may or may not have crossed your path in another life, but you had no connection to them emotionally; or they are brand new souls. He wanted you to know he is safe, and loves you just as much as he always has. He wanted you to know that you take the love with you. Where he is, there is nothing but pure peace and joy. The only sadness he feels is when he is pulled back to earth by your grief, and it has prevented him doing the things he is meant to do where he is now. He told me every soul has a choice to remain at Hiriarni or return to right any wrongs, or tie up any loose ends. Aaron has no plans to return here, as he lived a full and rewarding life and is happy with the legacy he left here, but he is waiting for you. He cannot tell you all the things he would like due to the fact you have no memory of past events, and he is bound by certain rules where he is. Is any of this making sense to you, Abigail, because it certainly isn't to me?' She picked up a New Idea magazine, wiggling down to the end of the bed to fan my toes dry.

'Frighteningly enough, it makes some sense to me.' Knots clenched in my stomach, my hands trembling as I thought of Maslow and all his ramblings, all too similar to ignore. I closed my eyes, confiding the awful details of Maslow's attack on me, and more importantly, everything he had said, including what he had told Aaron when he had assaulted him seven-months later. She remained silent, listening intently while nodding thoughtfully at times, her eyes glistening with tears she quickly brushed away. Given the gift Lilith possessed, I was able to speak freely without fear. She believed in the afterlife, and that souls could contact the living, and I did not know another who did, leaving no one else I could speak of this to without them thinking me mad, and soon after shipping me off to the Ararat Asylum.

'Well, at least you understand. There were several other messages, so be patient with me.' She put the magazine down before returning to my side, closing her eyes as she recalled what had passed between them. 'Aaron has been around you a great deal since he passed, and has watched you grieve deeply, causing him to shed many tears, while feeling such sorrow that he was unable to comfort you. He has been told you have the ability to see souls who have passed; however, your grief has prevented him showing himself to you. You have many gifts that haven't been revealed to you as yet given you started this life with a clean slate, so to speak. You must relearn everything you once knew, and that is not easy to do.' She exhaled deeply, her eyes still closed tight. 'He wants you to open your heart to Hamish and give everything to him. This is not the first lifetime where you have loved two men equally, or been forced to divide your heart down the middle. He tells me it's common to have more than one major love in the spirit world. Only you can resolve the guilt this brings you, and is one of the reasons you chose to come back and live yet another life cycle. You thought it would be different this time, and it can be once you choose to accept your circumstances and allow your heart to love without guilt or regret.' She opened her eyes and turned to me, gazing into mine. 'He wants Thomas to know he is always with him; however, there are things in life he must learn for himself. He will stumble and fall, but Aaron will always be by his side to pick him up and carry him where he needs to go. Most important is he wants Emmy to know he loves her exactly as she is. She will not be alone, and will find love on her own terms.' She sighed, turning away to stare up at the ceiling rose. 'It is all meant to be, the past, present and future. That was the most important message he asked me to tell you. Thomas and Emmy will live the lives they are meant to lead; therefore, you have no need to fret or worry as everything eventually falls in place just where it was meant to be all along. Tell his children he is proud of them, and loves them to the moon and back. He is releasing you to love again, knowing the love between you and he will never change. He wants you to have all the happiness in life that you deserve. You came back for a reason. Now you must continue on with your life and complete what you returned to do. Aaron is confident you will find happiness with Hamish; and yes, just as happy as you once were with him.' I rolled my eyes and grunted, while she laughed aloud. 'He warned me you wouldn't believe that part. All I know is he wants you to go with his love,' she murmured, while I wiped the tears from my face with my handkerchief.

I closed my eyes, sighing deeply, aware I would be forced to push this to the back of my mind for now, finding it all too overwhelming to think about. Relieved he was safe, while grateful he was happy, was all I had needed to know. He had shown me the sign he had promised, and in doing so, had taken the burden from me.

'Thank you, Lilith.'

'I hope it has helped in some way to ease you, Abigail. I must admit, I have found the entire experience quite intriguing. Aaron told me I was very dear to him in a past life; however, would again give me no more details than that, the cheeky bastard.' She smiled to herself, and I reached for her hand. What she had spoken of made sense; no matter how unbelievable. I did not believe in reincarnation; therefore, I would now be forced to reconsider.

'You have helped me more than you know, Lilith. I feel at peace, and able to move on with the rest of my life. Aaron will never be far from my thoughts, and he's forever in my heart; however, now I can be the wife to Hamish that he deserves.' She quickly put her hand to her head and slapped her forehead before turning back to me.

'I'm sorry. I forgot one last thing. Aaron wants Hamish to know how much he valued their friendship, and continues to do so, and wants to thank him for loving you as he does, and caring for his family as he would. He will never forget what he has done, which apparently you don't even know half of because he is too humble a man to skite about it. *Thanks, mate,* were his final words before he pulled away from me and left the room.' I felt tears prick my eyes, and I quickly brushed them away, sniffing loudly before she embraced me. 'Well, it wasn't his final word. He did mention he wished the poor man all the luck in the world when it came to managing you and Leonardo when in the same room.' She threw back her head and howled with laughter, while I snorted, raising my eyebrows in amusement, although slightly offended Hamish had his sympathy. One thing I knew for certain, she would never truly know or understand what a difference she had made in my life in so many ways, and I smiled.

After a decadent morning tea in the sitting room with my friends, Bessie had whisked me back upstairs to ready myself. Emmy had returned soon after, chafing at the bit to put on her new gown, her hair still tied up in rags despite her visit to the village. She bathed every night before bed, and washed her hair a few times a week so it was dry by the morning, just as I did since leaving the orphanage. Since she was small, she had always demanded the same products I used in my *toilette*, while little Mary acted more as a ladies maid and less like a nanny as each day passed, although, due to Emmy's age, her position had not formally changed as yet, and she was still considered their Governess until they turned sixteen.

Emmy lowered herself down carefully onto the chair at my dressing table, not used to wearing a restrictive corset, before Bessie set to apply just a touch of makeup on her porcelain skin, her nimble fingers soon untying the rags and letting loose her glorious red hair, the curls falling to her waist. After pinning half of it up, she stood and accompanied Bessie to the dressing room, and I followed to watch as she assisted my daughter into her first grown-up gown, taking my breath away as I looked at her, smiling back at me in the cheval mirror.

'You're the spit of your mother at the same age,' Bessie remarked, wiping a tear from her eye with the back of her hand. The lilac gown fell to the floor, the embroidered bodice covered in handsewn pearls intricate, while matching the shoes I had ordered especially for her months ago. Bessie led her back to the dressing table, pinning fresh flowers into her hair before standing her back up again to inspect her a final time. Satisfied, she nodded to herself before turning to order me to sit at my dressing table, while Emmy wandered over to the window to look out over the garden where our guests were already starting to gather.

'Are your nerves playing up yet?' Untying the rags in my hair, she smiled affectionately at me in the mirror before picking up the silver brush. Allowing my tresses to fall into loose curls skimming my waist, she pinned up the front in a similar fashion to Emmy's before fitting the tiara to the crown of my head securely. Leaving me there for a moment, she picked up the dainty lace veil, bringing it back to carefully attach just behind the tiara before slipping the pearl necklace around my neck and securing the clasp. Emmy clapped her hands as she wandered back to my side, thrilled to see me wearing the gift she had so thoughtfully chosen for my thirtieth birthday.

'I'm far calmer than I expected,' I replied after much thought. 'I was terrified upon waking this morning, and worried I was making the biggest mistake of my life; however, now I'm at peace with my decision.' I paused, wanting with everything in me to confide in Bessie as I did in every situation, but telling her Aaron had spoken to me through Lilith would cause her to sign me into Ararat Asylum herself, of that I was certain. Finishing my makeup, she assisted me to my feet and led me into the dressing room. My gown hung on a hook behind the door, the heavy ivory silk complimented with touches of lilac to match Emmy's dress, while the full skirt required a crinoline, the cage-like structure something I had avoided for years. Once satisfied my undergarments were in place, Bessie slipped the gown over my head, while Emmy ensured my hair was not ruined, before securing the pearl encrusted bodice, a large triangular section flowing from the back of my waist to the end of the train cut out and replaced with the lilac fabric, the long lace sleeves trimmed with touches of the purple hue.

Hamish had hired a photographer for the day, wanting to have pictures to remember the day in years to come, not only in our minds eye, as did I. Already planning to add a portrait of us on the wall in the hallway near the sitting room, where the faces of all I loved hung side-by-side, I had already ordered a frame from Harry. When we first arrived, the strangers staring back at us in most of the hallways had unsettled me, and Mr Masters had kindly relocated a small section from the hallway leading to the sitting room to another wing of the house, advising me when I complained in passing he believed I would feel far more at home if I hung my own portraits and photographs near the room I felt most comfortable, and he had been right, as he usually was in most circumstances.

Hearing the door of my bedchamber open, I stepped out of my dressing room to find Thomas standing by the table, and beckoned him to my side. Carefully kissing my cheek, I smiled up at him, while he narrowed his gaze, his eyes the colour of the ocean on a sunny day.

'All the guests are here, an' Da is gettin' nervous 'cause ya late, Mother.' I glanced at the clock on the mantle, before crossing the room to ensure it had not stopped.

'It is only ten past the hour. I've heard of brides keeping their grooms waiting far longer than a quarter of an hour.' I shook my head in disbelief while checking my gown one last time in the mirror. 'I'm ready now, anyway. You're such an impatient mob.' Emmy came to my side and took my hand, giggling to herself as her brother led us from the room and down the stairs to the front entrance, Bessie following behind before wishing us well and hurrying out ahead of us to join Danny.

'You look like a princess, Mummy. I am so glad you decided to dress as a proper bride. Da will be so very surprised. I bet my right foot he starts to cry when he sees you,' Emmy teased, still giggling as Thomas grinned affectionately at her.

'The poor bloke is as flighty as a cat on a corrugated iron roof. He thinks you've changed ya mind, Ma, so stop ya delayin' an' causin' the man ta worry.' A smirk touched his lips, the image of his father, and I smiled as Emmy took my hand, while Thomas offered me his arm, and I accepted, kissing them both on the cheek before stepping through the grand front door to meet my future husband.

We meandered down the path towards the back garden, chatting quietly between ourselves. Stepping around the corner, our family and friends came into view, all seated in rows on wooden chairs, while Hamish stood next to the minister, unable to stop fidgeting. He caught sight of us, his face relaxing into a smile as we stopped at the end of the long carpet laid out down the makeshift aisle, my bouquet of white roses mixed with lavender trembling slightly.

'Are you ready, Mama?' Emmy whispered, while Thomas gazed down at me, raising his eyebrows inquiringly as music started somewhere in the distance, startling me for a moment as I had not expected a full choral procession down the aisle to the makeshift altar as they did in the church.

'As ready as I will ever be,' I whispered back, our friends and family rising to their feet before turning to stare, their faces lighting up at the sight of us. Stepping onto the carpet, my children escorted me past our guests and towards Hamish, not a dry eye amongst them. Tears glistened in his dark brown eyes as he watched us walk towards him, the sound of Mendelssohn's *Wedding March* filling my ears, while drowning out the songs of the native birds and the sound of the bush, the winter sun warm on my face. Although this tradition was not started by Queen Victoria herself, I still lay all the blame at her feet. Despite German composer Felix Mendelssohn writing the piece for an 1842 production of Shakespeare's *A Midsummer Night's Dream*, it was performed at the wedding of Princess Victoria Adelaide Mary Louise, Queen Victoria's eldest child, for the first time when she married Frederick William IV of Prussia on January 25, 1858, in the Chapel Royal at St. James' Palace. Yet just another tradition left to us to follow to keep up with the fashion, or risk being seen as backward and behind the times. Despite the old Queen passing on January 22 of 1901 at the ripe old age of one and eighty, she was still mourned and treasured by her subjects as the longest reigning English monarch in history, yet I held a deep resentment of her I could not let go of, feeling forced to follow along by those around me, while wishing silently I had met her when she was young and given her a stern talking to regarding keeping her private life behind the walls of her castles.

I gazed up into Hamish's eyes as I stopped a few feet from the altar, and he stepped towards us, Thomas and Emmy handing me over, placing my hand in his before Thomas thumped him on the back, taking his place beside him, while Emmy kissed his cheek before moving to my side. The Minister, a short, rotund man I had only met once and whose name I had already forgotten, came highly recommended by Dana who attended a recent wedding in Geelong that he officiated. Welcoming everyone warmly, he began the ceremony, reading several passages from the bible before bowing his head in prayer. We had asked for a simple service, and had decided to say our vows in our own words, unlike my first wedding where Aaron and I repeated everything we were told like two school children, and looking back I was uncertain if we were capable of any more than that back then, both so young to marry and start a family.

'I promise I will be a loyal an' faithful husband tae ye, an' will show ye every day how much I love an' appreciate ye. I vow tae protect ye with me body, an' shelter ye when ye need comfort. I give ye me word I'll always be a lovin' an' gentle Da tae Thomas an' Emmy, an' will guide 'em through their lives as their father, Aaron, would've done. I love 'em with every part o' me, an' naw different than if they were o' me own blood, an' will continue tae do so fer the rest o' me life. I will stay beside ye 'till the time we must part an' leave this earth, knowin' I've lived every day o' me life happier than the last fer lovin' an' spendin' it with ye. I love ye, Abigail. I always have. I always will.' Several sighs rang out, and I glanced over at the guests, many openly sobbing, Leo's wailing the loudest, before turning back to Hamish, his hands held tight in mine.

'Hamish. I promise to be a kind and caring wife, and will always remain faithful and loyal, and promise to be your shelter whenever you need comfort. Thank you for loving me, and my children without limits. I will always be your best friend and biggest supporter, and will stand by your side until the day we must part, knowing we have had a full and wonderful life together.' A lump lodged in my throat, while tears pricked my eyes as I gazed up into his, a grin lighting his face. He squeezed my hand as the cheerful minister pronounced us man and wife, before picking me up off the ground and kissing me, his lips on mine, while not caring who he offended. The clapping and cheering deafened me, my hands over my ears when he placed me back down on my feet.

'Oh, for the love of all that is unholy. Keep the buttons on your trousers done up, Adonis. No one here needs to bear witness to such obscenity. Would you hurry yourselves up so we can start drinking?' Leo called out to much hilarity and cheerful banter as Hamish and I walked past them arm in arm, Thomas and Emmy following behind. Hurrying up the path towards the house, we left our guests in the garden, the local women we had employed for the afternoon already carrying trays, the crystal flutes filled with champagne we had taken from the cellar, left here by my great-aunt we assumed. Stepping into the grand entrance, I embraced Thomas, then Emmy, as did Hamish.

'We're a proper family now, an' have a father again. Now no one can say nothin' to us, or they risk gettin' a hidin' from our Da,' Thomas remarked, while Hamish threw back his head and howled, his laughter ringing down the empty halls.

'Please don't look sad, Mummy. We will never forget our Daddy, but it's so lovely to be able to say to the others at school that we have a Da who will come foot them up the arse if they annoy us,' Emmy added, her smile bright as I started to laugh.

Thomas pulled out a small box from his pocket, handing it to Emmy to give to Hamish. Unwrapping it to find a thick ring with two tiny pink diamonds embedded into the gold, tears glistened in his eyes.

'You are married to Mummy now and wear her ring on your finger, but you also married us, and we want you to wear this ring from Thomas and me to remind you we love you, and you are our Da,' Emmy said, his large fingers trembling slightly as he took it from the box.

'Och, there is no chance o' me forgettin', an' I'm sure I'll be reminded o' it in the future when I'm called tae defend yer wrong-doin's. Thank ye fer bein' so thoughtful. I'll naw take it off from this day 'till I take me last breath.' He slipped it onto the second finger on his right hand before gathering us in a warm embrace, kissing us one after the other on the forehead. 'Thank ye fer acceptin' me as part o' yer family.' We remained in his embrace for the longest time, grateful for the silence, before pulling away. Straightening our clothing as we stepped outside to return to the garden to enjoy the afternoon with our guests, Emmy and Thomas ran ahead now the formalities were over. We had given them a gift this morning, much to their delight, thanking them for their help today, Emmy receiving her very first pink diamond, the small stone hanging from a delicate chain around her neck, while Thomas wore his gold cufflinks, a small pink diamond set into each. Feeling the tension leave me, a peace and a sense of contentment settled on me for the first time in years, and I knew in that very moment, all would be well in our world. And I was grateful.

We returned to the garden to a crowd of well wishers congratulating us on our union, while a joy radiated from all present, and I sensed they were genuinely happy for us. Dana and Martin had not attended, and she had asked I not invite them, and I had respected her wishes, although I missed her dreadfully, aggrieved I could not share our special day given she had been present for every single celebration, and all the important moments, for fifteen-years.

Hamish stood beside me, his hand planted firmly on my waist, while beckoning a young woman over, the tray she carried full of crystal flutes filled with champagne. Offering us her congratulations, Hamish nodded, talking animatedly with her while passing me a glass, asking her to remember him to her father before taking one for himself and turning back to me. Nellie was notably absent, as Hamish had refused to invite her; however, she was the only one out of all our employees and their families, many whom we considered personal friends, not present. Hamish led me over to a carved wooden bench under the sprawling gumtree, and I laughed aloud, pointing at the skirt of my gown. Making it impossible for me to do anything but stand beside him as he lowered himself down to observe the guests, he chuckled to himself. I watched in admiration as the young women hired from a number of neighbouring farms in the district politely yet efficiently handed around trays filled with hot and cold savouries, all prepared especially to be eaten with fingers rather than knives and forks. Catching the eye of Jane, a lovely woman who had worked for the Bradley family for five-years now, she hurried to my side, offering the tray she carried to Hamish first, then to me. Picking up a lamb cutlet, a small piece of greaseproof paper wrapped around the bone, I bit into the charcoaled crust, the meat tender and sweet, the flavours exploding in my mouth. Jane hurried off to fill a plate for us with a selection of savouries, while I already looked forward to when the bite-sized desserts would be brought out. Ensuring I had already tasted everything that would be served to our guests earlier in the day, I found yet again Sally and Leo had outdone themselves, both working from the wee hours of the morning until late into the evening for the last week in preparation for today, the food they created fit to be served at Buckingham Palace, not only tasting magnificent, but every morsel beautiful to look at.

Mr Makenzie had voiced his concerns a number of times regarding our refusal to hold a lavish event, and was mortified when he learned we had invited our employees, only finding out through one of his kitchen maids who had asked for the day off to work at our reception. For weeks he had tried to persuade us to change our plans, pressuring Hamish to allow him to invite over five-hundred of his friends and business associates, and much to my relief, Hamish had flatly refused, advising his father he was welcome to attend; however, he was also free to stay home as long as his mother was present. Mr Makenzie had left in a rage, and we hadn't seen hide nor hair of him since—until today when they arrived dressed in their finest with Jemima in tow, almost ruining our special day before it began.

'I've never seen ye look as beautiful as ye do tae day, an' I dinnae expect ye tae dress as a bride.' He rose to his feet, gathering me into his arms, his eyes fixed on mine. 'I know ye did that fer me, an' I appreciate ye fer it, lass. I love ye, Abigail. Always have,' he whispered, his warm breath tickling my ear before he placed his lips on mine, and I melted into him, all around me fading into the background as I wrapped my arms around his neck and kissed him back.

The dining hall, decorated in shades of lilac and cream, had been transformed, and I suspected Polly had a hand in it given she was one of the few who had seen my gown. Our guests had been seated while Hamish and I remained outside, Thomas and Emmy impatient to join their friends, both whining at me constantly while waiting to be called, amusing Hamish while irritating me to no end. Sick of their complaining, I sent them inside ahead of us, no longer caring about following any tradition other than sitting myself down to enjoy the evening meal. Amelia came to the door and nodded, smiling at me before hurrying back to her seat, while Hamish took me by the hand

and led me inside, pausing in the doorway. Cheering, clapping and whistling filled the hall, piercing my ears as I took a half-step back.

'I'm here with ye, lass. Yer hand is tremblin'. I know ye dinnae like people starin' at ye, but all ye have tae do is walk beside me. Once we sit down, they'll all be far tae busy eatin' an' gossipin' about yer dress, an' all the things wrong with the weddin',' he whispered, and I smiled. Standing up on my toes, I kissed him gently on the mouth before he tightened his grip on my hand.

Making our way across the room to the front table where Thomas and Emmy waited, our guests continued clapping, some more restrained than others, while I lowered myself onto the chair next to Emmy, relief washing over me as Hamish sat down beside me.

'Are you well, Mama? You've gone pale,' Emmy whispered, reaching for my hand under the table. I smiled, my heart now slowing, my hands still.

'I'm perfectly fine now I am sitting with my family. There is nowhere in the world I would rather be.' Her face lit up, and she nodded, reaching out for a bread roll placed in a basket on our table, still warm from the oven, the butter churned from the milkings only this morning. I watched as she expertly broke the roll apart with her hands, spreading both sides thick with butter, before lifting half to her mouth and taking a large bite, crumbs sprinkling down over her dress, her eyes fixed on our guests drinking a selection of wine, beer and whisky placed on the long tables, many already taking their fill before the evening had even started. There was no denying my children were food orientated from the time they woke at daybreak until the time they lay their head in the evening, although, there had been many a time over the years they had woken in the middle of the night complaining their bellies were rumbling. It had become our usual habit to leave a plate of fruit and a selection of nuts from our own orchards on their side table when we tucked them in for the night. I was unable to cope with the thought my children went hungry no matter what time of the day; however, we were more concerned they would wake the entire household with their wailing, prompting little Mary to rise from her bed, often waking the kitchen staff to prepare a meal if that was what it took to make Emmy and Thomas happy. Aaron and I had never allowed it, despite their demands and tantrums when they were younger, and far naughtier, thinking themselves the children of the King and Queen of Willow Grove, a belief drummed into them by their Uncle Leo, who constantly encouraged their bad behaviour when they were far too small to know any better.

'How are you this evening, Mistress?' I looked up and smiled, while Jane placed the first course of four in front of me, a thick ham and pea soup, before setting down another basket of warm bread rolls and swiftly placing the empty basket on her tray, not waiting for my reply. Several others served Hamish and the children, hurrying off soon after, while Jane returned to stand in front of me, her eyes sparkling. 'And congratulations again. There is not a soul living or working at the Morgan property that isn't thrilled for you.'

'It was so very kind of Henry and Alice to allow so many of their staff the time off to help here today. I sent them a box of Leo's peppermint chocolates only yesterday to thank them for their generosity. They are here somewhere.' I glanced around the room while she nodded, her hand on her hip as she shifted comfortably from foot to foot, lingering to talk for a time. Jane was only one of the twenty women hired for today, and they had everything in hand.

'They feel indebted to you after what you've done for their grandchildren, as do Mr and Mrs Bradley.' She paused, waving discreetly at her employer's daughter, Regina, and son-in-law, George, sitting with our mutual friends at the end of a table nearby, their four growing children on the other side of the hall with their own mates, not only from their school here at Willow Grove, but several from neighbouring properties who attended school in Geelong, all the young ones here today growing up alongside each other since birth. Sitting quietly together while in deep discussion, they enjoyed the warm bread rolls, all on their second bowl of soup before I had even eaten my first. 'That new school teacher you hired is bloody magnificent, 'scuse me language. Until he came along, they cried before going to school, and they cried when they returned afterwards. They didn't even know what a half-caste was until a year ago when she started tormenting them, and I doubt any of the children raised here did either.' My stomach clenched, and I nodded, the guilt I felt laying heavy on my heart.

'I take full responsibility for what the Bradley children suffered at her hand, given I employed her. There is no excuse for it, but it was only when I took to my bed after Aaron died she showed who she truly was, only I did not see it. I was unable to check in on her or the children as I once did during that very dark time, and it seems she somehow felt she could do and say as she pleased without consequence. I only learned of her cruelty while away, and I'm sorry for it. It was not something I expected from her, as she never spoke that way before in my presence.' She stared down at me, a smirk touching her lips.

'No one knows what you threatened the old biddy with to turn her from a swine into a swan, but whatever that was, it did the job.' I smothered a smile as she giggled to herself. Much to his credit, David had thoughtfully stepped into the role of assistant teacher, and despite some initial tears and tantrums from the far older headmistress, within weeks he had slowly but surely started to win Albertina over. He was a hard man not to like, his wit and intelligence only overshadowed by his generosity and kindness, and his wife, Kate, was cut from the same cloth. In my eyes, he had the patience of a saint, and his tolerance was far higher than my own when it came to dealing with ignorance. 'He's only been giving lessons for near on four-months, and those children have gone from the bottom of the class in their testing to the very top.' I nodded, aware even my own children had benefited enormously under his instruction and often came home talking about how interesting they found the lessons from Mr Unaipon when he spoke of his culture, people, and traditions. We had done our best to raise the children here with an open mind, and expected kindness in their interactions and acceptance of all who crossed their path, no matter what their background; however, it was impossible for any of us to teach them what David could from his own lived experience, and I was grateful to him, aware he and Kate wanted to return to their kin, yet they had made a commitment to stay until we were confident Mrs McGinty would treat the Bradley children no different from the others. Although David and Mrs McGinty were not firm friends, nor did they associate with each other outside of the classroom, a mutual respect now lay between them, and they had both allowed themselves to learn from the other, and were far stronger teachers together than alone, although Albertina would never admit it, even to herself. 'Jarrah can't stop talking about perpetual motion, whatever that means.' She threw back her head and howled with laughter before wishing us well and returning to her work. I smiled at Hamish before picking up my spoon, the thick soup comforting on a chilly winter's evening. We were soon served the second course, then the third, the cutlery scraping on china plates mixed with a hundred different conversations, some serious, while most animated and cheerful. I gazed at Madeline sitting next to Emmy, their voices low, both so deep in discussion they noticed no other, and I wondered. Her family, unable to make the journey from Melbourne due to a family crisis, had asked if we would allow their daughter to stay several days longer than originally planned, and we had agreed without hesitation.

Glancing around the hall, my gaze moving from one table to the next to ensure our guests had all they needed, movement caught my eye. Standing in the doorway, a wide grin on his face, was my Aaron. Appearing as flesh and blood, no different from Hamish beside me, I closed my eyes, shaking my head to clear my mind. The same as the last time I had seen him on parting that final, wretched time at the Melbourne gaol what felt like a lifetime ago, only now he wore his favourite moleskin pants, and his leather hat, the brim still dusty from working out in the paddocks—the clothing I buried him in.

He leaned against the doorframe, his blue eyes, the colour of the ocean on a sunny day, locked with mine. Despite the distance between us, the room filled with people and loud laughter, all was silent, and I could hear him singing our song to himself as if no distance lay between us at all. He gazed across at Thomas, a smile touching his lips, a proud twinkle in his eyes before turning his attention to Emmy, his face further softening with love. He smiled, nodding his head at Hamish before blowing us all a kiss, one after another. I jumped slightly when I heard his voice for the first time since they took him from us, turning to see if he was beside me, despite his colossal frame looming in the entrance, unnoticed by anyone but me.

'Ya have ya sign, Abi, an' ya have all me love an' blessin' regardin' ya marriage. I'm safe, an' I'm around ya often, watchin' the nippers grow an' blossom under yer care.' He paused, while tears stung my eyes. Wanting to run into his arms, I forced myself to remain where I was. 'Enjoy this new start, *mo anamchara*. Ya deserve ta be happy, an' I'll be here waitin' for ya an' the nippers ta join me when ya own time comes, but there is no rush. I love ya all ta the moon an' back.' I lifted my fingers to my lips and kissed them, then opened my hand and blew, tears in my eyes. Aaron raised his hand in the air as if catching it in his fist, bringing it back to his lips before placing his hand flat over his heart. He grinned, his eyes sparkling, before waving one last time and turning to leave, his backside still firm as he casually strolled out without a backward glance.

I leaned back in my chair, staring after him while questioning if I had just seen and heard what felt so very real, or was I truly losing my mind as Leo often suggested to all who would listen. Considering what Lilith had told me earlier, it may have affected me far more than I realised. Aaron had sworn an oath to me that if he could send a sign he was safe, and life did indeed go on after death, he would find a way—and here he was on my wedding day, reassuring me of his love, while giving me his consent and blessing to marry Hamish. Any sadness I felt evaporated the moment I set eyes on him, and hearing his voice again eased me greatly. Knowing he still existed no different than he did in life, a peace settled on me, and I smiled to myself, the tears filling my eyes no longer from grief, but joy now filling my heart, healing me just a little more.

'Are ye well, lass?' Hamish asked, lifting my hand to his lips.

'Yes, Hamish. I'm happier than Leo when left unsupervised in my bedchamber.' He laughed aloud before I leaned closer and placed my mouth on his, no longer caring who noticed, while he kissed me back, Leo now the last person on his mind.

The village pub was filled to capacity, leaving many spilling out onto the verandah and down onto the town square where they sat together in groups, most men drinking beer while they laughed and bantered with their mates. Hamish had spared no expense, stocking the pub with every variety of liquor he could find, much of it thanks to Leo and the constant boxes of nonperishables imported from countries I had never heard of, while others were familiar. Leo had stockpiled ouzo from Greece, tequila from Mexico, whisky from not only Scotland, but Ireland, vodka from Russia, boxes of rum from Jamaica, and beer sent from the Cascade Brewery in Hobart, Tasmania, along with hundreds of bottles of wine he had imported from a vineyard in France over the last year alone—all bought and paid for by me, yet kept in the cellar under the kitchen as if it were his own personal treasure. Initially, he had refused Hamish's request to use some for the wedding, offering to sell it to him by the bottle; however, soon changed his mind when threatened that I would have him charged with theft, and gaining property by deception.

Before finishing up in the dining hall and we had eaten dessert, the women helping had forgotten all about the wedding cake standing ten-tiers high and panicked. Taking up an entire table on its own, the dense chocolate cake, filled with a vanilla custard, was a work of art. Jenny and Margaret, along with four men, had carried the table from the dining hall into the pub where they set it down out of the way in the corner to be cut later for supper. Although one of the largest cakes I had ever seen, I was confident it would all be gone by morning given the number of guests in attendance here to share our special day, many now drunk and impatient to dance, while some were more refined, sipping lemonade as they sat in groups at the tables talking quietly, others around them far louder, and far more cheerful.

'Please, naw whisky tonight, me beautiful wife. I want yer mind clear, so in fifty-years from now when we're sittin' in here havin' a beer, we can look back an' remember every detail of this night. Naw all here tonight will be there tae celebrate with us in 1955.' A lump lodged in my throat as he guided me past the bar, greeting the staff, before leading me towards a long table in the far corner where our friends and family sat together—a hundred conversations going at once—and I couldn't understand one of them.

'I have no need or urge to drink anything tonight, other than a lemonade. I feel so happy I could burst.' He kissed me before I slid into the chair next to Scarlett, while Hamish wandered off to the end of the table to have a drink with his mates. I hadn't mentioned what Lilith had told me today, or that I had seen Aaron. He knew nothing of my gift—or curse—all depending what beliefs another held regarding the matter. I had never once mentioned the golden glow I saw around those I loved, or those with black or grey swirling around them, just like his own sister, Jemima. Nor was he aware of my ability to predict the gender of an unborn child, or I had just seen my first husband, who I knew for certain lay beneath the heavy marble stone placed on his grave. I would be forced to tell him at some point, but now was not the time. I certainly did not want to risk him thinking me mad within hours of our marriage, and I worried he may consider signing me into an asylum as he now had the power to do as my husband—some poor souls locked up in there for years for the most minor of infractions without grounds other than the word of a father, brother or husband—or a man of the cloth if the woman had no kin.

'You look radiant Abigail. I have never seen Hamish so happy, and I have known him a long time,' Scarlett remarked, her hand on mine.

'You are a fortunate woman, sister. Not many get the opportunity to be with one gorgeous man in their lifetime, let alone two,' Victoria said, glancing over at Hamish at the end of the table, Angus beside him speaking quietly.

'He is handsome, isn't he? He has a way about him. A dark broodiness quite unique to him alone, yet when he is with you, Abigail, he just lights up an electric lamp,' Adele said, squeezing my hand before taking another close look at my engagement and wedding bands.

'We are all so very thrilled for you and the children, but also for Hamish. It is a joy to see you all so much in love with each other. We couldn't have asked for a better man to take care of you and the twins, and are truly happy for you all. Now, of course, we do not have to fret that Duke will race you off over the water to make you the queen of his castles,' Scarlett teased, and I smiled.

Although I had sent word to Reg, informing him of my betrothal to Hamish, he had already left England bound for Australia. I had received a letter only days after I had sent mine, telling me how much he looked forward to spending time with me again. He had arrived at the beginning of May, expecting to court me, only to discover Hamish and I were to marry on July the 6th, 1905. Although disappointed, he accepted the news far better than anyone expected, and chose to remain as our guest for three-weeks before reluctantly leaving us to return to his business commitments in Melbourne, then Sydney. During that time, he and Hamish had formed a friendship of sorts, and when it came time to part, Reg promised to return to visit with us in the future, now considering us all firm friends.

Watching Brian and Tamara stop to speak with Hamish, I wondered if she still had feelings for him. Confident she loved me and would never disrespect me by flirting with him, she valued our friendship as much as I, of that I was certain. Elizabeth noticed my stare, and moved to the seat beside me, kissing my cheek before leaning close to whisper in my ear so as not to be overheard.

'I've recently discovered Brian is not who I believed him to be, and my sister is just as badly behaved.' She paused for a moment, glancing around the table to find our friends deep in discussion and paying us no mind before continuing, her voice barely audible. 'I suspected they were not entirely faithful to each other, but I was certainly unaware when I stepped into their library last week in search of a novel to distract myself that they share the same lover. A man, Abigail, and the gardener at that. Upon further inquiries, a servant told me in confidence all she has witnessed for over a decade, and I'm sick with it, and cannot get the image of what I saw that day out of my head.' I smothered a smile, taking her hand in mine under the table.

'I know the shock of it well, Lizzy. You cannot unsee what you have seen, and you will never be the same again after witnessing anyone fornicating—man or woman—when brought up as a lady as you have been. I've walked in on Brian during a private moment at the most inappropriate times.' I collapsed into giggles, before telling her what I too had witnessed over the years.

'Abigail, I cannot believe you find this amusing. It is the most terrible thing that has ever happened to me. To see your own brother-in-law engaging in such a sinful act, and with another man—well, I am completely humiliated. My sister's behaviour is just as atrocious, and immoral. She has slept with every male servant in her household. Were you aware?' I feigned horror, while her cheeks burned red, clearly mortified and unable to laugh about the situation—and I doubted very much she ever would.

Hamish came to my side, taking my hand in his and pulling me to my feet.

'I've been ordered by Bessie tae cut the cake an' say a wee speech.' I kissed Elizabeth sympathetically on the cheek before he led me over to where the cake sat on the table in all its glory.

Leo had generously given so much of his time, care and attention, spending two full days baking then decorating each cake, from the largest on the bottom to the smallest on top. Magnificent, with its curls of chocolate decorating each layer, the crème pâtissière inside topped with raspberry jam, the dark ganache expertly covering every tier.

A hush fell over the room as our guests watched us slice through the bottom cake, our hands entwined on the large knife, while loud clapping and cheering filled my ears as Hamish cut two slices. He held mine up, encouraging me to take a bite, while I did the same to uproarious cheers, certain I had chocolate smeared on my face, a smile touching my lips as I reached up to wipe the side of his mouth with my thumb. I jumped as the photographer took a picture, almost blinding me with his hand-held flash.

'We'd like tae thank everyone fer comin' tae celebrate with us tae-day. It has been the best day o' me life. I truly have me own family now, who I'll love an' protect with all I have.' Hamish nodded, pausing for a moment as several clapped, while others refilled their glasses. Leo caught my eye as he rose to his feet and approached the cake. Stopping next to Hamish, he turned back to face the crowded pub, his hand up while inserting himself in between us.

'Oh, settle down. We are well aware how happy you are, no need to go on about it, Adonis.' My eyes went wide, while Hamish's mouth twitched, while memories of the speeches at my first wedding flashed through my mind. 'Now, back to me. That's right. All eyes off Hamish. I lost interest before he even finished his first sentence. Boring! The time has come for the father of the bride to deliver his speech.' I gasped, my eyes darting to the door, then quickly around the room, expecting to see strangers connected to me by blood stride into the room. 'I will be standing in for her father, Lord Christopher Howard, a man not unlike our own Mr Makenzie here.' His arm swept across to where Hamish's parents sat in the far corner, his father's face like stone, while his mother smiled affectionately at Leo, winking discreetly at me, her eyes twinkling in amusement. 'Old Christopher took a liking to a tavern trollop named Mary, had his way with her within a quarter of an hour of meeting, then the adulterer returned to his wife. Poor, dear Abigail was born that following January, and we all know what came after that.' He raised his eyebrows knowingly, several in the pub laughing, while Hamish did nothing, amusement in his eyes as he allowed my prick of a friend to humiliate us yet again. 'Eyes back to me! Quiet over there, fatty, I can hear you talking and I must have silence.' I gasped again, his finger pointing across at Bessie before turning it towards Polly. I placed my palms against my cheeks to cool them as I glared up at Hamish standing on the other side of the biggest moron ever to walk the earth, while he stood in silence doing nothing to prevent our reputation being ruined before my eyes—not to mention the impending bloodshed when my dear ladies maid could get her hands on him without witnesses. 'I want two-hundred and sixty-nine percent of your attention. Eyes back to me.' He sighed deeply, while I summoned all my strength not to strike him dead where he stood. 'Oh, dear. I was unaware how unfortunate looking many of you are from where I'm standing, and full of grog and bad intentions is far from flattering in this light, let me give you the drum. Given most here are spawned from convicts, I expect no less. We have all ended up living in a prison without walls, whether you came here freely or in chains. If you are not yet aware, the redcoats conveniently buggered off in 1868 to find other lands to send their criminals, leaving us to suffer the consequences. I've tried to make the best of it, but are you even aware of what you have done?' He widened his eyes in disbelief, while some listened intently, shaking their head in response, others laughing to themselves. My close friends among them did not appear surprised, many casting sympathetic glances in my direction. 'You have filled this village with miniatures of yourselves, that's what you've done, without thought or care for those of us who wake in terror night after night because of it.' My hands clenched into fists at my side, not only wanting to punch Leo in the throat, but Hamish, chuckling to himself as if he were at the theatre and enjoying a show. And he was. We all were, and not one person had said a word to stop him, not wanting Leo to embarrass them with his smart mouth in front of every soul we knew. 'I will be around later to speak to those involved, and have several suggestions that may be of help in preventing further damage to the innocent living here.' The pub, so quiet you could hear a pin drop, was warmed by the two fires in each hearth, although not the reason my cheeks burned. 'Pay attention, please. Back to me. All here at Willow Grove felt it highly unlikely any sensible man would be interested in taking Abigail as a wife. She cannot cook, chooses not to clean, and forces all who work here to chase along behind her no different from if she was a slave trader, while possessing the foulest temper I have ever had the misfortune witnessing. Good luck, Hamish. You haven't a clue what you have hitched yourself to, and had a far better choice of wagons, carts and carriages than most. I will always be here to support you when...' I brought my open hand down hard on the back of his head, the loud smack ringing out across the room as he stumbled, losing his balance, before falling forward and landing heavily, his face missing the ground by only a bee's dick as he landed on the floor at my feet.

Laughter filled the room as I gathered my skirt and stepped over him without a word, while he lay on the ground holding his head, his shrieks drowned out by the musicians resuming their place on the platform in the corner, many in the room ready to drink more and dance until the sun showed itself, no doubt most suffering for it in the next day or two. Hurrying back to my friends, I left him where he was, cursing under my breath when I saw Hamish bend down to help him to his feet. Carefully lowering myself onto the chair next to Catherine, I waited for her to compose herself, her musical laughter unhelpful given my current mood.

'Oh, Abigail, I have no idea how you put up with him. I've never seen Polly so thrilled as when you smacked him to the ground.' Aware of my fury, her face softened in sympathy, while taking my hand firmly in her own to prevent me striking him again as we watched him go from table to table, telling anyone who would listen he would have me charged and thrown in the cells at Geelong, while maintaining a safe distance between us should I break free of Catherine and come after him. 'I'm beyond thrilled for you, and for my Godchildren. They so adore him.' Tears filled her eyes as she gazed over at Thomas and Emmy standing by his side, all deep in discussion. Colin sat at the other end of the table with the men, while the women sat down the other, a comfortable habit we had formed over the years coming here together every Sunday night. Polly leaned forward and took my other hand in hers, her blue eyes glistening with tears.

'I still cannot believe you and Hamish are married. Not only are we sisters, or pretend orphanage sisters as your dickheaded friend likes to say.' She narrowed her gaze at Leo sitting two tables away, scowling before turning her attention back to me, squeezing my hand before releasing me and settling back comfortably in her chair. 'I will not ruin your day no matter how tempting it is to go over and strangle the wee bastard where he sits.' She sighed before smiling again, her face lighting up. 'You are now legally my sister-in-law. We used to dream about fanciful things when we were bairns, Abi, but never did I expect to be blessed with the life we have been blessed with.' She smiled, her teeth white from the baking soda she insisted on brushing them with once a week, a habit many here could benefit from. I did all I could by providing the very best three-row bristle brushes to all who wanted them, along with toothpaste tasting of peppermint; however, many ignored their teeth until they started to rot and cause them pain. I had read somewhere recently that despite toothpaste being available in various forms dating back to 5000 BC, prior to the 1850s, it was usually powdered. A new toothpaste in a jar called a *Crème Dentifrice* was developed during that time, and by 1873, mass production began. It was only when settled in Geelong for a number of years, Colgate introduced toothpaste in a tube, and we had used them ever since, finding them far more convenient. Yet still many walked around with yellowing teeth, despite all the basic toiletries available to them without cost, much to my chagrin; hover, it was not my place to insist.

Mr Cavanaugh returned to the other end of the table carrying two jugs of beer, his grin wide as he winked at me before sitting back in his seat. I always drew a great deal of comfort from him whenever he was near without a word passing between us. Richard and Jas waved from where they sat holding hands halfway down the table, while Hamish had joined the men and now sipped whisky, my children nowhere to be seen. He noticed my stare, and rose to his feet, placing his unfinished drink back on the table before striding over to my side. Taking my hand, he led me to the dance floor where one of our gardeners, Duncan, played the piano. A lovely man, he had originally been employed at Willow Grove by my great-aunt at the age of ten as a hallboy when she lived in the cottage, starting in 1860 before being promoted as an apprentice gardener at thirteen, leaving in 1866 to explore the world. Born to a Wathaurong woman and an Englishman, he had never met his father, and his mother died from fever. An uncle who lived at Willow Grove took the boy in for a time but was unable to manage him, and from what Duncan had told me directly, my aunt felt sorry for him, agreeing to provide him a trade, while ensuring he was fed and had a safe place to sleep. It was clear how fond he had been of my aunt, yet he refused to say much regarding the past other than the few details he had shared since returning to our employ in 1900, well-travelled and eager to settle back home. Mr Masters stood to the side of him, his voice sweet and low as he sang a ballad, while Hamish gathered me in his arms, his lips on my forehead for only a moment.

'I love ye, me fiery wee wench.' He bent down and placed his lips on mine, the couple dancing around us paying no mind. 'Ye an' Emmy appear tae be sisters all dressed up in yer finery, naw mother an' daughter. The lass looks far older than her years, while you could pass fer twenty.'

'Well, thank you, kind sir. You look dapper in your new suit, and far more handsome than I remember when we parted yesterday. I look forward to seeing you with it off later.' He chuckled, dancing as if we were the only people in the room.

'Stop teasin' me. Now I want tae race ye out o' here before the evenin' has even ended,' he whispered, kissing my earlobe and sending chills down my spine. Thomas and Emmy waved as they got up to dance with their friends, as did Mr and Mrs Cavanaugh. They regarded themselves as the parents of the bride this evening, and had made a point of speaking to every soul in attendance throughout the day and into the evening, while Mr and Mrs Makenzie barely acknowledged each other, his father watching us closely from their table where they sat separate to everyone, Jemima in between then, her current husband nowhere to be seen. I hadn't laid eyes on him since they arrived, and assumed she left him at home to care for the children. She was the only guest who had not congratulated or spoken to us directly, and I wondered for the hundredth time why they had even bothered to come, all but his mother making it clear they would rather be anywhere else but here. The aura still swirled around Jemima as dirty and grey as the day we first met, although now I viewed her in a different light. If I were to believe Lilith, Jemima and I were familiar long before we crossed paths in this life, but something had passed between us for her to feel such hatred towards me, and I, too, had disliked her from the very beginning. Mrs Makenzie caught my eye and smiled, a smile touching my own lips as I gazed back at her. Friends and family soon pulled Hamish and I apart to dance with our guests, Mr Cavanaugh smiling as he gathered me into a warm embrace, while Hamish danced a laughing Mrs Cavanaugh into the crowd alongside us.

'Abigail, you look as beautiful as the day you married me boy, an' it gladdens me heart ta see the sunshine back in ya eyes.' He kissed my forehead gently before I pulled away, my gaze fixed on his.

'I saw Aaron in the dining hall earlier, and he spoke to me. I swear he was as real as you standing here before me.' His eyes widened as he listened to me repeat every word his son had spoken, hoping it would bring him comfort. He danced me around the room, silent while deep in thought; however, I was confident he was one of the few in the world I trusted without question who would not immediately think me mad.

'Ya've brought peace ta a troubled soul, Abigail, an' me heart feels just that wee bit lighter. I can rest me head at night knowin' he goes on as he always did, an' me mind an' body can finally sleep without dreamin' the worst. Not knowin' has been the hardest part, an' I look for him in me dreams, but I can't find him. Ta know he's here lookin' on thrills me, an' now me imagination is runnin' wild.' Patrick politely stepped in, taking me into his arms while Scarlett danced away with Mr Cavanaugh.

By the time it came for Hamish and I to leave, I had danced with every male in the room, while he had saved the last dance for his mother, tears running down her face the entire time he held her, his chin resting on the top of her head. Picking me up in his broad arms, we called out our farewells to much cheering and good wishes before he stepped out onto the verandah, the door closing behind us. Holding me close to his chest, he walked down the street, passing the empty general store, the terraces lining the street dark apart from a lonely lamp burning in a window up ahead. The music and laughter faded behind us as the sound of the bush touched my ears ever so gently, bringing comfort and always reminding me of home.

'You can put me down. I did not even have a shandy.' I laughed, my arms wrapped tightly around his neck as he continued on as if I weighed nothing at all.

'Aye. If I want tae carry me wife home, drunk or naw, then I will.' A door opened ahead of us, and a woman stumbled out into the garden, her dark silhouette moving forward to the street.

'And here you are with that slovenly bitch who lured you into her fancy bedchamber in secret. Behind my back. She cast a spell on you, Hamish. I've heard the rumours about her and that witch, Lilith Arcadia. You don't know what you've gotten yourself into taking a whore like her to your bed. She has so many sniffing 'round her, it won't take long for her to lift her skirts for the next bloke who takes her fancy and you'll be out on the street on your arse before you can even grab your clothing,' she snarled, and I jumped, frightened as Hamish quickened his pace. I wondered how she even knew Lilith's name, let alone anything about her, true or not.

'Yer oot yer nut—mad wae it, ye drunken fool. Quiet yerself, an' get tae yer bed or I'll sack ye meself, ye foul mouthed troll,' he called out over his shoulder, while she screamed filthy words, her hand on the front fence to steady herself. Taking long strides up the hill, he appeared keen to put some distance between us and Nellie, his body tense, his face like thunder.

'Don't let her spoil a perfect day, Hamish. Let's just forget that even happened,' I suggested, his face softening in the moonlight, his shoulder relaxing slightly.

'Aye, yer right. I dinnae want tae waste another thought on the doolally. Me mind is with ye, where it will always be.' I placed my cheek against his neck, feeling not another soul existed, or ever had, other than us.

He stopped outside the stable, stooping for a moment to place me down on my feet, several lamps lighting the small stable yard. Pushing the heavy wooden door open, I remained where I was, my eyebrows raised as he turned back when realising I hadn't followed.

'The laundry maids are going to murder me in my sleep with their own hands when they see the state of this gown, and if they were to hear I was frollicking in the stables in the wee hours of the morning, well, they are likely to cut it up and use it for rags. I will go on to the main house and ready myself for bed while you attend to whatever you need to attend to.' I stepped towards the open door to embrace him; however, he threw back his head and howled with laughter.

'Och, ye dinnae think I'm takin' ye back tae our bedchamber fer our weddin' night?' He gathered me in his arms, still chuckling, before kissing the top of my head, my feet dangling off the ground.

'Well, I actually hadn't thought about it. But yes. I did assume that's where we were going until we departed on the honeymoon.'

'Aye, our honeymoon.' He gazed up at the low hanging moon casting silver shadows over the property, the dim lamps burning at the side of each door flickering gold. 'Did ye know the *honeymoon* dates back tae the fifth century when time was measured in moon cycles? Only it was naw called that then.' I nodded, aware of the custom of upper class couples partaking in what I had come to know as a *bridal tour*. A popular tradition since the early 1800s in England, the newly married couple were often accompanied by family and friends for a month after the wedding, travelling around the countryside visiting relatives who had been unable to attend. The practice soon spread to the European continent, catching on in France from the 1820s, and soon becoming known as a *voyagé à la façon anglaise*.

'I did read somewhere the word itself is derived from the Scandinavian tradition of drinking fermented honey during the first thirty-days of marriage. To increase the likelihood of the woman falling.' He held me close to his chest, my cheek on his as he stared out over the manicured back garden, an owl hooting in the distance.

'Aye. We call it mead back home.' He gazed up into the sky, finding the Southern Cross within moments. 'They believed it tae be a powerful aphrodisiac, an' the couple were given a moon worth o' mead an' expected tae drink only that for the month tae encourage sexual intimacy between 'em.'

'They'd be pissed as a parrot, and what's a moon's worth?'

'A month going by the cycles.' He placed me back down on my feet; however, did not release me from his embrace, his broad back resting comfortably against the door. I turned to look up at the sky, his arms around my waist, his chin resting on the top of my head. 'If ye go further back, the custom comes from a violent act.' I turned my head to stare up at him, a smirk touching his lips. 'I meself was tempted tae consider *marriage by capture*, as it was once known.' He threw back his head and laughed while my mouth twitched, the gentle breeze rustling the leaves of the shea-oaks dotted throughout the garden. 'Many before me not only considered it, they carried it out, kidnappin' the poor lass an' keepin' her in a secret location 'till her kin stopped lookin' fer her, or she was with child. Either way, she's ruined an' forced tae stay. An' then there's the dowry, often the reason behind them takin' 'em in the first place, an' somethin' I've managed tae avoid payin' without committin' a criminal act.' He laughed again, a possum startling me as it ran along the post and rail fence a few yards away.

'I heard the term was used in the 1500s to warn newlyweds about waning love. You know? *The moon will wane, and so will your affection.* How very terrible to place that burden on a young couple before they've even started.' He continued laughing, straightening up before taking my hand and leading me inside, the door closing behind us as the smell of sweet hay and manure filled my nostrils, the sound of horses stirring as we strolled down the paved walkway between the stalls to the workroom.

He entered a stall while I waited near the bench, returning several minutes later with a magnificent stallion he and Harry had been breaking in, the young beast, Samson, already bought and paid for before he was even born. Following him out, he kissed me before lifting me up, taking care to rearrange my skirt, his large frame swinging up behind me in one elegant motion, while I gathered my long train in my hand to save it from further dirt and damage. Turning Samson towards the house, we moved forward, ambling down the path and through the garden, soon passing Polly and Angus's cottage. Relaxing back into him, his hand around my waist, I gazed out into the darkness, Samson's pace slow and steady, almost lulling me into sleep.

'I had the staff bring our things tae the cottage where we'll stay fer the next two nights.' I could hear the smile in his voice before he clicked his tongue, the heels of his boots gently urging Samson into a canter, my gown streaming out behind us, the sound of hooves pounding onto the earth to the rhythm of my own heart.

Pulling our mount up to a walk, Samson wound his way through the thick scrub, soon stepping into the clearing next to the river, our cottage lit with lamps in every window. Lifting me down by the waist, he placed me on the ground only long enough to tend to the stallion, letting him loose to roam the small plot before carrying me to the front door, stepping over the threshold, and striding into the bedchamber.

He helped me out of my dress, the process long and painstaking, before carefully placing it on the chair to be taken back to the laundry house, while I stood in my shift, relieved to be rid of the corset and restrictive garments I had been forced to spend the day in. I was not confident the maids would get the stains from the hem and train, but if anyone could save the gown from ruin, it was them. Taking off my veil and tiara, he gently removed my pearl necklace, leaving them on the dressing table before taking the pins from my hair. I went to stand; however, he placed his large hand on my shoulder, keeping me there while he put his hand in his pocket, taking out the gold locket with my name inscribed before fastening it back around my neck, along with a pink diamond necklace, perfectly matched to my wedding bands.

'Thank you, Hamish. It's beautiful. I have something for you.' He helped me to my feet, gathering me into his arms, his lips on mine. I pulled away to find the gold cufflinks, identical to the ones we had given Thomas. Rummaging around in the carpet bag I had packed with what I needed at hand, my fingers touched the smooth box, and I straightened up, returning to his side.

'Thank ye, me precious lass. I'll keep 'em always, an' wear 'em on every occasion we celebrate fer the next hundred-years.' I laughed aloud, leaving him to wash and change in the bathroom, while I went to my small dressing room where the trunk Maggie had so thoughtfully packed for me sat in the corner. Stepping out of my shift, I slipped on a short, lace negligee Catherine had made, the emerald green silk the finest I had seen. I hesitantly walked back into the room to find him already in bed, his eyes widening slightly at the sight of me. Squirming under his gaze, I hurried to the bed, slipping in beside him under the heavy quilts. 'Where did ye get that?' His voice, deep and low, he slipped his hand around my waist, his fingers caressing the silk.

'Do you like it?'

'Aye. I like it. I've never seen anythin' o' the sort before, though. It covers nought, an' I can see every part o' ye through the lace. The shade o' it makes yer eyes so prominent, yer bewitchin' me. Maybe Nellie was right.' His mouth twitched as he pulled me up to sit on his thighs, his hands slowly running down my back. Bending forward, I kissed his chest, then his stomach before slowly making my way down further. As I took him in my mouth, I heard him gasp, then groan as I set to my task, his groans soon so loud I was grateful no one was within cooee of us to hear. Once his shudder and moans eased, I moved up the bed, kissing him for the longest time, my body prostrate on his. 'I had naw clue what I was missin' out on.' He gently ran his hands down the lace on my back, the lantern in the corner of the room casting gold shadows, while the wood in the hearth burnt brightly. His arms wrapped around me, he kissed me slow and deep. 'Now, I'm goin' tae make love tae ye, but I have one question.' I nodded, gazing up into his eyes. 'Can ye leave the nightgown on?'

Hours later, the moon high, I lay unmoving in his arms, his breathing steady as he slept. Feeling blessed I had married a man I cared for deeply, and who loved me and my children without measure. Seeing Aaron tonight and receiving his blessing, and his wish for happiness for all of us had unburdened me. Peace had been restored to my heart and soul knowing he still loved me, was safe, and waiting for me. As I drifted off into a deep sleep, I dreamed of a ship called *The Sophia*, a mansion—the sign out front declaring the place the *Emerson House*—and Hamish.

Chapter Ten

'IT'S LOVELY, HAMISH. I'VE never been on a boat this small, yet it is as comfortable as any ship I've sailed on. Have you?' We stood in our cosy cabin, the vessel he had chartered equipped with a full staff and luxuries I had not expected. Slipping my arms around his waist, my lips touched his throat before I gazed up at him. The floor swayed under our feet, the sound of the water crashing against the bow as it sailed out of Corio Bay towards a destination still unknown to me.

'Naw. I'm far fonder o' this than the steamships carryin' hundreds o' passengers. 'Tis private an' naw different than a floatin' cottage.' He smiled, reaching out to unbutton my heavy cloak, the winter sun fighting to break through the heavy dark clouds above. Slipping it from my shoulders, he bent down to kiss me. 'I told 'em we're in naw rush tae get there, so we'll spend two nights an' three-days aboard.' He raised his hand to my cheek, gently caressing me with his fingers, his thumb moving up my jaw before pulling away. 'While I go speak with Captain Pearson, ye can put on one o' those negligees, an' I'll soon be back tae see how comfortable the bed is.' He crossed the room to the door in three strides, winking at me before stepping outside and closing the cabin door, while I sat down on the end of the bed for a moment, worried I would fall, the boat rocking quite violently compared to the larger vessels I had travelled on.

I exhaled before carefully standing and making my way over to my trunk, finding the entire experience tedious as I stripped off my house dress. I had refused to wear the corset Bessie had packed, my shift and bloomers the only underwear I found agreeable this morning when Hamish helped me dress. After a great deal of difficulty, and several near falls, I returned to the bed in a white silk negligee as requested, climbing onto the comfortable bed and slipping under the heavy quilt to await my husband's return.

We had spent yesterday at the cottage, exhausted after the wedding the day before. Much to our delight, Emmy and Thomas had come to visit, bringing our lunch and staying with us well into the late afternoon until Leo returned with a box of food, providing us with a beautiful dinner we shared with them and breakfast this morning. Relaxing under the wide verandah on a comfortable lounge, a thick blanket around me while listening to my children and their step-father, the easy manner in which they interacted with each other brought such comfort, I felt a sense of family once again. I missed Aaron desperately, and always would until we were reunited; however, thanks to Hamish, I was now able to shut my pain away more often than not, and grieve when alone.

I was starting to relax, and no longer felt the need to keep my feelings so tightly controlled when it came to love as I had before I agreed to marry, and was far more affectionate and loving towards him than I had been, drawing us closer. He would tell me of things I did not know about him—of how he felt about the way he had lived his life, and the people he had hurt along the way—leaving me feeling terribly sorry for all of it. I wished others could see the sweet, gentle side he showed to me and the children. He hid it well, even from those he considered close, and it made me soften towards him further. I jumped as the door flung open and he hurried inside, closing it behind him before locking it securely.

'Aye. I'm pleased tae see ye take yer vow tae love, honour an' obey seriously.' He grinned as he pulled his woollen jumper off over his head while making his way to my side. I laughed as he tried to remove the rest of his clothes while trying to keep his balance, the rocking now far worse. He soon gave up, throwing himself down next to me to remove his trousers before lifting the quilt to peer down at me. 'I like this one the best.' He pulled the quilt over his enormous frame, his hand settling on my waist, his fingers caressing the soft silk, his feet hanging over the end of the bed.

'You say that about all of them.'

'Aye, I do.' His face lit up in a smile. 'I've ensured we have complete privacy durin' our time aboard, an' arranged with the captain tae meet in the mornin's tae advise o' our requirements fer the day. Naw one person will knock on our door fer three-days.' I snuggled close to his side, my arm across his bare chest.

'Do you really hate the busyness of home?' The last thing I wanted was for him to be unhappy; however, the reality was we had an enormous estate to run, and we needed a great number of staff who were present day and night to do that, the main house and property far beyond the management of a single family alone. I had come to love being surrounded by friends and family, many of our workers I considered to be both after so many years of loyal service.

'Naw, I dinnae hate it at all. It's busy as ye say, always someone wantin' yer or my attention all at once. I want tae spend time with ye uninterrupted fer as long as we can before I have tae share ye again.' He leaned closer, kissing the top of my head. 'Och, I still would've liked Thomas an' wee Emmy tae have come along. They're considerate an' give us our privacy, an' they would've enjoyed where we're goin' while spendin' time as a family.' I tried to smother a smile, failing miserably as I lifted my head to stare at him.

'Thomas and Emmy are perfectly fine where they are. Did you marry me for me or for my children?' I snorted, laughing to myself as a grin touched his lips.

'It's naw my fault I'm used tae havin' 'em around me every day since they first drew breath. Ye need tae remember it will naw be long now an' they'll have their own lives, an' will've forgotten about us. I want tae make sure they have fond memories o' bein' young, an' tae spend as much time as we can as a family before they take flight in tae the world without us.' I collapsed into giggles, while he rolled his eyes, grunting to himself before trying to push me away.

'Hamish, I've heard Leo tell you to your face that honeymoons are just an excuse for rooting every spare minute of the day and night. I cannot imagine the twins would have had any fun sitting around waiting for us to come out of the bedchamber, which is where I plan to spend a lot of my time with you.' He relaxed as I moved up to kiss his lips before laying my head on his chest once again.

'I still cannae believe yer me wife an' I can kiss ye whenever I like, an' have me way with ye at will.' He gazed up at the low ceiling before rubbing the top of his head where he had hit the doorframe when we first arrived, forgetting not all entryways were as high or wide as what we took for granted at home. 'I can talk tae ye about anythin', an' ye understand an' accept me without judgement. I've told ye things in the past few days I've never told a soul fer fear they'd think me an evil man. Ye seem tae be the only one who understands me heart.' He pulled me closer, his arm tightening around my back, while I lifted my head, gazing up into his eyes as I placed my hand on his heart.

'I have always known your heart, Hamish, and what a truly kind and decent man you are. You just got lost on the way for a time, and followed the wrong path. Maybe you should consider allowing others to see what you show me and the children instead of hiding your heart under that hard exterior.' He placed his hand on mine, and smiled.

'Aye. That may be a possibility now me heart is complete once again.'

My husband had been true to his word, and we had not been interrupted once the entire time onboard. Hamish would bring all our meals down to our cosy cabin, choosing to spend our days in bed. We would walk the deck in the early afternoon for a short time to enjoy the fresh air, while speaking with the crew. He had fished with them several times while I slept, and caught a small shark the cook prepared for dinner the same night. Accompanying me up on deck late in the evening to watch the moon while gazing out over the ocean, he held me close while whispering secrets of the heart.

I was thoroughly enjoying my time alone with him, and felt far more relaxed not having Bessie dress me or my hair styled every morning, free of everything but Hamish. He was loving and attentive to me in every way, confirming in my mind I had made the right decision in marrying him.

I stood beside him on deck, watching land draw near, the vessel following the shoreline. 'Are you going to tell me where we are now?' Although excitement filled me, a feeling of dread had started to rise in me ever so slowly as soon as I set eyes on the coast and the terrain that lay beyond.

'Tasmania, or Van Diemen's Land as 'twas once known.' He spread his arm wide, his eyes twinkling as we sailed on for a time, the boat soon anchoring in a deserted cove. A charming cottage set back a little from the shore stood alone—and nothing else for miles. Somehow, the place was familiar; however, I had never in my life stepped foot on this island at the bottom of Victoria. Just hearing the name caused my stomach to drop to the floor without warning or reason. Fear settled on me as I stared from a distance at this place I somehow knew.

'What part of Tasmania is this?' I bent down to pick up my carpet bag, while our trunks were loaded onto a smaller boat. Hamish took my hand and assisted me onto the vessel without incident before following, soon making himself comfortable beside me.

'Enjoy ya time here. I'll be back for ya in a fortnight,' Captain Jack Pearson shouted cheerfully from above, while Hamish called out our thanks before turning back to me. The great-great grandson of Edward Pearson, a well known seaman who had worked for Sinclair Shipping at the turn of the nineteenth-century transporting goods from England to Hobart Town, he had followed in his footsteps, and told us a great deal of the man he never met, but heard of constantly from when he was a bairn. The shipping company was still going strong over a-hundred-years later, and there were a number of Pearsons' in their employ to this day; however, Jack had decided to go out on his own, and now owned three pleasure boats chartered by the wealthy, along with a number of fishing vessels similar to what the Cavanaughs' used. 'This place is called Low Head, although 'tis naw a town in itself.'

I nodded before waving goodbye to the Captain, then took my husband's hand in mine while he chatted comfortably with the two crewmen who rowed us over to shore. Hamish jumped down into a foot of water before gathering me in his arms and carrying me up to the pristine beach, while the men pulled the boat up onto the sand before carting our trunks up to the cottage. Leaving them under the front verandah, they wished us well before returning to the boat. We stood side-by-side gazing out at the water for the longest time, our eyes fixed on the elegant vessel as it travelled back out to sea, soon fading from sight.

'Are ye ready tae go inside an' see what we're in fer?' He slipped his arm around my waist, chuckling to himself as he guided me towards the bright yellow door, the window trims painted in the same cheerful hue.

'Don't you know? I thought you had been here before.' He bent down to collect the key from under a pot before straightening up. Unlocking the door, he swung it wide, allowing me to step inside the small hallway while he picked up my trunk.

'Naw. 'Tis me parent's friends that own it. Me father told me 'tis nice enough fer somethin' so small.' He threw back his head and howled with laughter, and I smiled, knowing full well Mr Makenzie thought Willow Grove a cottage in comparison to the grand estates he himself had owned in the old country.

I continued on, thrilled to find every fireplace filled with logs and burning brightly, and although only four rooms in the main house, a small kitchen was attached by a hallway at the back, along with a servants' quarters, consisting of one tiny room—the charming sandstone cottage cosy and comfortable, the view of the ocean magnificent. On the table in the kitchen were three boxes filled with fresh food, along with several bottles of wine and whisky, the icebox containing a number of prepared meals we only had to warm. I returned to him where he stood on the verandah watching another boat sail past and towards the bend where it would soon be out of sight, no different from the first, our trunks now safely in our bedchamber. Slipping my arms around him from behind, I ran my hands up under his shirt on his bare stomach while kissing the back of his shoulder before moving around to the front of his warm body.

'It feels like 'tis only us here in the world. That's why I wanted tae bring ye tae stay. When me mother told me o' the place, she suggested I take the time tae get tae know ye again, just as we did when we first met. Only now, there is far more to learn o' what sits under the surface, an' what lays deep in yer heart.' He reached for my hand, intertwining his fingers with mine before leading me back inside to look around. The furnishings were from another time, the colours soft, the quality of every piece reflecting the owners great wealth given the property was only used on occasion.

'How long since you have seen your friends?' I ran my finger across the mantle in the sitting room, inspecting it to find not a speck of dust.

'Naw my friends, Abigail. Remember that should you ever meet. 'Tis owned by me father's friends who have a grand estate nearby in George Town. I assume they use this as their romantic hideaway, although they're beyond it, in me own opinion. The old bloke must be a hundred if he's a day.' He lowered himself down onto the leather armchair by the fire, beckoning me to come sit by him. 'Me mother kindly wrote tae them the day she heard o' our betrothal, an' they offered fer us tae stay as long as we liked.' I sat down on his lap, my arms around his neck before I placed my lips on his. 'Now, I plan tae keep the fires burnin' day an' night if ye promise tae only go round in yer negligées.' A slow smirk spread across his face, my eyes widening as I shook my head in disbelief.

'I will freeze.'

'Naw ye won't. I'll always be by yer side tae keep ye warm.'

The week had passed quickly, and I hadn't laid eyes on a soul other than Hamish. Every morning, he greeted a man at the front door, delivering the day's food and supplies, while I would listen to them from the comfort of our bed, chatting amiably for several minutes before my husband returned to my side. I found great comfort in waking next to a man I cared for, and to feel safe and loved once again by a man who held me in his arms like he would never let me go was a blessing. To be close with another man again, and to give and receive affection, gave me hope I had healed just a little more and would continue to do so.

We had spent the days walking along the beach, while I had gathered quite a collection of sea-shells to take home as a momento. On the cold and rainy days, of which there were many, we passed the time together sitting by the fire, while drinking wine and talking from the time we woke until the time we closed our eyes at night. Seeing a side to him even I was unaware of, he had shown me just how loving, gentle and kind he truly was, and I could not help but open my heart to him a little more.

Barely daybreak, I burrowed deeper into the feathered mattress, while voices floated in through the window. Several minutes passed before he crept into the room and quietly slipped in beside me. Turning to him, I smiled, his eyes lighting up.

'Good morning, my darling man.' I stretched, yawning widely before moving closer to the warmth of him.

'Good mornin', me fiery wee wench.' He gently kissed my lips before I had time to rinse my mouth with the peppermint water I kept in a small glass beside the bed. 'I've some news. We've been invited tae dinner this comin' Friday at Emerson House by me old man's friends, Sir Percival an' Lady Regina Emerson. Lucky fer us, wee Bessie packed a gown fer ye, suspectin' this'd happen, an' I brought me dinner suit along, feelin' certain we'd be unable tae avoid it.' He appeared relieved as I nodded, feeling it only polite to meet the couple who had been kind enough to allow us to stay, while looking after us exceptionally well. He picked up my negligee from the floor before expertly slipping it back over my head. 'This one really is me favourite outta the lot.' My mouth twitched as he ran his hand up my ribs, tickling me. Turning to lay on his back, he pulled me up on top of him, his hand gently taking the straps down from my shoulders, the silk slip falling to my waist, Caressing my breasts, I bent down to kiss his lips, the day outside dark and grey despite the sun doing all it could to break through. 'I love ye, Abigail. Always have.' I kissed him again, rendering him unable to utter another word.

We had spent the day together laying on the lounge in front of the fire, enjoying the food along with each other's company. Glancing at the clock on the mantle, I pressed myself deeper into his side while watching the flames dance in the hearth.

'How fancy will this dinner be tonight? I'm uncertain what to expect or how to behave.' He frowned for a moment before arching his eyebrows.

'I've met 'em only a handful o' times, an' that was many years ago now. They're nice enough, but knowin' what they're like, aye, it'll be elaborate, an' I imagine their property will be magnificent.' Gently running his fingers through my hair, I grimaced. After being so free here, it would be a chore to dress up; however, I looked forward to a night out with my new husband. 'Do ye know which gown Bessie packed?'

'The green one that you like with all the beads, and the jewelled band that sits across my forehead.' He smiled to himself, while I reached out to pick up another biscuit from the now empty tin on the table.

'Aye. Ye look like an angel in it.' He sighed deeply before kissing me. 'Emmy will be wearin' yer wardrobe soon enough, the way she's growin'.' He grimaced as memories of her filled my mind.

'I must talk to you about Emmy. I kept silent before now, not wanting to speak on the matter as I am uncertain how you will react, but she wants you to know.' He leaned back, his eyes locked with mine, his brow furrowed, only adding to my nervousness.

'Has somethin' happened to the lass? Is she well?' I nodded, going on to repeat the conversation that had passed between us the day we married, and how she had sobbed her heart out, fearing we would no longer love her. He remained silent for the longest time, while I listened to his heart pound against my cheek. 'It'll be a hard road fer her tae walk if she chooses that path, but she's still young, an' her feelin's may change in the next few years. She might meet a laddie she fancies who'll change everythin'.'

'I disagree wholeheartedly, Hamish. I truly believe she was born this way, and it is not a choice. Feelings like this do not usually change, from what I know about Leo, and all he has told me of the matter over the years. He, too, has always felt drawn to other men for as long as he can remember, and he fought against it for years, much to his own detriment. It wasn't until he was nearly a man that he was able to accept himself as he is, but he had to leave his home and everyone he loved to find his way in life alone to be truly free to live as he wished—until he met us. I will not allow Emmy to spend a moment alone feeling tormented by it until she can accept herself as she is.' He nodded slowly, still clearly surprised by it all.

'Aye, if she's like Leo, then that's how it shall be. Now we know, she naw longer has tae carry this alone or feel tormented by the matter, as I will naw allow it. I'll need some time tae think before I speak with her 'cause I want tae consider how her own father would have reacted had he been here,' Hamish murmured, causing tears to sting my eyes. Taking the news far better than I expected, or hiding what he truly felt, I was uncertain. I had complete faith he would take everything in hand when it came to Thomas and Emmy, my trust in him unshakable. He would never reject either of them for any of the choices they made in the future, although I was aware there would be times he did not approve. I leaned over and kissed him, reassuring him all would be well. 'Aye, I know. I wish I was there tae speak with her now. The poor lass must be fashin' over it.'

'Oh, you are a good father, Hamish, and they are lucky to have you.' Meaning every word, I lay my head back against his chest for the longest time, his arms around me, the room silent, each lost in our own thoughts.

'Och, we need tae move. If yer relyin' on me tae help ye ready, we'll need tae get a start.' He tapped my backside before I reluctantly struggled to my feet to organise myself. Following me into the bedchamber, he reached out and grasped my shoulder. 'We still have some time before we have tae leave,' he remarked before pulling me down onto the bed.

When he finally let me up, time had got away and we were running late. Rushing to ready myself, I pulled my hair up and pinned it to the top of my head, allowing several curls to fall loose around my face. Sitting down to apply the cosmetics Bessie had packed, I used very little in comparison to what she usually smeared on my face, before making three attempts to pin the jewelled band around my head until it was finally in place. Hamish, dressed in his dark suit, assisted me into the gown before clumsily securing the buttons down the back.

'Ye must ask Catherine tae make these bigger. Me fingers are like the sausages Leo makes, an' far too fat tae do these wee things up.' He laughed as he secured the last of them before stepping back to admire his work. 'I remember the first night I saw ye in this, an' was struck by yer loveliness yet again. It's naw only Lord Harrington who remembers admirin' ye in gowns made tae only enhance yer beauty.' He stepped back and smiled, reaching for my hand before leading me out to the waiting carriage.

The opulent carriage travelled down a long driveway lined in mature silver oaks standing a hundred feet tall, the branches casting shadows over the paddocks on each side, the moon full and hanging low. I stared out the window, Hamish's hand in mine, the swaying of the carriage almost putting me to sleep. The Martarinos they had not purchased from Willow Grove slowed before veering off onto cobblestones leading to the three-story manor, reminding me very much of Lord Harrington's imposing estate. Coming to a stop outside the grand entrance, I glanced at Hamish nervously, his smile reassuring before I turned back to gaze at the elderly couple standing under the portico awaiting our arrival, their full staff of servants lined up on each side ready to greet us.

The driver, appearing nearly as old as his employer, opened the door and politely assisted me down without uttering a word, while Hamish casually jumped out and took my hand in his. He guided me over to the entrance to meet our hosts, my heart pounding hard in my chest, my mouth dry.

'Welcome to Emerson House.' Sir Percival swept his arm grandly towards the enormous front door, while I stared up at the mansion, everything around me familiar yet foreign. Introducing us to their staff, we shook their hands one-by-one before they were ordered back to work. 'It's wonderful to see you again, Hamish, and what a beautiful bride you have caught for yourself.' The impeccably dressed old man reached for my hand before raising it to his lips, his kiss lingering far too long before I gently pulled away, not wanting to cause Hamish any embarrassment, despite this stranger's stare fixed firmly on my breasts from the moment I exited the carriage. Short and round like a ball, there was not a hair on his head, while his wife towered over him despite being far smaller than me.

Lady Emerson stepped forward, her arms reaching up to embrace me for only a brief moment in greeting before pulling away, her face kind, her manner warm and welcoming. She hugged Hamish for the longest time before cheerfully inviting us into her home. We followed behind them, their pace painstakingly slow as they climbed the stairs, their servants nowhere to be seen except for the butler standing near the open doors. Taking our coats, he hurried away, leaving us alone with our hosts in the grand reception room. Unable to take my eyes from the faint glow around Sir Percival, confusion settled on me. Many of my loved ones were shrouded in the brightest gold I had ever seen, but this was different, the aura so faint I barely noticed it.

'Follow us to the parlour, dear boy, and bring your lovely wife. We can sit and talk of all we've missed before we're called to dinner,' Lady Emerson announced, her voice strong and commanding in comparison to her physical appearance. Hamish nodded, taking my hand tightly in his before leading me through a number of elegantly furnished rooms into the large, very blue, parlour. Overwhelmed by how familiar everything was around me, a knowing settled in the pit of my stomach. I had been here before. To this estate. In this room. I had dreamed of it long ago, and somehow, I was reliving that dream while wide awake. Sir Percival invited us to sit on a blue velvet settee by the fire, while they made themselves comfortable opposite on their wingback chairs upholstered in the same fabric, elegantly placed side-by-side. Hamish caught them up on his parents, and of his own news since he last saw them. 'Oh, yes. What a terrible business that was when poor Harriet could not speak or visit with you for all those years. She wrote to me many times of her distress,' Lady Emerson said, sadness crossing her withered face, her white hair pulled back tight into a bun.

'Aye, 'twas a difficult time fer all involved, includin' Angus an' his wife Polly. Me father naw only prevented her seein' her own sons, he stopped her havin' any contact with her two grandchildren, Willy an' Bella. Me mother is a saint puttin' up with what she does,' Hamish said, sipping a dram of whisky from a crystal glass Sir Percival had poured from an eighty-year-old bottle.

'As long as it's sorted now, there is no need to speak of the matter again. Best leave the past in the past,' Sir Percival advised, his leathered face lighting up in a charming smile as he turned his attention to me. 'I heard this is *the* Abigail you have been breaking your heart over for all these years, and now I can certainly understand why.' I decided at that very moment I did not like this man at all. Shifting uncomfortably under his gaze, he blatantly leered at me, and no one else in the room seemed to notice.

'Aye, she is.' Hamish proudly slipped his arm around my shoulders, while I wondered if he had gone blind or was choosing to ignore how the old man, *his* family friend, was gawping at me. Telling them of our courtship, I was relieved he left out the fact we had been sharing a bed well before there was any courting involved, moving on to speak of our wedding day before my shoulders relaxed ever so slightly.

'Your children sound adorable, as do your niece and nephew. My mother-in-law, God rest her, called my husband William until the day she took her last breath, but never allowed anyone to call him Willy,' Lady Emerson remarked, only encouraging Hamish to go on and on about Thomas and Emmy and our life at Willow Grove, of which I was certain neither could have cared any less about.

'My dear, you do not look old enough to have any children, infant or grown. Hamish has been fortunate to marry such a beauty at his age,' Sir Percival said, my cheeks flushed, his eyes unblinking as they met mine for only a moment before I looked away, finding the painting above the fireplace far more interesting and pleasant on the eye. He noticed my stare, and relaxed back in his chair, while Lady Emerson poured herself another whisky, then did the same for her husband and Hamish, not bothering to offer me anything after my initial refusal. 'They are my parents, Lord Rupert and Lady Geniveve Emerson.' I nodded, unable to take my eyes from the pudgy, balding man staring down at me from the portrait, his eyes sincere, while a petite woman stood beside him, far taller than her husband by six-inches at least, and not unlike the woman their son had married.

Sir Percival was the spit of his father, and I would have assumed it was him when first married had he not told me any different.

'They appear to be a kindly couple,' I remarked, and he nodded, a smile touching his lips as memories flooded his mind.

'The kindest you could meet. They were among the first free settlers to arrive in Tasmania, and although they passed decades ago, Emerson House remains the same as it did when they first built the place in 1806, the year before I was born. It's the only home I have ever known.'

'Oh, you chose to stay with your parents after you married?' I inquired, and he laughed aloud, while Hamish nudged my waist with his elbow.

'Of course. Who else would have cared for them, or run the estate when they were beyond doing so? I was a dutiful son, and did what was expected of me. It is a heavy burden to bear being responsible for so many. We still have servants in our employ who are descendants of several men and women who were in service, or assigned, to my father to serve their sentence here rather than gaol. The truth is, in the early days, many of the prisons weren't built, and convicts were sent to work for the free settlers. It was criminals that built Emerson House, and most of the roads and buildings from that time.' He threw back his bald head and howled with laughter, while my stomach knotted up. Finding the man beyond irritating, I looked back up at the painting while he continued to chuckle.

'Do ye naw have a sister? I seem tae recall ye had a siblin' or two,' Hamish asked, his brow furrowed as Lady Emerson smiled at him before draining her glass and refilling it, along with his and Sir Percival's.

'Oh, Mollie is long gone, as are most of my family. We were never blessed with children, so once we are no longer, all this will be left to the people of Tasmania to do with as they wish.'

'A museum would be the most sensible, given the awful things that have occurred here,' Lady Emerson added, her husband's head snapping around to glare at his odd little wife, while he abruptly raised his hand to silence her. His shoulders slumped as he sat back in his chair, pausing for a time before exhaling deeply.

'The place has been cursed since the massacre that took place here in 1811, and we would rather not pass it on to any relatives or friends as a family home for fear they too will suffer. We considered leaving many a time; however, I was never able to bring myself to move away, or sell it and settle somewhere else. My parents adored the place, and were never bothered by the strange goings on, believing the spirits roaming the halls are those who were slaughtered within these walls.' My eyes went wide, and I sat back in my seat as if he had stood up and slapped me, a chill running down my spine, causing me to shudder.

'Cursed?' Hamish asked, his eyebrows arched in amusement.

'Oh, yes, dear boy. We do not speak of it, and neither should you,' the old woman warned before pausing as the doddering butler shuffled into the room to announce dinner was about to be served. Following them to the extravagant dining room, I was quickly seated between Sir Percival, perched proudly at the head of the polished wooden table, and Hamish, while Lady Emerson sat opposite me beside her husband. Within moments, the footmen had placed the first course in front of me, a comforting potato and bacon soup, warming me immediately. I concentrated on my food while listening to Hamish talk of our journey to England, Scotland and America, the Emerson's listening attentively, often interrupting him to ask not only questions that bored me, but prodding him for information that was not theirs to know.

I remained silent through every course, finding the food delicious and the company disappointing, the Emerson's far from what I expected. Finishing the last of my dessert, I let out a strangled scream and jumped to my feet, gasping for air.

'What's wrong with ye, lass? Are ye well?' Hamish pushed himself away from the table and rose to stand beside me, his hand on my waist, his brow furrowed.

'Something crawled under my gown and up my thigh. It's gone now.' I glared down at Sir Percival, while Lady Emerson screamed and raised her legs off the floor. Hamish bent down to look under the table before strolling around the room, checking behind the furniture. Catching my eye, his mouth twitched as he returned to my side and I lowered myself back onto the chair, as did he.

'Och, I cannae see a thing. Was likely a wee mousey.' He picked up his glass of wine, taking a slow sip before continuing. 'Whatever 'twas, best fer his own sake he naw touches ye again or I'll be forced tae stomp on him an' snap every bone in his wee body.' Hamish glanced across at Sir Percival, who lowered his gaze and returned to his meal, while I closed my eyes, wishing I was anywhere but here at Emerson House.

Returning to the bright blue parlour, the butler offered brandy to the men, his eyebrows shooting up in surprise—or judgement, I was uncertain—when Hamish requested a glass for me. He nodded, silent as he poured another, his disapproval clear. They seemed to have formed the opinion I did not imbibe after I refused a dram of whisky on arrival. If they only knew how many times I believed I had poisoned myself after a night at the village pub they would have no fear. The butler placed the round glass in my hand, every eye in the room fixed on me. Smothering a smile as memories flooded my mind, I made them wait, warming the brandy in my hands as the Emersons' spoke of Tasmania, and how much the place had changed since they were children nearly a century ago. Raising the glass to my lips, I drank deeply, swallowing several times as I drained the brandy while enjoying the warmth it left as it burned down my throat, a warm fire settling in my belly.

They were strange wee creatures, and different in their own way. I had not witnessed any interaction between them, and certainly no affection towards the other, both fixing their attention on Hamish and myself while saying very little of themselves. I found them cold and far too interested in finding out everything they could, suspecting it would be used against us at a later date when with their friends, and they could gossip freely.

'We are pleased Hamish has fallen on good times, and in more than one way,' Sir Percival remarked, glancing across at me, his eyebrows raised, before turning his attention back to Hamish. 'You are a fortunate man.'

'What do you mean?' I interrupted, feeling defensive now, but knowing I must behave.

'What I mean, my dear, is you are the great-niece of Lady Isabelle Delmont. I have been advised by a credible source that you are her sole heir. Although I never met the woman, we are well aware of her wealth. A very dear friend of hers, Abigail Sinclair, was a close confidant of my mother's. The poor woman was heartbroken when Abi, as she was known to all—here and in Hobart where she lived—returned to England ten-years after settling here. At Lady Delmont's direction, mind you. I assume you are named for her.' The fat little man stared out the window, the stars bright, while I clasped my hands together in my lap to stop them trembling, a lump in my throat. Casting my mind back to the dusty boxes stored under our house, the name was familiar; however, I had not ever expected to find someone who knew her, or the other faceless authors of those journals. 'My dear mother did keep in touch with Abigail, and even went to the mainland a number of times decades later to reunite with her. Abi accompanied Lady Delmont to Willow Grove several times over the years, and lived there for a time, not that my mother spoke anything of the place or the residents to us.' He wrinkled his nose in disdain before continuing. 'I digress. To answer your question, I feel it is quite obvious to all now Hamish has married you, my dear, he has gone from a farmhand to a wealthy property owner. I would say that makes him a very fortunate man, wouldn't you? Not to mention the fact he has you in his bed.' Sir Percival gave Hamish a condescending smile, and Hamish returned it, while I bristled, wanting to strike the man where he sat.

'I am the fortunate one to have him as my husband, Sir Percival. I could not have found a better man to love and protect me. Money cannot buy a love so deep, or the comfort and happiness he gives to me so generously and without measure,' I replied sweetly, while Hamish discreetly squeezed my hand, a smirk touching his lips.

'Oh, no harm meant, my dear, no harm at all. I am just surprised by your choice. Most are sensible and marry another who is just as wealthy. There is far more power in combining two fortunes rather than sharing one.' This awful little man made my stomach turn, and my skin crawl. Shifting uncomfortably in my seat, Lady Emerson held out her hand and clicked her fingers together several times to get Hamish's attention.

'I was wondering if you would have time to fix my spinning wheel while you are here, dear boy? I do not touch the thing myself; however, my ladies maid is quite distressed she is unable to use it.' Without waiting for him to respond, she slowly rose to her feet, tapping her foot on the floor as she waited for Hamish to do the same. He stood reluctantly, glancing down to grimace at me before shuffling out of the room behind her. I glared across at Sir Percival as he rose to his feet, and within moments he was sitting beside me, his hand on mine.

'I've never been in the presence of such beauty. Your father-in-law forgot to mention just how exquisite you are, my dear. I must say, I am surprised he did not choose to keep you for himself, as I would have should I have been blessed with a son who brought you home. My mistresses are plain in comparison.' I wrinkled my nose in disdain as he lowered his voice. 'I would very much like to meet with you in secret while you are here, and I am prepared to travel to the mainland to stay with you at The Delmont.' My eyes widened in horror as I abruptly pulled my hand away, rising to my feet to sit in Lady Emerson's chair.

'You filthy wee man! And at your age! I hope you know your parents would be ashamed of you.' I straightened up in my chair, prepared to defend myself should he leap across the room and pounce on me. 'Put your cock back in your trousers, Sir Percival. I am not interested in any secret meeting with anyone other than my husband, and never will be. I'm surprised your one-eyed snake still rears its ugly head at your age.' He threw back his head and cackled, an unpleasant sound causing me to grimace.

'Oh, you poor child. If you let me have my way with you, I promise you will scream and beg for more and forget you ever had a husband.' He placed his hand on his crotch, his erection bulging in support of his claims. He rose to his feet and stepped towards me, my boot kicking him hard in the thigh and causing him to stumble back onto the settee.

'Get away from me or I will strike you with whatever is at hand,' I threatened, my eyes darting around the room looking for the most effective object to weaponise.

'I see you like to play games, my dear. How wonderful to find a kindred soul who enjoys the same.' He smirked, a wicked glint in his eye as I heard footsteps coming down the hallway. He stood and quickly returned to his seat, as did I, not wanting my husband to add to the number of murders within these walls. By the time Hamish strode in, his face pale, a dazed look on his handsome face, Sir Percival and I sat opposite each other sipping our brandy. Not bothering to sit, he thanked them for their generosity and took my hand, apologising that we must leave as he was feeling unwell.

They escorted us to the front door, and we called out our farewells as we hurried down the stairs towards the waiting carriage, Hamish quickly assisting me inside before following and firmly closing the door.

'Drive on,' he bellowed, the carriage lurching forward. The Emersons stood at the door, waving cheerfully, while I turned away to face Hamish, pretending I had not seen them. Silence hung heavy between us, the sound of the hooves pounding on the wet ground filling my ears as the driver urged them on. It was not until the carriage passed the elaborate entrance gates and pulled out onto the road, I turned to Hamish, shaking my head in disbelief several times, unable to speak as I tried to compose myself.

'I have no words, nor do I know what to think.' Relief washed over me as the distance between us and Emerson House grew, the two mile journey from the mansion to the town not passing quick enough for my liking.

'Aye. If anyone knew what that filthy wee woman tried tae do tae me when she got me alone, I'd never hear the end o' it. I only just escaped with me virtue intact.' His cheeks flushed red, and I felt laughter start to rise in me.

'Did you fix her spinning wheel?' I stared out at a tavern as we passed down the main street of George Town, the horses now at a walk due to inclement weather, while I was grateful to be inside a warm carriage, no matter who owned it. The sign above the enchanting stone building, *Murphy Family Inn*, made me smile. Why, I was uncertain. Hamish had told me only last week of a family named Murphy who owned taverns all over Tasmania, the first inn built in George Town by their great-great-grandparents, convicts by the name of John and Mary—who birthed over a dozen children. From what I had been told, all of them lived well into adulthood and went forth and multiplied. As did their children. And theirs—spawning hundreds of Murphys still living on the island.

'Aye.' He nodded regretfully. 'It was pure trickery. The wicked auld woman waited 'till I fixed it before cornerin' me in her bedchamber.' I collapsed into giggles, tears streaming down my face as I took his hand in mine, given he appeared far more affected by the events of the evening.

'Sir Percival was not much better. I have no idea what he would have done had you not returned when you did, but I wasn't frightened, given the size of him. I cannot believe they wanted to bed us. They should be ashamed at their age. I have every intention of dobbing them into your mother.' I continued to laugh, his face stony as he stared out into the blackness, the town behind us.

'Aye. I was tempted tae smack Sir Percival in the mouth more than once tonight. I'm well aware it was he who touched ye in the dinin' room—an' I'm confused by it. I've naw seen or heard o' the man behavin' in this manner. Naw once.' He slipped his arm around my back, and I leaned into him, my head resting comfortably on his broad shoulder. 'Seems I'm destined tae spend the rest o' me days fightin' tae defend yer honour. Even the auld flapdoodles wanna have a shot.' His face slowly creased into a smile, and I laughed again, closing my eyes as I let myself melt into him, soon drifting off into a deep sleep, cathedral music filling my ears, while dreaming of a cemetery, and a place called Hobarton.

The waves crashed hard against the shore as I opened my eyes, the sky dark as the storm moved in. Turning to stare out the window while burrowing deeper under the heavy quilt, Hamish slept soundly beside me. Today we would head home, and although I had thoroughly enjoyed every moment here alone with him, I missed my children and my own bed dreadfully.

I had never seen Hamish so relaxed, blissful almost, and I appreciated that he did not ask any more of me than what I was able to give. He hadn't once asked if I loved him, despite telling me often how much he adored me, and accepted what I gave him without question. His breathing changed, and within moments, his large fingers stroked my hair before he kissed the back of my head, his hand running gently down to my backside. Turning over in his arms, I gazed up at him inquiringly.

'Och, yer awake.' He placed his lips on mine for a moment.

'I wasn't until you tried to wake me,' I lied, a grin spreading across his face, his dark eyes twinkling.

'Naw, I would never do that tae me wife. Ye must've been dreamin' o' me touchin' ye an' havin' filthy thoughts.'

'What a load of poppycock.' I laughed aloud, pushing him over onto his back before pulling myself up to sit astride him, resting back against his bent legs no different than sitting in a comfortable armchair.

'I've enjoyed havin' ye all tae meself, an' this fortnight will always be one o' me favourite memories, but I'm lookin' forward tae returnin' home, an' startin' our lives as a family with Thomas an' wee Emmy.' He caressed the lace trim of my negligee between his fingers, his face thoughtful as I nodded.

'I was thinking the same earlier.' I reached over to the small side table and selected an apple from the small bowl. Making myself comfortable again, he gazed up at me as I took a large bite, the fruit crisp and sweet.

'If yer tryin' tae get me one-eyed snake tae pop his ugly wee head out at ye, yer goin' the wrong way about it.' He chuckled as I continued to eat, his amusement clear. 'I was just about tae make love tae ye, but ye chose an apple over me, ye wicked we troll.'

'I was hungry, and I work far better with something in my stomach.' I threw the core towards the door to pick up later before leaning down to kiss him, my mouth sticky, although he did not seem to notice or care.

Standing on the beach side-by-side, we gazed out over the water at the small boat rowing towards us, the wind whipping my unbound hair around my heavy cloak. The large vessel where we would spend the next few nights waited further out from the cove, Captain Pearson already up on deck awaiting our arrival as he waved to us in the distance. Greeting the two crewmen cheerfully, Hamish lifted me into the boat before loading our trunks and climbing in after me. Soon after, I clung tightly to Hamish's back as he climbed the rope ladder up to the polished decks, placing me safely back on my feet without incident. Shaking hands warmly with the captain before he hurried off, the crew busy, Hamish placed his hand on my waist and guided me to the back of the boat to gaze at the cottage standing alone in the distance, the wild terrain shielding all sides from the harsh elements bar the front. Staring out over the ocean long after the cove faded from sight, Hamish tightened his arm around me before we made our way down to our cabin. I stretched out on the bed, feeling the sway of the boat underneath me.

'I fergot how these barques pitch about.' Trying to keep his balance, and failing terribly, he fell into the wall. Collapsing into giggles, he narrowed his gaze. 'Haud yer wheesht, ye wicked wee troll.' He stumbled across the cabin, giving up before lurching his heavy frame onto the bed, while nearly knocking me to the floor when he landed beside me. His fingers intertwined with mine, I stared up at the ceiling while sinking deeper into the feathered mattress, thoughts of home flooding my mind, and leaving a smile on my lips.

Our time on the boat sailing home was no different than our journey across Bass Strait to Low Head, and I enjoyed every moment. Having drawn even closer to Hamish, I was relieved we made a good match, sharing similar ideas and values I had only recently discovered. Most importantly, his only wish was to live a happy life with his new family, as was mine.

We had docked in Corio Bay, surprised to find Mr and Mrs Cavanaugh standing at the wharf waiting for us, an excited Thomas and Emmy beside them welcoming us home. I scrambled from the boat, missing my footing as I jumped across to the wooden jetty, while only just avoiding falling into the water below thanks to Hamish reaching out and grabbing me by the arm. Pulling me back up before gently setting me down on my feet, I broke free and ran to my children, their arms open wide, as were mine. Their grandparents strolled along behind them, watching as Thomas and Emmy ran into my embrace. Holding them for the longest time, Hamish came up behind me, his large hand on my shoulder, and within moments, Mr and Mrs Cavanaugh were by my side.

'We wanted ta be here to meet you with Thomas an' Emmy. Mind you, every man an' his dog wanted ta come, but we advised 'em ta let you all get settled for a day or two as a family before visitin' an' overwhelmin' you,' Mr Cavanaugh said kindly, his face lighting up at the sight of us. I appreciated how kind and thoughtful they were to meet us when they could have stayed home in the warm to await our return. I loved my father-in-law dearly and admired how considerate he was of everyone around him, just as his son had been. I wanted time alone with my little family to spend time together strengthening the bonds between us, given Hamish's role had changed from uncle and godfather to a father figure to my children.

'Mummy, I've been bursting to tell you Bessie birthed her baby the day after you left,' Emmy blurted excitedly, while I felt my heart would burst.

'Are they both well?' She nodded, as did Thomas, while Mr and Mrs Cavanaugh confirmed the same.

'Oh, yes. Her name is Lucy, and she is sweet as sugar. We've visited with her every day.' I nodded at my daughter, aware since placing my hands on Bessie's stomach months ago she would have a girl, and I was thrilled. Emmy and Thomas led me by the hand down the pier to the Cavanaughs' extravagant carriage waiting for us near Moorabool Street, while Hamish followed behind with Mr Cavanaugh, carrying our small trunks. After their new driver helped Mrs Cavanaugh into the carriage, followed by my excited children, Hamish came up behind me and lifted me off my feet before placing me down on the seat inside next to my mother-in-law. Mr Cavanaugh made himself comfortable next to his wife, while Hamish sat opposite with Thomas and Emmy.

'Did you enjoy your time away?' Mrs Cavanaugh placed her hand on mine as I nodded, happy to see her again.

'Aye, we did. Only we did have somewhat o' a strange experience.' Hamish leaned forward, his elbows on his thighs as he told them of the dinner we attended at Emerson House. The carriage was soon filled with uproarious laughter, causing Hamish to grimace at the memory.

'It's that green dress, Mummy. Every time you wear it, men turn into lunatics and lose their heads over you. I still wish to wear it when I am older,' Emmy remarked, her sweet little face beaming at me. I smiled, reaching across to hold her hand for a moment before settling back in my seat, a storm in the distance nearing, the sky darkening as the paddocks took over from the town.

'We missed ya, but it was fun havin' Willy an' Bella stay with us. Uncle Angus an' Aunt Polly didn't make us eat in the dinin' room once. We got ta take every meal in the kitchen,' Thomas said, and I laughed aloud. It was something we had done since they were small, ensuring we had at least one meal together as a family in the dining room at night. 'An' we got ta spend a lot of time with our grandparents an' cousins.' He glanced across at them lovingly and grinned before Mr Cavanaugh reached out and affectionately tousled his sandy blonde hair, so much like Aaron's. Chatting animatedly all the way from Geelong until we were trotting down the driveway of Willow Grove, I was surprised how fast the time had passed, and relieved Mr Hinkle was nowhere in sight as we went by his cottage. Pulling up the horses at the bottom of the front stairs, Hamish jumped down to help the driver unload our trunks, the children hugging their grandparents before following him out.

'Will you come in and take morning tea with us?' I asked, while they smiled back at me, affection in their eyes. Mr Cavanaugh stepped down from the carriage before turning to assist his wife, then offered his hand to me.

'Not today, sweetheart. Enjoy some private time before you are inundated by your brothers and sisters, who will give you no peace. Go along and we will see you tomorrow,' Mrs Cavanaugh replied, kissing the twins once more, then myself, before kissing Hamish with affection on his cheek, while Mr Cavanaugh thumped him on the back.

'Ya part of our family now, Hamish, an' just as much of a son as the other bludgers we have, an' no doubt ya'll give me just as much cheek,' Mr Cavanaugh said, thumping him on the back again, while Thomas and Emmy laughed before bidding their grandparents farewell. They ran up the stairs and into the house, calling out over their shoulder they would ride over after school tomorrow to visit with them. Mr and Mrs Cavanaugh returned to their carriage, the driver quickly moving the four Martarinos forward, while they waved out the window as it elegantly turned in the circular driveway before making its way towards the front gates and out of sight.

Hamish carried the trunks up, leaving them by the stairs to take up to our bedchamber later before we made our way to the kitchen. Stepping inside the warm room, the staff cheerfully called out their greetings. Hamish strode over to the table to join Thomas and Emmy, while Leo came towards me, his arms outstretched. Grabbing me roughly by the shoulders, he pulled me into his embrace, my face squashed hard to his chest and leaving me unable to breathe.

'Oh, my darling, sweet Abigail. I've missed your unfortunate looking face, but am thrilled to see that you appear well-bedded. I take it the honeymoon was full of fabulous fu... I mean, fabulous fun.' He smirked wickedly as he winked, and I couldn't help but smile.

'Tell us what you did while away?' Emmy called out as Leo guided me over to the table, his hand on my waist.

'We know what they did,' Thomas said smugly, and I blushed, restraining myself from reaching over and giving him a clip around the ears for his cheek.

'I do not want to know about that. That's disgusting, Thomas. To even think of them doing such things makes my stomach turn. My mother isn't like that at all,' Emmy snapped, her nose wrinkled in disdain.

'Oh, my poor, dear, simpleminded Emmeline. It's clear you do not know your mother at all. The stories I could tell you about her would burn you pretty little ears off. There was this one time...' Leo went to say as Sally came up from behind him, firmly placed her hand over his mouth, and promptly dragged him backwards to the other side of the kitchen where she spoke sternly to him, her tiny finger waving about, while I admired the strength of the woman given his size.

'We had a bonny time walkin' on the beach every day. Yer mother has brought home so many seashells, I dinnae know what she'll do with 'em all,' Hamish said, changing the subject calmly as Leo and Sally returned to the table.

'Well, *I* know what I am going to do with them. I plan to put them all in a crystal vase and keep them in our bedchamber to remember our honeymoon.' I leaned over and kissed him across the table as Sally lowered herself into the chair beside me.

'You're so sentimental, Abigail. That is just beautiful,' Sally murmured before ordering Leo to return to the kitchen to serve the food warming in the oven and awaiting our arrival. Soon, the table was full, not only of food, but the staff wanting to hear every detail of our time away. Closing my eyes for only a moment, I thanked the heavens for all I had been given, and the souls surrounding me who felt like family. I was truly grateful.

After spending the evening in the sitting room with our friends, Hamish and I accompanied the children up to their rooms to retire for the night. Hamish followed Emmy into her bedchamber and quietly closed the door behind him, while I walked alongside Thomas into his room. I lay down and waited for him to change in his dressing room before throwing himself down beside me.

'How are things with Hannah? You seem to have drawn closer since the Delaforce family came to stay.' I stroked his hair, his head on my chest.

'I really like her, Ma. I think I might even love her, but then, I may be too young to know for certain.' He sounded confused as I kissed his furrowed brow.

'I knew I loved your Daddy when I was only a little older than you, and I will always treasure the years we spent together. I would not trade any of it for all the tea in China. If Hannah treats you kindly, and loves you deeply, but most of all respects you, then she may be the girl for you. Just take it slow and see what happens. There is no rush, sweetheart. I was in a very different situation than you are, my darling boy.' I kissed the top of his head, while thinking back to how angry I felt being forced to marry Aaron, and I smiled, amused how stubborn I had been on the matter.

'Ya don't like tea much, Ma, but thanks for tryin'. I'm happy yer home. Wasn't the same at Willow Grove without ya.' Thomas sat up, encircling me in his growing arms.

'We're glad to be home with you.' I rose to my feet, tucking him in before kissing his cheek as Hamish walked in to say goodnight, tousling his hair. Leaving him to sleep, I crept into Emmy's room to check on her. She had beamed up at me, her face tear stained as she kissed me goodnight.

Grateful she would sleep well tonight, Hamish led me by the hand to our room. After helping me undress, I went to my dressing room, selecting a negligee I had not worn yet, and quickly slipped it over my head. He was already in bed when I returned, settled into the feathered mattress where I had slept for so many years. Climbing up onto Aaron's side of the enormous bed, I placed my head on his shoulder, remaining silent as I gently caressed his smooth chest.

'Me poor, wee Emmy. She was frightened I would naw love her anymore.' He gently kissed my forehead, sadness in his eyes. 'I sat on her bed, an' I told her I knew o' her feelin's. She burst in tae hysterics, sobbin' so loudly I had tae hold her till she calmed herself. I told her much the same as ye did.' He sighed deeply, pausing in thought for a time. 'I think yer right, Abigail. That she was born like this, I mean. Emmy confided how long she's been feelin' this way, an' I'm surprised it goes right back tae when she was small.' He shook his head in disbelief, and I nodded silently. I had never noticed anything different in Emmy than other girls her age, and told him so. 'Ah, well.

I'd rather the sweet lassie be happy than tae live in misery the rest o' her days, forced tae live a lie. We can protect her here within these walls, an' help her come tae accept herself fer the lovely lass she is.'

'You were never this understanding when I first met you. You were terrified Leo would take you by force if you bent down to pick something up, and you thought far too much of yourself.' I laughed at the memory. His opinions back then on those in service and stations in life, and how everything must remain as it was or there would be chaos were far removed from the man he was today. Now, he counted some of the staff and workers at Willow Grove as his closest friends, and enjoyed their company as equals.

'Och, I was naw that bad.' I rolled my eyes at him, his laughter filling the room.

'Oh, yes you were. You were a terrible snob for the first few years I knew you.'

'Aye, it's true I have naw been the man I should've been over the years. I've learned a lot; although, I never got it right when it came tae women. 'Till now.' He slipped his large hand down to my backside, resting it there as he kissed my nose.

'Do you think you will be tempted to return to old ways as the years go on?' I felt a lump rise in my throat as he stared back at me, before giving me the sweetest smile.

'Abigail, me precious girl. Ye need naw ever think o' that again. Naw other woman in this world could catch me eye, or own me heart forever the way ye do. I'll never put me hands on another woman again, an' I give ye me word on the matter.' He turned towards me, his eyes on mine. 'Should ye ever leave me, I'd stay by meself fer the rest o' me days 'cause I could never replace ye.' My heart melted as he rolled on top of me, careful not to lay his full weight. 'I love ye. I always have,' he whispered before sliding down the straps of my negligee. Taking me in his arms, his lips on mine, all thoughts of anyone but him disappeared.

As I lay in his warm embrace much later, I dreamed of macadamia nuts, a place called Boolarra, and a little boy with a crown atop his head named Alistair.

Chapter Eleven

TIME HAD PASSED SO quickly, and today, January 6th, 1906, was six-months since we married. Everything had been going wonderfully well, and I no longer felt I carried the load by myself anymore. Hamish and I were closer than we had ever been, and Thomas and Emmy appeared happy and settled with Hamish as their Da, and my husband. Once the twins had left for their grandparents Friday afternoon, Hamish would come and get me and take me to the dining hall to eat, and we would spend the night at the pub dancing, drinking, and talking with the workers, many of whom I considered friends. The poor man would often have to carry me home on his back when I was far too drunk to stand, but we enjoyed ourselves immensely every time.

I was getting to know the new, younger families who had moved into the village, and as the first group of children born here were growing up, the bairns were starting to arrive again, and we were all delighted. Assuming the school would close within the next five-years, it was now clear it would be of continued value. David and his wife, Kate, had left us three-months ago to return to their mob in South Australia, and although it had been a sad day for all who lived within the boundaries of Willow Grove, it was a joyous occasion knowing they were moving on to greater things. David had talked to Hamish of a shearing tool he had invented, and although in the early stages, promised Willow Grove would be the first to receive them once he had perfected the device he believed would change the industry, cutting time and cost.

Bessie had thrived as a new mother, and Danny doted on their sweet daughter, Lucy. Although I had been absent at the birth, I shared a close bond with the wean, and saw her daily when I visited them in the village. How different it could have all turned out, but it hadn't, and Danny loved her as his own, the infant never far from his arms when he had finished work for the day. I had told Bessie to take all the time she needed, and continued to pay her wages while she stayed home to care for her brown-haired, brown-eyed little girl, only a few days from turning six-months of age. Bessie enjoyed very much being a first-time mother, and felt she could not return to work just yet, unable to tear herself away from Lucy. She would come to the house with Lucy if I needed my hair done, or was going somewhere special, and I appreciated her doing so.

Little Mary had taken over organising my wardrobe; however, I had not felt the need to replace my ladies maid, as I was capable of doing most things myself, and if I couldn't, Hamish would usually help me. I kept Bessie on because she was my friend, and I enjoyed having her with me every day, but I would easily cope without a maid to do all my bidding. I enjoyed our long talks as she would get me ready in the mornings, and I was missing that part of my day dreadfully. On the other hand, I had Hamish to help me dress, to which there were benefits.

I turned around to stare at his face, his eyes still firmly shut, his breathing rhythmic. He truly was a striking man, his broody dark looks only enhanced by his large, muscular frame. I leaned over, placing my lips on his.

'Good mornin', me precious lass. Did ye sleep well?' His yawn wide, he placed his large hands on his face and rubbed vigorously before yawning again.

'Like a baby. Although, I have no idea why we even say that. Weans do not sleep well at all more often than not,' I pondered, and he grinned, still rubbing his handsome face. 'Are you being truthful when you say you're not sad about missing out on having your own?' I gazed into his eyes, my hand stroking his cheek as he yawned again before gathering me into his warm embrace while kissing the top of my head.

'Naw, not at all, me angel.' His eyes widened as they often did when discussing the subject. 'I'm naw sayin' it would naw have been nice had we married when we were young an' had our own family, but it dinnae turn out that way, an' the past cannae be changed.' He pulled me in closer to his chest. 'I feel I do have two bairns who belong tae me, an' that's the honest truth. 'Tis naw as though ye married a man ye only knew a short time. I've been there fer Thomas an' Emmy since the day they drew breath, an' I've watched 'em grow every day since, an' loved 'em naw different than if I planted the seed meself.' He kissed me, his hand sliding down my side to my waist as I cuddled in closer to his warmth.

I still had not been able to tell him that I was in love with him, or believed myself to be—the words sticking in my throat when I would try to speak of my feelings. The thought of him ever leaving me caused my stomach to drop to the floor, and my heart would race away from me. I lit up at the sight of him, setting off a hundred butterflies in my stomach. His touch thrilled me, as it always had; however, now we were close in every way two people could be. I depended on him more and more as each day passed, allowing my frozen heart to melt bit by bit as his love warmed me once again for the first time since I lost Aaron.

Loving Hamish had not lessened my love for Aaron. I still visited his grave and that of our sons every day to talk to them, and grieved they were no longer here with us. Settling myself under our tree for a time, memories of him would flood my mind as I relaxed against the thick trunk of the gumtree while gazing out at the water he loved so much. Thoughts of Harrison and Jack, and how they would have been had they lived, tormented me often. Once I returned to Hamish and the children, only occasionally would there be moments when I yearned for Aaron, or longed for my boys, as now I truly felt content with my lot in life.

'Have ye noticed Thomas has been melancholy since Ron an' Irene moved tae their property, an' it's only been a week,' Hamish remarked as he turned to lay on his back, his arms still tightly wrapped around me.

'I know, and I'm sorry for it, but we all agreed Hannah can come and stay, as long as they behave. Have you talked to him about that?' He sighed deeply, the early morning summer breeze floating through the open windows, the lace curtains billowing and dancing about the darkened room, the shutters outside pulled closed in preparation for the hot day expected, but still allowing the air to flow through.

'Aye, an' although he says they will, I know what young men are like when it comes tae a lass sleepin' under the same roof. Especially one he's in love with. Surely ye remember when we met?'

'That's exactly why I am so worried.' He smiled, gently stroking my face with his fingers.

'Och, he's a good lad, an' he respects her, so I doubt anythin' will come o' it yet. I am o' the opinion he'll marry her as soon as they're old enough, an' ye'll have tae prepare yerself fer it, Abigail. I know better than most what yer like.' His eyes twinkled in amusement as he tightened his embrace, while I snapped my head up to glare at him.

'What is that supposed to mean? What *I'm* like?' I attempted to sit up; however, he held me where I was, chuckling to himself while only infuriating me further.

'Ye speak without thinkin', an' say the first thing that comes tae ye mind naw matter what the consequence. I dinnae doubt fer a minute ye'll try tae talk him out o' it when the time comes. I'm attemptin' tae get ye comfortable with the idea years afore it happens, an' tae prevent ye causin' a deep rift between ye an' the lad.'

'You do not believe I should give my own son advice regarding such an important matter?' I snapped, irritation rising in me as I glared up at him.

'Naw. Ye need tae keep yer mouth shut fer yer own sake. If Hannah makes the lad happy, in which she appears tae, an' we both like the wee lass, why should he wait? What would ye have done if someone tried tae stop yer weddin' tae Aaron?' I widened my eyes, my finger pointing at his face accusingly as he threw back his head and howled with laughter. 'Aye, I did give it me best shot, but ye would naw listen tae me anyway, an' neither will he, naw matter how much he loves ye. Get used tae the idea now is all I'm suggestin'.' I knew he was right, but Thomas was my baby boy, an' I wanted him to step out with a few girls before he chose one. To travel and go to university, if he so wished, not be stuck with a wife and children here at Willow Grove, tied down for the rest of his days without going out into the world to explore and go on adventures as I had always dreamed of doing myself. I knew I shouldn't think this way given I was happy living here, and wanted no other life—I had not considered the possibility Thomas felt the same way.

'The best I can do is give you my word I will try,' I promised, and he gently kissed my lips. He always knew how to calm me, whereas in the past he had been the one to lose his head in anger. I had never seen the man so relaxed and serene throughout the entire time I had known him, and it thrilled me no end.

We had walked home from the pub only last week to be confronted by Nellie, so drunk she was barely able to stand while hurling insults at us. This time, it was me who told her to hold her vicious tongue, and threatened to smack her if she did not mind me. She had stepped away, her mouth opening and closing in shock, silent as we continued past her. Times like these, I considered us mad to let her stay on, although I still held out hope she would calm in time; however, her behaviour would not be tolerated much longer. I understood that it must have been torture for her to watch us together, and for that reason alone, I overlooked her lashing out at us far more often than I usually would.

'Aye, that's sorted then. We have a few hours tae waste before we have tae get up, an' I've naw plans tae go back tae sleep.' He kissed my neck, slowly making his way up to my ear, his lips gently sucking my lobe, while desire rose up in me as I slipped my arms around his neck, and allowed myself to melt into him, all thoughts of Thomas and Hannah long gone.

I relaxed back in my chair at the kitchen table taking breakfast with Leo, Thomas and Emmy, along with Jasper, Lilith and their boys Eros and Poseidon, or Ross and Sid as they preferred to be called. They had moved in with us over seven-months ago after hunting high and low for the perfect property to settle on, and much to their continued disappointment, they had been unable to find it as yet. We had assured them they were welcome to stay at Willow Grove for as long as they wanted so as to prevent them rushing to purchase a property they would later regret. They had already made the acquaintance of many like-minded people around the Geelong district, and those they had befriended in Melbourne during the short time they had stayed there had also relocated to Geelong, waiting for Jasper and Lilith to set up their new community, a place where they would live side-by-side just as a tribe would, supporting, caring for, and loving each other.

'Is it okay with ya both if we ride over ta Grandpa an' Granny's after school today?' Thomas asked. Hamish and I both nodded in unison, our mouths full.

'Make sure you give them our love, and the same to your aunts, uncles and cousins,' I reminded them, both nodding as they rose to their feet to kiss us goodbye, Ross and Sid following them out of the kitchen to meet Willy and Bella at the back door, who shouted out their hellos and goodbyes before they all departed. Leo reached over and poured us all another coffee before sitting back in his chair to settle in for a gossip.

'Tell me, Jasper. When will you have your nudist colony set up? I am beyond excited about visiting with you so I can take a good look around, especially at the squiggly snakes wiggling round all over that property. I will be the first to visit your rude, nude and glorious property that must be named Mammoth Python Estate, after me.' Leo handed the mugs of coffee around the table while Jasper smirked, his eyes twinkling in amusement.

'Leo, I have told you a thousand times we are not nudists. We are currently considering a property near Hamilton in Victoria, just on the border of South Australia. It is already set up for the lifestyle we and many others have chosen as it was the longest running commune in the history of Australia; however, they disbanded several years ago. We've been told all it needs is some effort and skilled hands to restore the buildings that have fallen into disrepair, and once we are able to travel to see the place with our own eyes, the purchase will depend on the soil and if we are able to establish our crops. That's only one of many things I need to check to enable us to be self-sufficient, and hopefully once we are settled where we are finally meant to be, I expect the place to be running smoothly within a year.' Leo nodded, appearing bored as he yawned, not bothering to cover his mouth.

'Oh, stop coating your words in sugar, Jasper. You forget I knew you in your past life in Chelsea, and I'm well aware you are both mad rooters, and will lay with anyone who is willing,' Leo teased, while I cringed at his brashness.

'We do believe in being free to love whomever we choose, despite our commitment to each other, but you will be disappointed to hear that we do most of that with our clothes on.' Jasper smiled at Lilith as she giggled quietly to herself, while Hamish appeared embarrassed as he glanced warily at Jasper, then Lilith. Leo and Lilith were well acquainted, becoming familiar years before I met Leo myself. Lilith had been his soothsayer when he lived in London, and although they had never been friends, they had been excited to see one another again when we arrived home from our travels.

'What do you mean by free to love whomever? Free to bump uglies without the threat of being poisoned or strangled in your sleep by your husband or wife is what you really mean. Oh my, I cannot believe you pass your wives around to each other no different than doing the *Brown Jug Polka*, and I find it not only fascinating, it's fabulous!' Leo clapped frantically, applauding them both as he bowed his head in admiration before continuing, despite me wishing he would be silent on the matter. 'I've come across some in Paris not unlike yourselves who have the same inclinations as you to fornicate with anyone willing; however, to the outside world, they are respectable married couples. I'm thrilled our Abigail is finally making friends with people far more exciting than she.' Lilith laughed aloud as I narrowed my gaze at him, my hands clenched into fists under the table. 'The friends she surrounds herself with up until now, while forcing them on the innocent among us, are as boring as brown paper.' He leaned forward in his chair, his eyes glinting wickedly as he waved his finger around. 'Go on. Swap wives now, Jasper. You take Abigail here into the panty, while Lilith can take Adonis down to the cellar just beneath us. I'm conflicted as to which couple to go and observe first only to ensure you all know what you are doing.' Leo clapped again, his backside bouncing up and down on his chair as I watched Hamish grimace.

My husband was well aware of Jasper and Lilith's ways and the ideologies they held dear; however, chose to ignore their beliefs, finding them far too open-minded and confronting to discuss. They were certainly free in many of their ways, including sharing their bodies with those they were not married to; however, I could not have cared less, finding them honest, creative and expressive, and they fascinated me living so very differently to anyone I had met.

'Are ye at the orphanage taeday, or spendin' it at home, Abigail?' Hamish asked, quickly changing the subject.

'Home today. I plan to visit with several friends I haven't seen lately, and there are things I need to do here.' I smiled across at him as he sipped his coffee. 'Why? Do you need me to do something for you?' I bit into a piece of warm toast as he nodded.

'Aye. Can ye meet with me back here in the kitchen 'round mid-day? I want tae take ye out fer a late lunch? I've a lot tae do this mornin', but I'll be back tae get ye as soon as I've finished.' He winked at me, reaching across the table to squeeze my hand for a moment before helping himself to some more bacon.

'You are becoming just as promiscuous as Jasper and Lilith. I'm well aware they fornicate at least five times a day with each other, and goodness knows how many times more with anyone else who is willing, the delightful deviants. I'm beyond thrilled you allowed me to listen to your perverted secrets, instead of sending me away on some quest to search for things I've never heard of. I hate Australia.' Leo beamed across at me as they all howled with laughter.

'Like the time you were sent down to the laundry house to bring back a bucket of steam?' Lilith said through her giggles.

'That was not funny at all. I spent over an hour arguing with that new tyrant of a head laundry maid, Prissy, over that,' Leo spat, his arms crossed against his chest defensively.

'Her name is Prudence,' I reminded him, smothering a smile.

'Prissy, Prude, Fatty, or Prudish, it matters not, and does not improve her unfortunate looking face for the better, trust me,' he replied, scowling at the thought of her.

'Or there was that time he went looking for elbow grease when I told him to put a bit of effort into scrubbing the workbench,' Sally interjected to more howls.

'Naw, when he spent hours lookin' fer the glass axe an' the left-handed shovel was the best out of the lot,' Hamish added, wiping tears from his face as he continued to laugh.

'I have several favourites,' Jasper interrupted, a slow smirk spreading across his face. 'Sending him out to collect ant milk with that tiny bucket in hand, well, I nearly had a conniption. And then back to collect dry water in that enormous pail made me laugh until I cried, and gave us all close to six-hours peace that day.' Leo gasped, clearly offended as he threw a bread roll across the table, while Jasper raised his hand and caught it expertly before continuing. 'Then there was the tartan wool he searched all over Geelong for, while abusing the shopkeepers for not having it in stock so Bessie could crochet a blanket for Lucy, along with the polka dot paint to redo the kitchen walls, but I've left the best until last. The wire mesh watering can he still hasn't found to this day.' Jasper sat back in his chair, threw back his head and laughed loudly, tears pouring down his handsome face, while many in the kitchen stopped their work to join in.

'I am still in the room, you rude funts. My point was, I was being very nice in thanking you all for trusting me with your private escapades, no matter how filthy or immoral, and this is how I'm treated? You should all be ashamed. Any goodwill I had, you can now bang the entire lot up your backsides.'

'Only some escapades, Leonardo, an' only the ones we dinnae mind travellin' along yer passionfruit vine,' Hamish said, still laughing as he rose to his feet, his kiss on my cheek before he called out his goodbyes and headed out to the stable to start his workday. Sally returned to the kitchen, while Jasper and Lilith stood, excusing themselves to go riding down to the ocean. Leo slid into the chair beside me, while the staff carried trays filled with food into their own dining room just off the kitchen, leaving us alone.

'Finally, we are free to talk.' He took my hand in his and smiled before settling himself into what I had come to know as his gossiping pose, his chin resting on his hand, his legs crossed, his eyebrows arched expectantly, while I remained silent, sipping my coffee, unimpressed, although the bright scarf wrapped around his head holding his hair back off his face looked divine. 'Oh, come on, Abigail. Tell me what happens in the privacy of your bedchamber. I want every detail from last week to this very minute.' I shook my head, taking another piece of toast; cold now, but still edible. 'You're not acting like my best friend at all. You know Brian hasn't visited here, or there, in forever.' He pointed to his groin as I spat my coffee, quickly scanning the room to ensure we were still alone. Tamara's children had all been sick one after another, and in truth, they had only missed one of their monthly visits. As usual, Leo was exaggerating. It had not been forever at all. 'If I went outside and the wind blew on my enormous cannon, well, you know what the outcome would be.' I laughed loudly, remembering Aaron once saying the same to me before we married.

'Leo, how do the details of my rumpy-pumpy help improve your rumpy-pumpy, or lack of it?'

'As your friend, it is my responsibility to ensure you are enjoying yourself in the boudoir. I like to imagine what stamina that brute of a man must possess, and I am so easily able to visualise him in the nuddy after our recent conversations.' He smiled, while I rolled my eyes.

'That in no way relates to me at all, and if he knew I told you anything about it, or foolishly described his naked body to you, he would strike me dead where I sit, and you shortly after. The thought of you fantasising about him as you do, well, if he knew it would give him nightmares.' I laughed aloud as he collapsed into giggles, tears streaming down his handsome face.

'I do find his reaction amusing, I must admit. The look on his face if I allude to anything of a sexual nature often leaves him silently wondering if it was directed at him.' He squealed in delight, kicking up his feet in the air as if he were running on the spot before relaxing back in his chair. They were getting along famously; however, I was of the firm belief Leo was secretly thrilled he had the power to make Hamish squirm at whim purely for his own entertainment. 'Does he rip off your bodice and lift your skirts whenever he feels the urge no matter where you are, or does he take the gentler approach?'

'I'm not telling you, Leo,' I repeated for the millionth time in the last six-months.

'If you just tell me one filthy thing, I promise I won't ask again.' He glanced at me slyly as Sally placed a fresh pot of coffee on the table before raising her hand to cuff him over the ear.

'Mind your business, you nosey gossip.' He grunted, dismissing her with his hand as she returned to her workbench, before leaning closer, his voice low.

'One thing.'

'Oh, for the love of all that is holy, one thing, but you are to ask nothing more ever again. If you do, you will have to sleep with a woman.' Making him promise, I leaned closer and whispered in his ear while he sat still as stone, listening intently. Once I finished, he threw himself back in his chair, his eyes closed, a blissful sigh emitting from his lips.

'You lucky birch tree,' was all he could say, waving me away while he summoned up filthy images of my husband in his mind. Allowing me to leave him to his thoughts, I silently crossed the empty kitchen and stepped out the backdoor, before making my way down the meandering path towards the charming cottage I still to this day held deep regret over not claiming for myself.

I found Polly sitting under the verandah out the back where she loved to watch the native birds in the early morning, while doing her needlework, embroidering everything from handkerchiefs to cushions.

'How lovely to see you, dear Abi.' She rose to her feet and gathered me into a warm embrace before offering me the seat next to her. Talking of our children, and commiserating how independent they had become, we spoke amiably of the day-to-day occurrences around the property.

'Do you think Hamish will return to his old ways? With women, I mean?' Feeling embarrassed within moments of the words leaving my mouth, Polly gazed back at me, her brow furrowed, concern in her eyes as she set her embroidery down on the table.

'Why would you even ask that? Has he given you reason to think he would?'

'No, not at all. It has bothered me since the day I met him when he told me how he behaved when it came to women. I've come to believe that what stops me loving him completely and without limits is the chance he will leave in the future when he gets sick of me, and another catches his attention.' I held back the tears threatening to fall, sniffing loudly as I tried to compose myself.

'Oh, Abi, that's never going to happen. Not ever. Hamish adores you so very much, more than I have ever seen him love anything or anyone. Even Angus says so, and he knows everything about the man. If that's all that's holding you back from him, you must forget this nonsense. He is now the man he was always meant to be since marrying you.' She took my hand in hers, while giving me a reassuring smile. 'Angus says he's never seen Hamish so content. He is devoted to you, and the bairns. Our husbands are handsome men, and they do not go unnoticed by the women from the surrounding properties who approach them at the pub, often when we are not present. Some of the trollops freely and openly offer themselves as mistresses, but they are faithful and return home to us. You know that as well as I do, Abi. You must let this go if it's the only thing holding you back. He deserves to be loved, and receive the same love back he so freely gives to you.' A cockatoo on a nearby branch screeched, startling me.

'Oh, I am trying, Polly. I am acutely aware I will not cope if my heart is broken once again, and it's the reason I have tried to protect myself from the pain of it.'

'I know you trust him completely in every other way, so you may just have to take him at his word and believe him when he says he will love you as he does now for the rest of his days. I accept his word on the matter, and now you must do the same. The time has come for letting go of all that no longer serves you.' I nodded, squeezing her hand before she stood to go and make a fresh pot of tea. I stayed by her side for hours, swapping secrets and stories before I kissed her goodbye, and slowly made my way back to the house feeling like a weight had been taken from my shoulders, a peace settling over me as

I stared out over our garden and the paddocks beyond. Our property. Our home. My everything.

It was nearing mid-day; however, I was not expecting Hamish for at least another half-hour, and returned to the kitchen. Finding Sally at the worktable preparing the vegetables for tonight's dinner, I stopped beside her, placing my hand gently on her shoulder.

'How are you, Sal? Are Johnathon and the children bonny?' I pulled up a stool to watch her knead a lump of dough I assumed would soon be a loaf of bread.

'They are well, Mistress, the young scallywags they are. Growing fast, as you are witnessing with your own. Thomas looks so much like his father, and Emmy is the spit of you, no different than when I laid eyes on you my first day here as the scullery. We were all so young. Where has the time gone?' She shook her head in disbelief as I nodded in agreement. Lowering her voice, she stopped what she was doing for a moment. 'We are all very grateful and want to thank you for moving Neville's Ian and Molly into their own terrace. It is kind of you to help get them away from that awful woman. She's not a stepmother's arseh... Sorry, I'm enraged by the thought of her. The noise and the skerrick that used to come from that house, with her screaming at those poor bairns day and night and never letting them play or behave as children should. Their only value to her was carrying out all the chores in the house, and treating them as if they were her personal slaves. Well, we were all right disgusted by her. Everyone told her so to her face, and even the men got involved, talking to Neville. He's as useless as tits on a bull when it comes to that Trixie, or Trickster as all in the village have started to call her.' She placed the dough in a tin before sliding it into the oven. Straightening up, she returned to my side, placing her hand on mine. 'Thank you for asking the women to keep watch over Ian and Molly. We all take it in turns, but they are sweet young people, and give us no trouble. They are much happier with the new arrangement.'

'I'm pleased things have improved. I know Hamish is going to speak to Neville about paying more of an interest in them now they are no longer living under his roof.' Although trying to be cheerful, I believed he would be unsuccessful no matter how he handled the matter. Neville was a quiet man and would never stand up to his bad-tempered wife, and I understood completely. Not a soul in the village liked her, finding her argumentative with the other women over the smallest of issues, and then there was the way she treated her stepchildren, infuriating many, including myself.

Leo stepped back into the kitchen, panting loudly as he gripped the back of the chair while trying to regain his composure.

'What's wrong with you? Have you been running or rooting?' I inquired, while Sally collapsed into giggles.

'Very funny, Mistress Abigail. I can only wish I had the opportunity to be a mad rooter like some here in the room.' He eyed Sally suspiciously before returning his attention to me. 'As if I would be running. You know how much I hate any form of exercise. I had business to attend to, if you must know.' He strolled over to the stove to warm a pot of chocolate milk, my very favourite.

'Oh, really? You can have secrets, but I cannot?' I called back over my shoulder as I crossed the room to sit down at the table. Soon after, he approached me, tray in hand.

'That's right. Now be quiet and drink your chocolate.' He placed the steaming mug down in front of me before sitting down opposite. Chatting animatedly for a time, Hamish strode towards the table, bending down to kiss me before glancing at Leo suspiciously.

'Why would ye be takin' hot drinks on a warm day such as this? 'Tis like a furnace in here.' He shook his head in disbelief before wiping the sweat from his brow with his sleeve. 'Are ye ready?' I stood and took his hand, his grin wide as I followed him out the back door to find Delly saddled and waiting, his stallion nowhere to be seen. Taking me by the waist, he lifted me onto her broad back before swinging himself up behind me, the reins firm in his hands.

'May I ask now where you are taking me?' Delly ambled down the winding path and through the manicured garden, Hamish's lips on the back of my neck sending chills through me.

'Aye, ye may. We're goin' tae our cottage tae enjoy a private lunch. I'm finished fer the day, an' 'twas the reason I was busy this mornin' gettin' it out the way so I could spend the rest o' the day with ye.' We slowly rode past Angus and Polly's cottage towards the thick trees that would eventually lead to the river. I enjoyed riding with him sitting behind me, his arms around my waist, occasionally kissing the back of my neck as he whispered crude things into my ear. It reminded me of all those years ago when I could not ride to save myself, and Aaron always sat behind me. Now it was Hamish, and I felt just as safe and secure leaning back into his arms—only a recent realisation among many I had experienced of late.

Delly stepped into the clearing, the shutters on the windows of the charming cottage closed to keep out the midday heat. He quickly dismounted, helping me down before stripping Delly of her saddle and bridle, allowing her to roam the fenced plot. Following him up to the house, the smell of roasted meat wafted out onto the wide verandah, and I hurried to the kitchen to check. Finding our lunch warming in the oven and a peach pavlova chilling in the icebox alongside several bottles of champagne, I returned to the verandah to join him. He stood stone still gazing out of the river as I came up behind him, encircling my arms around his waist.

'Ye celebrated yer anniversary monthly with Aaron, an' 'tis the reason I've avoided all mention o' it, but I count the days I've been wedded tae ye. I planned tae wait 'till we'd been married a year, as most do, but I could naw let it pass without commemoratin' our six-months taegether as man an' wife.' He reached into his pocket, pulling out a small box before turning to face me. Placing it in my hand, I gazed down in surprise before flipping open the top to find a pink diamond mounted in a thick intricate gold band, a small opening at the back. I tried to slip it on my pinky; however, the ring stopped half-way. A nervous smile touched my lips as I stared up at him, careful not to offend him.

'Thank you, Hamish. It's beautiful.' I held my hand out from under the protection of the verandah, the hot sun causing it to sparkle as I admired the stone.

'Naw, Abigail. 'Tis fer yer toe.' He chuckled to himself as he took it from my finger, then dropped to his knees in front of me, removing my left shoe. Bending the gold band open a little, he slid it onto my second toe before gently tightening it. I had never seen anything like it, nor seen anyone wear one—not that I ever really saw any bare feet but my own.

'How on earth did you think of it?' I smothered a smile as we sat down on the outdoor lounge.

'Och, weel, I asked Mr Dawson fer a suggestion. He knows I give ye pink diamonds, an' had a perfectly round one tae suit. I thought he'd make ye a wee pendant or a ring out o' a diamond o' three-carats, but he surprised me with this. I'd mentioned tae him in passin' how ye spend all yer time in the house an' garden without shoes, an' only wear 'em when ye have tae, so he made this.' I held my foot up in the air to admire the brilliant stone, while he slipped his arm around my shoulder, proud as a peacock. 'Do ye like it?'

'Oh, Hamish, you are so thoughtful, and I adore it. I feel terrible I did not think to get you a thing,' I apologised, his handsome face breaking into a wide grin.

'There's nought I need or want. I have everythin' I ever wished fer.'

Hamish had asked me before we married if it would remind me of Aaron, or cause me pain, if he continued to order jewellery from Mr Dawson. I admired and appreciated Mr Dawson's unique pieces, and felt anything Hamish bought for me from him, and him alone, just as the pieces I continued to treasure from Aaron were. He lay down on the lounge, pulling me down on top of his large frame, my head resting on his chest.

'Happy six-month anniversary,' he murmured, kissing me for the longest time. Soon after, we took our luncheon down by the river while watching the pristine water rapidly flow downstream. The mood jovial, we chatted about stuff and nonsense, our loud laughter ringing out through the bush, while finishing every bottle of champagne in the icebox. Laying side-by-side on a blanket spread out over the grassy riverbank, the trees above sheltering us from the hot sun, their leaves rustling in the gentle breeze. 'Aye then. Yer naw opposed tae celebrating twice a year if I promise I'll never bring ye a cupcake?' He lifted his head, his eyes twinkling.

'Aye, Hamish. I'm naw opposed.' I ran my fingers along his cheek, caressing his face before melting into him, his lips on mine, while cupcakes were the furthest thing from my mind.

'Hamish, I'm in love with you.' Feeling choked up, this was something I had not said in many years. He stared into my eyes for the longest time, tears welling in his own, the room silent bar the river outside the bedchamber window and the sounds of the bush vying to be heard. Pulling me close to his chest, he held me tight, uttering not a word as he gently placed his lips on mine.

'I've told ye me feelin's many a time, an' accepted ye'd never really love me the same way I love ye, an' I was still the happiest I'd ever been. Tae hear it from yer lips made me heart stop fer a moment, an' question if I heard ye right. 'Twas somethin' I never expected or demanded from ye, but I'm more than thrilled tae hear it.'

'Hamish, you have been by my side ever since Aaron died when you had no obligation to be, and loved me through everything. I have stopped myself from loving you because I didn't want my heart broken again. I was so worried that if I let myself fall in love with you, I could no longer love Aaron. I have discovered only recently I have enough room in my heart for both of you, and I can love you as you deserve. I've come to realise I am now deeply and completely in love with you.' Tears trickled down my face, his thick fingers gently wiping them away, his eyes locked with mine.

'Aye, an' I love ye more than life itself. Always have.' A sharp knock rang out, and I jumped, startled as Hamish sat bolt upright. 'I'm naw expectin' anyone. Are ye?' He swung his legs out of bed and rose to his feet as I shook my head, quickly pulling on his trousers before hurrying to the front door. Leo's voice drifted down the hallway, and I rolled my eyes, his footsteps becoming louder before he burst into the room, Hamish close behind him. Not bothering to take off his pants, he slipped back into bed beside me, Leo watching on, his eyes twinkling in amusement as he stood at the foot of the bed.

'Good afternoon, mad rooters. I am the bearer of good news. There is no need to rush home as Thomas and Emmy wanted me to tell you they've decided to sleep over at their grandparents for the night. They had no idea it was six-months today since you wed, and wanted to give you time to yourselves, the thoughtful babies they are.' He made himself comfortable on the bed, his eyebrows arched expectantly. 'So, tell me what you have been doing?'

'We've been playin' *Key Tae The King's Garden*, an' sittin' in our rockin' chairs reminiscin' about the auld days. What do ye think we've been doin', Leo?' Hamish inquired, grinning widely.

'Well, Adonis, surely you understand that when you wed Abigail, you married me. I'm entitled to hear all the dirty details. I am quite willing to give my opinion and offer any suggestions for improvement if I find you inadequate in the boudoir, as I suspect.' Hamish struggled to sit up, the quilt clutched to his bare chest, his eyes glinting dangerously. 'Oh. Yes, alright then.' Leo scrambled to his feet, fear in his eyes. 'I'm off to do far more funner things with people who are not so serious, but I will be back this evening to bring your dinner, and breakfast for the morning. Don't do anything I wouldn't do. Kisses,' he sang out as he quickly made his way out of the room and back to the front door, leaving it open behind him.

'I've naw doubt he'd sleep at the foot o' our bed every night if we allowed him.' Hamish laughed loudly as he watched Leo out the window, so eager to leave he slipped to the ground several times as he tried to mount his horse. Soon after, he galloped away, while I collapsed into giggles.

'Now it's time for me to give you your anniversary present.' I gently kissed his chest, slowly moving my way down his body.

'Aye. I love anniversaries,' he groaned.

Expecting my friends to take afternoon tea in the garden, Hamish and I had only just returned from our cottage to meet them. Quickly changing our clothes, we made our way to the kitchen to await their arrival. Lowering myself down onto a chair, Leo poured me a coffee, his face glowing.

'I must say, I could not believe my luck yesterday when Hamish opened the cottage door with no shirt on. I am such a jealous silver birch, and am still green with envy. How you can keep your hands off that Adonis of a man, I have not a clue. I was tempted to run my hands all over that broad chest of his, but he would strike me dead, of that I am certain. Can you ask for his permission on my behalf?'

'Oh, stop. And do not mention it to Hamish, or you will never see him in the kitchen again,' I warned, my mouth twitching at the thought.

'As if I would tell anyone but you I now have a picture of his naked torso stored away in my memory forever that I can call on anytime I feel the need, even when he is wearing his shirt. He would smack that perfect vision straight out of my head if he knew. Shhh, and promise not to ruin it.' He winked at me before sitting down opposite, and I smiled.

The leaves above rustled gently in the warm breeze, the sun burning down over the manicured garden where the staff had set up an extravagant afternoon tea under the shade of the ancient gum tree standing proud amongst its English neighbours, insisted on by many of the new arrivals to this foreign land over a century ago when building their homes, despite finding the climate harsh and unsuitable compared to their homeland. Lilith and I were in deep discussion over their plan to travel to the south-west of Victoria in the coming weeks, when movement caught my eye. Turning to find Catherine and Beatrice walking towards us, hand-in-hand, their shining hair the colour of wheat, I rose to my feet to welcome them.

'Hello, my dear friends.' I embraced them warmly before encouraging them to join us at the enormous table. The staff had outdone themselves, the white linen tablecloth laid out without a crease, crystal vases filled with white roses and lavender placed down the centre from end to end, a silver candelabra standing in the middle dripping with crystals, while the breeze continued to blow the candles out much to my chagrin. I had advised Sally not to bother after watching them go back and forth lighting them a dozen times within a quarter of an hour, reassuring her the table looked exquisite.

Beatrice had started to visit quite often now she was living with Catherine, and Emmy could not have been happier. She had taken a shine to Beatrice as a small child, and they had formed a close bond, and now that friendship was blossoming. Despite Beatrice still not uttering a word from that dreadful day in London sixteen-years ago to this, Emmy appeared to have no difficulties in communicating with her. She would take her horse riding and show her the property when they visited, and would sit by the river teaching her to fish for trout, aware she was Beatrice's only friend in the world other than Catherine and her immediate family. Despite their conversations always being one-sided, Emmy spoke as if she had received a reply, while Beatrice communicated with a nod or shake of her head. Beatrice still to this day possessed the sweetest of nature, and although soon to turn twenty-and-six, her terror of men remained; however, that fear lessened only slightly when in the presence of those she knew and trusted. Although still wary when around Hamish, she would give him a shy smile now and then when he asked how she was, easing me a little. All I could hope was that she would improve in the future now she was surrounded by family and friends who loved her and showed her much affection and attention—unlike her parents. Mr and Mrs Montague had always placed their own needs above their children, and continued to do so to this day, constantly travelling around the world to promote their business.

Catherine, now famous in her own right for her unique, and increasingly eccentric gowns, along with her naughty nightwear, was known by all of high society's elite here and across the water, and her business was thriving. Colin had earned the reputation as the best tailor in Geelong, and many would travel great distances to attend the shop to place their orders. Their marriage was a happy one, and their two children, David and Imogen, were growing into lovely young adults who wished to follow their parents into the clothing industry. We only saw William on rare occasions now he had married and opened his own law firm in Collins Street, Melbourne. He was living his dream, exactly as he had planned, and I was pleased for him.

Catherine sat close to me as the footman held out a tray, offering her a choice of white wine or champagne. She politely picked up a crystal flute and took a sip.

'Oh, you've brought out the good stuff. Bollinger, no less.' She paused, taking another sip before placing it down on the table. 'Are you still receiving those letters from Detective O'Neil?' Her voice low, her brow furrowed in concern, I reached over and took her hand in mine.

'Do not fash, dear friend. He sends them far less frequently, every month or so now; however, I do not bother to read them anymore. I file them away unopened just in case I ever need to use them.' She nodded knowingly, a smile lighting her face as she noticed Dana and Victoria walking towards us. We both rose to our feet to embrace them, their laughter filling the air.

'What a joy to see you all together. Isn't this a luxury? No men. We can say and do as we please,' Dana called out cheerfully as she lowered herself down onto the seat opposite me. Mrs Cavanaugh arrived shortly after with Scarlett and Adele, followed by Maggie and Irene. Soon after, Polly and Amelia sat down at the table, enthusiastically joining in the spirited conversation.

Mr Masters stood at the far end of the table supervising the footman passing around plates filled with finger sandwiches, while the maids carried trays of glasses filled with alcohol Leo had mixed with his secret ingredients that made it taste like heaven; however, went down far too easily.

'Isn't this civilised?' Irene remarked, taking a glass of champagne and drinking half before biting into her sandwich. She had become so relaxed since living at Willow Grove, I was confident her newly appointed staff would benefit greatly. She had become accustomed to interacting with our own workers as equals, and by the time they reluctantly moved out, the entire Delaforce family took nearly every meal in the kitchen with us.

'How is the new mansion?' I asked, and her face lit up in a brilliant smile.

'Oh, it's wonderful, but I do so miss living here. I could have stayed forever if Ron had let me. It feels lonely, though, not having you all around. Poor Hannah is suffering the most.' I squeezed her hand, knowing full well how much my own son was fretting. Maggie sat beside her, chatting with Lilith animatedly. Although she and Mark were still living in Melbourne, they spent an extensive amount of time either staying with us, or now Irene, where they would remain for another fortnight. She was still alone—and lonely—and had not worked up the courage to take a lover, despite desperately wanting to. I was thrilled we would get the opportunity to visit often while she was staying at the Delaforce Estate.

'How are you, my dear friend?' I asked, taking Dana's hand across the table.

'I am well, my sweet Abigail. I must say, you look radiant. What's on your toe? I noticed it sparkled when you greeted us.' I lifted my bare foot up onto her lap under the table, and she laughed aloud before examining the pink diamond and the exquisite gold band closely. 'It's absolutely flawless. Where did you get it?' I squirmed under her gaze, while quickly placing my foot back on the grass, reluctant to even say my husband's name in her presence, and had avoided it at all costs whenever we visited with each other.

'It was an anniversary present,' I mumbled, my face becoming warm.

'Ah, that's why you're embarrassed. Has it been a year already?' I shook my head, while she reached over and took my hand back into her own.

'Only half.'

'You can tell me when good things happen for you, dear girl, even if it is *him* behind it. I want to hear about your happiness, as joy shines from you like I haven't witnessed since Aaron was alive, God rest him. Although I will never have anything to do with *that* man, I am grateful he has brought you back to us, my sweet Abigail.' She smiled affectionately as tears stung my eyes. Relief washed over me as there had been many times I so desperately needed her advice and her sense of humour to guide me; however, held back for fear of upsetting her.

'Did you hear about the scuffle at school over Emmy the other day?' Victoria asked, a smirk touching her lips.

'No. I haven't heard a thing,' I replied, surprised Emmy hadn't told me herself.

'Well, I heard there are two boys who have a crush on Em, one of them being Amelia's Mathew.' Victoria waved her arm down at Amelia, who nodded before rolling her eyes. 'The other lad, and I won't say who he is in case it gets back to his parents, refused to heed Emmy when she said she did not want to eat lunch with him in the dining hall, and he became upset and took her by the arm. Once he laid hands on her, Mathew stepped in and shoved the boy to the ground, threatening to punch him if he went near her again. I doubt this is the last time she will witness boys fisticuffing over her. The sooner she is married to a good man the better.' I nodded, knowing that the path many expected Emmy to follow was not the same one my daughter was forced to walk, and they would all have to accept the fact without knowing the reason behind it.

Mr Masters had ordered the savouries be passed around, and soon after, a selection of tiny tea cakes, much to everyone's delight, while most at the table sampled as many as they could without fear of judgement. Once the plates were empty, within moments they were replaced with a new assortment, including miniature cheesecakes in various flavours.

'I agree with you, Victoria, and am of the firm belief our sweet little Emmeline is going to experience something similar to her mother when it comes to men fighting over her,' Dana remarked, winking at me as she smiled. Catching sight of Hamish out of the corner of my eye, his large frame lurking beside the house discreetly beckoning me, I excused myself and went to him.

'Is everything all right?' I stood up on my toes to kiss him.

'Aye. I came out tae see if everyone is stayin' fer dinner, but stopped when I saw ye with Dana. I dinnae want tae upset her by comin' out, an' was just about tae leave an' send Leonardo out tae take his chances.' He chuckled before grabbing me around the waist and lifting me up into a passionate embrace. After the longest time, he put me down on my feet, kissed my nose, and prepared to leave.

'Where is your mother? She told me only two-days ago she would come.'

'Aye. She sent word she's feelin' poorly, but I suspect that's tae do with the latest scandal me father's caused with one o' his mistresses. She's with child, or so the rumour goes.' I shook my head, my heart heavy for my dear friend, Harriet, and all she suffered behind closed doors and in public because of that philandering bastard.

'I would bet money on it there are a hundred bairns out there fathered by Colin Makenzie, and this latest betrayal proves just what a cheating, lying funt the man has shown himself to be.' Kissing him again, he bid me farewell before I slowly made my way back down the garden to the table and returned to my seat.

'Oh, Abigail. He is such a good-looking bear of a man, isn't he? I know our husbands are built like brick thunderboxes, as was Aaron, but Hamish is that touch bigger, and he has that dark reckless thing about him that is so very attractive,' Scarlett remarked, swooning before she continued. 'When he picks you up and kisses you, I can feel the passion from here.'

'I think it's lovely you are so happy together, Abigail. It's clear how much he adores you,' Adele added kindly, and I smiled at her. I heard singing in the distance, and turned to find Leo dancing as he made his way down to the table to join us. He was greeted with cheers and clapping as my friends thanked him for the delightful afternoon tea. Bowing before taking a seat at the end of the table, he relaxed back in his chair, his handsome face mischievous, a lock of dark hair hanging loose over his brow.

'It was my pleasure, as always, although if I had known Polly would be here benefiting from my hard work—well, let's just say I would have sent a very special cake just for her flavoured with almonds.' He widened his eyes at her while she glared at him, her hands clenched into fists in her lap.

'How dare you threaten to poison me with arsenic, you big mouthed lunatic. You are fortunate there are witnesses or I would strike you dead where you sit.' A slow smile spread across his lips, while eyeing the safe distance between them.

'Oh, of course you would. That makes you the lunatic, Polly Wolly, and we know it well. Now hush your mouth and let the adults speak.' He raised his hand, his palm pointed towards her, while she shook her head, using all her restraint to not embarrass herself in front of our friends; however, I had no doubt Leonardo would suffer for this at a later time. 'Why are there no eligible men here at these fancy garden parties? Why does it have to be only sheilas, as the Australians say? I cannot have any real fun with any of you with those two things on your chest and your missing bits and pieces. I love you all, apart from Pollyanna—and possibly Dana if she doesn't behave herself—but you can keep yourselves to yourselves.' He paused for a moment, a wicked glint in his eyes. 'And you can stop flirting with me right now, Mrs Cavanaugh. I see the lust and longing in your eyes when you look at me, and I'm telling your husband, you tavern trollop.' Laughter filled the air, my mother-in-law the loudest amongst us, while Polly ignored his presence. Leo was not unlike a court jester from long ago who would pop out on occasions to entertain the residents of the castle before returning to his business, and, although it would be far less embarrassing if he quietened down and behaved himself, I loved him as he was, as did most living and working at Willow Grove. It was only when we were forced to hire new workers Leo was the brunt of their jokes—and the object of their hatred of anything and anyone not like them—and those men did not remain in our employ for long; however, I was aware some hid their disgust of him and kept their opinions private on the matter only to keep their job.

We rarely held parties where we entertained strangers, and this allowed my darling Leo to be himself and be comfortable in his own home, a feeling that had evaded him for most of his life. Catherine adored him, and willingly made all his clothes, taking great pleasure from the fact he would wear anything she designed, often turning up to deliver packages of loose pants made from soft, flowing materials unlike any man would wear on the streets of Geelong, along with matching shirts, all brightly coloured to compliment his headscarves. To me, he looked beautiful, always brightening up my day with his own sense of style. Slowly rising to my feet, I made my way to the empty seat beside my mother-in-law, still wiping the tears from her face while trying to compose herself and failing miserably, her laughter delighting me.

'It gladdens my heart to see Hamish has brought you such happiness, and peace has been restored, my dearest daughter. The children are thriving, and they adore him as if he were truly their father. I appreciate that very much.' Sadness settled on me for a moment, and she reached over and took my hand in hers. 'They haven't forgotten their Daddy, and miss him still; however, they need a father who is here and able to guide them. We love and respect Hamish for accepting them as his own. He has proven me wrong, as I was deeply worried he would return to his old ways, but he has convinced me he is committed and a man of his word. Our Aaron would be pleased, Abigail, wherever he is, as this was his last and only wish for you.' I smiled through my tears, her hand on my cheek. 'There are not many years between now and when I will see him again, and I promise to tell him everything about you he has missed. And how deeply you still love him. I give you my word, my dear girl.' She squeezed my hand, tears in her eyes as a lump lodged in my throat.

'You have many years before that time comes, and who knows? I could go before you. Not one of us knows what life has in store for us, and we have very little control over the matter.'

'And you, my darling daughter, can be confident that you will die old and happy in your bed, having lived the wonderful life you truly deserve.'

I stepped through the backdoor and staggered into the kitchen feeling lightheaded, far too hot, and a little unsteady on my feet from the champagne. Thomas and Emmy took no notice of me as I approached the kitchen table, both deeply involved in a game of cards with Hamish.

'Have yer friends departed?' Hamish asked, not taking his eyes from the cards in his hand, while I sat down heavily beside him.

'Yes. Irene and Maggie were the last to go. They stayed until they finished off the rest of the champagne.' I groaned, placing my head in my hands for a moment.

'Seems ye helped 'em. How many bottles were left? A dozen?' He chuckled as he watched me straighten up, swaying in my chair. Reaching out to steady me, he continued to laugh, the card game now forgotten.

'Thomas and Emmy. Take a good hard look at your mother. Blind Freddy can see she's stonkered, and it isn't even dinner time,' Leo announced as he placed a mug of black coffee on the table in front of me.

'I'm sorry. I cannot drink that. I will take a jug of lemonade and raspberry syrup to our room, and try and sleep it off,' I slurred apologetically, uncertain if they understood me as I placed my head on the tabletop, the wood-grain cold against my warm cheek.

'Abigail, you are so easily led into mischief by your friends when it comes to the grog. You should be ashamed, allowing yourself to overimbibe in this manner. And in front of your children at this hour, too. Well, you're no better than that tavern trollop, Trixie, whose enormous backside is planted on that bar stool twelve-hours a day, every day, down the village pub,' Leo teased, my children's laughter filling the room, while my head had started to ache.

'Oh, what a hypocrite,' I spat, my face still firmly pressed against the smooth table. 'You are behaving as if you have never been pissed in the garden during the day. I've had to carry you to bed and go without dinner because you're such a boozer.'

'I am not. You take that back now, Abigail. It's you that forced me to drink with you every single time, always bothering me and dragging me away from my responsibilities.' He stood over me, his hands firmly placed on his hips, his nose wrinkled. 'Hamish, your wife corrupts everyone around her, and I am of the firm belief you need to give her a hard smack to keep her in line,' Leo advised, nodding his head adamantly as Hamish raised his eyebrows in amusement, while Thomas and Emmy clearly found the entire situation hilarious.

'Ma would hit him back. When he's sleepin'. With an axe.' Thomas laughed at his own wit, while Hamish choked on his cider.

'Leo, go bang it up your backside,' I slurred as the room spun, and I gripped hard onto the table.

'Oh, Mummy. You don't look well. Do you need me to come and tie back your hair in case you are sick?'

'Aye, dinnae worry yerself, lass. I'll do it, as I've done many times before over the years.' Hamish mockingly widened his eyes, his tone woeful as she collapsed into giggles. Lifting my head, I tried to glare at them before rising unsteadily to my feet. My vision blurred, my thoughts fragmented, Hamish gently took my arm and guided me out of the room and down the hall to the bottom of the stairs. Seeing I was at risk of falling if I attempted to climb them without assistance, he gathered me into his arms and carried me to our bedchamber before placing me down gently on the bed. Emmy soon followed him with the jug of lemonade and raspberry, along with a basin should I be sick.

'Thank you, my beautiful Emmy,' I murmured, stroking her face as she kissed me.

'You're so funny, Mummy. You look so happy. I hope you have lovely champagne dreams.' She kissed me again before silently making her way back to the kitchen, while ensuring the door was firmly closed behind her.

'The lass is very sweet. So much like ye, me precious girl.' Hamish stood me up before stripping me naked, while leaving me holding the sideboard to steady myself, the room spinning. He strode into my dressing room, soon returning with a black silk negligee and dressing gown, apparently unable to find my plain cotton nightgown. Slipping the negligee over my head, he placed the dressing gown beside the bed within reach should anyone come in. 'There, ye look respectable enough if ye put yer dressin' gown over the top an' keep it closed.' I slid into bed with his assistance, a smile on my lips as I tried to focus my gaze on his handsome face.

'Oh, Hamish. Every single person who loves me—well, except for Dana, of course—is so thrilled I married you. Sister Josephine, and Mr and Mrs Malcolm, especially. Even Lord Harrington. He's coming to stay again next month . Did I tell you that yet? I only received his letter this morning,' I mumbled, my eyelids heavy as I yawned.

'Naw angel, ye dinnae, but it naw matters. Reg is welcome here, as he was the last time, an' I look forward tae seein' him again now I'm yer husband.' He smiled innocently as I raised an eyebrow in suspicion. 'Naw, I like the man. Fer an aristocrat, he's a nice bloke.' I closed my eyes, while he stripped off his clothes and climbed in beside me. 'I've been waitin' all day tae get ye alone. I was tempted tae drag ye away from yer garden party when ye met me down the side o' the house.' Kissing me forcefully, he pulled me close. 'An' yer far more affectionate when yer drunk an' I would naw miss bein' here tae witness it fer quids. Thank the Lord above fer champagne an' garden parties.' He grinned as I kissed him, my fingers entwined in his curly black hair as I loosened the bind, his hair soon hanging loose around his broad shoulders.

'I feel very blessed. The last time I was truly this happy was when we stayed at Heavenly Hideaway all those years ago,' I whispered, memories flooding my pickled mind.

After Aaron had been killed, I could not bring myself to return to our property in Gippsland. We had only ever been there once and stayed a fortnight when it all was sparklingly new, but had never been back since. I had such wonderful, special memories of Aaron and everyone we loved spending time there, it would only make me melancholy should I return, of that I was certain. Hamish had arranged for the guest cottages to be boarded up, and all the furnishings covered, along with securing the main house in the same manner. All remained as it was the day we left the property, not knowing then it would be the first and last time we would ever visit. Hamish organised for a neighbour to care for the property, and I was content to let it stay as it was until Thomas and Emmy were of an age to decide if they would holiday there. The thought of it all was far too painful for me, and I pushed the memories to the back of my grog addled mind.

'Rest now, precious girl,' he murmured in my ear, his hand resting on my heart as I nodded, allowing sleep to take me. Soon after, a man named Michael and a woman called Martha entered my dream, their four children at their knees running towards a river—one I recognised, yet unfamiliar—while visions of a noose, a book filled with blank pages, and a painted canvas tormented me.

Chapter Twelve

DECEMBER 25TH, 1907

I had woken this morning well before daybreak, excitement covered in joy leaving me unable to sleep a minute longer. I had dreaded Christmas when living at Emiliani House as a bairn, finding the day always left me feeling melancholy having to see the village children in their new clothing, flaunting their sweets and playing with their new toys, while we trudged through the streets to attend mass and thank the Lord for providing the little we had, holes in our shoes and all.

Our loved ones were invited to join us for lunch here today, as was our custom every year. I had carefully chosen presents for every soul attending, and placed them under our enormous tree in the sitting room weeks ago. Hamish had continued our Christmas tradition and cut down a Geebung tree to decorate, as had Mr and Mrs Cavanaugh every year since they first arrived in Australia in 1875, selecting the native plant for its pine-tree-like leaves and yellow flowers that bloomed at this time of year. Maturing to around forty-feet tall, I understood its attraction, and had adored them since Aaron had proudly dragged a Geebung through the front door for our first Christmas in Australia. Soon after, he had planted a number of them along the boundary of our property, attracting a variety of native animals and birds throughout the year. The round, fleshy fruit it bore was ripe to eat once they turned a deep purple in winter, and was a favourite of Leo's.

Sitting at the head of the elaborate table next to Hamish, I gazed around what had become one of my favourite places to spend time, the dining room always reminding me of family, while those seated at the table engaged in cheerful banter. Decorated beautifully with flowers from our own garden, candles flickered and burned on every surface, the table filled with platters of decadent food the kitchen staff had been preparing for over a week. Bowing our heads, the room soon fell silent as Hamish said a prayer, before our guests erupted in rowdy conversation, everyone helping themselves to the feast laid out before us. Our Sunday lunches and celebrations of any kind held here over the years weren't much different, the food always placed out on large silver platters from which we could serve ourselves. Although similar, it was not quite the same as I remembered the Malcolms' family lunches I so wanted to replicate as a young girl once blessed with a family of my own—the food here far more indulgent as a direct result of Leo and his expensive taste—and then there was the fact we employed an army of staff, while the Malcolms only had Mrs Shank to cook such a wonderful repast all by herself. Atop a silver trolley, Mr Masters standing beside it observing critically, sat flagons of wine, whisky, and beer, along with lemonade and fruit juice, the footmen replacing the empty bottles as swiftly as the guests drank them. Our loyal butler had never been comfortable with the lack of formality in our home; however, he was a tolerant man regarding my countrified eccentricities, as he politely called it. Mrs Cavanaugh sat by my side, her husband opposite, while Mr Makenzie had chosen to sit at the other end of the table with dear Harriet, who appeared distracted. Grateful Jemima had chosen not to attend, I smiled at my new mother-in-law, her eyes lighting up as she nodded in acknowledgement, a smirk touching her lips.

'Do ye remember the Yule an' the daft days after we spent at Castle Leod when we were lads, Hamish?' Angus called out from where he and Polly sat halfway down the long table, my brothers and sisters-in-law seated around them.

'Aye, although I rarely think o' those days in the old country anymore. I do remember 'twas naw the happiest o' times.' Hamish glanced at his father for a moment, then smiled sympathetically at his mother.

'Oh, Angus has the fondest memories of staying with your grandparents in that castle when you were bairns,' Polly remarked, while Hamish nodded slightly, continuing to eat, a hundred conversations going on around us. 'Why are you so angry, Hamish? I can see it in your eyes.'

'Best we leave the past where it belongs, dear Polly,' Harriet called out cheerfully, her husband abruptly turning to glare at her.

'Fer Christ's sake, what are ye moanin' about now, woman?' Without giving her time to respond, he fixed his gaze on Angus, then Hamish. 'Ye'd all be nothin' without me an' me family name, an' ye have the nerve tae whine about it? Yer mother here would've ended up naw different than the trollops down Little Lon openin' their legs fer a shillin' had I naw plucked her from the sewers, an' she knows it well.' I watched as Hamish's large hands curled into fists on the table, his broad shoulders tense, while Harriet looked down at her plate, her bottom lip trembling slightly, her cheeks flushed. I quickly placed my hand on my husband's leg under the table, his brown eyes glinting dangerously. Silence hung over the room, while Mr Masters averted his gaze, the footmen Jonathon and Samuel silent as they waited near the sideboard for yet another family argument on Christmas day to pass.

'That's naw true, an' *ye* know it well. Our mother is the granddaughter o' Michael Ferguson an' Freya Stewart from the village o' Prickwillow, an' she has every right tae be proud o' her kin fer their hard work an' fortitude.' Mr Makenzie sat back in his chair, his lips curled into a sneer as Hamish turned to address our guests. 'Our great-grandfather was once the head gardener at Castle Howard, while our great-grandmother ran the shop in the village sellin' gemstones—an' they made a good livin' from it an' were far from peasants as me father likes tae make out tae anyone who'll listen.' Mr Makenzie widened his eyes sarcastically, his broad arm slung over the back of his chair, while the scraping of cutlery on the china plates the only sound in the room as our friends and family tried to behave as if this was not the most awkward of lunches we had ever experienced.

'Aye, that may be so, but did she naw tell ye the state her grand-mother was in when she arrived in that village as a wean? Naw, o' course not. An' she's naw English, despite bein' born in York. Yer mother's great-grandparents hailed from Cromarty, an' were naw better than the beggars I'm forced tae spit on in the streets o' Melbourne. The story goes they were dressed in rags an' pleadin' with the parish priest tae feed an' house 'em. Am I a liar, Harriet? What say ye?' My stomach knotted up as I watched my dear friend lower her gaze, summoning all my strength not to rise to my feet, take the carving knife, and cut the old bastard's throat in front of witnesses at my very own table. I had always suspected he beat my friend; however, Harriet refused to speak of anything that passed between them within the walls of their mansion from the day we met to this. It was clear he tortured her mind, humiliating her constantly in public and private in word, thought and deed, and although I had never seen a bruise or a mark on her, I would not be surprised if he not only harmed her soul with his words, but her body with his fists. Harriet raised her head to meet his gaze, her hands trembling slightly, her voice barely above a whisper.

'I say, you need to question your own conscience, Colin, instead of attempting to tear my family apart. Have you told Angus that Polly may well be his sister?' My stomach dropped to the floor as several guests gasped aloud, while others remained silent. My eyes met Polly's, her face white as a bedsheet, while Angus remained where he was, unmoving, his face like stone.

'Haud yer wheesht, ye wicked bitch,' Mr Makenzie roared, startling me. Rising to his feet, he drew back his arm high above his head before bringing his fist down on the table, shattering the silence, along with several crystal glasses. He strode out of the room without looking back, the door slamming hard behind him. Harriet glanced at Angus, before fixing her stare on Polly, tears in her eyes as she watched her collapse into loud sobs.

'I apologise for my careless words. They were said in anger, and I am beyond ashamed. I need a moment to myself.' Harriet struggled to her feet and excused herself, seeking permission from Hamish to retreat to the drawing room as I prepared to follow, and take Pollyanna with me. He nodded, pushing away his plate as most of our dining companions had done. The leftovers were promptly removed, and the oversized plum pudding was carried in, flaming in brandy, and placed on the table by Mr Masters, the footmen setting down large bowls of custard to serve. Samuel glared at Leo as he slammed a jug of thick cream down in front of him before abruptly leaving the still silent dining room. There had been many a tense moment in the house since things had soured between them.

'I feel all the words inside my head will cause me to burst if I do not speak,' Leo said far too loudly as I narrowed my gaze.

'Well, do not let them spill from your lips or you will be in a thousand pieces right here on the dining room floor, of that, I give you my solemn promise,' I warned him, my face flushed.

'Although I am reluctant to speak, I feel I must,' Mr Masters interrupted, quickly approaching Hamish, who nodded. 'Mr Makenzie did not sire Pollyanna, of that I am certain.' Polly turned her head sharply, tears streaming down her pretty face, while I wiped my own with my handkerchief, feeling wretched for not only Polly, but Angus and their children witnessing every word.

'Aye, I hope yer right,' Hamish murmured, his eyes locked with Angus, while Mr Masters nodded only once.

'Pollyanna is my daughter, and I will no longer stand by in silence saying nought. Nor will I allow her mother, Anna, to be shamed, or her integrity questioned by any man, woman or child brave enough to do so—Makenzie or cook, it matters not.' I gasped, as did Leo, only for very different reasons, our gaze fixed on Mr Masters as he bowed his head for a moment, first to Polly and Angus, then Hamish and myself, before hurrying out of the room and quietly closing the door behind him.

'How *dare* Pollyanna's new Daddy disrespect me in front of witnesses? I am *not* a cook!' shrilled up into the silence, and I closed my eyes, wishing I was anywhere but here.

We met our staff in the back garden, as we had done every year since arriving at Willow Grove, to present them with their gifts and their yearly bonus of ten-pound. Providing refreshments of beer, wine, and fruit juice, they stood with their mates, or sat together on the lawn with their friends while enjoying afternoon tea, many looking forward to partaking in their own Christmas dinner in the dining hall tonight with their friends and families, along with free grog at the pub afterwards, paid for by Hamish from the farm account. We had experienced enormous profits from the sales of the Martarinos and were acutely aware Willow Grove would not be anywhere near as successful without our employees—their tireless hard work, dedication and loyalty valued by all who lived here, while openly envied by other large estates in the district.

Hamish jumped up on the old cart, shouting out to get their attention. A hush fell over them, many listening in silence as he wished them a Merry Christmas and thanked them for their hard work over the last year, a great number of them clapping and cheering once he finished. I had purchased gifts for every child who lived here as we always had, and the excitement of seeing their faces when they opened them was worth more than gold or silver.

My husband called up the unmarried women first, then the men one by one, passing out wrapped parcels for every soul living here, their names on small squares of cardboard tied with ribbon. It had taken me months to organise all the presents, and I had quickly tired of the long journeys into Geelong, along with frequenting Amelia's store, determined to purchase the perfect gift for each person. Hamish smiled as he handed the envelopes to our workers, the joy on their face when they opened them the only thanks we needed. I knew what a difference this money made in the coming year, allowing them all to have funds at hand should they be required for goods, services, and a few luxuries they would typically be unable to afford.

Moving around the garden, I mingled with the workers and their families before they excused themselves, some slowly making their way back to the village, others lingering for a time to chat, while I ensured I wished each and every one of them a happy and peaceful Yule.

Still suffering shock as a result of our luncheon, Polly and Angus had returned to their cottage, and Mr Masters had accompanied them at their request, while our family and friends relaxed in the garden, many sprawled out on the sun lounges, their stomachs too full to move, the gumtree above sheltering them from the warm sun. I smiled across at Lilith as she beckoned me, soon making my way to her side.

'Well, if that wasn't the most horrifying Christmas dinner I've sat through I will eat my hat. My own family gatherings are like attending Sunday mass in comparison.' Her voice teasing, her lilac eyes sparkling, I watched her collapse into giggles before lowering myself onto the comfortable lounge beside her, grunting to myself while rolling my eyes.

'I've put Harriet to bed in a guestroom. The poor darling was beside herself, but is resting fitfully now. I wish she would consider our offer, and leave that pig to drown in the shit he surrounds himself with.' I shook my head in frustration as Lilith's face darkened for a moment.

'Mrs Makenzie is a loyal soul, one of the most gentle and loving I've been fortunate to meet, but she will never willingly leave that man. She is an intelligent woman, and is aware she is at far greater risk of being seriously harmed in every way should she take that path, rather than remain until he tires of her and chooses to set her free under his own terms.' I frowned, not surprised at all by her response, before shaking my head in an attempt to clear the image of my father-in-law from my mind.

Joining us alone this year, I no longer saw my dear friend as often as I would have liked. Early last year, Jasper and Lilith had purchased over six-hundred hectares of land in Western Victoria. Leaving us in August 1906 and taking over seventy like-minded friends with them to embark on this new adventure, I missed her company dreadfully still. Finding myself quite drawn to the property they had purchased, its history fascinated me when they returned shortly after to tell of their good fortune, and the fact they would soon leave us.

Johann Fredrick Krumnow had been the charismatic and self-appointed leader of *Herrnhut*, Australia's first commune based between Penshurst and Hamilton in Western Victoria, settling on the land that now belonged to Jasper and Lilith.

On the 27th May 1853, Krumnow and his followers had acquired the 642 hectares of crown land for £1,584—less than half what Jasper and Lilith paid for it. However, they had purchased the property just over six-decades later—the land abandoned several years prior, while all the buildings still standing required some form of repair and were in a terrible mess.

Jasper and Lilith had set about to remedy that, and after living there for just over a year, had managed to restore over thirty buildings on the property, some small, while others were built to house hundreds and hundreds of people, reminding me of an enormous orphanage. They had gained another forty members since moving, and going by their frequent letters, had found the peace they were seeking—our dear friends were now able to live without fear, while free to do as they so chose without judgement, and this alone brought me great joy. It all sounded wonderful to me, while a farfetched dream to Hamish, who would chuckle loudly when reading their letters at the kitchen table to all who would listen.

Lilith had fallen in love with a member of the commune who had not gone to Utopia with the same motivation as the others, this man finding solace while attempting to escape his past. I had met Mr Sam Amess when they had all travelled to Melbourne to attend the Supreme Court for a hearing involving one of their members. They had stayed for several months on and off, and Hamish and I had taken the opportunity a number of times to travel to Melbourne to join them at *The Delmont*, where we had offered them safe lodging without recompense for the length of the trial.

I personally found Mr Amess to be a lovely man who clearly adored Lilith, and he was handsome to boot with a calm confidence about him. Angus and Hamish had known him for years, and were mates long before he found himself at Utopia, the black highland cattle on our property sold to Angus from his father's herd on Churchill Island after the old man died—with or without the family's consent, we were still uncertain. Jasper and Lilith's relationship was complicated, and not one I interfered with, nor did I comment on their lovers' given I still struggled to understand their arrangement.

The previous commune run by Krumnow had been part of the Moravian Church, an evangelical Protestant movement originally from Bohemia in Germany, although Kromnow had been initially based in Melbourne after immigrating to Australia, and had converted most of his followers while based in Collingwood—predominantly farmers, carpenters, blacksmiths, saddlers, masons and other craftsmen, along with their families.

This had resulted in the most exquisite buildings, all finely crafted and solidly built in the way of a village back in their homeland. Despite being left abandoned and empty for a number of years until Jasper and Lilith stumbled across the property, their commitment and the hard physical labour of all who lived there had slowly but surely restored the place to what it had once been.

All who lived at Utopia were expected to contribute in some way, whether that was working the land to produce items of value that could be taken to market—art, wool, furniture, and grain were highly sought after, as were the animals they raised to slaughter, some of the excess meat sold when they could spare it—while others spent their time carrying out domestic chores to ensure the residents were fed and the place spotless. Working together for the greater good and the group as an entirety, they produced most of their own food, while making items to trade or sell to generate the money needed to run the property and ensure the basic needs of all who lived there were met.

They had restored a building quite similar to our dining hall, where they cooked and ate together. A small but dedicated group of women had volunteered to work in the kitchen as their contribution to Utopia, and those who were too old or infirm to carry out physical work were excused; however, a great number chose not to be idle and kept their hands busy knitting, crocheting or embroidering items to be sold at market to earn their keep.

Although I dreamed of visiting with them and seeing the place with my own eyes, Hamish had bluntly refused me when told of their invitation, concerned they would corrupt me in every way. We had met a number of the residents who travelled with them on occasion, and found them all to be lovely, albeit wonderfully strange in their freethinking ways. Jasper and Lilith had visited with us as often as possible when their responsibilities brought them back to Melbourne; however, this was becoming less frequent, and due to the great distance that lay between us now, we had rarely seen them in the last few months.

'I thought there would be bloodshed in my own dining room. I've never experienced a dinner like it, nor do I wish to again.' She nodded thoughtfully, her gaze on Polly and Angus in the distance as they slowly made their way hand-in-hand towards us, pausing at times to enjoy the fragrance of the roses while in deep discussion.

'Do you think it a coincidence that Mr Masters found himself in your employ?' I exhaled loudly before shrugging my shoulders, while a smile touched her lips. 'I do not believe in happenstances myself, and I did have my suspicions when it came to your butler that all was not what it seemed. I tried a number of times to offer him a reading when we lived here, but he bluntly refused, and now I understand why.' Her musical laughter rang out across the garden, our friends and family sitting together in groups enjoying the warmth of the late afternoon sun, while Polly stopped beside me, a weak smile on her lips.

'May I sit beside you, Abi? I don't feel like talking with anyone else at the moment.' Lilith nodded sympathetically before rising to her feet and embracing Polly warmly, while Angus prepared to join the others. He bent down and gently kissed her cheek before grinning at me as I rose to my feet to embrace Lilith. We waved them off before sitting back down on the same sun lounge, our shoulders touching, the sounds of the bush and native birds competing to be heard.

'How are you, Polly?' She sighed deeply, her eyes fixed on Willy and Bella in the distance sitting with Thomas and Emmy, their heads close while in deep discussion.

'Oh, Abi. I don't know where to start.' I took her hand in mine, squeezing gently in reassurance, my eyes locked with hers.

'At the beginning. Always at the beginning.' She nodded, her face relaxing into a half-smile before taking a deep breath, her complexion still pale.

'I don't really know what the beginning is, to be honest. Mr Masters... I mean, my father... oh, that sounds so ridiculous, even to me.' She paused, shaking her head in disbelief, while I smothered a smile at the thought. Her breath slow, she rested her head back against the lounge and closed her swollen eyes, while I gazed across at our loved ones in the distance, paying us no mind in our quiet corner of the garden. 'He only told me what he felt he must, given the shock of it all, but has promised over time to explain everything. He feels it's his duty as my father, and Willy and Bella's grandfather, to correct the gossips who have taken great pleasure in slandering my mother's character and questioning her morality since before I was even born. His one regret in life is not coming forward sooner and identifying himself publicly, and of course, missing out on the bond we would have shared from the beginning as father and daughter. The experience of being part of a real family that we so desperately yearned for, Abi.'

'Are you certain he is your father?'

'He knows far too much, and he has nothing to gain from lying.' I nodded, while joy mingled with peace settled over me that my dear sister finally knew something of her kin. What she chose to do with that information was entirely up to her, and I would support her no matter what her decision, as she had so loyally done for me. I had felt pressured by many an opinion over the years regarding the Howard family, and my decision to remain estranged from all connected by blood was often questioned; however, I had my reasons and felt it was no one else's business what they were—and Polly had always agreed, and spoken up on the matter, if forced, on my behalf.

'I heard the rumours, as have most who live here, but never did I once consider any of them to be true, Polly.' She nodded, her eyes still closed.

'Oh, I thought Leonardo had made them all up to spite me, finding it best to ignore his passionfruit vine and all who eat from it, rather than be taken to trial for cold-blooded murder,' she murmured as I laughed aloud, a smile touching her lips, 'but the wee dickhead wasn't far wrong.' She opened one eye for only a moment as I collapsed into giggles, pausing for a time until I composed myself. 'He told me of my mother, Anna. She was your mother's older sister, Abi, but he didn't find out until much later exactly who you were.' A lump lodged in my throat. We weren't sisters, but cousins, the invisible thread that had always connected us unknowingly forged by blood. She squeezed my hand, her eyes still firmly closed as several tears trickled down her face, while I openly sobbed. 'My father had a short love affair with Anna Campbell. It was when he travelled from England with his master to Castle Leod in 1873 to visit the

Makenzies for a month.' She paused again, raising her hand to quieten me, her eyes still closed as I wiped my face and settled myself back beside her. 'Before you say anything, I'm aware how serendipitous this is given we married into that clan, but it seems my mother was in service there for a brief time before leaving to work at Merinda Manor, *your* Lord Harrington's estate, shortly before I was born. I had heard mention over the years that Mr Masters... my father... was in their employ for over a decade before coming to Australia to start a new life, but now I know that is not entirely true. He came here for me, Abi. He only found out I existed after I had already passed my first birthday, but by then I was already considered an orphan and living at Emiliani House under the authority of the kirk. The poor man tried to claim me a number of times when I was a wean, but Sister Mary Monica would not take him at his word and refused, saying he had no proof, and given he could not produce my mother to speak up one way or the other, the wicked bitch dismissed him every time.' Memories flooded my mind of the last time I set eyes on her in the hallways of the orphanage, and fury clenched at my stomach while I summoned all my strength not to curse out loud. 'It was common knowledge downstairs at Merinda Manor he sired me, and that my mother broke his heart and ruined him for all others, but the servants were willing to keep his confidence and help where they could. He spoke fondly of the cook there at the time, Agnes Fraser, who offered to care for me as her own, suggesting he snatch me away under the cover of darkness; however, it mattered not, and all his attempts failed.' I smiled softly at no one in particular, a new admiration for my inflexible, solemn, and overly conventional butler growing exponentially. 'He kept track of me over the years through one of the Sisters, who kindly sent him a letter twice a year in secret to ease his mind, while he waited for the day I was old enough to leave and he could claim me. He had planned to secure a position for me under his supervision, and *your* Lord Harrington's own father had given his consent on the matter, even taking the offer of employment to Sister Maleficent Monica herself. But the cunning bitch lied, telling them I would stay until I turned sixteen. It was only when he received a letter a month after I left, telling him I had been sent to England and my whereabouts was unknown, did he realise just how depraved *that woman* truly is.' She grunted to herself, while visions of Sister Mary Monica being struck down by lightning where she stood brightened my mood ever so slightly. 'He took leave from his position shortly after to look for me, with the blessing of *your* Lord Harrington's father, and eventually found himself in Suffolk discreetly asking after me at Somerleyton Hall. He had heard whispers when still in Scotland I had been taken there against my will and forced into service, but by the time he arrived to save me, I was long gone.' My stomach dropped to the floor, images of this Somerleyton Hall flashing through my mind, the stables and gardens so terribly familiar, yet I had not stepped foot on the place as far as I knew. Nausea overwhelmed me for a moment, and I quickly sat up and reached for a glass of water, taking several slow sips as the odious castle faded to the back of my mind.

'Reg is not *my* Lord Harrington, so stop it, Polly,' I pointed out abruptly, and she laughed aloud. 'What I want to know is how on earth he arrived here before us? Was that by chance or intent? I'll remind you that he secured the position at Willow Grove months before we stepped off that ship.' I gazed across the garden at Hamish, beer in hand, his dark eyes twinkling as he swapped banter with Patrick and Aiden.

'Weeks, not months. It was by luck he found me in the end, but not here in Geelong. He saw us that day going into the zoo with Richard in London, then followed us around the place at a distance. We obviously paid him no mind, as I have no recollection of it, but he listened to the conversations between us—and we were not discreet, going by how he tells it. Well, until I noticed that customer from the tavern.' She cringed while my stomach lurched at the memory. So long ago now, yet it seemed a lifetime had passed. 'He says we spoke of Geelong that day, and of your lawyer here, although not by name. I cannot recall any of it if I were to be honest.' She sniffed loudly before rubbing her nose on the back of her hand. 'I'm grateful he didn't find me when I was at the tavern, but he knows about my time there. He had been in London for weeks looking for me, and had asked around the docks daily, and been told by many a similar lass worked for Leroy. I wasn't there, of course, when he went looking, but he was confident it was me and I was still with the unknown red-haired woman reported to have kidnapped me.' Her musical laughter surrounded me, my head filled with memories. Some I chose not to relive and push to the back of my mind, while others made me smile and lightened my heart. 'It was by pure luck he was walking near Regent's Park that day, as he had exhausted his funds and was set to return to Merinda Manor until he could earn enough to look for me again.'

'You talked of everything but what I asked you.' She continued to laugh while I leaned back and closed my eyes, enjoying the warm air softly tickling my skin.

'Oh, he arrived here only weeks before us, Abi. After visiting a number of solicitors in town the day his ship docked, he soon tracked down Mr McPhee, who was not a discreet man when he was amongst the living. Thinking him there to apply for one of the positions advertised, he confirmed Willow Grove would soon have Isabelle Delmont's heir in residence, and we know what happened after that.' I nodded, feeling not a pang of guilt or grief for the recently departed Mr McPhee; however, I had liked Mrs McPhee a great deal, and was saddened to hear she followed him only weeks later, God rest her.

'Did he mention if he is aware Maisie is Anna and Mary Campbell's younger sister? I was only told of the connection myself when staying at Merinda Manor, and I have wanted to ask him a thousand times since out of sheer curiosity.' Her eyes fluttered open, widening in disbelief as she shook her head.

'Are you teasing me?' It was my turn to shake my head, laughter bubbling up inside me.

'No, but I understand why you would think so. I thought the same when I would hear whispers on Leo's vine saying as much; however, it was confirmed when I met their brothers who are still in Reg's employ. Our uncles.' My voice low, she closed her eyes once again, before raising her hand to her head to gently rub her temples.

'It seems we are all somehow connected, whether we know it or not, Abi, and it is not an unpleasant feeling.' She took my hand in hers once again, resting our entwined fingers on her stomach before turning to me and meeting my gaze. 'Unless I am yet to discover Leonardo is my long-lost brother. The thought is far too awful to contemplate or accept, even when said in fun. Then there's the fact I would be forced to spend the rest of my days behind prison walls for his sudden disappearance... and subsequent murder.' Our laughter rang out across the garden, the afternoon sun low, while several of our loved ones turned to stare, their smiles bright as we laughed louder, while content in the knowledge we had always been family, and always would.

Chapter Thirteen

APRIL 1909

The smell of coffee filtered up my nose, a smile touching my lips as my eyes fluttered open, while Hamish slid back into bed after placing a tray on the table beside him holding a silver pot and two clay mugs.

'I've brought ye somethin'.' I struggled to sit up, my yawn wide while making myself comfortable against my pillows. He leaned over to kiss me before handing me the freshly brewed coffee, a smirk on his lips. 'I cannae believe the twins are eighteen taeday. Where did the time go?' He stared out over the garden, the lace curtains billowing out in the gentle breeze floating through the open windows.

'I have not a clue. How old do you think I feel having carried and birthed what are now two fully grown adults? I'm not blind and see the wrinkles on my face getting deeper every morning in the looking glass.' I grinned at him while rubbing the sleep from my eyes. I had turned thirty-four in January and had started to feel my age.

'Och, ye look like Emmy's older sister. Naw her mother. Do naw say such scaffy in me presence.'

'Oh, I love you for saying it, Hamish, but unfortunately you are slightly biassed when it comes to my appearance.'

'Naw, that's a furphy. I can naw walk down the streets o' Geelong with ye without folks starin'. Naw doubt they're wonderin' what business an old man like me has with a beautiful young lass like ye. More than likely they suspect ye've escaped from the asylum.' He smirked wickedly, while I leaned across and playfully punched him on the arm before reaching over to fill my cup.

'You're not even forty yet, and I cannot find one silver hair in that thick mop of curls on your head. You are far more handsome now than the day I met you, my darling man.' His kiss deep, I encircled him with my arms, not wanting to let go. I had been a bundle of nerves for the past month, as I expected Thomas to ask for Hannah's hand within days, if not this evening. Dedicated to each other, their bond had grown even stronger since first meeting four-years ago on the ship. Their betrothal and impending marriage was inevitable, and I had decided to be gracious when it occurred, while trying to be happy, despite feeling far from it.

Thomas had confided in me months ago that Hamish had taken him to Mr Dawson to have Hannah's engagement ring made, along with both wedding rings designed to match. My son, unable to hide his excitement, had shown me the flawless diamond—elegantly set in a wide gold band surrounded by a dozen smaller stones—the very same evening he returned from Melbourne after collecting the expensive jewellery.

We had experienced an influx of young gentlemen, from Willow Grove and districts near and far, seeking permission to call on Emmy; however, she refused them all, choosing to spend her time with friends at home, or staying with family. She would travel to Geelong during the week to stay the night at Catherine's when she would visit with Beatrice, their bond growing strong over the years despite their age difference. They enjoyed a close friendship, as strong as what Catherine and I shared, and it lightened my heart to see Beatrice at her most relaxed when she came to stay at Willow Grove, sometimes for weeks until Catherine demanded she return home.

'Come here, auld woman. Come talk tae me. Thomas an' Emmy'll be here within a couple o' hours tae get their birthday presents.' I turned over, placing my head on his shoulder while he gathered me in his arms and pulled me close. Memories of my children bursting into my bedchamber and bounding onto the bed, particularly on their birthday and Christmas morning made me smile. 'This'll be the only opportunity I'll get tae have ye tae meself taeday an' I plan tae enjoy every minute. Yer goin' tae be far too busy runnin' about the place organisin' this party, an' everyone'll be wantin' yer attention, despite naw needin' it. I know better than most exactly what it'll be like here. Chaos.' He smiled; his face close to mine as he gazed into my eyes. 'Leo said tae tell ye good mornin', an' sends his congratulations tae ye on bein' the mother o' two fine adults who'll contribute tae the world far more than their mother—an' he made me promise tae remind ye that within the comin' year or two, ye'll likely be a granny.' He laughed aloud, his arms tightening around me as I rolled my eyes.

'That man has a beastly tongue and a wicked mind.' I smirked at the thought of him as I struggled to sit up, picking up my cup to drain the last of it before pouring another.

'He made me promise to repeat it word fer word three times before he'd hand over yer mornin' coffee .' He sat up beside me, chuckling to himself. 'He gets great satisfaction out o' teasin' ye, but then I've seen ye give it back tae him far worse over the years, naw different than if ye were brother an' sister. I've naw doubt he'd pull yer hair if he got mad enough with ye.' He threw back his head and laughed, while my eyes went wide.

'Have you lost your sight and not told me? He has always yanked my hair at every opportunity. You were in the room last week when he grabbed a handful of it, and pulled it so hard I screamed, but he ran away before I could grab him by the balls.' I sneered at no one in particular as my husband continued to laugh.

'Aye, I remember, but I dinnae realise he had pulled yer hair. I thought he pinched ye, an' I know I witnessed him try tae trip ye over on purpose the same day, naw different from what most older brothers do tae an annoyin' younger sister.' He chuckled as his eyes twinkled and I smiled at him.

'He *is* closer than a brother, which is the only reason I tolerate his awful behaviour. Who would have thought that night on the ship when we met by accident during that silly dance we would still be friends all these years later?' Leaving out the fact Leonardo was surrounded by the golden glow, I hadn't yet opened up to Hamish about the auras I saw, or what I had learned when I was married to Aaron after he confided in me his conversation with Maslow. If I spoke of what I had witnessed with my own eyes, and heard with my own ears since Aaron's death, I was confident he would take me to the Ararat Asylum and sign me over himself.

'I cannae believe 'tis comin' up twenty-years since ye moved into this house. Ye really did make Willow Grove yer own, me precious girl.' He shifted comfortably, leaning back on his pillows before placing his empty cup on the tray. 'From the way ye treat the staff, tae the buildings an' improvements ye've made here. Ye went against what was expected o' ye from the start, an' I could naw be prouder o' ye, Abigail.' I leaned over and placed my cup next to his before slipping back down under the heavy quilt, while listening to him talk of times now gone, his thick brogue lulling me to sleep. 'Ye could have secured the ear o' the most powerful in the country, an' befriended those who are connected tae anyone worth knowin', but the closest ye come tae mixin' with the likes o' that lot is when we attend *The Cosmopolitan Theatre* when stayin' in Melbourne.' I yawned, not bothering to cover my mouth as I pressed my body deeper into the feathered mattress while he continued on. 'The newspapers an' magazines print every picture they can get o' ye, whether they ask yer permission or naw. I watched me parents all me life with their wealthy friends, attendin' balls an' fancy parties, an' I formed the opinion that was how me own life was tae be. An' that was me plan. Tae be like me father an' own an estate with hundreds o' servants, an' take a timid wife who'd naw speak back, knowin' her place, an' that she's fortunate tae be there tae supervise the Nannies raisin' our eight bairns. I'd planned tae make powerful connections, while keepin' me mistresses a secret an' away from me family. Then I met ye, an' everythin' changed. I know now the way I was raised was naw the best. Through naw fault o' me mother's. I was never a happy lad, an' the truth is, I favoured me father fer far too long, an' followed in his footsteps without conscience.' Mr Makenzie continued to shame Harriet on a daily basis by openly flaunting his lovers around Geelong, and there was talk he had fathered a dozen children with numerous mistresses, their ages ranging from eighteen down to a month old, much to my disgust.

Mr and Mrs Makenzie visited every week without fail on a Wednesday for luncheon, and I could barely stand it. I loved Harriet deeply, and felt wretched for what she suffered at the hands of that bastard she was bound to, but I also felt hopeless, and unable to help my dear friend. Lilith had advised me a number of times not to interfere, or I would place her in great danger, so I kept silent on the matter. All Colin Makenzie did was criticise Hamish, pointing out all he did wrong, from running the property to how overfamiliar we were with the servants. Hamish had made me promise to hold my temper no matter what passed between them or how his father behaved. He loved his mother deeply, and was acutely aware his father would cut her off from us again in a heartbeat if displeased, and it was only for his sake I held my tongue. Hamish had not once invited them to our Sunday lunches, preferring the company of those who had joined us from the very beginning when we first moved to Geelong, along with the new friends we had made here over the years.

'You are nothing like your father.' I lifted my hand to his handsome face, his gaze fixed on mine. 'Hamish, you are loving, thoughtful, compassionate, and a kind and wonderful man. You favour your sweet mother and don't you ever forget that. You deserved to be loved more as a bairn, and I'm sorry for it, I truly am. Your father did not set a good example for you as a lad to follow, but you took another path by choice because you are not like him. I would not love you as I do if you were.' I gently kissed his lips, feeling terribly sad for him, while his arms tightened around me as I stroked his back reassuringly.

Although he was a sweet and sensitive man in private, he had behaved like his father for a long time—and everyone throughout the district and beyond knew it well—while there were a handful who would not allow him to forget his past, or accept the change in him was genuine. Believing his father's treatment of others was customary of a man in his position after witnessing his bad behaviour during his tender years, he made some terribly poor choices when it came to the women he had loved and lost before we married. In the years we had been together, I could not fault his conduct, nor did I doubt the love held for us. Always thoughtful and romantic, he often took me to Melbourne to spend the weekend for no reason at all, or whisked me away to our cottage with little or no warning. He was affectionate and loving, often sneaking away from work during the day to meet with me because he missed my company, and I found his actions spoke far louder than his words when it came to love.

'Thank ye fer trustin' an' believin' in me, Abigail. Me greatest fear is turnin' out like the man. 'Tis naw somethin' I ever wanted tae be.'

'You are safe, my love. You have nothing to prove to anyone.' A slow grin spread across his lips as he held me to his chest and closed his eyes. After so many years seeking his father's approval, while searching for something he could never find, a sense of peace finally settled on him—and I was grateful.

The door burst open, and I turned to find Thomas and Emmy running across the room, their footsteps heavy, before my grown daughter threw herself down across the foot of the bed, no different from when she was a wean. Thomas much more sensibly lowered himself down next to her, their smiles wide as we wished them many happy returns of the day.

'Och, now how does it feel tae be free o' yer parents, an' o' an age tae make yer own choices, good or bad?' Hamish teased, propping himself up against his pillows beside me.

'Oh Da, we'll never be free of you and Mama, nor do I wish to be.' Emmy laughed aloud, her hair spread out over the pillow I had passed her and glimmering like silk in the early morning light, while Thomas smiled up at me as I smoothed my hair back from my face.

'Well, I don't wanna be free of either of ya, but I'm a grown man now, Ma.' My son stared back at me fondly, before turning to Hamish and rolling his eyes knowingly, my lips twitching as I relaxed back on the pillows propping me up.

The spit of his father, Thomas was tall, broad and handsome, possessing the same scruffy sandy blonde hair and big blue eyes, always reminding me of the ocean on a sunny day. At times, I felt I was looking at Aaron back when I first met him all those years ago. Even his smile was the same. He was blessed with the easy going manner and good nature of his father—always making friends wherever he went—and had stayed in touch with every single person he considered a mate, as had sweet Emmy.

I rearranged my pillows as I watched them swap banter with Hamish, while hoping someone would soon bring a pot of coffee. Glancing at my daughter, I smiled at her likeness to myself, not only in looks, but in temper. We had experienced a constant stream of young men calling at the house over the past two-years wishing to court her. She was tired of it, and now refused to entertain any of them. Although placing herself in a position where she was at risk of being considered rude, or far worse, she no longer cared what anyone had to say about the matter. Hamish and I supported her decision to no longer receive visits from anyone other than family and friends, and her step-father was now the one to politely turn them away at the door, advising anyone who would listen that Emmy was already promised.

I quickly rose from my bed and hurried to my dressing room to find their wrapped gifts. Returning soon after, I passed two parcels to Hamish, while keeping the other two with me as I climbed back into bed.

'Here my darling boy. Happy birthday.' Handing my son a small box, he thanked me before bending his head to open it, tears in his eyes as he caught sight of what was inside, while causing my own to fill and spill over. He turned to embrace Hamish as I wiped my face with the back of my hand, thanking him before gathering me in his arms. Now he was a man, the day had come for me to pass over the gold watch his father never took off until that day when they arrested him. 'That's from your father. Wear it with his love, Thomas. He would want you to pick the best memory you have of him to keep close in your heart, and remember him often.' He nodded, pulling away to slip the gold band on his wrist, while Hamish squeezed his shoulder in comfort. Handing Emmy a large flat box, I sat back in silence to watch her open it, a gasp coming from her lips as she gently pulled back the tissue paper.

'Oh, Mummy. I cannot believe it. It's your gown. The one I have always adored even more than chocolate.' She clutched the emerald green silk to her chest, her eyes closed, her face lit up in a brilliant smile. 'Thank you so very much, Mama. I will wear it tonight, but

I do hope Mary knows how to fit this headpiece.' She gazed down at the gemstone strand, struck by its beauty, the emeralds embedded on the gold chain glittering as she caressed them with her fingers. Little Mary had been assigned as Emmy's ladies maid two-years ago when my children outgrew the need for a nanny, rendering her position with us redundant. They adored each other, and enjoyed a close friendship, no different than Bessie and myself. Hamish cleared his throat, startling me from my thoughts as he handed Emmy her present, then the remaining parcel to Thomas.

'We give these tae ye with all our best wishes. When ye look at them, we hope it reminds ye o' us, an' how much we love ye. Naw matter where life leads ye, we're never far away.' Hamish paused, full of emotion as he watched them open their gifts. We had travelled to Melbourne to see Mr Dawson, requesting he craft an identical gold chain to the one I had buried Aaron with, although without a diamond so Thomas could add his own once he was married and the bairns came along. Emmy squealed when she opened the small box to find a gold ring, the pink diamond far smaller than mine; however, she appeared thrilled as she slipped it onto her left hand.

'Oh my. I cannot thank you enough, Da, and of course, Mama. It's too fantastic for even me to believe. I have my very own pink diamond.' She turned her face up to the ceiling and squealed in delight. 'This should stop the blokes turning up here to seek my affection. It looks as if someone has asked for my hand, and I accepted.' Emmy waved her finger around in excitement, her eyes shining as she admired the ring, before embracing us all at once. I slipped the chain around Thomas's neck, securing the clasp before gently kissing his cheek.

'Thank ya, Ma. I love ya more than ya know. Ya've been the best mother any bloke could ask for, an' nothin' scares me as I know ya've always got me back. As for Da, well, I love ya as much as I love me own Daddy, God rest him. Thanks for being there for us. I'll never take this off, an' always be reminded of me three parents who loved me without limits or judgement.' Thomas and Hamish hugged for the longest time, while Emmy and I fiddled with the emerald headpiece, neither of us having much luck to our great amusement.

Making our way through the wide corridors connecting the distinct wings of the grand mansion, Thomas and Emmy walked ahead of us, deep in discussion. Turning into yet another hallway, this one leading directly to the dining room, a portrait of a young boy caught Emmy's eye, and she paused, calling for Thomas to stop while she waited for Hamish and I to catch up. Pointing to the smiling child, his tiny frame painted standing in front of a shop, his boots, overalls and thick coat immaculate, the initials *B H* were signed on the bottom right corner, the large sign above the shop in the background written in black and identifying the business inside as *K & B Hinkle Fashion House.* A sad smile touched her own lips as she stood on the tips of her toes, elegantly raising her hand to lift the picture down from its hook—surprising me when she took the one next to it of a pretty young girl, dark-skinned and dark-haired, standing in front of what appeared to be Polly's cottage. Dressed in a plain skirt and white shirt, a shawl pulled tight over her shoulders, she was flanked by an older Aboriginal woman in native dress, their arms around each other, a strong resemblance between them.

'Dear Mr Hinkle told me the most dreadful story last week about this poor lass.' Her voice barely above a whisper, she traced her finger over the young woman's features before leaning back against the wall.

'It would be nice if the *dear* old bastard was as helpful to everyone else forced to tolerate him as he is to you, Emmy. I've invited him a number of times over the years to join us for a meal so I could ask him about the history of the place, but he runs for his gun every single time,' I complained, while Hamish and Thomas threw back their heads and howled with laughter.

'Oh, Mummy. He's harmless, and has you all bluffed. He loved your great-aunt very much, and she viewed him as her own nephew. The poor man was used to living a certain way, and holds strong opinions on the matter, one of them being you have all sullied Lady Delmont's memory and reputation since the day you stomped onto the soil of Willow Grove without care or conscience.' Emmy laughed quietly, her eyes twinkling, while I wrinkled my nose, feeling highly offended.

'Our father used ta say that opinions are like arseholes. Everyone has one, but it doesn't mean others need ta see or hear about it,' Thomas interrupted, and I rolled my eyes, leaning back on the opposite wall while Hamish studied the faces lining the hall with renewed interest.

'We have been nothing but kind to that man, despite his awful threats to anyone unfortunate enough to pass the gates when he is outside. He would have been forcibly removed years ago if he tried his scaffy on any other property,' I spat, while Hamish looked back over his shoulder, his eyes twinkling in amusement. I tried to compose myself, not wanting to ruin their birthday before it even began.

'Why does the auld man hold such strong feelin' towards yer mother?' Hamish called out, not taking his eyes from the wall for a moment.

'Well, he was looking forward to meeting Mama for months, but when all the servants turned up here the day after she arrived, he knew then she was nothing like her kin, and wanted no part in it.' She turned to me, widening her emerald green eyes teasingly. 'He believes you think far too much of yourself and likens you to Queen Victoria. Without a drop of royal blood running through your veins.' She snorted, clearly amused. 'He often refers to you as Lady Regalia—a pretender of the worst kind—a beast of a woman who should be ashamed of keeping those who have no choice in the matter as servants. Enslaved for the sole purpose of having them chase after you day and night, carrying out chores you are too slovenly to do for yourself. He is of the firm belief you were born under a lucky star to come into such fortune, but wishes to remind you money is the only thing that separates you from those you employ to carry out your dirty work. You didn't earn a penny, nor do you deserve it any more than they do.' My head snapped around to glare at my daughter, my cheeks flushed. Opening my mouth to defend myself, she raised her hand to stop me, drawing our attention back to the portrait in her hand. 'This young woman turned up here looking for her mother after suffering a terrible tragedy.' I summoned all my strength not to march outside and up to Mr Hinkle's cottage to shoot him in the foot with his own gun, dropping my gaze to study the picture.

'If it's too awful, I would rather not know.'

'Oh, Mama, I cannot get the story out of my head, and must tell someone,' Emmy pleaded, and I nodded, relenting as Thomas wandered off to catch up to Hamish, now studying the bronze statue ten-yards away near the entrance to the dining room, the plaque embedded in the marble identifying him as George Howard. 'The younger woman is named Ruby, after the lady standing by her side in the picture. That's her mother, but they hadn't seen each other since Ruby was a wean. This was painted the day she arrived at Willow Grove and reunited with her kin. The poor lass was taken by her Da when still at her mother's breast. He sounds like he was a good for nothing sod.' She sniffed loudly, while a lump lodged in my throat.

'What did he do to the poor child?'

'It's what he didn't do. He was a convict, sent over from Ireland for thieving, and when he got his ticket of leave, he travelled from place to place begging for work, while really looking for opportunities to steal and take advantage. He met Ruby's mother and stayed with her people for a time, promising her the world when he found out she had fallen with his child. But when things soured between them weeks after Ruby was born, the bastard snuck away in the night and took the baby with him. Abandoned her within weeks, he did. Left her with an English couple and was never heard of again.' Dread sat heavy in the pit of my stomach, my mouth dry as I cleared my throat.

'Well, I hope they loved and cared for her after such a terrible start in life.' She shook her head vigorously, and I swallowed hard.

'That respectable, and very wealthy married couple, showed not a drop of kindness, Mama. They didn't take her in as their own child, they paid that pig money for her, no different from purchasing livestock. They owned a large sheep station in South Australia, and used the Aboriginal people as their personal slaves, paying the adults only in rations and providing a bed, never money, expecting them to feed their children from what they were given, even though the young ones worked alongside their parents. From how Mr Hinkle heard it, they started taking in orphans to learn the way of the English before going into service, not only at their own property, but they sold them to their friends, and most were not orphans at all.' Her eyes wide, she tapped her finger gently on the chest of the young woman. 'Ruby spent her first eight-years being raised by an ex-convict, alongside seventeen other children, give or take a few, all in a two-room cottage set away from the main house.' She stopped once again to compose herself, before gazing into my eyes. 'The woman given the task to care for them was transported out from Scotland, and spent twenty-years at the female factory in Hobart for baby farming before finding her way into their employ once she served her time. Mr Hinkle reckons she killed hundreds of babies before she was caught, and continued doing so when the urge overtook her once she gained her freedom, but that's another story.' She shuddered, a chill running down my spine as I closed my eyes for a moment and prayed she would summarise what she so clearly needed to purge from her head and heart, while cursing Mr Hinkle for befouling my daughter's mind with his awfully blunt retellings of the past that had nought to do with us. 'Poor Ruby started as a scullery maid at nine, but was sold to a friend of the master four-years later. They sent her away to a small household twenty-miles outside of Adelaide to carry out domestic chores and assist the cook. That's all they want to train them to do, Mama, still to this day. I often hear Mrs McGinty's words in my head all those years ago harping on about how they're only good for labouring and domestic service, and even then they need a whip held to them. Thank goodness for Mr Unaipon stopping here for a time to open her mind, and change her heart.' I nodded, smiling to myself at the thought of David and Kate, who had recently come to the attention of the nation after his hand-held shearing tool had changed the way of the wool industry, a box of them arriving only a month ago addressed to Hamish.

'You can see the sadness in her eyes, even though it's a painting. Some of these are very detailed, and done by the same hand, I suspect.' She nodded as I ran my finger over the cottage in the background, our heads almost touching as we stared down at the women, strangers to us but so very familiar.

'Mr Hinkle said there was once an artist here who painted everything from memory. As if he had the ability to take a photograph in his mind, and recall it in every detail even months later.' I nodded, trying to gently hurry her along given Hamish and Thomas had already wandered into the dining room without us, while wishing Mr Hinkle would bang his thoughts and opinions up his own arse.

'I hope this Ruby found only happiness here after what she suffered.' She shook her head, reaching up to place the portrait back up on the wall.

'Oh, Mama. I doubt she found any peace at all until she took her last breath. The poor girl was not only forced into service to a cruel master and his wife at the age of thirteen, she bore his daughter only days after turning eighteen, the exact same age as me.' Tears filled her eyes as I dug around in my pocket for a handkerchief, finding a clean one within moments and passing it to her. 'Two more daughters arrived in the following years, and although the mistress of the house knew what lay between them, she never spoke of it, appearing content enough to treat the children as unpaid house servants from when they could first walk. Ruby remained only as long as she did because they had nowhere else to go, but then the most awful thing happened.' She slipped her arm through mine, wiping her eyes once again before slowly guiding me towards the double doors at the end of the hall. 'The mistress had sent her into Adelaide town on foot to run some errands, and when Ruby returned in the evening, she found her three daughters dead in their beds. Poisoned. The master was hundreds of miles away inspecting a property in Mount Gambier they wished to purchase, while the ten-year-old daughter he shared with his wife had travelled with him, leaving Ruby and the bairns at that woman's mercy.' She shook her head in disbelief, her face pale, while I thought back to a similar tale I had once heard from Mrs McGinty regarding her own childhood; however, I had been furious with her that day, and my memory was fragmented. 'The only reason the poor lass escaped with her life was that cruel bitch wanted to see Ruby live out her days suffering the heavy burden of grief she so cruelly placed on her, knowing she would mourn her daughters until the day she joined them. As punishment for her own husband's sins, Mr Hinkle believes. What's worse, it's said she forced Ruby to bury her own children in the bush, and threatened to find her relatives and kill them one by one if she ever told a soul, or returned to cause her further trouble. The poor lass ran for her life, and somehow, she ended up here reunited with her mother. At least something good came from such an unbearably tragic and terribly sad situation.'

Stepping into the elaborate dining room, we were greeted by a fairly understated cake by Leo's standards, the eighteen candles on top nearly burnt down to the wick. Leo rose to his feet, as did all the house staff who had come to wish the twins a happy birthday. Singing to them, Thomas and Emmy stood beside the vanilla custard cake until we had finished, then bent down in unison to blow out the last of the burning candles before thunderous applause filled the room. Leo whisked the cake away to the sideboard to allow the staff to serve our breakfast.

'How long until you make them grandparents, Thomas?' Leo called out over his shoulder, a wicked smirk spreading across his lips, before glancing over at me. I ignored him as I thanked Sarah and Erin for the sweet, creamy porridge and tall glass of apple juice they placed down in front of me.

'Won't be for a while yet, Leo. I've too much ta do with me life, an' far more ta still learn meself. I can't bring a nipper into the world 'till I know enough ta teach the poor wretch,' Thomas teased, giving nothing away, the smart boy, and reminding me of his father not only in looks, but in his manner.

'When you do decide to sow your wild oats, Thomas, the best advice I can give you is not to leave any resulting produce with your mother unsupervised under any circumstance, at least until old enough to protect themselves. We all know she is not only hopeless in nearly everything she does, but she's beyond careless, and likely to drop your bag of porridge on its head. You do know she enjoys a tipple in secret, and would live at the pub if we would let her? Gets drunk at every opportunity, and smokes her green buds until she laughs no different than a lunatic, while giving no care or consideration to the fact she bursts my eardrums, and I cannot hear a thing for days after. You can only imagine what she would do to a helpless wee haggis.' His voice low, he spoke to my son secretly as if no one else was in the room.

'Shut that fat mouth of yours right this minute before I get up and smack you sideways. *You* are the one who steals my green buds to use in secret, and *you* force me to smoke it with *you*, or threaten to get me into trouble with Hamish with *your* lies. I could kill you with my bare hands, you sneaky wee shit. Keep going, Leo, and you will feel my boot up your backside in front of witnesses.' He widened his eyes, taking a half-step back into the sideboard, while rage rose in me. The staff hurried out of the room after wishing Thomas and Emmy many happy returns of the day, while I placed the palms of my hands on my cheeks to cool them.

'Hamish, control your wife, please? I have far more important things to deal with than her outbursts and tantrums over the most trivial of matters. The doctor at the *Ararat Lunatic Asylum* is already well versed on her case, and recently sent me a list of symptoms on which they admit the feebleminded for care and treatment. Out of the fifty disorders listed, our Abigail has forty-seven.' I grunted aloud, and went to jump to my feet to knock him to the floor; however, Hamish swiftly and without warning placed his arm across my chest, pinning me to my seat.

Leo ignored me as he placed the last of the breakfast trays on the table, the room far quieter now only our family of four remained, while chatting to Hamish and my children of the party this evening, along with going on and on about the five-tiered chocolate cake layered in cream and filled with raspberries he had baked especially for the occasion.

I calmed myself, choosing to concentrate on how much time and effort he had put into making this such a special day for my children, and decided to let him live another day. I rose to my feet to help myself to a piece of birthday cake, returning to the table several times to place a slice in front of Thomas, then Emmy, and finally Hamish, Leo offering no assistance as he sat his backside down on the other end of the table, while casting a critical eye over me.

'You cannot eat that for breakfast, Abigail. To this day, I do not understand why you are not the size of this house.' I devoured the delicious cake without guilt or regret, enjoying every mouthful and choosing to ignore Leo and Hamish's teasing as they shook their heads, while I flicked through the Geelong Advertiser until I found what I was looking for and passed it to Emmy.

'It's a notice congratulating us on our birthday. From our parents. The three of them,' Emmy murmured, tears in her eyes as she leaned over to show Thomas.

'Ya've already made today special. Thanks Da, an' ta Ma, too,' Thomas said, his thick fingers caressing the chain around his neck before glancing down at his wrist. I had slept clutching that watch to my chest for months after Aaron died, and I was relieved to see it now on his son's wrist where it belonged. I knew without doubt if Aaron could have been here today, nothing would have stopped him, and he would be proud of the adults they had become in his absence.

I still visited and attended Aaron and our boys' graves every day, always taking fresh flowers, and I still sobbed for them. Once I had gathered my thoughts and composed myself while relaxing under the old gumtree at the edge of the water, I would make my way back to the house, and return to the life I enjoyed with Hamish and the children, while the grief faded into memories of a time now gone that I spent with Aaron. He had not shown himself to me since my wedding night to Hamish, and I desperately missed seeing him, and often wondered since if he would ever return.

Aaron had been turned into a hero by his countrymen after his execution, but instead of the attention fading away as the years went on, he was now the stuff of myths and legends. An Australian folk hero, many said. Some of the stories I occasionally heard described him almost as a mythical creature standing twelve-feet tall, while ten-times the size of a normal man. Many believed him to be a freedom fighter who had stood against injustice his entire life, while others merely exaggerated the events leading up to his trial and subsequent murder. Not a soul had revealed to this day where Aaron hid for nearly two-years, and as a direct result, the fables only grew.

The odd journalist approached me on occasion asking for an interview, thinking I would reveal more of my private life than they already had in their newspaper articles; however, they had all failed. Aaron had become the working man's ideal in a system that was oppressive, and what many viewed as unjust, and we would often hear strangers mention his name in passing on the streets of Geelong and Melbourne. The letters still came, although had dwindled to fifty a week at most, arriving from all corners of the world. Most were from people who had written to me consistently over the years, and I had replied to every one.

My most favourite letters of all came from Mrs Sarah Stewart, a young woman who had contacted me months before Aaron passed, and all these years later we still corresponded weekly, despite the fact we were considered strangers. Sarah and her husband Lawrence were only a day's travel away, yet we had never met in person, both finding circumstances preventing it every time we tried. We had become quite close through our letters, sharing secrets we usually kept for only our most trusted friends and confidants. After suffering a tragic loss themselves, they had gone on to have several healthy children, and Sarah was happy with her life, despite the poverty they endured.

I felt that after all these years we shared a friendship, and I was confident they were not out to use me, so I started to include a few pounds in the envelope to help ease their burden. Three times Sarah returned the money with her letters, thanking me profusely, but stating they lived adequately, and as long as she could keep her family's stomachs full, they were happy and required nothing else in life. They were proud people, and I admired that very much, so promptly wrote back, pleading they accept the money enclosed from one friend to another for the sake of the bairns.

After much consideration, I received the most heartfelt letter I had ever read from both Sarah and her husband, advising they would accept our kind offer, and how much of a difference it would make. As time went on, Lawrence had been able to buy a buggy to go into Garfield when he needed to transport their produce to market, and they had purchased a further fifty-hectares adjoining their property to raise their own stock, not only to keep them fed, but to sell the excess for profit. Lawrence had fenced off five-hectares to plant an orchard, along with vegetable gardens producing enough to feed their entire district, while still growing several varieties of potatoes on the original fifty hectare plot. Sarah had sent me her measurements, confused why I had asked for them to begin with; however, was thrilled to receive a half-dozen elegant but serviceable house dresses in the post made especially for her by Catherine, along with several respectable nightgowns with matching dressing gowns of the finest quality. For her last birthday, I had sent a thick woollen coat that fell to the ankles with a fur-lined hood, amongst other things, and she was thrilled, thanking me profusely with the winters being so very bitter on the farm.

The connection I felt to the Stewart family made no sense to me, or those around me, many of whom were suspicious of their motives. Without conscious thought or warning, they had become just as close as my dear friends I had known for almost two-decades, and although Hamish and I had talked of visiting them, I was not ready to go anywhere near Gippsland. As they were unable to leave their farm due to their own work and family commitments, the letters continued.

'We have things ta do, an' people ta see,' Thomas called out cheerfully as he and Emmy stood in unison, both coming to my side to kiss the top of my head before hurrying off to start their day.

'Ye've been daydreamin' again all through breakfast. Are ye worryin' yerself about taenight?' Hamish reached over and placed his hand on mine. 'I've sent word tae all who'll be attendin' from here, an' I've dropped in on a few o' our neighbours tae spread the word tae all the young ones that they're tae behave 'emselves.' I nodded, my mind wandering back to this moment eighteen-years ago when I was screaming in my bedchamber for death to take me, while thoughts of what had happened the night before sent chills through me, a vision of Devil's Point flashing in my mind.

'Oh, Thomas and Emmy have chosen their friends wisely, and we know every single soul coming tonight, even those who are travelling great distances to be here. Most attended the village school at one time or another, and many are from the district who were sent here for their schooling. They respect us very much, and still view the adults here at Willow Grove no different from their own aunts and uncles.' He nodded before picking up his cup of tea and took a long sip, while I finished the last of my toast.

'Aye, there's nought tae be concerned about, yet yer mind was a hundred miles away.'

'I was thinking of Sarah and Lawrence.' He leaned over and kissed my forehead, before gathering his things to wander down to the stables to meet with Harry regarding the recent death of a foal.

'Och, aye, Sarah an' Lawrie. I agree that ye need tae visit with 'em, but only once yer ready tae travel back tae Gippsland. Yer own property is far beyond Iona, an' 'tis a shame they carry the full burden o' the farmin' on their own. Yer tied tae the land day an' night when ye have no kin tae help, or tae give ye some respite an' time tae rest. 'Tis unlikely they'll ever be in the position tae accept our invitation tae stay as our guests at Willow Grove,' he remarked, not without sympathy. 'I know yer unlikely tae want tae hear this, but keep in mind they may naw be what they say in the letters. We never truly know what others think, or what motivates 'em, an' ye need tae protect that big heart o' yer's, me precious lass.' I grunted to myself before rising to my feet to prepare to accompany him to the back door, before forcing myself to go about my own tasks for the day. 'I know yer busy, an' it'll be chaos here in a matter o' hours, but come sit with me in the garden this mornin' fer a time before ye start preparin' fer the party an' goin' an' gettin' yerself in a tizzy.' He chuckled loudly as he took my hand in his and led me from the empty room, my gaze finding Ruby and her mother as we made our way down the wide hallway—and I said a silent prayer, hoping wherever she was, she had found the peace she deserved, and had somehow made her way back to the loving embrace of her daughters.

I stood at Emmy's dressing table applying a final coat of soft pink paint to her rosebud lips, while little Mary twisted sections of her thick hair to pin up at the crown of her head, allowing several tendrils to fall loose around her face and down her back, skimming her waist. Mary and I fiddled with the jewelled hair-piece far longer than we wanted to admit; however, stepping back to admire our work, I sighed at her beauty, while little Mary gazed down at her with pride, and great affection.

'You resemble an Indian princess I once saw in London, only far more beautiful, Mistress. With them glittering green gems running across your forehead and into your glorious hair, I've never seen the colour of your eyes look so striking. The lads will be lining up tonight to get your attention,' Mary remarked as she helped Emmy to her feet. Dressed in her shift, her face void of emotion, she followed the little maid over to where her corset, petticoat and stockings sat neatly at the end of her bed. Well aware of just how deeply assumptions like little Mary's hurt and irritated her, it cut me to the core that my daughter would never be able to openly love another in the same way had she been attracted to men. Hamish, Thomas and I had kept her confidence for nearly four-years now, and would continue to do so given how dreadfully the world treated those attracted to the same gender, most considering them filthy deviants corrupting the moral fabric of society. Despite the majority living a lie and forced to keep the deepest yearnings of their heart a closely guarded secret, there were some brave souls who tried to live truthfully for their own sake; however, they placed themselves at risk of imprisonment and death, and were in far greater danger of being rejected by those they loved the most, shunned by friends and strangers alike, discriminated against in every situation. Some beat them for fun, while others were murdered in cold blood. A great number took their own lives, unable to stay in such a cruel world where it had been made clear there was no place for the likes of them.

I sniffed, composing myself before wandering over to the four-poster bed where little Mary pulled on the laces of my daughter's corset, her cheeks flushed, while Emmy held tight to the carved post, showing no emotion, her eyes closed, her body rigid. The pink diamond ring glittered when it caught the sunshine, casting bright shadows around her bedchamber when she moved her hand. Taking a box from the dressing room, Emmy carefully carried the beaded gown over to the bed, and I helped her into it, gently lifting the beautiful emerald silk over her head. Stepping back to admire her as little Mary secured the tiny buttons on the back, I was not surprised it fitted as if made only for her. Thinking her the most beautiful woman I had ever seen in my life, the tears I had been fighting back since I woke trickled down my face as I reached into the pocket of my skirt and pulled out a small, velvet bag.

'I wanted to give you this in private.' I held out the bag as Emmy's eyes widened, while little Mary discreetly left the room to find something to busy herself with for a few minutes. 'I do not know the history of it, other than it was found with me the night I was abandoned at Emiliani House.' Emmy gently accepted the bag, her eyes widening further as she carefully slid the necklace out and gasped aloud.

'I've never seen you wear this, yet it must be one of the most beautiful pieces you own.' She held the glittering emerald up to the light by its delicate gold chain before motioning for me to place it around her elegant neck.

'It is truly beautiful, yet the rare times I have put it on, a dark cloud of sadness settles over me.' Emmy abruptly turned her head and narrowed her gaze at me.

'And so you decide to pass on those storm clouds of grief and sorrow to me? How very thoughtful, Mummy,' she teased, her eyes lighting up in amusement as I shook my head, a gentle smile touching my lips.

'It has nothing to do with the emerald itself, sweetheart, and I would never do such a thing to my most precious and only daughter.' She touched the emerald where it now hung just above her décollage while admiring the flawless necklace she had only ever seen a handful of times. 'This will bring you nothing but protection, comfort, and love when you wear it.' I gently placed my hands on her shoulders. 'I feel connected to this emerald, and when I hold it between the palms of my hands, I can feel the love between whomever originally gave the piece to the unknown person who owned it. How it came to be in the hands of the heartless person who left me on the front steps of the orphanage, we'll likely never know.' My frown deepened as I held back tears of rage and deep, deep pain. 'I've never been able to part with it, yet the mere sight of this emerald hurts my heart. It reminds me of how I was thrown away by my own mother, no different from a piece of scaffy, when someone clearly had the means to raise me just by selling that emerald alone. But they chose not to.' My voice faltered for a moment, but I was determined to finish. 'Seeing it on you only brings me a sense of comfort and peace that I hope when you wear it will bring you that and more. I've always felt this necklace belonged to you from the moment I found you breaking into my jewellery box when you were barely two-years-old. It was the first piece you would reach for and demand I place around your neck. I was forced to put it in the vault once you started taking my belongings as your own at the age of eleven. Without a doubt in my mind, I knew it would go missing sooner rather than later, and the risk that some poor innocent would be accused of theft was far too high.' We both collapsed into fits of giggles, thoughts of all the times I blamed Leo for stealing my clothes and jewellery coming to mind.

'I must be more like you than I realised, Mummy, as I often get similar feelings about objects and people. I remember this necklace before it suddenly disappeared from your collection,' she teased before her expression turned to one of confusion, 'and I still remember how I felt the first time I saw the emerald that time you speak of. It's one of my first and clearest memories.' She paused, appearing to be trying to find the words she needed to express a feeling she couldn't understand to this day. 'When I touched it, I saw you standing in front of me like in a moving picture at the theatre, and I saw myself at the same age I am now. We were standing in the great hall at Merinda Manor and you were crying—well, sobbing really, but you were maybe ten-years younger than you are now. There was a small bag at my feet, and I wore a plain dress but in the old style like you wore when we were bairns.' I remained silent as I listened intently, fascinated and a little miffed all at once that she hadn't confided any of this in me sooner.

'Is that why, when we were staying at Merinda Manor and you all assumed I would marry Reg, you asked if I would ever send you away should I marry again?' She nodded as my stomach sunk.

'I couldn't tell you when we first arrived at Merinda Manor after Daddy was murdered that I had seen the place before. You were in no fit state to hear what I'd imagined as a bairn, and I didn't want you to think me possessed by the devil.' She threw back her head and laughed as I bent down to gently embrace her where she sat by the window. 'Entering the great hall brought it all back to me, and I worried the vision I'd seen had been a prediction for the future and I would be sent away at eighteen by your husband. In the vision, you were bereft, and did not want me to leave. I was crying, and when I went to bend down to pick up my bag, you ran to me and removed the emerald from your neck and placed the necklace around my own. Then the real you walked in and caught me and there was hell to pay.'

I stared down at her, unable to stop myself from bursting into tears, the thought of her carrying this burden alone for all these years was far too much for me to bear on such an emotional day. 'Oh, please don't cry, Mummy. Today is a happy day, and one of celebration. Do you know that Daddy is here and can see me? And you? He hated it when you cried.' I nodded, quickly wiping the tears with the back of my hand and forcing a smile. 'He told me he would be here for all my special days, so we need to be on our best behaviour.' She rose elegantly to her feet, her hands on the windowsill as she gazed down over the gardens, a brilliant smile on her pretty face, and I laughed aloud, drying my face with a clean handkerchief before checking my reflection in the cheval mirror.

'I know he's here, sweetheart. He wouldn't miss today for quids.'

'Run along now, Mama. You must get ready, or I will be late to my own party,' she teased, turning to usher me out of her room. I graciously relented, kissing her goodbye before making my way back to my own bedchamber. Stepping inside, I was surprised to find Hamish and Bessie sitting at the table in deep discussion, neither noticing I had joined them, while Lucy played on the floor with a basket of toys I kept there just for her.

'Oh, just wait until you see Emmy tonight,' I called out before Lucy squealed, and promptly ran into my arms for a hug. 'She looks like a princess. I've never seen a more beautiful woman.'

'I have,' Hamish called back, his eyes twinkling as I stopped beside him, while Bessie greeted me cheerfully. He grabbed me around the waist, pulling me down into his lap before kissing me deeply. After some time had passed, and much rolling of eyes and disgruntled whining coming from the direction of my ladies' maid, she ordered me into the dressing room to ready myself, her hand firm on my upper arm.

Making myself comfortable at my dressing table, she ran the solid silver brush through my hair until it shone, then applied the cosmetics I had recently purchased at Amelia's store sent all the way from France, while laughter floated in from the bedchamber, the sound of whinnying bringing a smile to my lips. Hamish and Lucy often played with the miniature wooden stables and the Martarino horses Harry had carved as a gift when Lucy was born, the sweet wee lass choosing to keep them here as they were her most favourite thing. Bessie touched the back of my head, and I stood for her to assist me into the bronze gown Catherine had made especially for this evening. The wide neckline sat just off my shoulders and flattered the cinched bodice, while the skirt required no thick petticoats and draped elegantly to the floor, creating a slim silhouette—while minimising the risk a candle would set me on fire. Memories of several women I was acquainted with in Melbourne during our early years here met that same fate when attending formal events, and all any of the guests could do was stand back and watch them burn to death in the ballroom. I considered myself fortunate I had not been there to witness such horror; however, even when told afterwards by Dana, the thought haunted me to this day, and I pushed it to the back of my mind. Compared to the crinolines and wide skirts we were all forced to wear up until recent years, I considered these straighter skirts far more practical, although many formal occasions still called for the cumbersome ballroom gowns; however, never at Willow Grove no matter what the occasion.

'You look pretty, Auntie Mistress,' Lucy called out as Bessie and I stepped back into the room.

'You can call her Auntie, or Mistress, but not both together, sweetheart,' Bessie said through her laughter, bending down to pick Lucy up. Cuddling into her side, Lucy grinned at me, her baby teeth so tiny and white.

'Or Mrs Makenzie, or Mrs Cavanaugh, or Abigail. As long as it's not bitch or witch.' Bessie gasped aloud, grasping her daughter's hands in her own. The face of an angel, her brown ringlets were loose today and hanging to her tiny shoulders, ironically reminding me of a halo, her pinafore already displaying smears of dirt here and there.

'Hush your mouth, you wee fiend, before I take you down to the laundry house and have Miss Prudence scrub your tongue with the tallow soap. Where did you hear that?'

'Uncle Leo said it yesterday when he was talking about you and Auntie Polly in the kitchen, Mama. He says other bad words about you that I don't know the meaning of yet, but he promises to teach me every one.' Without another word, Bessie turned and marched out of the bedchamber, Lucy clinging to her hip for dear life, before the door slammed behind them, the room now silent bar the native birds calling in the trees.

'The house is busier than Flinders Street Station, so I came tae hide in here.' I sat down on the end of the bed, while Hamish stretched where he sat near the fireplace, the wooden horses scattered around his feet.

He wasn't far wrong. All our friends and family were staying here, including Brian and Tamara with their cavalcade of servants, along with Victoria and Eric, and their brood. Many of Thomas and Emmy's friends had made the long journey, not only from the furthest parts of Victoria, but across the country—these friendships formed long ago when they lived here while their parents were in our employ. A great number of families had passed through the gates of Willow Grove over the years, some remaining still, while others stayed for only a time before moving on to make their life in another part of Australia. Several friends they had made during our travels over the years had taken ship from America, France and England, arriving weeks ago to join in the celebration of all that was Thomas and Emmy.

For the first time in recent memory, every guest room was spoken for, and the staff quarters were filled to capacity, as were the accommodations in the village for the guests. Many of the servants accompanying their employers were forced to sleep cramped above the stables, while others slept four to a room, sharing with our own staff.

Rising to my feet, I studied my reflection for a final time, checking all was in place as Hamish came to my side. Taking my hand in his, he led me through the halls and down the stairs, slowing his pace as I carefully hitched up the front of my gown to avoid injuring myself. Finding Thomas and Emmy already waiting in the reception room, their eyes fixed on me as I gripped the railing while slowly descending the stairs, Hamish greeted them loudly, their faces lighting up. We had decided to walk down to the village together as a family to enjoy the last moments before they officially left their childhood behind, and had asked the guests to be there half-an-hour before we planned to arrive.

I stepped away from the staircase to embrace them both at once, while Hamish wandered over to the long fireplace. Looking particularly handsome this evening in his new shirt and the trousers Catherine forced Colin to tailor a little tighter than usual across his backside, I smothered a smile, my stomach grumbling loudly for a moment.

Both kitchens, here in the main house and the village, had been running day and night for the last week, the kitchen staff working from the wee hours until late into the night to make the miniature creations, or finger food as my children called it, that Leo liked to serve so very much. He often told us it was his preference, as then there were fewer dirty dishes for his staff to worry about, nor did he suffer the irritation of serving people where they sat, demanding the staff pay them their full attention, and demanding they return at whim to serve them a hundred times within a few hours. It was far easier to have the staff walking around casually with trays of various dishes, while guests helped themselves as often as they liked from the time they arrived until they left to find their beds. We found our guests enjoyed the food far more when served this way, many reporting they preferred this rather than consuming a heavy meal at the beginning of the night, then nothing for hours.

We stood together in a circle at the grand entrance of our home, our arms entwined around each other, our heads close.

'Always remember this. We love ye. We're proud o' ye. An' we'll always be here as a safe haven fer ye both, naw matter what happens in the future or where life takes ye.' Hamish smiled down at them, gathering us closer one last time before we turned towards the door. I smiled to myself, ready to celebrate the two very people who made life worth living in a world that was often the last place I wanted to be.

My mouth dropped open as I stepped inside the village pub, delighting me when I heard Emmy gasp, while Thomas stopped to gaze around at the thousands of candles burning on every surface.

Hundreds of pink roses and royal bluebells filled the vases sitting on the tables, the cream linen tablecloths pressed to perfection and showing not a spot. Several enormous bouquets were placed on the windowsills and side tables, along with a tall vase filled with the same flowers sitting on the table at the back of the room, the stage where the musicians played a little too close for my liking. Their five-tiered cake loomed large next to the flowers, and I worried it would be knocked over the moment the guests got up to dance; however, pushed the thought to the back of my mind as it was far too troublesome and heavy to move now.

'Oh, Da. Mama. It's beyond fabulous,' Emmy exclaimed, her eyes flitting around the room, while Thomas nodded, the side of his mouth turning up into a lopsided grin. I had never seen a room so transformed. Although a beautiful building, the pub had been turned into something magnificent, and almost unrecognisable. Pink silk had been strung from the ceilings, the luxurious material draping down the walls to the floor where thick carpets had been laid. A number of tables and chairs were replaced with oversized cushions scattered on the floor to sit on, the pub now no longer a pub and transporting us to some far off *khayma* or *suradeq* in the desert of Egypt long ago. I had witnessed ceiling draping at Merinda Manor with my own eyes, the ballroom transformed into a white silken paradise for an upcoming event only days before we departed.

Excitement filled the room, and I was pleased at the turnout, most of their friends and cousins here tonight between the ages of fifteen and twenty—apart from dear Beatrice, who had just gone eleven when Emmy was born. We knew every soul who they considered a friend, and although I would not go as far to say any of them were truly bad, there were a few that left a little to be desired. Most were good natured rascals, while others just out to cause harmless mischief; however, I already had my eye on a couple I believed would soon find themselves behind enormous bluestone walls if they were not careful.

We wandered over to Polly and Angus sitting at the corner of the long table, allowing them a clear view of the entire room, while Willy and Bella jumped to their feet to embrace their cousins, soon wandering off to sit on one of the thick carpets together with their friends. Lowering myself down onto the chair next to Polly, Hamish went to the bar to get a jug of ale.

'Thank you for doing all this, Polly. You've created something truly beautiful.' Her face lit up as she reached over and took my hand in hers.

'Oh, it was nothing, Abi. Thank you for giving my Da the time off to come help me for a few hours. He is the master when it comes to setting a grand scene, and it's him who ensures not a thing is out of place. I'm not that fussy, and consider myself fortunate not to have inherited his pettifogging.' Her musical laughter filled my ears as I glanced across at Mr Masters standing behind the bar near the entrance to the small kitchen, his cheeks flushed as he took a young maid to task for the grubby apron she wore.

'Does he ever relax in your presence? I cannot imagine it myself.' A smirk touched my lips as she rolled her eyes good-naturedly.

'Of course, Abi. He is my father. You only ever see him working, but he is most himself when at home with his family. Who would have thought when I first held Henry as a wean, I was swooning over my own brother.' She glanced over at our children, then Henry and his brother George sitting beside them, their younger sibling Reginald and sister Charlotte relaxing opposite them with several of their school friends.

'And cousin,' I reminded her as she grimaced.

'Oh, Abi. I find it terribly hard even now to view Maisie as our aunt, and it's clear she finds the entire situation as uncomfortable as we do given she's not much older. She was unaware Da even knew her sister until that Christmas day she found out about me, alongside everyone else, the poor lass. I know she hates our mothers' for leaving the four of them in the workhouse for as long as they did, and credits the former mistress of Castle Howard for saving them. She thought your stepmother more saintly than the blessed virgin herself, and is still grieving the loss of her. Lady Eugenie was close with *your* Lord Harrington's mother, and the reason our uncles secured such grand positions at Merinda Manor.' I pushed the Howard family to the back of my mind, along with the rumours on Leo's passionfruit vine that Christopher Howard had somehow hastened the death of his wife decades before her time, many of the opinion he refused her requests for a divorce out of spite. The man kept several mistresses; however, his heart belonged to one, and he wanted to make her his wife, but did not want the irritation of the first. As Lady Eugenie had never been sick a day in her life, and reported to have been stronger than most men with the constitution of a young lass, many were suspicious when she died in her sleep for no apparent reason.

'No one ever speaks of Ailsa. Did tragedy touch her?' Polly shook her head before taking a small sip of wine.

'She's still amongst the living, from what I hear, and they get the odd letter on occasion, but the woman is said to be a black widow.' She lowered her voice and leaned closer. 'Ailsa married the first time at fifteen to a wealthy landowner, but he died in his sleep two-years later, they say from an apoplexy. Not three-months after putting him in the ground, she wed a shopkeeper, surprising many who knew the woman well. He was comfortable enough, and supported her in every way while she waited for the sale of the first husband's estate, and to receive his investments and savings from the bank after a lengthy probate process. They say she had a daughter with the second man while biding her time waiting to inherit that small fortune, but no one is certain. It was only when the second husband's parents were tragically killed in a carriage accident she discovered they were even wealthier than her first husband's family, and he was their only son and sole heir. She remained with him longer than she first planned, and soon sweet talked him into selling his shop, and they moved to the family estate in Hertford. Ailsa was thrilled to find when claiming not only a substantial amount of money, half the buildings in the town were owned by her husband's parents. Soon after, he too suffered an apoplexy in his sleep, and as there were no kin left to dispute his last wishes, Ailsa got the lot. The way I heard it was after everything was sold, she quietly disappeared and was not heard of again for a number of years. Not until she married a sea captain who owned a small fleet of boats. Did you know she's been here to Australia to visit with Maisie?' My eyes went wide, and I shook my head.

'They are a secretive family, more so since they became aware of our connection to them.' She nodded, a wistful smile on her lips.

'Aye, they are. It's not Maisie telling me this, though, but my Da.'

'Has Ailsa been here recently?'

'Nah. This would be five-years ago now. They met in Port Melbourne where their private vessel was docked for a week, before continuing on to Tasmania. Maisie took a few days off and went to stay, but returned the next day, telling Da her sister was no better than their mother had been, and the man she was married to—Captain Steve as he demanded to be called—well, apparently he had the morals of a tom cat. The letters still came, and a year later poor Captain Steve passed peacefully in his sleep.'

'From an apoplexy?' She nodded, collapsing into a fit of giggles.

'I do believe we are related to a murderess, Abi. A wealthy one, but a manslayer no less.' I laughed aloud, my gaze fixed on Thomas and Emmy's Cavanaugh cousins, the rowdiest of all as they congratulated them before scattering themselves down on the three large carpets they now took up.

Our friends and family sat with us, the adults filling one long table running the entire length of the pub, the room bursting with cheerful banter, smiling young people, and love. Hamish rose to his feet in one elegant movement before making his way to the table at the front of the room, calling for quiet, the cake looming over him.

'I want tae say a few words while yer all still sober enough tae hear 'em. Come join me up here Abigail. Ye too, Thomas, an' wee Emmeline.' A hush fell over the room, and I made my way to his side while my children jumped to their feet. 'We'd like tae welcome ye all here tonight, an' thank ye fer comin' tae celebrate their birthday with us. We as their parents, an' I speak fer their father, Aaron also, are proud o' who they've become. We've watched 'em grow in tae fine adults, an' could naw have asked fer a more lovin', respectful, an' kind son an' daughter than we've been blessed with.' He paused, raising his glass before gazing down at Emmy, then Thomas. 'Yer three parents wish ye the happiest o' lives, surrounded by people who love ye fiercely, an' who ye love back just as much. Happy birthday. We love ye more than chocolate.' The room erupted into cheers and thunderous applause, while tears trickled down Emmy's face.

Movement caught my eye, and I glanced over at the entrance to find Aaron leaning against the door-jamb, the golden glow surrounding him brighter than I remembered, his smile mischievous as he gazed across at us. My heart pounded hard in my chest, his presence so very real it took all my strength not to run to him, not to scream his name and wrap my arms around his broad frame and never let him go again. Pride shone from his eyes, the colour of the ocean on a sunny day, his stare fixed on his children for the longest time. Turning his attention to Hamish, he nodded in thanks before his eyes locked with mine, the love he felt for us palpable. Although the room was filled with laughter and good cheer, I heard nothing but silence, the guests in the room fading to grey while all I could see was Aaron. I smiled as he blew his mother a kiss, warming my heart as he turned back to me and I heard his voice, startling while thrilling me all at once.

'I love ya, Abi. I want ya to know I'm always around ya. Tell me Ma she has nothin' ta fear when it comes ta dyin'. It's nothin' like she imagines. I plan ta come ta ya when the time's right, *mo anamchara*, 'cause I need ta explain some things I believe ya need ta know. Tonight is a celebration, an' I want ya ta wish me precious nippers a happy birthday, an' tell 'em I love 'em with all me heart. I've always kept me whispered promises ta them, an' been by their side whenever they've thought of me. Tell 'em they've made their old man proud, an' nothin' will ever change me love for 'em.' He grinned and placed his hand over his heart. 'Please tell me sweet Emmy, I know she frets that she's disappointed me, but that's impossible. I'll love 'em no matter what they do or the choices they make. I do know this. Emmy has always chosen ta return ta earth in female form, despite only ever lovin' women. She was truly born like this, an' has nothin' ta be ashamed of. I love ya, me darlin', Abi, an' them, ta the moon an' back. I thank ya for raisin' 'em the way ya have, an' I'm eternally grateful ta Hamish for loving 'em as his own. I'm the proudest man in Hiriarni.' He patted his heart several times, his grin wide as I beamed back at him.

Lifting his hand to his lips, he blew me a kiss before gently waving as he turned and slowly walked away without a backward glance, gone from my sight once again. A sense of peace settled on me seeing him again as he once was, while knowing for certain he was safe and remained close thrilled me, and gladdened my heart he lived on.

Without warning, I was pushed aside, and as I took a half-step back in an attempt to regain my balance, I stumbled, my backside hitting the ground with a thud. I grimaced in pain as I looked up to find Leo standing where I once stood with his back to me, while making himself comfortable between Hamish and Emmy. Neither appeared to have noticed I was no longer there, while Thomas stood to the other side of Hamish, his attention fixed on Hannah smiling back at him as if no one else was in the room.

'All eyes on me. Shhh, enough. You back there. The unfortunate looking woman with two backsides. No, not you. It's clear I must be more specific given the crowd we have here tonight. You there. Shut the daffodil up. Thank you. Now, back to me.' I grunted loudly, unable to move without knocking the table over, and ruining their cake. 'I have been Uncle Leo to Thomas and Emmeline from the moment they first drew breath. Oh, what a day that was. I nearly witnessed their birth; however, the midwife ordered me out because I said the word vagina in polite company. Well, that's the excuse Dr Richards told me when I tried to break my way back in when Abigail was shrieking like a banshee. Such a whiner. Anyway. Poppycock I say to Dr Richards and his evil sidekick, who, by the way, are not present tonight, or I would not be able to speak freely due to fear of repercussions.' I relaxed back against the hard floor, my hands curled into fists by my side as I slowly counted to ten. 'Anyway, back to me. I was blessed with two beautiful children that day. They are the only weans in the entire population born here at Willow Grove who haven't been unfortunate looking, or caused our eyes to bleed and fear to well up inside us at the sight of them creeping round the village. Thomas and Emmy are my pride and joy, and they love me very much as I have always fed and cared for them as a mother would. I've always done the hard work when raising them, while Abigail sat on her barge of an arse sipping whisky and smoking her green buds. Without me, they wouldn't have turned into the upstanding citizens they now are. They have so much to thank me for, but I don't mind my sacrifice. Thomas, Emmy. I just wanted to say...' I kicked his legs out from under him before he could finish, causing him to crash backwards onto the floor, landing right beside me.

Uproarious laughter filled the room as Hamish leaned down and picked me up by the waist just as I tried to grab Leo by the balls. Shrieking that his back was broken, Hamish carried me to the furthest side of the room in an attempt to calm me, while the twins helped Leo to his feet. Angus hurried to his side to escort him away and out of my sight before Hamish would put me back down on the floor.

'He's such a fat headed moron. This is not the end of it, Hamish, of that I give you my solemn oath. He has ruined every single celebration we've ever had with his ridiculous speeches,' I spat, while he chuckled, his arm still firmly around my waist as we gazed across at our children still standing at the front of the room.

Thomas and Emmy gave a poised and extremely touching speech, while I stared after my beloved husband and their father. They thanked us for all we had done and went on to thank all present for celebrating with them—while all I could think about was the many and varied ways in which I would torture and kill Leo for ruining the moment yet again.

The guests were asked to stand and sing happy birthday, while Thomas and Emmy each took a knife and cut into opposite sides of their enormous cake. I shook Hamish off to go and find Mr Masters, wishing to speak to him as a matter of urgency. Returning soon after, the guests had taken their seats and quietened down by the time I slipped into the chair beside Hamish, leaning close to whisper in his ear. His eyes widened slightly as the staff wandered around the room offering hot savouries, while several platters had been laid out along the table for those too old to sit on the floor, or stand around in groups.

'Are ye certain, lass?'

'I am.' He bent down and gently placed his lips on mine for only a moment, his arm resting on my thigh. He rose to his feet, my hand in his as he addressed our guests.

'Me wife an' I will lead Thomas an' Emmy in the first dance o' the evenin'. We ask fer ye tae join us after this ballad.' Leading me to the dance floor, Hamish placed my hand in my son's, before gathering Emmy in his arms as Mr Masters began to sing, the musicians playing along beautifully.

'And I will love you until the sun no longer shines, the earth no longer turns, the seas no longer rise. Our hearts will be together beyond the end of time, our souls will never die and I will love you for eternity and for all time.'

Thomas stared down at me, his eyes wide, while confusion crossed Emmy's face. 'This is a special night that requires a special song,' I murmured as he slowly danced me around the room, tears in his eyes. Hamish kissed Emmy's forehead, his voice low as she cried tears of joy, while listening intently to her stepfather's reassuring words, along with the love song she had heard hundreds of times when a bairn.

Tears streamed down Mr Masters face, his voice faltering several times while a great number of guests sobbed openly. Most were aware this had been a special ballad, a song just for Aaron and myself, and it touched them that I was sharing it with Thomas and Emmy as a gift from their father and I. The song ended far too soon, and Mr and Mrs Cavanaugh came to claim the next dance with their eldest grandchildren, passing me back into Hamish's arms.

'That was a beautiful act from a mother tae her children,' Hamish whispered, kissing me softly on the lips. I told him of Aaron and what he had said. 'Och, I knew he'd be here somewhere taenight. Nothin' would keep him away, the same as our weddin'.' I took a deep breath, leaning close to his ear before telling him of the golden auras I saw around those I loved, right through to what Maslow, and then Lilith, had told me. Remaining silent for the longest time, he swept me around the crowded dance floor, his face thoughtful. 'Do ye mind if we talk o' this in the mornin'? I need some time tae think.' I nodded, relieved he hadn't thought me mad, laughed, or completely dismissed me, as so many others would. Thomas and Emmy were passed between their aunts and uncles, along with our friends, until they had danced with every person present. 'It's bonny tae have ye back in me arms. Ye've been as busy as a bee.' Guiding me back to the table, we watched the young ones dance while drinking our beer. Poor Emmy clearly felt obligated to accept every invitation from the young men who were brave enough to ask, and being as kind and sweet as she was, she cheerfully danced with every one of them.

'Do you think they will ever stop chasing her?' I asked, placing a sweet tomato meatball in my mouth as I watched her intently.

'Naw. Not ever. Naw different than if ye were still free.' He bit into a savoury tart filled with onion and cheese, while no longer overly concerned about men paying me attention as he knew I wore his ring. Unless someone dared touch me, resulting in him flying into a jealous rage, and often ending up in a fist fight. I had always assumed by now, especially at his age, he would have softened, but he hadn't, and guarded me ferociously whenever we were away from Willow Grove.

Most of our friends and family had returned to the table, leaving the young ones to dance. I stood and made my way to Aaron's mother, lowering myself into the chair beside her. Telling her what I had witnessed earlier, and the message her son had asked me to pass on, her eyes welled with tears.

'I knew deep in my heart my boy was safe, and lived on in spirit, but it comforts me greatly to hear it. I have no doubt the words you speak come from his own lips, as he is one of the few aware of my morbid fear of death. It seems I have nothing to worry about.' Out of all Aaron left behind, Mrs Cavanaugh would continue to grieve deeply for her son until the day she was reunited with him, of that I was certain. The hole his death had left in our lives would never be filled, in her or myself. I embraced her for the longest time before excusing myself to sit with Tamara and Brian. Leo rose to his feet, unaware I had overheard them attempting to convince him to resign from his position at Willow Grove to enter their employ, before hurrying away and preventing me from hurting him in front of witnesses.

'You and Hamish appear so very much in love. I must admit, I was the biggest doubter of them all at the very beginning of your courtship, but he has proved me wrong, and I'm more pleased for you, dear Abigail,' Tamara said, her hand on mine as I smiled at her.

'How are you, sweet Tamara?' I embraced her warmly, her smile bright as she pulled away, not a hair out of place, her dress exquisite, and a Montague no less.

'Oh, my life is as exciting as I allow it to be.' She leaned in to whisper in my ear. 'I've discovered only recently that I prefer my lovers to come from the middle classes. The men I've taken to my bed whom I consider of equal standing lack passion, nor do they try as hard as a working man.' She paused, a wry smile touching her lips. 'They seem to appreciate women far more than those powerful types.' I tried to smother a smile and failed miserably. Tamara had devoured more lovers over the years than I had eaten hot dinners, so many I had lost count. They ranged from her servants to the upper classes—a judge and a number of prominent politicians amongst them—while I suspected Leo was not the only lover Brian kept during their time together.

Brian and Tamara seemed to get along far better the older they grew, and enjoyed an amicable friendship of sorts that appeared to suit them both, allowing them to live separate lives and seek their own happiness, but come together when required as a respectable family for the world to see. Hamish caught my eye, beckoning me over. I excused myself and made my way to his side, promptly sitting down on his lap and wrapping my arms around his shoulders.

'I fetched ye another beer. Angus was forced tae step in an' stop an argument before it started between two lads vyin' fer Emmy's attention. The lass did naw even notice, an' is havin' a fine time.' He chuckled to himself as I gazed across at my son in the distance, a thousand candles casting a romantic glow over the room.

Thomas had not left Hannah's side since the party began apart from the few minutes they were separated when they cut the cake. They looked so happy, so very much in love, and it was driving me to drink. It was not that I didn't like Hannah, in fact, the opposite was true, and I loved her like my own daughter. My only wish was for my son to experience life before taking a wife and having a family of his own. I was proud Thomas treated Hannah in the way his father had shown him by the way he cherished me, and it was obvious to all he loved her deeply, as she did him. I felt wretched behaving so selfishly, yet I was unable to change how I felt.

'Come fer a walk tae get some air?' Hamish suggested, winking at me. I nodded and stood, smoothing my dress before he took my hand in his, leading me outside where he slipped his arm around my waist, while taking a lantern in the other. It was a beautiful autumn night, the stars twinkling brightly, not a cloud in the sky and as we walked away from the pub. Stopping to watch a koala, her baby clinging to her back, she quickly climbed the trunk of a gum tree as I watched in awe. The native Australian animals were like nothing I had ever seen, and no matter how many times I came across them on our property, I never failed to stare in wonder.

Hamish had come across a joey early last year, her mother found dead on the property shortly after, shot by an interloper trespassing on our land. I had nursed her with warm milk initially, then native grasses as she grew, and she had attached herself to me no different than a housecat. No longer allowed in the house now that she was almost fully grown, the pretty grey kangaroo would wait for me in the back garden in the mornings to accompany me as I went about my day. Although she lived as a wild animal and found her own food, she would spend her day hopping alongside me, even escorting me across to the island when she could be bothered getting into the boat. I had named her Kanga, and she was loved by some; however, had become a source of much hilarity to others. Most found her fascinating, and were greatly amused to see her jumping along beside me down the cobblestone street, or waiting outside their houses for me to return when visiting with friends in the village. Hamish and I wandered down past the dining hall towards the schoolhouse hand-in-hand, the stars brighter the further away we ventured, the moon full and casting a silver shadow over the land. I heard a rustle behind us, and quickly glanced back to find Kanga beside me.

'I was just thinking about you, sweetheart.' I smiled to myself as I bent down to stroke her lovely face.

'I've never seen a wee beastie so dedicated tae a man, woman, or bairn.' He paused, his brow furrowed. 'Och, apart from ol' Dingo.' I smiled at the memory of the yellow dog, so very loyal to his master until the end. 'Ye cannae be like everyone else an' choose tae keep a wee kitty or pup fer company, can ye, Abigail? O' course naw. Ye must have the native ones who're as wild as Mr Hinkle himself, yet somehow, they end up as tame as that cantankerous old barn cat, Mrs Dingie.' He grinned as he kissed me on the mouth, and I laughed aloud.

'Leo calls her Mrs Dyngalyng Dingie.'

'Ding-a-ling?' He pointed to his temple, moving his finger in a circular fashion, while pulling an odd face.

'Yes, Dyngalyng, but he insists we use the exotic way in the spelling of it. Anyway, he not only believes her to be the most unfortunate looking cat he's ever laid eyes on, but the fattest, with the stumpiest of legs that look set to snap under the weight of her. And he is of the opinion the poor creature possesses the most vindictive and malodorous disposition he has ever encountered in a feline. Not to mention he finds her coarse striped coat repugnant, and feels she would be far more attractive if she stopped lying around in the sun, or ran a brush through it on occasion.' We continued on for a time, laughter rising in me as we came to the white fence surrounding the playground, the headmistress's cottage in the distance shrouded in darkness, the school house further down, but long before the bend in the river where the children liked to swim, the pristine water slowing into a shallow pool. Mrs McGinty had made a special effort to attend tonight, and it was lovely watching her perched on her chair in the corner with her students, past and present, tending to her every need, while I had formed the opinion she would be one of the last to leave. 'Did you know, Leo truly believes if Mrs Dingie were a person, she would work as a junior clerk in some boring solicitors' office in the middle of bumfuck nowhere? Way out the back of Bourke, he insists. An incompetent pencil pusher at best, or so the story goes. He often imagines her waddling around the streets speaking badly of everyone she encounters, and she has the nerve to look up her nose at her betters. A terrible gossip, she is. Well, from how Leo tells it.' My voice low and secretive, I mockingly widened my eyes, a mischievous smirk on my lips as Hamish threw back his head and howled with laughter, while I wiped tears from my face, my stomach aching as I continued to giggle.

'Does he only imagine another life fer the cat, or all the beasties livin' here?'

'Oh, all of them. He expects Delly would be tall and beautiful, and of royal blood should she be human, while I would be her least favourite pet snake.' He sat down heavily on a wooden bench near the school gate, placing the lamp at his feet while still chuckling to himself. I stared up towards the stables in the distance, just out of sight over the hill, the moon blanketing the valley in a silver glow so bright there had been no need to carry a torch to light the way at all. 'That poor barn cat...'

'*Mrs Dyngalyng Dingie*, thank ye kindly,' he interrupted, before continuing to laugh. 'We do naw want tae bear the brunt o' her wrath if we can help it. Sounds tae me she could be one o' *the Erinyes*, but we have naw clue if she's *Alteco*, the wrathful one, *Tisiphone*, the avenger, or *Megaera*, the fierce an' most frightenin' o' 'em all. Let's naw take our chances.' He slapped his knee, clearly amused by his own wit, while I rolled my eyes.

'Well, poor Mrs Dingie doesn't mean to irritate Leo as she does. She was stepped on as a wee kitty, and although she survived, you'd think her a touch soft-heided if she really were a person.' We both collapsed into each other, our laughter ringing out over the paddocks. I reached down to stroke Kanga sitting on the ground between us, my mind wandering off to times long gone.

'Stop daydreamin' an' concentrate on me. 'Tis naw often there's this much distance between us an' the hundreds who live here.' Pulling me up onto his lap by my waist, he kissed me deeply as I slipped my arms around his neck, his hair running through my fingers like silk. 'Feels like 'tis just us in the world, an' I'm holdin' on tae the thought 'till some bastard comes along tae ruin it.' I placed my lips on his, melting into his solid body as thoughts of all else faded from my mind, and all I saw was him.

We strolled back inside the rowdy pub, the room full of dancing and great merriment. Catching my eye from his chair in the corner, Leo smirked in our direction, and I stopped where I was, turning to march to his side to smack him upside the head; however, Hamish tightened his grip on my hand before pulling me in the opposite direction. The beer, wine and whisky flowed freely as we expected; however, most had refrained, including myself, choosing to stick with the large barrels of the delicious fruit punch on the bar. Without stopping to sit back at the table with our friends, Hamish pulled me up onto the polished floorboards at the front of the room to dance a jig with Thomas and Emmy, the young ones surrounding them appearing to be having a fabulous time. Dancing until sweat dripped down my brow and I could move my feet no longer, I hobbled over to sit between Maggie and Lilith at the long table, while my husband wandered off to order more beer.

'You and Hamish are so very wonderful together,' Maggie gushed as I sat down before embracing Lilith and thanking her and Jasper for making the long and arduous journey to celebrate with us. We chatted animatedly while I watched Mark dance with my daughter. Maggie, in consultation with her son, had decided to move to Geelong. Despite remaining in Melbourne in the mansion she shared with her husband, the years after his death had been the most miserable for them both, and they had spent more time in Geelong at Willow Grow, or as guests of Irene and Ron's, than they had in their own home. Maggie had accepted our offer to stay until they found their own property, and planned to move within the coming month. I looked forward to her company and hoped their time here was not fleeting.

I smiled at Jasmin and Richard across the table, their offspring also dancing and paying them no mind. Still so very much in love, I was thrilled he was content with his lot in life, and enjoyed their company often. Jas and I would visit several times a week, at her home and mine, while Richard always accompanied her to our Sunday lunches with the children, and more often than not, joined us at the pub afterwards. Richard managed my often complicated business dealings in Australia more than competently, while Mr Malcolm continued to keep an eye on my affairs in England. I trusted them both completely and ensured I compensated them above what they asked of me for a job well done.

Thinking of the Malcolms' always led me to thoughts of Sister Josephine. She was still waiting to receive permission to travel to Australia to visit with us. After four-years of writing a letter a week to Mother Mary Bernadette with my own hand, pleading the Order of Saint Emiliani to allow her to come, along with Sister Josephine's own requests whenever she had the opportunity, our efforts had come to nought. I believed the only reason behind their blatant refusal to even consider the matter was Sister Mary Monica. She held such contempt for me, and had told me to my face it pleased her to hear I suffered, and hoped tragedy and sorrow would follow me all my days, while knowing the only way she could truly hurt me was through my love for Sister. We wrote to each other every second day, and it thrilled me to read about the day-to-day lives they enjoyed, along with news of the Sisters and bairns. I moved down several seats to sit with Dana and Martin, smiling at them warmly as my dear friend placed her hand on mine.

'Don't all the young ones look radiant? So full of life,' Dana remarked softly, her gaze fixed on her grandchildren and their cousins dancing, their laughter filling the room.

'They are all lovely, sweet souls. We've been fortunate.' She smiled wistfully, no doubt thinking of the grandchildren she was robbed of when Charlotte was put to rest in that muddy graveyard that grey day, what felt like a lifetime ago. 'We are heading back to the house soon and leaving the young ones here to have their fun. I would bet my right arm none of them will be in their beds until well after the sun rises,' I teased, her hand still on mine as she laughed aloud.

'Oh, to be young again, Abigail. I miss it more and more the older my bones grow, but I bloody well had fun.' She had certainly lived an interesting life, although marked with tragedy along the way, as we all came to experience. I noticed Hamish handing Thomas a beer and Emmy a glass of champagne, preparing to leave. I embraced Dana, bidding them farewell before hurrying to his side, our children's friends surrounding them.

'Enjoy yer night, but behave yerselves—all o' ye—or I'll come back down here an' ye can expect tae feel me boot up yer backsides.' He thumped Thomas on the back, bidding him goodnight before gathering Emmy in his arms. Our nieces and nephews waited in turn to be embraced in their drunken stupor, and Hamish and I were forced to spend a quarter-of-an-hour hugging them before we managed to make our escape.

Spilling out of the pub and onto the street, they called after us, waving frantically as their parents joined us outside, many glancing back dubiously at their offspring before they moved up the street in groups to take the short walk back to the main house, our children soon forgetting us and returning to the warmth of the pub. I had no doubt they would enjoy a memorable night together, one full of fun and laughter, and saw no cause for concern that they were tipsy, as it was a special occasion. Hamish reached across and took my hand as we passed the terraces. He had convinced me to sack Nellie when she had tried to kiss him at the pub months ago, and along with her continued attacks directed at me, I had reluctantly agreed. Although I had become accustomed to her ranting while drunk when she would catch us on our way home from the pub, it had infuriated Hamish to a point I was forced to relent.

'Tis a bonny night, is it naw? Look how bright the Southern Cross.' Hamish reached up, his other hand holding me around the waist as I leaned back against his chest, a memory of Aaron coming to mind as he pointed up into the sky, the stars like diamonds on black velvet. He kissed the top of my head as our friends and family trudged past us, some far more unsteady on their feet than others, while Leo paused to turn back, a wicked glint in his eye.

'You may want to hurry it along. There is safety in numbers, and if you lag behind and get separated from the pack, especially anywhere near the stables, that maleficent Mrs Dyngalyng Dingie will have no hesitation in taking you down without fear or warning, while leaving not a trace you were ever here. She is an evil lunatic, but far more clever than we suspected. I admire that very much.'

We caught up to him, uproarious laughter ringing out across the moonlit paddocks as we headed up the hill towards the main house—to the grand building that sheltered us from more than the ever changing weather—to the only place I ever wanted to belong to, and would forever call home.

'What a wonderful night.' Scarlett sighed, dreamy eyed as Patrick held her in his arms, while we sat around the kitchen table eating oversized pots of crème brulee. Spending far longer than we intended laughing and gossipping about the night, our guests started to wander off to bed, several at a time, until all that remained were Hamish and myself. Leading him out the back door, we made ourselves comfortable side-by-side on the same lounge, while I pulled my pipe from my pocket to share while we talked.

'Did ye enjoy yerself tonight, lass?' Hamish relaxed back against the thick cushion, his arm around my shoulders while holding me close, my head resting against his shoulder as we gazed up at the sky.

'Oh, yes. It was lovely to see Thomas and Emmy so very happy, and to hear Aaron's voice again and look into his eyes gave me such peace.' I relaxed back into his arms, while gazing out over the silver paddocks. A horse ambled past carrying Thomas and Hannah, their voices low as they silently moved beyond the paddock and disappeared into the bush.

'Ye know o' his plans?' Hamish murmured, his hand stroking my arm as I grunted to myself.

'He told me. All I can wish for them is happiness, and a long and joyful life together.' I sighed deeply as he kissed my nose, his eyes twinkling in the soft glow of the night.

'We could be grandparents in the naw too distant future.' His voice teasing, I smacked him playfully on the arm, before nuzzling my face into the side of his neck while planting small kisses along his collarbone.

'I love you, Hamish. Thank you for standing by my side, but more so, for being *on* my side in every situation.' I reached up and affectionately stroked his cheek.

'I love ye, Abigail. Always have.' His lips on mine in unbridled desire, he gathered me in his arms and rose to his feet, carrying me to bed without another word spoken.

Much later, as the sun began to rise, I drifted off into a deep sleep, while dreams of a ship, a world with no men, and a field of red poppies overlooking an ocean filled with blood tormented me, yet still I was unable to wake.

A Word from the Author

THANK YOU FOR TAKING the time to read my series 'Samsara-The First Season'.' It's been nearly a decade since I wrote the first sentence of Abigail's story, and it is a privilege to share it with you.

If you have a few moments, I would be deeply grateful if you left a review on your chosen platform or website. It will help other readers find books that they may never have discovered otherwise. Your feedback means the world to authors and we cannot thank you enough for your support! Thank you for investing your valuable time and money in this story and I hope you enjoyed reading it.

If this series was not for you, that's perfectly okay. We all have different tastes as readers and we can't please everyone all the time. Thank you again for your support and I wish you well in finding novels that bring you joy. Much love to all xx

To find out more,
go to www.jlmartinauthor.com

SAMSARA

THE FIRST SEASON

Soul Connections
Volume One Book Eight

What if you could remember a past life?
Or worse, what if you couldn't?

War breaks out, and Abigail is left to manage Willow Grove while the men she loves fight for their country, leaving her to console those who have lost while suffering her own torment.
Abigail meets Sarah Stewart, and a deep friendship is established, bringing a very special child into her life who will change the course of her future. Abigail again faces one of the most traumatic events of her life, leaving her unable to cope or find peace, despite a loved soul on the other side showing themselves to her and revealing some interesting information about the golden glow.

Continue your journey with Abigail in the epic new Australian historical fiction series spanning a lifetime. Based in Geelong, this debut series by J L Martin spans a lifetime, from 1890 to 1968. Join thousands of readers accompanying this cast of characters through each decade, sharing their joy and sorrow, their triumphs and tragedies, while trying to find out the meaning of the golden glow. The first series of twelve full-length novels are available in ebook, audiobook and paperback from all good bookstores and on-line platforms, and the author's website.

www.ingramcontent.com/pod-product-compliance
Lightning Source LLC
Chambersburg PA
CBHW060738190726
48285CB00001B/257